JOHN FENLEY

ONE MORE MIRACLE

LOUSARAH PUBLISHING GROUP

ACKNOWLEDGEMENTS

Special thanks to my life-long friend Ms. Yvonne Toney, who encouraged me to finish this book. You were the first person, to whom I introduced Allen and Teresa. Thank you Ms. Yolanda Tezeno. Your input on this project has been invaluable. My heart-felt thanks to Dr. Olinda Johnson, for helping me convey to the reader what goes on in the delivery room. I couldn't have done this without you! Much gratitude to Harris County Deputy, Charles Ferguson, for enlightening me on the intricacies of police work. Enormous thanks to new-found family member and friend, Nomsa H., for helping me complete this mission. Thank you Aaron Cotton and Symone Pellerine, for giving Allen and Teresa a face. For technical support, special thanks to Patrice Kirksey, Johnathan Fenley, Asha Price, Dekoiya Jackson, and Mia Butler. Last but not least, thank you Professor Donna Kilgore, of the Texas Southern University (TSU) English Department, your academic expertise was priceless!

In loving Memory of

Sarah Lou

Steve Fenley

Ethel Cobb

Octavia Williams

Allen Williams Sr.

Marvalyn Motley

Prologue

At 8:12 a.m. on January 8, a squalling wind blows outside of Atlanta's Northside Hospital. Inside, an eardrum-piercing scream emanates from Delivery Room 7. Twenty-nine-year-old Teresa Williams is in her twelfth hour of labor and about to give birth to her sixth child. Her contractions are running three minutes apart. With each contraction, she clenches her fists in excruciating pain, and a heavy stream of perspiration flows down her forehead. The heat from the incandescent lights in the delivery room adds to her discomfort.

At Teresa's bedside is OB-GYN resident Dr. Tracy Blanks, the delivery team, and Teresa's husband, Allen. He is suited up in scrubs, breathlessly holding her hand. He is coaching her on the art of breathing to minimize the pain of childbirth, just as he learned in their Lamaze classes. Dr. Blanks grows concerned because Teresa's been in labor for over twelve hours. She's also concerned about the baby's dropping heart rate. The doctor is well aware of the risk factors of prolonged labor, which could lead to postpartum hemorrhaging. If necessary, she has Pitocin on hand to help control any excessive blood loss after the birth.

Finally, at 9:25 a.m., Dr. Blanks says to the medical team, "I think we have about a thirty-minute window. Just in case this baby doesn't start to move, let's go on and prep her for a C-section."

Teresa's contractions become more intense, running two minutes apart.

She begins to scream loudly, "Oh, oh, ouch, oh…um-um oh, I think the baby is coming!"

"Come on, Teresa—push, push, push, push harder," Dr. Blanks encourages.

"I am pushing!" Teresa shouts in pain as she holds on to her husband's hand in a viselike grip.

When Dr. Blanks sees the baby's head emerging ("crowning," as it is technically called), she repeats, "Push, Mommy. We're almost there."

"Yes, sweetie, push. Push! Push," Allen echoes. Teresa looks

1

at him with angry eyes, as though all of this were his fault.

Roughly five minutes later, the agony of childbirth comes to an abrupt conclusion as the baby emerges from Teresa's womb. Dr. Blanks cradles the child in her arms.

"It's a girl!" the doctor announces excitedly, before placing the crying infant on Teresa's chest.

Allen looks on in amazement, displaying a broad smile visible even behind his surgical mask. The sound of the crying baby girl fills the room, along with cheers and congratulations to the proud parents. Dr. Blanks lets the father cut the umbilical cord.
Obviously, it is love at first sight for the father.

"You are so beautiful, little one. I love you. Yes, I do. Daddy loves his little girl," Allen coos.

Within seconds, joy is transformed into desolation when Dr. Blanks shouts urgently, "Bolus he Pitocin. She's bleeding too much."

The nurse whisks the baby to the nursery. Allen is ushered out of the delivery room to a waiting room a few doors down the hall.

Dr. Blanks starts an IV on Teresa, shouting at one of the nurses, "Get the Methergine. I've got to massage the fundus."
But then she corrects herself. "Oh no, we can't use Methergine because of her blood pressure."

She continues to bark out instructions to the medical team. "Bring the Hemabate."

After a few minutes of administering the medication and persistently applying fundal massages, Dr. Blanks checks the clock and yells, "Five minutes of medical and fundal massage, page for an upper-level stat. Take her blood pressure."

OB-RN Sandra Jackson responds, "Yes, Doctor."

Dr. Blanks calls for anesthesia. "Hey, start another line in her left hand. Give her one liter of saline and send a stat Hgb level. Patient's estimated blood loss has exceeded nine hundred ccs."

Dr. Blanks further instructs the team. "Take the patient up to the OR and get her in stirrups. There are no retained fragments, and her uterus is remaining boggy."

The site from where the blood had been drawn continues to ooze after the needle is removed.

Dr. Blanks shouts to RN Jackson. "Better check her clotting

factors. Teresa! Teresa, are you okay?"

No response.

"B/P unable to obtain. Rechecking," RN Jackson chimes in.

"Someone get the cardiac monitor to the room now. The patient isn't responding, isn't breathing, and has no pulse. Start CPR. Call the code, call the code. Bag her. Bag her!"

Within minutes, the CPR team fills the room. When Allen hears the page operator over the intercom call, "Code Blue to Delivery Room Seven," he leaps from the chair and runs back to the delivery room. When he pushes the door open, he witnesses the cadre of medical personnel performing CPR on his wife.

"Oh my God, no!" he cries, panic-stricken. He turns to Dr. Blanks. "What happened? What went wrong? Please, please, Tracy, please don't let her die!"

Tears roll down his face.

The chief resident screams, "Get him out of here now," as Dr. Blanks and RN Jackson continue chest compressions.

Within minutes, the security team arrive and sternly escort Allen from the delivery room. After learning that Teresa has coded, Dr. George Joubert, chief of cardiology, joins the CPR team. Dr. Joubert takes charge immediately. The cardiac monitor shows Teresa is in cardiac arrest.

"Let's prepare to shock her with three hundred sixty joules. Clear! Clear! Clear," says Dr. Joubert to one of the interns.

Again, Teresa doesn't respond; hope is fading. The continue CPR for what seems like an hour. Dr. Joubert looks at Dr. Blanks. "Doctor, she's been down for well over thirty minutes. Let's call it. We've done all we can."

Dr. Blanks shakes her head forcefully. "No! No! We can't stop now. We can still save her."

Minutes later, when the heart monitor's screen flat-lines, it is as though someone pushed a mute button. The room is totally silent, except for the sounds of the machine still pushing oxygen into Teresa's lungs. Dr. Blanks is visibly upset, tears rolling down her cheeks. She stands with her hands on her head, reliving the sequence of events in her mind and trying to determine what just happened.

Her mind races. How am I going to tell Allen his wife didn't make it? she asks herself.

This is more than an ordinary doctor-patient relationship. Dr. Blanks and Paul, Allen's brother, dated when they were classmates in college. Her lips quiver into a melancholy smile, remembering the good old days. Then she continues to sob. She is about to leave the delivery room to break the grim news to Allen when, miraculously, Teresa's heart monitor begins a slow beeping sound.

The team crowds back around her, ecstatic.

Dr. Blank's voice, loud and strong, exclaims, "We're back in full code. Check the pulse. Check the pulse!"

The team resume their positions, and the anesthesiologist, in tearful relief, softly replies, "We have a faint pulse."

RN Jackson blurts out, "And a B/P of sixty."

Dr. Blanks instructs her to give Teresa 0.5 mg of Atropine and a bolus of saline.

"Call CCU," Dr. Blanks orders. "And let's get her up, stat! I hope she hasn't lost any oxygen to her brain, but at least she's back."

To herself, Dr. Blanks sighs in relief. Thank God for that.

Once in CCU, Teresa regains full consciousness, and her heart rate stabilizes. Dr. Blanks orders a CT scan and an MRI to determine whether any brain damage has occurred during cardiac arrest. Fortunately, the tests are all negative. What had taken place in Delivery Room 7 was nothing short of a miracle. Teresa had been clinically dead, but suddenly she has come back to life.

Later on that evening, in a family room at the hospital, Allen graciously thanks Dr. Blanks. "Tracy, I am eternally thankful to you for saving Teresa's life."

Dr. Blanks explains to Allen that the amniotic fluid seeped into Teresa's circulatory system, causing her to suffer an amniotic fluid embolus. The mortality rate for this condition is usually high.

With that in mind, Dr. Blanks quickly points out that medicine played only a small part in saving Teresa's life. "I believe, without a doubt, that a higher power intervened: the power of God." Smiling, she says, "I'm a Christian first and a scientist second. I believe in the power of medicine, but I've witnessed the miracles of prayer. Allen, it gives me chills to say this, but Teresa was a dead woman in the delivery room. We did everything medically possible to save her, and I truly

4

thought we had lost her in the end. But every now and then, God lets us know who has the final say. We thought it was over, but God said, 'Not so fast—I'm still in charge here.'"

"Tracy, I'm emotionally drained. I know that I'll be forever thanking God. Please convey my gratitude to your staff," Allen says as he gives Dr. Blanks a heartfelt embrace. "But right now, I need to go see my wife."

"Okay, go see your wife. I'll check on her later."

When Allen enters the CCU, all he can do is stare in amazement at Teresa as she sleeps in a medicated state. After such a close call, he refuses to leave. Later on that evening, Dr. Blanks makes arrangements for him to sleep in an unoccupied patient room.

The next morning, Allen went by the nursery to check on his new baby girl. Teresa is stable enough to be moved out of the CCU and into a private room on the OB floor. When Allen goes to check on her, she is sleeping soundly. So he quietly closes the door behind him and makes his way over to her bedside. He stands for a long moment, gazing at his wife with the deepest affection.

In his mind, he thinks, I am so lucky and so thankful I still have the woman I love in my life.

He knows the outcome could have been so different. He moves closer to the bed, leans down, and kisses her gently on the lips. When she feels his moist lips pressing against her dry, chapped ones, and smells the pungent scent of his cologne, without even opening her eyes Teresa smiles, knowing it is her beloved Allen.

CHAPTER 1

The six-foot-three, well-built man with straight black hair and engaging blue eyes whispers in a baritone voice, "I love you so much."

Teresa sluggishly opens her eyes. "Hi, Daddy."

"Hello, Mommy," he says, his eyes glossy with tears. Suddenly, his mood becomes pensive. Teresa senses a shift in his facial expression.

"What's the matter, Allen?"

"Oh, nothing. Yesterday was one of the happiest days of my life, seeing our daughter being born. Yet my joy was diminished when I almost lost you. I've never been so scared in all my life. I love you so much."

Even though she's in pain, Teresa reaches out to hug him. It is a loving embrace. She instinctively places his head gently on her breasts. She wants him close to her. She whispers in his ear, "I love you, too."

He continues to rest his head on her breasts and mutters, "Sweetheart, I can only imagine what you were going through yesterday in the delivery room."

"Allen, you're going to find this hard to believe, but I had a very spiritual encounter. It was so strange…so surreal. When I was in the delivery room, I was aware of everything that was going on—all of the chaos, the noise.

"But you know me; whenever there's a crisis, I automatically go into prayer mode. At first, my body was experiencing extreme trauma. Then I began to have an out-of-body experience. Who knows? Maybe it was medication, but my mind was totally at peace. I was talking to God the whole time, asking Him not to take me. I was praying, asking Him to let me live to see our children grow up to be adults and let me live to see our grandchildren one day. Baby, then I heard the most calming, soft, and loving voice I've ever heard in my life. It said to me,

ONE MORE MIRACLE

'My child, this is not your time; go back to your family.' That's when I woke up in the ICU."

With a perplexed stare, Allen slowly raises his head from her chest. He thinks, it must have been the medication; she was probably hallucinating. He nods slowly, placating her by stating, "That's incredible, really incredible."

Allen is not one to quickly embrace what he doesn't understand. He certainly could be called a pragmatist. As a lawyer and an astute businessman, he tends to rely more on tangible facts rather than on the supernatural. So he is somewhat relieved when Teresa says she will share this story with him only. Still trying to grapple with his wife's ethereal experience in the delivery room, he finds the story to be more abstract than substantive. Because of his love for her, his dedication to her, however, he has never challenged or questioned anything that is important to her. He is far too smart to patronize her.

Feeling the residual effects of the medication, Teresa continues to slip in and out of consciousness. Two hours later, when she is fully awake, Allen is gone. He has left her a note on the bed, so she unfolds the piece of paper and begins to read what turns out to be a poem he has written:

What makes you so beautiful is your capacity to forgive time and time again.
You are the consummate friend.

What makes you so beautiful is your touch, your stride, your voice, your physique, your face, and your warm embrace.

What makes you so beautiful is your prowess to carry a child inside of you for nine months, to remain committed to that child for life, and to see it not as a sacrifice but as a pleasure, because your children are your treasures.

7

What makes you beautiful is your total being.
I am so blessed to be seeing what God has created, just for me.
What makes you so beautiful is your way of revealing something
new about you that makes me love you more each day.

What makes my life so beautiful is you.

When she finishes reading the poem, she folds the paper
back and clutches it in her hand. Suddenly Allen walks back into
the room; he had gone to the car to get some business
documents.

Teresa smiles bashfully at him. "I love the poem you
wrote for me. How can you think of such beautiful words?"

He smiles. "It's so easy when the inspiration is right in
front of you."

"I'm so blessed to be married to the sweetest man in the
world."

He smiles proudly. "Well, if you say so."

"I say so." Teresa falls back to sleep.

Another hour passes before she wakes again. She
focuses her eyes on Allen and mutters, "You're still here?"

"Where else would I be?"

"Thank you for not leaving me," she replies weakly.

With tender emotion, he says, "Oh, sweetheart, you
don't have to thank me. It's my pleasure to be here."

"Daddy, can you do me a favor?"

"Sure, Mommy. I can do ten favors for you."

"I want to see my baby. Please call the nursery and ask
them to bring her to me. I want to hold her and feed her."

"Sure, sweetheart, I'll call right now."

A short time later, the door opens quietly. It is a member
of the neonatal staff, pushing a bassinet with their baby inside.
Allen's eyes follow the bassinet over to where Teresa is sitting
up. Before the nurse can hand the baby to Teresa, Allen

whispers, "Please, may I hold her first?"

The nurse smiles and looks at Teresa, who nods. The nurse then hands the baby to Allen. His face is all aglow as he holds his infant daughter. He coos softly, "Hi, princess. How is Daddy's little angel? Daddy loves you. Daddy loves his little girl."

Needless to say, the newborn isn't impressed with what her father has to say. She begins to cry loudly, smacking her lips, obviously ready to eat. Allen willingly hands her over to her mother. Teresa gently takes the baby from Allen, resting her back on two pillows, and opens the buttons on her gown to expose her right breast. Her new daughter suckles greedily, her eyes closed in contented bliss.

During the feeding, Allen asks Teresa, "Have you decided on a name for her yet?"

"No, not really," she replies.

"I have a name."

"Okay, let's hear it."

"Let's name her after my grandmother, Mary Lee."

Teresa shakes her head. "Oh no, there's no way I'm going to name my child Mary Lee. It's an old-fashioned name. You know, Allen, if my memory serves me well, I let you name both of the boys when they were born. We agreed if we ever had another child, I would get to name him or her."

"Teresa, did we sign a contract?"

"Of course not." She laughs.

He responds, "Oh, well then, the agreement we made isn't binding. That's what the law says."

"Forget the law. I'm naming this child, and I have the perfect name."

"Okay, dear, what's the perfect name?"

"I'm naming her Mallory Jassiah."

He smiles. "I'm pleased."

Sister Jassiah and Sister Mallory were two nuns at the

church where Allen and Teresa were married. They also taught Mia and Kendria in the fourth grade. They were instrumental in aiding Teresa and the girls when they converted to Catholicism. The nuns were the girls' godmothers as well, so what better way to honor them?

"Teresa, that's wonderful. That's really sweet of you. I'm sure they will be pleased."

It is eight thirty in the evening, and both mother and child are soundly asleep. Allen relaxes in a reclining chair and reminisces about the first time he laid eyes on Teresa.

CHAPTER 2

It was almost six years ago when Teresa was employed as a maid at an uptown building where Allen leased an office. He was filing some papers when she came into the office to empty the trash. Even dressed in her dull denim uniform, in his eyes she was gift-wrapped in elegant splendor. Allen was spellbound by her raw beauty and her plump derriere, not to mention her small waistline and shapely legs, especially for such a petite frame. Allen, being the quintessential ladies' man, knew he had to get to know this brown-skinned doll immediately.

At twenty-eight, Allen had been an attorney for only four years and was already a successful millionaire. His fortune was made mostly through several prudent real-estate ventures, so he was under the illusion that money could buy anything. He pursued Teresa persistently for more than three months, but to no avail. Teresa had become increasingly uncomfortable with his advances, although they were never sexual in nature; Allen's conduct was more annoying than aggressive. However, when he offered her three days' pay to go out on a date with him, that was the last straw.

With a voice loaded with disdain, she approached him menacingly. "Mr. Williams, let's get one thing straight: I'm not for sale. I find your offer offensive and degrading. I'm sure if I weren't a black woman, you never would've approached me in this manner."

"Wait! Wait! Please, Teresa. You've misinterpreted my offer. I only wanted to take you out and show you a good time. In retrospect, I shouldn't have approached you that way. I realize now that it was tacky. I'd never intentionally disrespect you or any other woman. I'm truly sorry."

Teresa gave him a cold stare.

"You're not really sorry. You're just sorry you didn't get the response you wanted, so I'm declining your offer of becoming

11

your personal whore."

Allen pleaded even harder. "Teresa, you've got me all wrong. You're blowing this out of proportion."

As she walked away, she looked back at him with a frosty stare. "Out of proportion? I don't think so. Please don't say anything else to me ever again."

Allen quickly followed behind her, begging her to stop and hear him out. Teresa was so determined to get away from him that she ran to the elevators. The first elevator that arrived was crowded almost to capacity, yet Teresa maneuvered her way into a small space as the doors closed, leaving Allen still trying to plead his case.

Two weeks elapsed with no sign of Teresa. Allen desperately wanted to see her to try to make amends. So he decided to do some investigative work. In a roundabout way, he asked the new cleaning lady what had happened to Teresa. She told him she had heard that Teresa had been transferred to another office building.

A few days later, Allen, still committed to finding Teresa, offered the new cleaning lady one hundred dollars to help him locate her. In this case, money did the trick. She told him exactly where to find Teresa. She had been transferred at her request (for obvious reasons). Her new place of employment was located in downtown Atlanta. Armed with that information, the unrelenting young lawyer journeyed over to Teresa's new workplace.

He made several trips to the downtown building, only to have the misfortune of not seeing her. He was forced into using the power of money once again. He gave the maid another one hundred dollars for more information.

She admitted that she had failed to tell him that Teresa was working a new shift, from three in the afternoon to eleven at night, which explained why he kept missing her; Allen had assumed she was still working mornings.

ONE MORE MIRACLE

As he sat parked in his car across from the office where Teresa was working, he felt optimistic that he would have a chance to apologize to her. He began to wonder, what will I say to her? How will she respond to me?

Soon, he would have his answer.

When Allen saw a security guard unlock the first-floor doors to let the workers out of the building, he noticed Teresa among the last group leaving the premises. She walked briskly alone, bundled in a long wool coat and wearing gloves and a scarf around her neck. The night air was bitterly cold as she proceeded along Peachtree Avenue to the bus stop. After observing her for a moment, Allen turned on the car's engine and took off behind her. When he caught up with her, she was at the bus stop.

He rolled down the window and said, "Hi, pretty lady. Can I give you a ride home?"

Teresa grew concerned when she saw a strange car following her, so Allen had to repeat his request two more times before she realized who it was. When she saw it was Allen, her attitude toward him was just as cold as the night air.

"Oh, it's you, Mr. Williams. The man who thinks money can buy anything."

"Teresa, that's not fair," he protested. "I need to talk to you. Would you please let me take you home?"

She shook her head. "No thanks, Mr. Williams. I really don't know that much about you. I can't let you take me home. Anyway, how did you find me?"

"I have my sources. I can find anyone I want to. It's not important how I found you. Are you going to let me give you a ride home?"

"No. I'm fine. Please, leave me alone."

"Teresa, your bus must be late. It's cold out here. Why don't you just let me take you home? Come on, get into this warm car," he pleaded with her.

13

"My bus will be here in a few minutes, so go on and leave, please."

He became frustrated, so he abruptly opened his car door and got out.

"Teresa, can you drive?" he shouted angrily.

"Yeah, I can drive," she shouted back.

"Then here, take my car and drive yourself home. I'll get a cab. Go on, take my car."

Teresa, bewildered, scoffed. "You're telling me you want me to take your car?"

"Yes, you can take my car and drive yourself home. There are some business cards in the glove compartment. My phone number is printed at the bottom. Call me in the morning and tell me where to pick up my car."

She decided to call his bluff. She looked at him and said, "So I can take your car and you'll take a taxi home, right?"

He nodded as he stepped away from his car. Teresa got in, adjusted the seat, and secured the seat belt.

Before rolling up the window, she said to him, "Well, Mr. Williams, thanks for the use of your car. I'll call you in the morning."

"Okay, that's fine," he mumbled.

She then put the car into drive and sped off.

Allen quickly walked down Peachtree Avenue, shivering from the cold, and in search of a cab. Teresa drove around the block and then came back and stopped the car next to him. She rolled down the window and yelled, "Hi, Mr. Williams, going my way?"

He stared at her and then laughed. "Hell yes, I'm going your way." He quickly got into the car, and she drove off.

During the drive to Teresa's place, he got his chance to apologize, explaining to her that he was grossly misunderstood when he offered her money for a date. He really wasn't expecting anything in return; he just wanted to compensate her

14

for possibly missing a day of work. Teresa accepted his apology and then posed a question to him.

"Is it typical of you to offer money to women when they refuse to go out on a date with you?"

"Well, you're the first woman to turn me down."

She looked at him and laughed lightheartedly. "You're nothing but an egotistical playboy."

During the drive to Teresa's apartment, the conversation became more personal. Teresa revealed that she was married and was the mother of three children—twin daughters and a son.

"Mia and Kendria are five, and Carl Ray Jr. is two," she said. "My husband, Carl Ray Sr., is incarcerated in the Georgia State Penitentiary, serving a twenty-five-year sentence for his part in a robbery where a bank teller and a security guard were killed. Carl was the getaway driver. The mastermind behind the robbery, Eddy Miller, was the shooter. I convinced my husband to turn himself in to the police. He aided the police in catching Miller. You see, this guy was a career criminal who vowed not to be taken alive, and he made good on that promise. When the police surrounded his residence and ordered him to come out, Miller came out shooting and was gunned down in a hail of bullets. Since Carl Ray had never been in trouble with the law before, his cooperation with the police and the district attorney earned him a reduced sentence."

After hearing Teresa's story, Allen replied sympathetically, "I'm sorry your husband is incarcerated."

She muttered sadly, "So am I."

Allen told her that he had been married briefly, but didn't go into details. A half hour later, they were parked in front of her Grady Homes apartment.

She thanked him for allowing her to drive herself home and was about to get out of the car when Allen reached for her hand, gazed into her eyes, and asked, "Please, do you have a minute?"

"Yes, I guess I have a minute. What's on your mind, Mr.

15

Williams?"

"Let me start by saying, you're so beautiful. I don't want you to go inside right now."

She laughed cynically and repeated, "Oh, I'm so beautiful. You don't want me to go inside? Is that your best line? Mr. Williams, why do men play silly games?"

"What games?"

"You know what games. The players' games. You men use the same old smooth, tired lines. 'Heaven must be missing an angel,' or 'Where have you been all my life?' or 'Oh baby, you look so good!' or 'You smell good,' or 'I like the way you walk,' or 'I like the way you talk.'"

To her surprise, he responded, "Teresa, those games are necessary."

"Whoa, I'm shocked by your candor."

"What you don't understand is that the games are all part of the process. The compliments are just a precursor to dating, marriage proposals, and procreation. God forbid if one of these so-called players happens to meet that special lady, fall deeply in love, and realize that she is the center of his universe and that he can't breathe without her. So, Teresa, in order for all those things to fall into place, a man has to get a woman into bed, right?"

She stared at him for a brief moment, repelled by his comments, and then shook her head as she responded, "All right, whatever."

"Oh, Teresa, why are you such a skeptic? You're not one of those people who can't stand to hear the truth, are you?"

"Your interpretation of the games men play has nothing to do with the truth. I've come to the conclusion that you're like most lawyers—you like hearing the sound of your own voice."

"That is ridiculous."

"No, Mr. Williams, I'll tell you what's ridiculous. What's ridiculous is you thinking I'm silly enough to believe what you're telling me. Look, it's getting late, and I'm tired.

16

Unless you have something earth shattering or important you need to tell me, I'm going inside now."

With a huge smile, he responded, "What if I told you my grandmother was black?"

Teresa frowned. "Shame on you, Mr. Williams. You don't have to stoop to the level of lying, just to get a black woman to go out with you."

Allen looked at her, shaking his head as he reached into his wallet. He retrieved a picture of a fair-skinned black woman and showed it to Teresa. She looked at the photo, unimpressed, and tossed it back to him.

"This lady is about as much your grandmother as the Queen of England is mine."

"Believe it or not, she is my grandmother, so help me God." He then made the sign of the cross, adding, "She really is my grandmother."

"Yeah, right." Teresa smirked. "Come on, Mr. Williams, be honest. What do you actually want from me?"

"Like I said earlier, I'd like to get to know you."

"Are you deaf? Senile? Like I've told you before, I'm a married woman. There's no way you can get to know me."

"Hey, Teresa, I was hoping we could be friends."

"If friendship is what you're really after, I'm sure there are plenty of other people you could turn to."

"Oh okay, I see that you don't believe me."

"Well, what else do you want to know about me, Mr. Williams?"

"What are your plans for the future, then?"

"I've got dreams and aspirations. I'm in school, but I'm only taking six hours. At this rate it will take me a while to get my degree."

Impressed by what she had revealed, he smiled. "Teresa, I think that's wonderful. What's your major?"

"Education. I've always wanted to be a teacher."

Allen looked at her with serious eyes as he said, "I admire you, and I think that's wonderful."

Curious, Teresa asked him to tell her more about himself.

"I come from a family of three children. I'm the oldest. Both of my parents are physicians."

"Do you have a girlfriend?"

"No, not really."

"What do you mean, no, not really? What do you do for sex?"

Rather surprised at her bluntness, especially since she had shied away from all of his advances, he replied hesitantly, "Teresa, sex is secondary to me in a relationship. If I don't connect, spiritually and emotionally, with a woman, then sex is really not an option."

Chuckling, she responded, "Well, I had no idea I was in the company of such a pious man. Do you feel spiritually and emotionally connected to me?"

Staring deeply into her eyes, he replied, "Yes, most definitely."

She laughed. "Mr. Williams, tell me how I knew the answer to my question would be yes."

"Perhaps because you are a very perceptive lady?"

"You're really full of it."

They both laughed. Allen nonchalantly reached into his coat pocket and removed a little black book from inside. He flipped through the pages. After not finding his client's phone number, he put the book back into his pocket.

This prompted Teresa to ask, "What's that, your g-book?"

Looking at her curiously, he replied, "This book contains my clients' names and phone numbers. Is that what you're referring to as a g-book?"

She laughed. "Yeah…yeah, that's what I was referring

to."

He leered for a moment. "For some reason, I don't think you're being honest with me. Come on, Teresa—tell me what a g-book is."

"It's a girl thing."

"Can't it be a guy thing, too?"

She shook her head. "Oh, it's really not that serious."

He smiled. "Okay, lady, I'm all right with that."

Teresa had first heard of the term "g-book" from a girlfriend, who said she once dated a guy who knew more women than a gynecologist. Her inner voice echoed. This man is not only good-looking; he's also rich and charming. I bet he's seen more vaginas than a gynecologist, too.

With a strained smile, Teresa said, "Why don't you just cut to the chase? You just want to take me to bed; that's all. You're no different than the average lustful man. You see a woman with a decent body and ordinary looks, and we're all just fresh meat to you."

He shook his head somberly, saying, "I must challenge you on everything you just said. First of all, there's nothing ordinary about you. When I look at you, these words come to mind: angelic, mellifluous, phenomenal. When it comes to your body, on a scale of one to ten, you're a twelve. The intangible aspect of your being, your core, is three times greater than the human eye can perceive."

Teresa's stern expression was soon transformed into a blushing smile. She thought, this guy is either the best BS talker I ever heard, or he's the most romantic man on the planet.

Whichever was the case, Teresa was mesmerized by his compliments. But she was persistent. She asked again, "You never answered my question. What do you do for sex?"

Allen, taken aback again by her straightforwardness, answered with a smile. "I think that's personal."

She nodded. "Mr. Williams, you are certainly right. I'm

19

sorry."

"Well, you should be. What if I were to ask you the same question?"

"I would answer it honestly and tell you I'm not having sex with anyone."

"Teresa, I can be honest, too. I'm dating two ladies, but it's nothing serious. I'm not in love with either of them."

"Oh, as long as you're spiritually and emotionally connected to those women, I'm sure they don't really care whether or not you're in love with them," she said with a facetious smile.

Allen thought, Damn, I've really put my foot in my mouth.

Trying to correct the bad impression he felt he must have given her, he continued, "Teresa, the relationships are not just sex. I take them out, we go on trips, and we have fun."

Teresa remarked dryly, "Oh, that's nice. Tell me something. These two women you're seeing—do they know about each other?"

"Of course they do. I don't believe in lying."

Teresa stared at him for a moment before saying, "From a male's point of view, I suppose you must be on cloud nine, having two sexual partners at your disposal."

"Oh, I think it's Heather and Wendi who are on cloud nine."

She shook her head again, and glared at him with obvious disgust. "You know…that's repulsive."

Surprised by her response, he laughed. "Oh, are you that much of a prude? You really think sex is disgusting?"

"On the contrary, sex is beautiful when it's between a husband and a wife, or with two people who love each other. Have you ever had a monogamous relationship?"

Allen, beginning to feel as though he was on a witness stand, answered her question with a question.

"Teresa, what place does monogamy have with two single adults looking to have a good time? Especially when both parties are consenting to do whatever it is that pleases them."

"There is definitely a double standard. When men sleep with multiple women, they are called ladies' men and players. However, when a woman does the very same thing, she's called a whore. In reality, there is no difference. He's a male whore, and she's a female one. Therefore, to answer your question, monogamy has no place with whores at all. It doesn't matter if they are male or female."

Allen, usually quick-witted, was at a loss for words. He thought, Damn, she's beautiful and brainy.

"Are you always this judgmental?"

"No, I am not judgmental at all," she scoffed. "I'm simply stating the facts. My aunt Liza warned me about men like you."

"Men like me? What are you saying? Why are you judging me? You don't even know me."

"I know enough about your kind, and I still say my aunt Liza wasn't wrong about men like you."

"What? Was your aunt Liza an authority on men or something?"

"In a way, I guess you could say she was. When she was in the world, she dated her fair share of dogs."

"What do you mean 'she dated her share of men when she was in the world'? Has she passed away?"

"No, she's not dead."

"Okay, is she living on the moon, Mars, or somewhere else in the galaxy?"

Teresa rolled her eyes slightly. "Hey, since you want to be funny, when I made the statement that my aunt was still in the world, I was referring to an expression that some Christians use when describing unsaved people."

"Unsaved from what?"

"Unsaved from sin...aren't you a Christian, Mr. Williams?"

"Yes, of course I am. I'm Catholic. Have you ever attended a Catholic church?"

"Yes, once, and the only thing I got out of the service was sore knees. All that standing and kneeling just made my knees hurt. The worst thing about it was the sermon was conducted in Latin. The Catholic Church isn't for me."

"Obviously you went to the wrong Mass. Most of the Masses are celebrated in English. When we get married, you'll have to convert to Catholicism," he said, with a coy smile.

With a sardonic gaze, she said, "You know, I must commend you."

Out of curiosity he asked, "Oh? Why?"

"Because you mask your mental illness quite well. You must be insane to associate the word 'marriage' with you and me."

He smiled. "Well, I've been called worse things than insane."

"Mr. Williams, I'm married, remember? Now, please excuse me. I really must go inside. Thanks again for the ride and take care. Have a nice life."

She opened the car door, quickly stepped out into the cold wind, and raced toward her apartment.

Allen called out to her, "Teresa, Teresa! When will I see you again?"

Without breaking her stride, she yelled, "Count to a billion. When you're finished, click your heels three times and I'll appear."

Allen laughed hysterically and called to her, "Teresa, that makes no sense."

When she reached her door, she turned in his direction and said in a loud voice, "It makes about as much sense as the statement you made about us getting married." She then entered the building as Allen drove off, still laughing.

22

ONE MORE MIRACLE

Once inside, Teresa rushed over to a space heater in the corner of the living room to warm her chilled legs. Her mother called out to her from a bedroom down the hall, "Teresa, is that you?"

"Yes, Mama, it's me."

"You're home a little early tonight?"

"Yeah, Mama, I got a ride home."

Like a typically inquisitive mother, she asked, "Oh…with whom, baby?"

"Just a guy from work. You don't know him."

Teresa tore herself away from the space heater and walked down the hall to her mother's room, where she found her watching television. Lying next to her, sound asleep, was Carl Jr.

"Do you want me to take Little Carl and put him in his own bed?"

Her mom shook her head. "No, it's all right; he can sleep in here with me tonight."

"Okay, I'm going to take my shower and go to bed. Good night, Mama. I love you."

"I love you too, baby," her mother responded.

Ms. Hunter was in her midforties but was often mistaken for a woman ten years younger; she looked more like Teresa's older sister than her mother.

Teresa walked across the hall to her daughters' room to look in on them. They were cuddled together, fast asleep. Teresa kissed them both on the forehead and then closed the door behind her. She went straight to the bathroom, took a shower, and went to bed.

CHAPTER 3

At eight forty-five the following morning, Teresa was awakened by the sound of the phone. After it had rung five times, she picked it up, answering in a raspy voice, "Hello?"

On the other end of the line, Allen greeted her cheerfully. "Good morning."

Not recognizing his voice at first, she said, "Who is this?"

"It's me, Allen."

She paused in frustration for a long moment. "Mr. Williams, how did you get my number?"

"Let's just say a little birdie gave it to me."

"I'm not in the mood for jokes. What do you want?"

"I'd like to take you to lunch today."

"Mr. Williams, I can't go to lunch with you today, or any other day. Good-bye." She hung up.

The phone rang again. She picked it up, irritated. "Hello?"

"Teresa, why did you hang up on me?"

She shrilled, "Urm…ohm…ahhhh…ohhhh." (She often made those sounds to keep from cussing.)

"I hung up on you because I didn't want to talk to you. Man, what's your problem?"

"I don't have a problem. I just want to take you to lunch."

"What is it that you don't understand? I don't want to go to lunch with you."

"Why not?"

"Are you crazy? You know, this borders on harassment."

"I'm not harassing you."

"Sure you are."

"No, I'm not."

"Yes, yes, you are too."

This verbal sparring match lasted for several minutes. An impasse was finally reached. Allen, being a great litigator, made her an offer she could live with. "Teresa, do you want to never hear from me again?"

She answered sharply, "Sure. How can I make that happen?"

"If you go to lunch with me today, just for an hour, I promise you I'll never, ever call you or come by your job again. I'll even put it in writing. If for any reason I should go back on my word, you can sue me."

She responded carefully. "Okay, you're saying if I agree to go to lunch with you, you'll never call me or come by my job or house ever again?"

"Yes, that's what I'm saying. You have my word."

"Okay, I'll go, but bring the contract. No contract, no date."

"Fair enough. I'll pick you up around one o'clock."

After hanging up, Teresa uttered again, "Ooooh! Urm! Ahhh! Ohhh! I can't believe I let that man talk me into going to lunch with him. I don't even like him. In fact, I think I hate him."

A few hours later, Teresa was getting ready for her date. Her mother had no idea the man calling on her daughter was white. Teresa wasn't about to tell her either because she didn't want to spoil the surprise she had in store for her mother. Teresa was known as a practical joker, but the pranks she played were always harmless, and mostly done for shock value.

At a quarter to one, Allen pulled up to Teresa's apartment. He killed the engine, got out, walked up to the door, and knocked. From her bedroom, Teresa looked out her window, saw him, and called out to her mother. "Mama, I'm not quite dressed yet. Can you get the door please?"

"Sure, baby," her mother answered. She opened the door and came face to face with Allen. "May I help you?"

Allen smiled politely. "Yes, I'm here to see Teresa."

Teresa's mother was stunned. "You're here to see Teresa?"

"Yes, ma'am," Allen affirmed.

"Excuse me for a minute, sir," said Teresa's mother. She

immediately closed the door in his face. She then rushed to her
daughter's bedroom. "Teresa! Teresa! There's a white man at the
door looking for you."
"Mama, he's my date," Teresa said, laughing.
"Teresa Gail, you're not going anywhere with that man."
"Mama, please go and let him in. Don't leave him standing at the
door. That's rude."
"All right, little girl, but we've got some talking to do."
Teresa's mother raced back to the door and apologized, saying,
"I'm sorry, sir. Please come in. Forgive me for taking so long to
come back to the door."
She then greeted him. "Hi, I'm Teresa's mother, Ethel Hunter."
        "Hello, I'm Mark Williams, Teresa's date," he extended
his hand. "Nice to meet you, Ms. Hunter."
"Pleased to meet you too, Mark."
"Please, everyone calls me by my middle name, so call me
Allen."
"Sure, Allen. Please come in and have a seat. Teresa will be with
you shortly. She's getting dressed. May I take your coat?"
"No, thanks, ma'am. I'm fine. I'll keep it on."
"Okay, then, young man. Would you like some coffee?"
        "Yes, ma'am, I'd like some. Thank you."
        He took a seat on what was obviously a well-used sofa.
The moment he sat down, he felt a protruding spring pricking the
right side of his leg, causing some discomfort. He moved to the
center of the sofa to get some relief.
        Ms. Hunter brought a tray with a white mug filled with
coffee, a dish with sugar, a small pitcher filled with cream, and
two giant cookies on a napkin.
"Do you take cream and sugar with your coffee?"
"Only cream. These cookies are huge." He smiled.
"They're not cookies; they're called tea cakes."
He bit into one of them. "They are very good. Where did you
buy them?"

She smiled. "Oh, I made them."

"You made these?" he asked, surprised.

"I certainly did."

"Perhaps I can get you to make some for me one day."

"Just say when," she replied. She then left him to enjoy his snack and headed out of the room.

While eating the second tea cake and sipping the coffee, Allen's eyes scanned the room, looking at the dull green concrete walls. He glanced up at the ceiling where flakes of peeling paint covered a large area of the surface.

He could feel a heavy draft sweeping into the room from the threshold beneath the front door, causing flames in the space heater to flicker. As he gazed down at the missing floor tiles, he thought, Gee, what a dismal place to live.

Suddenly, Teresa entered the room. Her mere presence seemed to transform what he first perceived to be a dismal dwelling into the Garden of Eden. She was tastefully attired in a cranberry suede skirt and a black turtleneck sweater. Her gorgeous, shapely legs were clearly visible above the ankle-high black boots, which appeared to be new. Her clothes weren't extravagant by any means, but in Allen's mind, her aura transcended any apparel she could have adorned. It was hard for him to take his eyes off her.

Teresa brought him out of his trance when she said, "Mr. Williams, please forgive me for taking so long to get dressed."

"There's no need to apologize. I was a few minutes early. You look absolutely stunning."

"Thank you, Mr. Williams and may I say you look good also. But you look good all the time."

"Thanks, Teresa...hey, I have a favor to ask of you. Would you please call me Allen?"

"Yeah, sure," she said, smiling. "Allen, if you're ready, we can go now."

She walked over to a walnut-colored coatrack near the

27

door and got her coat. He helped her with putting it on. She was impressed; it had been a long time since a man had done that for her. Before leaving, Teresa yelled to her mother in the kitchen, "We're going! When the children wake up from their nap, tell them I'll see them when I get back."
"Okay, baby, enjoy yourself," Ms. Hunter replied.

They headed out of the door. Once outside, Teresa noticed several inquisitive neighbors standing in the cold, just to get a glimpse of the man who owned the silver BMW. Teresa found it amusing to see adult women acting like children. It was no secret the women were drooling over Allen.

As he opened the car door for her, he too noticed that all eyes were on them. "Are they friends of yours?" he asked.

She shook her head. "Nope, they're a bunch of nosy women. When they see a strange man in an expensive car, they're like hens in heat."

Allen shook his head. "Hens in heat. I've never heard it put that way before."
"Allen, you being white and all, I can only imagine what they must be thinking, seeing the two of us together."
He looked at her and smiled. "Something tells me you couldn't care less about what they think."

She winked. "You do know something about me, don't you? You know what's funny? Let somebody's apartment get burglarized around here and those same hens looking at us now could see it happening, but when the police come around asking questions, they'd be like Ray Charles: haven't seen a thing. One day I'm going to get out of these projects, and it can't come fast enough."

He gave her an approving look and said, "I believe you."

Changing the subject, he asked, "What would you like to eat?"
She answered, "It doesn't matter. Why don't you choose the restaurant? When it comes to food, I'm not hard to please. I like

28

beans and rice, spaghetti, barbecued ribs, and chicken."
"Well, do you like steak or seafood?" he asked.
She nodded. "Seafood is fine with me."

Allen knew just the place to take her, La Cove de la Mer, a four-star restaurant outside the city. He started the engine and drove off.

As soon as they pulled up to the restaurant, a valet approached the car from the passenger side. He opened the door for Teresa first, then made his way around to Allen and received the car keys. The couple strolled under a bright red canopy through a pair of gold-plated doors, where a doorman held the door open for them.

When they got inside, they were welcomed warmly by a hostess, who escorted them to a cozy table for two with a view overlooking a botanical garden and an artificial waterfall. Teresa was awestruck by the opulent surroundings. Once seated, her eyes scanned the room. The smoked-glass windows overlooking the waterfall and the sound of a live jazz band created an atmosphere for lovers. When Teresa gaze came to rest on Allen, he was staring at her.

"Why are you staring at me?"

"Forgive me. I used to imagine what it would be like to be with an angel. Thanks to you, now I know."

She smirked. "Oh, Mr. Williams, do you always pour it on so thick?"

"My dad once said, 'What's in a man's heart will eventually filter out of his mouth.' If I don't feel something inside, I won't say it."

"Well, in this case, it's a pleasure to know a man who means what he says."

The waiter soon came with bread, wine, and cheese, then quoted them the specials of the day.

A few minutes later, he returned to take their order. Allen ordered for the both of them. As the waiter took their order, Teresa sat in silence, carefully observing Allen's every move. She began to admire how perfectly his necktie was tied, and how every strand of his hair was in place. As she took a deep breath, she noticed how his cologne complemented his body chemistry. She couldn't help but think that Allen could have any woman he wanted. Great-looking men like Allen always intrigued her, yet made her wary. They love the pie, but they rarely love the baker. She was a fervent believer that as long as women kept serving it up, the booty calls would continue. Teresa's mind drifted back to her original thought. Allen could have any woman he wanted, so why was it so important for him to take me out to eat? He's definitely not a fool, and he knows that nothing is going to come out of this date with me. He'll never have a chance to sample this pie in a million years.

When the waiter left the table, Allen focused his attention on Teresa. He touched her hand gently and said, "You appear to be in deep thought…a penny for your thoughts." She smiled and said, "As a matter of fact, I was just thinking about what a fabulous place you brought me to."

A few minutes later, their food arrived. Teresa was served first. Her dish was a seafood platter, consisting of grilled sea bass with crabmeat/lobster sauce, jumbo grilled shrimp, and fried oysters and clams. Allen had ordered blackened red fish, oysters Rockefeller, and steamed lobster. During the meal, Teresa thought to herself how she was glad she didn't give in to her initial reservations about Allen. She pondered, If I never see this guy again, at least I had an excellent meal.

CHAPTER 4

After enjoying a superb lunch, the couple sat and talked for close to two hours. Teresa mostly talked about the loves of her life, her three children: the twins, Kendria and Mia, and her son, Carl Ray Jr. Teresa referred to her son as her miracle baby, because doctors had given him a slim chance of survival. Tears brimmed in her eyes as she told Allen that Carl Jr. was born three months prematurely. His little lungs hadn't developed normally and he still had a host of medical issues, including severe asthma. Allen took a silk handkerchief from his pocket and gave it to Teresa to dry her eyes.

She held the handkerchief tightly in her right hand and said to him, "I can't use your handkerchief, it's silk. If it gets wet, it'll be stained."

"Who cares? I have lots of silk handkerchiefs."

He removed it from her hand and dried her tearstained eyes.

She apologized, saying, "I'm sorry; I didn't mean to get so emotional."

He said gently, "It's okay."

Teresa forced a smile. "On a brighter note, let me tell you about Kendria and Mia. They are my little women. They love to help me clean the house. They want to help with the cooking, but I told them they're too young right now. When they turn eight, I'll teach them how to cook. I was eight when my mom taught me. I have so much fun with my children. I love them more than I love myself. Only God knows where I'd be without them. Allen, do you ever think about getting married again and starting a family?"

He sighed. "If I can find a woman who will put up with me, but I don't think children are in the cards for me."

"Why not? Please don't tell me you don't want children."

"No, that's not it at all."

31

"Well, what is it, then?"

"I have a low motility count. Unusually low," he lamented.

"Oh, that's too bad." Her voice softened.

"Teresa, you don't have to feel sorry for me. I have a great career; my life is fantastic. Who knows, maybe the woman I marry will already have children. If not, we can always adopt. I think I'd be a good father."

Teresa replied, "I'm confident you will be."

He smiled. "Thanks."

"I want to ask you something, but please don't be angry. The picture you showed me last night of that black lady, she's not really your grandmother, is she?"

"Absolutely. Of course, she is. Why would I lie?"

"Your grandfather actually married a black woman way back then?"

"No, I can assure you they weren't married. Let me explain something to you. My grandfather was the chief of police in Savannah, Georgia. His name was James Williams, but everybody called him Big Jim. The relationship was neither amorous nor consensual."

Teresa gasped. "He raped her?"

"Yes, that's about the size of it. My grandfather's wife couldn't conceive. Big Jim desperately wanted children, so that caused him to go outside of the marriage. My dad wasn't the only mixed-race child he fathered. Big Jim had affairs with two other black women and he fathered two daughters with them."

"Whoa! He impregnated two other black women? He couldn't find a white woman? Please don't tell me that he raped those other women."

"That I can't answer. According to dad, one of the ladies rented a house from Big Jim. The other lady taught school in Savannah."

"You know; I don't think it was children Big Jim was after. I think he had a thing for black women."

"That may be true. However, to add insult to injury, Big Jim

32

took Dad away from my grandmother. He and his wife raised Dad as their own son."

"That was so wrong. Your grandmother couldn't have gone to the police to get her child back?"

"Big Jim Williams was the police, my dear. Grandmother was a teenage black girl. Big Jim was a rich, middle-aged white man. Who was going to go against him for some poor black girl? Nobody. You have to realize my dad was born in 1941 in the South. That was a perverse time and place for blacks."

"How did your grandmother come to know Big Jim?"

"She worked for him and his wife, cleaning their house, and washing and ironing for them," he answered.

"Why didn't Big Jim take his daughters from their mothers?"

"Actually, Dad looked whiter than his two half-sisters. Grandmother's dad was also white, which made her mulatto."

"I would've been devastated if someone had taken my child."

"Oh, Grandmother was devastated. That's why she packed up and left Savannah and never returned."

"Where did she go?"

"Dad said she moved to Florida with a relative. In spite of all that happened, Dad still had a good life. Big Jim sent him to medical school, so obviously Dad became a doctor. The irony of it all is that on the day that Dad graduated from medical school, Big Jim had a massive heart attack and died en route to Dad's graduation.

"As fate would have it, in less than two years, Big Jim's wife also died. However, on her death bed, she revealed to Dad that she wasn't his real mother. She told Dad the entire story about Mary Thomas, his biological black mother. To say he was devastated was an understatement. It was hard for him to come to grips with the fact that his mother was black. When Big Jim's wife saw how upset Dad was, she was actually sorry she had told

33

him. But once Pandora's Box had been opened, it could never be closed. The psychological damage had already been done.

"Dad didn't look black, and his eyes were green. He had all the physical characteristics of a Caucasian. His stepmother told him it would be best if he just forgot about everything she had told him. He agreed, but after she died, Dad had a change of heart. Something inside of him compelled him to go and find his real mother."

"Your dad was really determined, wasn't he?"

"Yeah. He went to Florida and hired a private investigator, who found her. She worked at a restaurant as a cook. After the investigator gave Dad the information, he went to her job and stood outside for over an hour. He was nervous and apprehensive about going inside. People began to look at him strangely. I guess they were wondering why a white man was looking in the window of a black restaurant. After drawing so much attention to himself, he finally went inside and asked to see Mary Thomas. It was just his luck—she was off that day."

With a chuckle, Teresa asked, "What did he do next?"

"Dad asked her boss if she knew her address, and without reservation, she gave it to him. Dad took a cab to her house. When he arrived there, he got out, walked on to the porch, and knocked on the door. He heard a woman's calm voice ask, 'Who is it? May I help you?'

"Dad responded nervously. 'I'm looking for Mary Thomas.' She opened the door slowly and said, 'I'm Mary Thomas.' Dad took a deep breath and said, 'I'm your son, Rob.'"

"Wow!" Teresa gasped.

Allen continued. "Her eyes remained fixed on Dad for a long moment. There he stood, at six foot four, a dominating figure. A mirror image of Big Jim. She was astonished and found it difficult to speak. Dad's nervous smile resembled that of a bashful little boy. She just couldn't keep her eyes off him. She suddenly staggered backward, as though she were about to faint.

ONE MORE MIRACLE

Dad rushed in and held her in his arms, until she regained her composure. Dad repeated, 'I'm your son, Rob.' She found herself too emotional to speak, as tears streamed down her face."
Teresa sighed. "Oh, I bet."
"When she finally spoke, she revealed to Dad that God had answered her prayers because she desperately wanted to see her child once more before she left this world. She told Dad she thought about him often and always carried him in her heart. It was gratifying to her that Dad wanted to see her, especially after learning that she was a black woman."
Teresa smiled. "That was awesome."
"They embraced again. She held on to Dad. She didn't want to let him go. They sat on the sofa, where they literally talked for hours. Dad said she had a kind and gentle spirit, but he still felt awkward. He asked, 'What shall I call you?' She replied, 'Why don't you just call me Mary?' He wasn't comfortable calling her Mary, but she insisted that's how it had to be."
Teresa propped her hands under her chin, intrigued, as Allen continued talking.
"Dad spent two days with her. They found out a lot about each other. Grandmother had been married, but she was separated. Her husband was abusive and a drunkard. She lived in an old, run-down house. Dad tried to convince her to move back to Savannah, but she refused. She told him in the eyes of the world he was a white man—an educated white man, a doctor, and the sky was the limit for him.
"Grandmother told him it would only bring shame to him, and ruin his chances of success, if people knew he had a black mother. It wouldn't matter how white he looked or how much education he had; he would be just another fair-skinned black man."
"Sad, but true," said Teresa.
"Grandmother was a philosophical woman. She was convinced something good could come from a bad situation.

What Big Jim did to her traumatized her, in more ways than one, but she felt that if she had to be raped in order for Dad to be born, that was God's will. God must have had a purpose for Dad's life. She believed God had a way of blessing hundreds of people through one person."

"Yeah, that's so true."

"Dad said he was perplexed by her statement. He didn't fully understand the meaning of what she was saying until years later, when he and mom built two clinics in Jamaica. Those clinics are still in operation to this day. A lot of poor people receive medical help, even if they don't have any money."

"How did your parents manage to serve the poor and not receive any money? Isn't that a financial burden for them?"

"No, not at all. You see, they built a larger clinic in Kingston for people with money and insurance. The clinic in Kingston supported the other clinic in the rural area of the island."

Teresa agreed, "Your grandmother was right. A lot of people are still being blessed through your mom and dad."

"Big Jim was a wealthy man, though most of his money came through shady dealings. He owned real estate in Savannah and here in Atlanta. When he died, he willed everything to his wife and my dad. When she died, everything went to Dad. When Dad found out that most of Big Jim's money was made by less than honest means, he was determined to do some good with that money.

"He even built my grandmother a new house because the house she lived in was in a deplorable condition, with terrible plumbing. Dad bought a vacant lot three blocks down from Grandmother's house and hired a contractor to build her a new house. Everything was done in complete secrecy. Grandmother would walk by the construction site every day on her way to work, oblivious to what was going on. Obviously, Dad wanted to surprise her. Trust me, he did.

36

ONE MORE MIRACLE

"When the house was completed, Dad flew back to Florida and picked her up from work that day. They drove to the new house and Dad graciously gave her the keys. To say Grandmother was stunned would really be putting it mildly. She just broke down and cried, thanking Dad over and over again. It brought tears to his eyes to see how happy and grateful she was."

"Your father is a very good man," Teresa said in admiration.

"Yes, he's quite a guy," Allen agreed.

"After that day, Dad and Grandmother didn't see one another for almost a year. They kept in touch by phone and letters. Dad went on to complete his residency. That's where he met Mom. They both worked at King's County Hospital in Brooklyn. Mom was a second-year intern. Mom says it was love at first sight. The two of them dated for less than a year before Dad proposed and she accepted. They married in secret and had a small wedding. Dad wanted it that way for professional reasons, but shortly after the wedding, Dad sent Grandmother a plane ticket to come to New York to meet his new bride."

"I bet that was a shocker."

"No, Mom and Grandmother hit it off right away. They were crazy about each other. Mom said Grandmother stayed a little over a month before going back home to Florida. The next year I was born. Grandmother came back to New York to help out with the new baby, that being me.

"Sixteen months later my brother, Paul, was born. Grandmother was there again to help Mom. Soon after Paul was born, I recall Mom saying Dad took a job at a hospital in Jamaica. He was hired as chief of staff.

"Two years later my sister, Kathleen, was born there. Once again, Grandmother came down to Jamaica to help Mom. She was such a sweet lady, always willing to lend a hand whenever asked. She loved Jamaica, especially the water. This time, my parents asked her to come and live with us. She agreed, but on her terms. It was like she felt she wasn't good enough to be Dad's mother."

Teresa responded, "Aw, that was too bad."

"Mom says Dad tried hard to make her feel secure with the fact that he was her son, but Grandmother was old school. She knew how racist and cruel people could be, so she was determined not to bring disgrace to Dad. In the end, Mom and Dad relented, saying they would introduce her as their nanny. We all called her Mama Mary. Dad mainly wanted her to stay because he was concerned about her health. See, Grandmother was an avid smoker. After being around her a while, Dad noticed some difficulty with her breathing. He admitted her to their hospital and ran some tests. Grandmother was diagnosed with emphysema and congestive heart failure. She lived fifteen more years with her ailments, and through it all she never complained. Her philosophy was that life should be lived to the fullest, and that death is as natural as birth."

"Well, you can say she died the way she lived, on her own terms."

"A month before she died, Mom and Dad called us all together. That's when Mama Mary told us she was Dad's biological mother and our grandmother. We were stunned, to say the least, but delighted. We couldn't have loved her any more. My eighteenth birthday was bittersweet. Grandmother died that day, around four o'clock in the afternoon. The whole family was at her bedside. Mom and Kathleen took it the hardest. Well, I should say they were the only ones who showed their emotions. Dad just stood there, with a stoic expression on his face. Paul started to choke up and left the house. I tried not to cry. I wanted to be strong like Dad, but I couldn't. I went into the bedroom and cried. In my heart, I knew our lives were better because of Grandmother."

Chuckling, Allen continued. "My sister says she benefited genetically being Grandmother's granddaughter. She inherited her big butt and chest. Grandmother showed us some photos taken when she was in her twenties—she was quite a looker."

Teresa smiled. "Yeah, that chocolate does have a way of surfacing."

Allen smiled. "Teresa, your thoughts are naughty!"

"Yes, I know. By the way, what do your brother and sister do for a living?"

"Paul is a doctor and Kathleen—we call her Katie—is a lawyer. As I alluded before, both of my parents are physicians. My dad is an orthopedic surgeon and my mom is a cosmetic surgeon."

"That's awesome! You come from a very successful family."

"Thanks. I believe that with hard work, anybody can succeed."

Teresa nodded. "I agree. Did you grow up here in Atlanta?"

"Yes, for the most part, but we also lived in the Caribbean. We lived in a house overlooking the ocean."

The subject changed quickly when Teresa asked, "Allen, have you ever dated a sister before?"

He replied readily. "Of course I have. Color is not a factor."

"Where did you meet her?"

"I met her when we were in college."

"Well, that's one thing you had in common. Allen, why don't you describe both of the ladies you are currently dating?"

"Why do you want me to describe them? What exactly are you trying to find out?" Allen inquired suspiciously.

"I am merely curious about their appearance. However, if it is going to be a problem for you, you don't have to tell me anything," Teresa muttered.

"It's not a problem. I'll tell you. Heather has red hair, and Wendi is a blonde."

"I presume both are white?"

"Yes, both are white, but what does that have to do with anything?" He laughed. "Why are you so color conscious? Why can't you just see me as a man first, and not focus on my color? When I look at you, your race isn't the first thing that comes to mind. Teresa, when I see you, I see a beautiful woman with a beautiful soul. I know that we'll never be more than friends. I hope you can just see me as a man."

"Allen, if I've offended you in any way, I'm truly sorry. I'm not a racist. I've never had an intimate relationship with anybody white. But I'm no different from most white people who are suspicious of blacks. It's 1984. Don't forget we're in the South."

"Yes, you're right. But black people have made a lot of headway here in Atlanta."

"That's true, but we haven't got there yet. So if you must judge me when it comes to interracial relationships, just say I'm a bit naïve or not well rounded. I can say that I love all people, even people who hate me."

Allen looked at her sincerely. "Teresa, in my world I just see people. I try not to see black or white. I know that you're not a racist."

Teresa squeezed his hand gently and said, "Thank you for understanding me."

She then closed her eyes for a brief moment. When she opened them, she smiled softly.

"Now I don't see a white man sitting across from me; I just see a man."

With a smile, Allen said, "Well, at least you see me as a man. Okay, now that you are familiar with my family tree, you know I'm not as white as you thought I was."

With her lips pursed, Teresa grabbed his hand, held it next to hers, and quipped, "Man, if you were any whiter, you would be Frosty the Snowman."

Allen laughed. "You're a funny lady."

She smiled. "Yes, I've been told. Allen, you come from the

corporate world, and white men rule that world. I'm positive the
two ladies you're seeing have professional careers. If you desire
to date a black woman, there are plenty of professional black
women here in Atlanta. Why not choose one of them? A man
with your intellect and swagger shouldn't have to come to the
projects looking for love."

Allen said, acerbically, "Thanks for those words of
wisdom, but I think you should embrace love wherever you find
it. Sometimes you don't go looking for love, it has a way of
finding you."

Teresa smiled. "Amen. I won't argue with that."

Teresa's attitude toward Allen was softening slowly. Her
initial opinion of him had been that he was arrogant. However,
after spending two hours with him, she could see he was an
honest and sensitive man, who loved his grandmother and wasn't
ashamed to say she was black. Teresa was indeed impressed by
that.

Their eyes seemed to be drawn to each other like magnets.

Uncharacteristically shy for him, he asked, "Are you
seeing anyone, by chance?"

She took a deep breath before saying, "Yes, I have a
friend named Rodney, whom I'm interested in. We've known
each other our whole lives, but have only been seeing each other
for close to six months. Let me tell you something about myself.
I'm twenty-three years old, and I've only slept with one man, my
husband, Carl Ray. I was eighteen the first time I had sex, and a
month later we were married. I don't give myself easily."

"So this relationship with Rodney—is it platonic?"

"I wouldn't say platonic; I am very fond of Rodney. We hug, we
kiss, and I have deep feelings for him."

Allen was amazed. "The two of you have been seeing each other
for six months, and you haven't slept together? He's a
remarkable man."

"I couldn't agree with you more. He's special for

41

waiting. It shows that he really cares for me. Allen, sometimes a woman needs intimacy more than she needs sex. That's not to say I don't miss sex. Who knows? It may happen or may not. After all, I am still a married woman."
"All I can say is, Rodney's a lucky guy."
"Oh no, I'm the one who's lucky. It's difficult for a woman with three kids to find a decent man. Most men tend to shy away from a woman with children. Rodney wants me to divorce Carl Ray and marry him. I can't lie; I've thought about it—I've thought about it a lot. Could you marry a woman with three children?"
He hesitated for a moment and then said, "Teresa, when love is the common denominator, anything is possible."

After Teresa revealed to Allen she was seeing someone, in a bizarre way, he felt a sudden sense of loss. In reality, he shouldn't have. As the old saying goes, you never miss what you never had. For one of the few times during the date, Allen let his eyes drift away from Teresa and stared into a half-empty glass of wine.

Teresa interrupted his moment of solitude, saying, "I really enjoyed the food, and the company wasn't bad, either."
He smiled. "Thanks. I am happy you had a good time." He quickly glanced at his watch. It was ten after three. He signaled the waiter to bring the check, saying that he had an appointment with a client.

Half an hour later, Allen and Teresa were sitting in the car in front of her apartment. Their final conversation was brief because he was pressed for time. Before stepping out of the car, Teresa asked with a smile, "Oh, by the way, where's the contract you were bringing?"

Allen smiled as he reached into the glove box and retrieved it. He handed it to her. It was indeed a contract. Teresa read it, and when she finished, she immediately tore it up and stated, "You are truly a man of your word."
He replied, "A man is only as good as his word."

ONE MORE MIRACLE

Teresa hated to see the date end. She got out of the car reluctantly. He soon followed. They stood for a quick moment, staring into each other's eyes. Teresa thanked him again for a fabulous lunch. Unexpectedly, he took her right hand, drew it to his lips, and planted a soft kiss. He then said good-bye and casually walked back to his car. Teresa, still caught up in the moment, managed to whisper, "Good-bye."

Allen had mixed feelings about how the date had ended. In his heart, he wanted to kiss her, but he didn't want to force the issue because he felt it wasn't the right thing to do. In his mind, he realized that he and Teresa were as different as day and night. The chance of their having a future together was against all odds. All he needed to do was to convince his heart.

Although he had been gone for about five minutes, Teresa was just finding her way into her apartment, still ruminating over what conceivably was the best date of her life. In the two hours she had spent with Allen, she found him to be a genuine and caring man, but by the same token, she never thought he would be her Prince Charming.

Teresa definitely wasn't into fantasy. She never envisioned a knight in shining armor coming to rescue her from a life of poverty. She was well aware that the only way she was getting out of Grady Homes would be through education and hard work. She knew that a college degree was the key to a better life for her family.

CHAPTER 5

Teresa lived on what little money she made cleaning offices. Her mother received a pension from Teresa's deceased father, and they split the monthly bills. The Hunters were a proud family who never accepted welfare, and Teresa wasn't about to break tradition.

Sometimes in her despair she felt there was no light at the end of the tunnel, but her faith kept her going. She believed deep in her soul that God had a better life in store for her.

Once inside the house, Teresa ambled over to the coatrack near the gas heater and hung up her coat. She stood in front of the heater for a brief moment to remove the chill from her cold legs. The concentrated smell of coffee brewing permeated from the kitchen. The twins soon bounced into the room, dressed in dark-blue corduroy jeans and red Mickey Mouse sweaters. Teresa's mother had found the sweaters at a resale shop for a bargain price of four dollars apiece.

When the two beautiful little girls laid their eyes on their mother, they began to chant ecstatically, "Mommy, Mommy, Mommy, you're home!"

With extended arms, Teresa squatted down, saying, "Yes, Mommy's back. Did you miss me?"
Speaking in what seemed to be identical voices, they replied, "Uh-huh, we did," as they ran into her arms.

She gave them a bear hug. When she stood up, she grabbed both of them by the hand and proceeded to the kitchen.

Teresa's mother was sitting at a small white table. Above her head hung an eight-by-ten-inch print of Jesus. She was doing a crossword puzzle, her favorite pastime. She glanced up at Teresa with serious eyes. "Hi, baby, how was your date?"
Teresa blushed slightly. "Oh, Mama, it was nice, real nice. Is that coffee ready?"
"Yeah, it should be; turn the fire off and pour us a cup."

44

ONE MORE MIRACLE

Teresa nodded and said, "Okay, Mama."

"Teresa Gail, I need to talk to you, little girl."

She knew whenever her mother addressed her by her middle name something was on her mother's mind or she was in trouble. She went to a cabinet and took out two zodiac coffee mugs, one bearing a Leo and the other a Sagittarius sign. She filled the Sagittarius one first and set it in front of her mother. She then filled her cup and sat down across from her mother. The twins joined her, occupying both of her knees.

Teresa said, "Mama, how long has Little Carl been asleep?"

"For a while, baby."

"Did you give him his asthma medicine?"

"Yeah, I gave it to him right after you left to go on your date."

She suddenly stopped doing the puzzle, laying the pencil on the table, with one eyebrow raised. She looked at Teresa and asked, "Now tell me, what on God's green earth possessed you to go on a date with that white man?"

Teresa pondered for a second before saying, "Mama, I know this is probably going to sound crazy to you, but I went on that date with him so he would leave me alone."

Ms. Hunter replied, "Yes, you're right; that does sound crazy."

"Hold on, Mama. Let me finish. There's a method to this madness. I went out with him because I really didn't want him calling me or coming by the job anymore; besides, he made me an offer I couldn't refuse."

Frowning, her mother responded, "He made you an offer you couldn't refuse? What kind of offer was that?"

"Let me put your mind at ease. The offer was that if I went out with him just once, he agreed not ever to call again or come by my job. He put it in writing in the form of a contract."

"Teresa, this still doesn't make any sense. You could've said no to him. He doesn't have any leverage over you."

Teresa suddenly cut her eyes at her two daughters, saying to them, "Mia, Kendria, go to your room. Granny and I are having an adult conversation."

The girls scurried off to their bedroom. Teresa continued. "Well, I guess subconsciously I wanted to go out with him, just to see if there was any difference between a black man and a white man."

"Well, is there any difference?"

"No, Mama, I don't think there is. Men are men. They're after the same thing. All they want is the prize, and of course the prize is the cookie, the candy, the biscuit, the doughnut, and the pie."

Ms. Hunter laughed. "When it comes to a woman's certain body part, most men have an enormous sweet tooth. Teresa, as far as white men go, they have been secretly wanting black women for years. They don't mind getting with us in the dark, but they don't want to be seen with us in the light of day. Once they get our goods a few times, then we're damaged goods, and they have no use for us anymore."

"Well, that applies to all men. I don't have a problem with interracial dating. I think people should date and marry whoever they love. Color shouldn't be an issue."

"Are you saying you could date a white man?"

"No, Mama, that's not what I'm saying at all. Personally, I'm not attracted to white guys. Believe me—the day I lie down with a white man, hell will freeze over, and the devil will go ice skating."

Ms. Hunter laughed. "If I've told you once, I've told you twice: you should be doing stand-up."

Suddenly there was contempt in her voice as she continued. "Oh, baby, let me tell you before I forget. That Rodney Boyd called you while you were out on your date."

Teresa was defensive. "Mama, why can't you just say Rodney called? Why does he have to be 'that Rodney Boyd'?"

"I just don't want you getting mixed up with a man who still

46

lives with his mother and parks cars for a living."

"There is nothing wrong with parking cars for a living. It's an honest job, Mama. Rodney is a decent man. Besides, he and I are just friends."

"Well, I'm certainly glad to know that, because I didn't want to see you getting involved with any more losers. Much as I hate to admit it, we both know what a loser Carl Ray is."

Teresa's voice escalated in anger. "You just can't resist the opportunity to bash Carl Ray. You do this to me all the time. Carl Ray is paying his debt to society. Can't you just let this rest? I know you feel that I made a mistake marrying Carl Ray, but I don't. I love him, and that's not going to change. He is the father of my children. Mama, when you say these unkind things about him, it hurts me deeply, and it angers me."

Ms. Hunter sat speechless. Her eyes displayed the remorse she felt in her heart. Teresa got up from the table abruptly, went into the living room, grabbed her coat from the rack, stormed out of the door, and headed toward the park across the street from the apartment.

She took a thirty-minute walk to clear her head and calm her emotions. When she returned to the apartment, Ms. Hunter was sitting in the same place, with a cup of coffee in front of her. She instantly made eye contact with her daughter. "Can I get you some coffee?" she asked quietly.

Teresa nodded gently. "Yes, Mama."

Her mother rose from the table, went over to the stove, and poured a cup of coffee. She moved her chair next to Teresa's, put her arms around Teresa, and said, "I am so sorry that I upset you. I hope that you can forgive me. I'm going to have to keep my feelings to myself. I am truly sorry."

Teresa's response was short and subdued. "It's okay. I forgive you, Mama."

Ms. Hunter looked at her daughter with a half-smile. "Now, do you want to finish telling me how your date went?"

After calming down, Teresa said, "Sure, Mama. I had a marvelous time. He took me to a seafood restaurant. The place was very elegant."

"How was the food?" her mother asked.

"It was superb. I had a seafood platter. It had everything on it: huge shrimp, large oysters, crab cakes, clams, and grilled sea bass. It was delicious. And Mama, I caught a glimpse of the check. Our bill came up to eighty dollars!"

"What? Eighty dollars! My goodness, Teresa, we could eat off eighty dollars for a month."

Four hours later, Teresa finished ironing the twins' clothes and her work uniform. She went into the twins' room to check on them, as was her nightly ritual. She found them still up, coloring in a book. She asked in a firm voice, "Why aren't you two asleep? Go to bed, and I mean right now."

The girls whined. "Okay, Mommy."

Teresa turned off the light, quietly closed the door, and walked a few feet down the hall to her mother's room. She knocked softly on the door. Not waiting for an answer, she slowly entered the bedroom. Ms. Hunter was sitting up in bed, reading her Bible. Her concentration was not interrupted by Teresa's surprise visit.

"Mama, I just wanted to say good night. I love you."

Her mother's eyes remained buried in the Bible as she murmured, "Okay, baby, I love you, too. Good night."

Teresa closed the door and went back to her room. She took off her terry-cloth bathrobe and laid it on the exercise bike at the foot of the bed. She proceeded to wake Little Carl so he could use the potty. After he finished emptying his bladder, she tucked him back into his single bed next to hers. She then got in bed and turned off the lamp, but she didn't fall asleep right away.

She was still on an emotional high, reflecting on what was possibly the best date of her life. She could still smell the manly scent of Allen's cologne. Her luncheon date had exceeded all of her expectations. Before drifting off to sleep, she thought,

48

some woman is going to be lucky to have Allen for a husband.

CHAPTER 6

Two weeks later, Allen was visiting Heather Sinclair at her high-rise condominium. The 2,900-square-foot apartment could easily be described as an interior decorator's showplace. The salmon-colored walls, the robin's-egg-blue carpet, and the ornate contemporary furniture were tastefully coordinated. As the couple relaxed on a navy leather loveseat in Heather's bedroom, sipping champagne, she noticed the bottle was getting low. She got up and went into the kitchen to get a fresh bottle from the refrigerator. When she returned to the room, she found Allen taking off his pants.

After stripping down to his underwear, he placed his pants neatly on the edge of the sofa. Heather replaced the old bottle of champagne with the fresh one, sat down with anticipation, and watched Allen finish undressing. He soon joined her on the sofa, and they began to kiss wildly. Allen pulled away from her for a moment to take a sip of champagne. He leisurely laid back on the sofa as she straddled him. He removed her pajama bottoms as she frantically unbuttoned her top and threw it on the floor.

He proceeded to kiss her nipples. Heather began to fondle him below the waist and kiss his body all over. She gradually moved up to his lips. As they exchanged positions, he ended up on top of her. He then picked her up and walked over to the bed, laying her down gently. She opened her legs and accepted him, her face contorted in pleasure as they made love for hours. Allen and Heather had an insatiable appetite when it came to sex. They fell asleep in exhausted bliss.

A few hours later, a rainstorm woke them. Heather got up to get a drink of water. When she returned from the kitchen, Allen's eyes were focused on the rain as it hit the top of the skylight.

"Enjoying the rain?" Heather asked.

ONE MORE MIRACLE

Allen appeared to be in deep thought. He didn't respond as he continued looking up at the ceiling. She got back into bed, and laid her head on his chest. Moments later, she asked, "Are you okay? Is anything wrong?"

"No, I'm fine. Nothing is wrong," he said.

She raised her head from his chest, glaring at him, but he refuses to look her in the eye. So she said sarcastically, "Your sudden change of mood reminds me of a song I once heard: 'Your body's here with me, but your mind is somewhere else.'"

"That sounds so cynical."

"It was meant to be. You seem preoccupied. You're thinking about that bimbo, Wendi, aren't you?"

He shook his head. "Heather, Heather, baby, why must you put a dent in our perfect evening by bringing up another woman?"

Heather exclaimed angrily, "Because I know that you are involved with another woman, that's why."

Allen, trying his best to appease her, said, "Please let's not get into this right now. You knew from the beginning I was seeing Wendi. It wasn't any secret, and you were seeing that Todd fellow. So what do you want me to do, just drop Wendi?"

"Yes, that's exactly what I want you to do. I ended things with Todd a month after I started seeing you."

"That was your choice. I never asked you to."

"No, you didn't ask me to. I did it because I fell in love with you. Allen, am I not enough woman for you?"

"Sure you are," Allen laughed. "There are times when I believe you're too much woman for me."

"Don't play with me! Being facetious only makes matters worse."

He shrugged his shoulders. "I don't get it. Pay a woman the ultimate compliment, and she doesn't even take you seriously. I don't believe this."

"Allen, do you love me?"

"You know I care deeply about you."

51

"That's not what I asked you. Do you love me?"
Becoming irritated, Allen turned his back to Heather and said,
"Look, I'm not in the mood for a serious colloquium with you at
two in the morning."

Heather raised her head and poked him in the back. She
shouted, "Allen, this is my damn house! You just finished
screwing me like a drill, but when I asked you if you love me,
you couldn't tell me? Then you had the nerve to give me that BS
answer, 'I'm not in the mood for a serious colloquium.' Mr.
Williams, let me tell you something: if I want you to, you'll
engage me in a diatribe, a song, a sermon, or a powwow. Allen, I
don't know what to make of you. Sometimes you can be quite
the Lothario; other times, like now, you can be an inconsiderate
bastard."

He interrupted her, saying, "You seem to have a short
memory; I told you less than an hour ago that I love you."

Heather's childish attitude transitioned into a sardonic
sneer. She lowered her head and blurted out, "Oh yeah, you
mean you told me you loved me when you were on top of me.
I've noticed the only time you tell me you love me is when my
legs are open."
Allen shook his head and said, "That is certainly not true."
"Yes, Allen, that is very true, and you know it."
"Heather, are you finished now?"
"No, I'm not! And another thing, when I woke up, you were
staring at the fucking ceiling like you were in a trance. You
won't admit it, but I know you were thinking about that hussy,
Wendi."
He laughed. "Oh, I suppose you're psychic, and have the ability
to tell me what I'm thinking."

Allen's demeanor could sometimes be described as
remote and aloof, but in the courtroom he was dynamic,
animated, and razor sharp. Having grown accustomed to
Heather's temper tantrums and fiery tirades, he knew just how to

defuse her. He turned around and said, "Heather, I can't help it if I am not as loquacious as you are most of the time."

She mimicked him. "'Heather, I can't help it if I am not as loquacious as you are most of the time.' You really tick me off when you do that shit. You are a damn lawyer. You get paid for talking. You know what else ticks me off? Whenever we get into an argument, you always want to show me what an excellent vocabulary you have. You are not dealing with a fast-food counter girl flipping burgers. I can compete with you lying on my back or standing on my feet. Have you forgotten that I have an MBA?"

He sighed. "I can see that you are in a bad mood. I think it is time for me to go."

Heather stared at him angrily and riposted, "Go on…I really don't care. This is what always happens when you refuse to hear me out."

An hour passed and they continued to lie on opposite sides of the bed, consciously trying not to touch each other. Allen thought, It's time for me to end this stalemate. I'm getting hungry, and I'm going to need her to fix me something to eat. He pinched her butt softly, but she didn't respond. He then caressed her, and that was when she gave into him. They began to kiss, and he apologized for not being attentive to her needs. They locked into each other's gaze, and Allen asked, "Do you still want me to leave?"

Heather gave him a sensual kiss and murmured softly, "I don't ever want you to leave."

He grabbed her hand. "Baby, I didn't want to leave. Look at me. You know I wouldn't lie to you. I wasn't thinking about Wendi. That's the honest truth."

Heather looked at him with seductive eyes. "Allen, I believe you. I'm just so jealous and insecure. I want all your time. You know that."

He hugged her. "Okay, as of now, all of my time is

53

yours."

He kissed her softly. After the kiss, Allen said, "I'm famished. Do you have anything to eat?

She replied, "Sure, I have chicken salad, ham, and corned beef in the refrigerator. What do you want?"

"Chicken salad sounds good. Do you have wheat bread?"

"Yes, I bought it today, so it's fresh. I'll make you a sandwich," she said. She got up and went to the closet to get a robe, and slipped it on. Then she went into the kitchen.

Moments later she returned with two sandwiches and soft drinks for each of them. After the meal, they went back to bed. Heather fell asleep in his arms.

It took a while for Allen to drift off. As many times as he slept over at Heather's place, he never felt completely comfortable there. Tonight he felt especially guilty, because he found himself thinking of another woman.

He hadn't lied when he told Heather he didn't have Wendi on his mind. In fact, it was Teresa he was really thinking about. In his head the question kept popping up: why was he still thinking about Teresa? She had made it clear they could only be friends. He continued to ask himself, why can't I get her off my mind?

Sure, she was beautiful, but Heather wasn't chopped liver either, at five foot ten and 150 pounds, with a thirty-six-inch bust, a twenty-four-inch waistline, and dazzling, emerald-colored eyes. She was a physically glamourous specimen.

In Allen's eyes, all the women with whom he shared sexual liaisons were "physical specimens."

In addition to Wendi Heller, his other Atlanta love interest, there were voluptuous Mercedes Romero, his Latina princess, who was a Chicago stockbroker; and the stunning Natalie Chung, a San Francisco lawyer. Allen made five or six trips a year to visit the "Windy City" and the Bay area, to see these ladies.

ONE MORE MIRACLE

All of the women in Allen's life were truly beautiful. Teresa was equally as lovely but she possessed an inner beauty that the others couldn't hold a candle to, and she was morally sound. However, considering Allen's usual MO when selecting women, Teresa wouldn't fit the bill. She wasn't a college graduate, and she was married with three children. But for some strange reason, that didn't seem to be an issue with Allen. Perhaps the logic behind it all was that he wanted something he knew he could never attain.

The next morning the alarm clock sounded at six. Allen raised his head lethargically from under the satin comforter. Heather was missing from the room. The bathroom door was ajar; the shower was running, and the steam filled the bathroom. Allen reached over to the nightstand and hit the snooze button to silence the alarm. The bathroom door swung open, and Heather emerged, dressed in her bathrobe, with a white towel wrapped around her head. Allen rolled over on his back, rubbed his eyes, then said with a yawn, "Heather, why did you get up so early?"

She walked to the bed and sat beside him, saying, as she kissed him, "Allen, let's get married."

His sleepy eyes suddenly opened wide. "Did you say get married?"

"Yes, Allen."

"Heather, who knows what life has in store? Life takes you through so many twists and turns, peaks, and valleys. Who can say what the future holds? I can't see myself getting married in the foreseeable future."

She looked at him dejectedly. "I guess I should take that as a no. You gave a rambling excuse, when you could've easily been honest and said, 'No, we are not getting married.'"

She got up from the bed abruptly, went to the vanity, and began to apply her makeup. She mumbled in a low voice, "This SOB makes me sick. He can never give a straight answer."

Allen assumed she was talking to him, so he inquired,

"Heather, did you say something, baby?"
She smiled. "I was just saying how much I love you; that's all."
Allen looked at the clock and muttered, "Oh, I'd better get up. I need to go down and get my blue suit from the car."
"You don't have to. I went down and got it for you."
"Thanks, my dear; I appreciate it."

CHAPTER 7

Two days later, on a Thursday morning, Allen boarded a plane for Phoenix to sell some real estate. He'd purchased the property three years earlier from a client who'd fallen on hard times. Allen was excited about the potential sale of the property. Its location in downtown Phoenix had made his colleagues think he'd made a bad deal because that area was considered depressed, and businesses were relocating. However, Allen believed that one block of property, downtown of a major city, was a deal he couldn't afford to pass up. His instincts had paid off.

He had paid a mere $400,000 for the lot, and he was now being offered $2.4 million for it. City Hall's recent effort to revitalize that part of the city had been a huge success, and businesses were moving back to the area. A Los Angeles–based consortium wanted to buy the property to build a department store. Allen had already agreed, in principle; the object of the trip was to finalize the deal.

When Allen's plane landed at noon, he took a taxi, and forty minutes later he arrived at his destination, the law firm of Clay, Hale, and Grant, which occupied the entire first floor of an office building. He stepped out of the cab and entered the three-story building. Once inside, he was greeted by a secretary. He informed her of the nature of his visit. She offered him a seat, and then buzzed her boss. Within minutes a tall, husky man came out of an office to greet Allen.

"Allen Williams?" the man said, looking him in the eye.

Allen stood up. "Yes, that's me."

"Hi, I'm Kenneth Clay, one of the partners with the firm, but everybody calls me Big Ken."

Allen extended his hand and gave him a firm handshake, and then said, "Pleased to meet you, Ken."

"Same here. Please come into my office; we've been expecting

57

you."

Allen followed him to his spacious office, replete with framed degrees and awards covering the burned-pine paneled walls. Ken took a seat at a large oval-shaped mahogany desk. Allen sat in front of him in a burgundy, Old English–style chair. Ken handed him a set of documents. Allen studied each page, reading them carefully.

"Is everything in order?" Ken asked.

"Yes, it is," Allen replied. He smiled and signed the papers.

Ken happened to notice Allen's class ring. "I see you attended Harvard."

"Yes, I did."

"So did I," Ken said proudly.

"I kind of figured the chemistry in here was more than coincidental," Allen replied.

"Yeah, we Harvard guys do share a special camaraderie," Ken said.

"So true!" Allen grinned.

"Do you agree with the figures?" Ken asked.

"Yes, they are all accurate."

"Well, then, here you go," Ken said, handing Allen an envelope.

"Thanks."

Allen opened the envelope. Inside was a cashier's check for $2.4 million. He put the check inside his briefcase, then turned to Ken and stated, "Counselor, I'd like to wish you and your clients all the luck in the world on this business venture."

"Thanks, Allen. I believe they'll do just fine."

Ken took him up to the bank on the third floor, so he could wire the money back to his bank in Atlanta. After the transaction Allen headed back to the airport, but mechanical issues had delayed the incoming flight in Miami for an hour. He didn't mind; in fact, he was bubbling inside. He wasn't sure which was more satisfying, making an immense profit, or proving his colleagues wrong about the land deal.

ONE MORE MIRACLE

At 4:25 p.m., the plane finally arrived. Allen boarded. When the plane landed back in Atlanta, waiting for him was a statuesque, Nordic beauty with short blond hair. Wendi Heller was a former foreign exchange student from Germany who had graduated from Georgia Tech with a degree in architectural engineering. After meeting the debonair Allen Williams, she was in no hurry to return to her native Germany.

Allen stepped off the plane, went through Gate Thirty-one, and entered the airport's waiting area. He soon spotted Wendi among the throng of people. She was wearing knee-length, black spandex workout tights, a racer-back halter top, and a matching jacket. She looked as if she had been poured into her clothes. She had the body of a fitness instructor, and the tight suit certainly complemented her curves.

He called out to her. "Wendi! Wendi! Over here."

When she made eye contact with him, she rushed into his waiting arms, and bombarded him with kisses. The embrace was long and passionate, as he lifted her off her feet.

"I should go out of town more often. This is such a nice welcome."

"No, you don't have to go out of town to be greeted this way; you just need to visit me more often."

"I can't argue with that."

"Should I take that as a yes?"

Looking deeply into her eyes, he said, "Baby, if my schedule permits, of course I will."

Wendi shook her head as she thought, Damn it! When that man looks at me that way, I believe anything he tells me.

Four hours later, Allen lay in Wendi's bed with a towel around his waist and Wendi giving him a massage. Wendi's profession was engineering, but she was also a licensed masseuse. As a masseuse, she knew all of the pressure points of the human body, as well as the erogenous zones. Allen's pet name for her was Magic Fingers, because her style was unique.

59

The massage would begin firm and intense, and at the end it was soft and tender. Her galvanic touch was physically and mentally gratifying. Sometimes Allen grappled with the thought, which is better? The massage or the sex?

After an intense sexual encounter with Wendi, there was never room for doubt, the massage was good…but the sex was incredible.

When she finished massaging his back, she removed the towel from around his waist, exposing his naked body. She then proceeded to take her clothes off, and got in bed with him. Wendi was extremely vocal when making love, which always turned Allen on. When the lovemaking was over, they went to dinner. He didn't plan to spend the night; he intended to drop her off and head home. He escorted her to the door, but after a few hot and heavy kisses, she convinced him to stay.

The next morning, after a prolonged preliminary session in the shower, the lovebirds stepped out, and went back to the bedroom to finish what they had started. Afterward, they sat having a late breakfast on the terrace. The view from twelve stories up was quite breathtaking.

Wendi's apartment wasn't nearly as ornate and spacious as Heather's. It paled in comparison, but Allen felt more at home at Wendi's. It was cozier and warmer, with less furniture. If Allen had to define Wendi's apartment, it would be a sui generis love nest.

Wendi had prepared homemade waffles, Canadian bacon, and scrambled eggs. Since Allen didn't eat red meat, he ate only the waffles and the eggs, and had a glass of orange juice. On the table were two small pitchers of syrup, one maple, the other strawberry. Allen reached over, took the strawberry syrup, and poured some over his waffles. He ate a mouthful, then looked over at Wendi.

"Mmmm. These are fantastic. They taste incredible, Ms. Wendi. You're a superb cook."

ONE MORE MIRACLE

She beamed at the compliment. "They're just waffles. Anybody can make them."

"No, I beg to differ. These waffles were made with love. As sweet as this strawberry syrup tastes, your lips are sweeter. As smooth as this orange juice is, and enriched with vitamin C, my darling Wendi, you are the only vitamin for me."

Wendi looked at him quizzically. "Come on, Allen, you can do better than that. You write lovely poems."

Ever since Allen was a child, he'd had a knack for spontaneously composing poems. He smiled. "Okay. When I finish my breakfast, I'll write you a poem. I'll try, anyway."

When he finished eating, he made good on his promise. As he gently caressed Wendi's hand, he gazed deeply into her eyes and recited these words:

A woman's value can never be calculated, not her allure, intrigue, and intellect.

Her pulchritude can't be over exaggerated.

Foolish men describe her as being complicated.

To fools, nothing makes sense. But I am convinced of her smile, her style beguiles.

Her charisma, luster, and mystique are immutable.

It began when she was a little girl.

Her light is the glow that illuminates the world.

Love without her is useless.

A woman's value is priceless.

61

Wendi smiled sincerely, saying, "Oh, Allen! You're awesome. That's why I love you so much. You never cease to amaze me."

"My darling, I'll do anything to please you."

"If you're not doing anything Friday night, some friends of mine are having a party. Will you come?"

"Sure, I'd love to."

CHAPTER 8

Three months had passed since Allen and Teresa's date. He was leaving a downtown department store with a shoebox in his hand, walking across the street to a parking lot to fetch his car, when the Marta bus stopped at a red light. Suddenly, a passenger banged frantically on the window, trying to get his attention. He finally looked in the direction of the knocking; it was Teresa, waving and smiling. His heart skipped a beat. He couldn't hear the sound of her voice, but he read her lips. She said, "Hello."

He shouted with a smile, "Hey! It's good to see you." But before he could utter another word, the light turned green, and the bus took off. Teresa waved zealously. Allen yelled, "Take care!" His eyes stayed fixed on the bus, and, as it turned the corner, he said under his breath, "I love you."

Allen's mental faculties seemed temporarily impaired. He stood at the light for a few minutes, then proceeded down the street, in the opposite direction of his car. He finally came to his senses, realizing he was going the wrong way. He turned around, and went back to his car.

Allen had the luxury of having two places to stay. He owned a condominium in downtown Atlanta, but he also maintained a bedroom at his parents' estate. Later on that night, he visited his parents. Like most mothers who observe their children's behavior, no matter their age, his mother noticed Allen's demeanor had been somewhat wistful all evening. She compressed her concern for as long as she could. Finally, she asked, "Bug, what's on your mind?"

Bug was the name that his father had given him when he was a boy, because Allen was never in a hurry to do anything. With a scrutinizing stare, she repeated, "Bug, is there something troubling you?"

"No, Mother. Why do you ask?"

"Because mentally, you appear to be in another place."

"No, that's certainly not the case. I'm right here with you and Dad."

"That's good to hear because you shouldn't have any major concerns. You have a thriving business, and I hear your love life isn't suffering—any man who is called the Don Juan of Atlanta must have remarkable rapport with the ladies."

With a bashful grin, he blushed. "Where are you getting that from, 'the Don Juan of Atlanta'?"

She smiled. "That's what a couple of ladies at the beauty salon called you when I was there the other day."

"What is the world coming to? I try to be cordial to the ladies. I always say hello with a smile, and I'm always willing to lend a hand whenever needed. Now I've become infamous."

"Son, being compared to Don Juan doesn't make you infamous. It means you are a ladies' man, or you're nubile of the male persuasion."

He laughed. "Mother, I don't want to be Don Juan, or nubile of the male persuasion. I just want to be known as a nice guy, who's really shy, and looking for a nice girl. And I don't want to be taken advantage of."

Allen's mother looked at him and glowered. "Oh, it's getting deep in here, and I don't have my boots on. Obviously you're not going to tell me what's really on your mind."

She got up from her chair, kissed her husband on the lips, and bid him good night. She then advanced over to Allen, kissed him on the cheek, and wished him good night, too. She wound her way upstairs to her bedroom.

Allen's dad left the room for a moment. He came back with a bottle of white wine and two glasses. "Bug, would you care to join me for a glass of Chardonnay?"

"Sure, Dad."

His father filled the two crystal wine goblets and handed one of them to his son.

64

ONE MORE MIRACLE

"Thanks, Dad."

Allen asked his father, "Dad, is Mom the only woman you've ever loved?"

With a puzzled look on his face, his father answered, "Yes, she's the only woman I've ever loved. Hey, son, where are we going with this?"

"Well, I think I'm in love."

His father felt relieved to know where his son was going with his questioning. "Son, who is it: Heather or Wendi?"

"It's neither."

"Then who is it?"

"No one you or Mom know, but if you'll permit, let me paint a picture."

Allen's dad interrupted him. "Wait a minute, Bug. You're going to create a hypothetical situation and expect straight answers?"

"Let's say my summation is part hypothetical and part factual."

He shook his head. "Okay, son, let's hear it."

"This woman is beautiful. She's intelligent. She's a ray of sunshine. She's charming and morally sound."

"Will we be hearing wedding bells any time soon?"

"No, because technically, she's married."

"Bug, you're in love with a married woman?"

"Yes, but her husband is sort of indisposed at the moment."

"Is he ailing or incapacitated?"

"No, sir. Perhaps I used the word out of context, and a word I shouldn't have used to a doctor. I'm going to say, he's out of the picture, for now anyway."

Allen's father tried again. "Out of the picture? Are they separated?"

"One could say that."

"So they're legally separated?"

"Ah, you could say legally, but probably physically separated would be more correct."

65

"Bug, would this man possibly be incommunicado?"
Allen nodded. "Well, yes, he is, but I'm not going to elaborate on him any further; he doesn't matter."
"You shouldn't be focusing your attention on a married woman. It's not right."
Allen's dad stared at him, then continued. "I guess you're forcing me to become something that I'm not."
"What's that?"
"A cryptographer. This conversation we're having appears to be loaded with cryptic messages. If I didn't know any better, I wouldn't think I was communicating with a lawyer, a Harvard lawyer at that, who usually articulates better than he's doing tonight."
Allen laughed. "Yes, Dad, I do sound sort of silly, don't I? I can say with all honesty this woman and I are just friends. She's a young lady who used to work in my building. We went out only once, and she made it perfectly clear we could never be more than friends."
"She sounds like a sensible woman. Bug, take it from me, the moral thing to do is forget about her."
"What does morality have to do with any of this?"
"Morality has something to do with all things, Bug."
"Dad, who's to say what's moral and what's not? My morals may differ from yours, or the next guy's."
"Son, morals don't belong to me or you. Morality happens to be God's rules. In His divine wisdom, He set the standards for us to follow because man's thoughts and conduct seldom coincide with God's. We're truly blessed that God doesn't emulate us."
With an affirming gaze, Allen said, "Okay, I won't argue with that."
"Bug, you're almost thirty. Why don't you settle down with one woman? Do like your brother and sister and get married."
"Would that make you proud of me...if I were to get married?"
His father replied artlessly. "No, but it would make your mother

66

and I happy because we're already proud of you. Bug, you've been a great son. As a matter of fact, Deni and I have been blessed with three wonderful children. I can recall the time when you, Paul, and Kathleen were little. I'd peep in your rooms at night to watch you. Just seeing the three of you sleeping made me feel so proud, and good inside. I love the three of you so much."

"Dad, we love you, too," Allen said with a tender smile. "I'll make you a promise. Before the end of this year, I'm going to do everything in my power to find a wife."

"That's wonderful. If I had to wager, I'd put my money on Wendi."

Allen smiled slightly. "We'll just have to wait and see."

His father took what he said with a grain of salt, because Allen had made this declaration before in the past.

CHAPTER 9

Eighteen months later, Tuesday, June 14 would prove to be one of the grimmest days in Teresa's life. She received a phone call from the warden at the Georgia State Penitentiary, calling to inform her of Carl Ray's death. He had been stabbed in a fight with another inmate. The state of Georgia was transporting his body back to Atlanta. Teresa's mother had a nest egg saved for rainy days. At Teresa's request, Ms. Hunter depleted her savings so Carl Ray could have a proper funeral.

The service was held in a small chapel inside the mortuary. Few people attended. Carl Ray was eulogized by the funeral director, who happened to be an ordained minister. Teresa's mood and facial expression epitomized all the grief and hurt in her heart, yet she showed great composure. She hid her tear-filled eyes behind a pair of dark sunglasses. After the service, Carl Ray's remains were taken to his hometown in Alabama for burial. Teresa and the family could not afford to make the trip, however, so they said their good-byes and watched the hearse drive away.

Now that Carl Ray was gone, Teresa's outlook on life changed drastically. Her focus was on consummating her relationship with Rodney. Two months after Carl Ray's death, Teresa spent the weekend with Rodney, but lied to her mother about it; she didn't want her to know she was spending time with Rodney. She told her mother that she and a girlfriend were driving to North Carolina. Teresa might have been an adult woman with children, but she had the utmost respect for her mother.

Teresa's relationship with Rodney seemed to blossom for a few months, and she began to pressure him to get married. When she asked about setting a wedding date, he would evade the issue. Teresa then gave him an ultimatum: if he wanted to sleep with her again, he'd have to marry her. That was when

ONE MORE MIRACLE

Rodney became indifferent. He abruptly stopped coming to see her, or calling her. Teresa was heartbroken.

A few weeks passed and Teresa had not seen Rodney, so she decided to visit his place of work, the Downtown Parking Garage. When she got there, he had just finished for the day. He was about to get into his car, when she called out to him. He waited for her. When she tried to reach out to him and hug him, he was cold and aloof.

"Rodney, what's the problem? Have I done anything to you?"

He shook his head. "No, you haven't done anything to me."

"Why haven't you called?"

He looked down at the ground and replied, "I've been busy."

Teresa continued, "You've been busy! That's a cop-out."

Rodney eventually made eye contact with her, saying, "Hey, Teresa. I think you should find somebody else because I don't want to get married. I'm not ready to be a father to your children."

Teresa responded angrily, "Oh, you had to sleep with me first, before you determined that?"

"No, it was never like that. I care about you, but I'm not ready for a serious commitment."

Teresa recoiled at his words, then sighed deeply. "Thanks, Rodney. Thank you very much. You could've called the house and told me that. You could've saved me a bus ride down here."

"I'm sorry, Teresa. Really, I am. Please let me give you a ride home."

"No, Rodney, no more rides from you. You've already taken me for the biggest ride of my life. Take care of yourself."

She turned and walked away, her chin quivering with despair, as she took what seemed an endless, solitary stroll to the bus stop.

Teresa wanted to break down and cry, but she thought, No, Teresa, you're not going to do that. He isn't worth it.

The bus soon arrived. She boarded it and took the long ride home.

It was three o'clock in the morning. The house was silent and dark. Teresa was in a deep sleep, in the midst of a dream of dancing with Carl Ray in a rose garden. She was wearing a sparkling new white wedding dress; he was wearing a black tuxedo. Violins were playing, but there were no musicians present. When the dance was over, Carl Ray's image slowly began to vanish.

Teresa called out to him. "Don't leave me! Where are you going?"

She reached for his hand, but his image began to fade into the wind as his voice reverberated faintly. "Teresa, please be happy. Forget about me. Be happy."

She fell to the ground, sobbing. "No, no, come back! Please don't leave me. I want to be with you."

Allen suddenly appeared in her dream, in a white tuxedo. He bent down, picked her up, and held her in his arms, saying, "Come on. Let's go home now."

She resisted him, crying hysterically. "I can't go with you. You're not my husband."

The twins then appeared. They were laughing and playing. "Mommy! Mommy! Let's go home, Mommy!"

Teresa shouted in panic, "Where's Little Carl?"

Kendria answered. "He's gone, Mommy. The man in the white robe took him."

Teresa screeched, beseeching again. "Where's Little Carl?"

Kendria repeated, "He's gone, Mommy. I told you, the man in a white robe took him."

Teresa shouted even louder. "What man? He needs his asthma medicine…and oxygen."

Mia said, "He doesn't need it anymore. The man made him well. He's not sick anymore. That's good, huh Mommy?"

Teresa screamed hysterically. "Where's my baby? Where's my

70

baby?"

She woke up abruptly. She was perspiring profusely. She climbed out of bed and looked at Little Carl, sleeping safely next to her. Shaken to her core, she spent the rest of the night tossing and turning, thinking how real her dream had been.

Four months later, Little Carl died in his sleep of an acute asthma attack. Teresa's dream had been a sad premonition. Still, she was not prepared for it. Emotionally, Teresa was at her lowest. She lost her zest for life. In less than nine months she had lost her husband and her son. She was devastated, and to exacerbate matters, she didn't have money for a funeral, nor did she have burial insurance. Fate had truly dealt her a serious blow.

CHAPTER 10

The following Monday, Allen was out to lunch with two of his junior partners. They were celebrating a $25 million judgment that the firm had won for a client. Allen treated his two junior partners, office manager, and secretary to a lavish lunch at Trader Vic's, in downtown Atlanta. After lunch, he gave them the rest of the day off. Allen, content, was last to leave the restaurant. He stood outside a moment, waiting for his car, feeling devoid of any worries or cares the world had to offer. He looked up at the blue sky, reflecting on just how blessed he was. Another thought occurred to him. He realized that he was obligated to bless others. His intention was to give his church a $300,000 donation for the poor in the parish. He was like his parents; they always gave generously and anonymously to the church.

The valet soon brought him his car, a shiny new, blue Corvette convertible he had bought himself as a reward for sealing the deal. Allen tipped the young man fifty dollars. The shocked valet thanked him effusively. Allen then slid into his car and headed home.

However, the car seemed to have a mind of its own, for within minutes he found himself three blocks from where Teresa worked. A strong urge compelled him to stop and say hello. He pulled into the parking lot next to her building, got out of his car, and entered. Once inside, he encountered a lady wearing the same type of uniform Teresa wore. She stood about five foot seven, with black shoulder-length hair. She spoke with what he guessed to be a New York Puerto Rican accent.

Allen introduced himself. The lady told him her name was Bernice Bonilla. She was Teresa's friend and coworker. When Allen inquired about Teresa, Bernice informed him that she was out on a funeral leave. When she delivered the grim news about Little Carl, the crest of euphoria Allen had been

72

climbing all day became a sea of despair. For some strange reason, he felt guilty because everything in his life was going so well. He had money and a thriving business; Teresa's life was marred by poverty and the sudden loss of her child.

Allen stood silently for a long moment; then he began to shake his head. As he looked at Bernice, his voice dropped. "I'm so sorry. I am sorry to hear about this."
He turned slowly, heading toward the door.
Bernice called out to him. "Sir, forgive me for being forward, but would you like to contribute to the funeral fund? We're collecting money to help bury Teresa's child."
Allen, still shaking his head in disbelief, replied, "Sure, of course, by all means."

He reached into his pocket and pulled out his wallet. Although he had several one-hundred-dollar bills in his wallet, he told her he had only a few dollars. He assured her, however, that he would go to the mortuary and leave a donation in the form of a check. Bernice gave him the name and address of the funeral home.

"When you talk to Teresa, please tell her she has my heartfelt sympathy," he said.
Bernice assured him that she would give Teresa his message.

He immediately drove to the Eastside of town, going to Andrews Mortuary. When he arrived there, he entered through the front doors of the building, and walked down a short hallway. Soft organ music played over the intercom. When he came to the end of the hallway, he noticed a teenage boy, wearing thick bifocal eyeglasses, sitting at a black lacquered desk, reading a book.

When the boy noticed Allen approaching, he closed the book, looked up, and said, "Sir, may I be of any service to you?"

He sounded far more mature than his age.
Allen asked, "Do you have the remains of Carl McCray Jr. here?"

"Yes, sir, we do, but the arrangements are pending at this time."

"Well, I'm here to expedite the proceedings."

The young man got up from the desk, walked over to an adjacent office, and returned seconds later with a tall, thin, dark-skinned man, whom he introduced as his father.

The man extended his hand to Allen, and said, "Hello, sir. I am Cleveland Andrews, the proprietor and funeral director."

After their introduction, Mr. Andrews invited Allen into his office, and offered him a seat. They began discussing the funeral arrangements.

"Mr. Williams, I take it that you're familiar with the family's financial situation?"

Allen responded, "Yes, sir, I am. That's why I'm here. I want the child to have a proper funeral."

Mr. Andrews handed him a price list of various funeral plans. Allen vigilantly looked at the list and discovered that the cheapest funeral plan was $1,700 and the most expensive was $8,000. After he handed the price list back to Mr. Andrews, he removed his checkbook from inside of his suit pocket. He wrote a check for $9,000 and handed it to Mr. Andrews.

Mr. Andrews recognized at once that he was being overpaid for the services, and quickly pointed out to Allen that he had made an error in calculation in the amount of $1,000. Allen convinced him that the amount of the check was not an error, but rather a bonus specifically for him.

Mr. Andrews looked bewildered. He asked, "What exactly have I done to earn this bonus?"

Winking conspiratorially, Allen told him, "Just make sure that Mrs. McCray doesn't ever find out who paid for the funeral."

Smiling brightly, the funeral director gushed. "Oh, I certainly will do that, Mr. Williams, but what shall I tell her when she asks?"

ONE MORE MIRACLE

"I'm going to leave that entirely up to you."

"Sir, don't worry; I'll handle it."

A curious Mr. Andrews then asked, "Mr. Williams, is Mrs. McCray one of your employees?"

Allen replied, "No, she is not. She's just a friend, a dear friend."

"I'll call Mrs. McCray at once and tell her everything has been taken care of."

"Yes, I think that's what you should do. No need in having her worry any further."

"So, Mr. Williams, do you plan to attend the service?" Mr. Andrews asked.

"Ah, I don't know. I'm really not sure."

"Well, sir, just in case you want to attend the funeral, it is going to be held at the Friendship Baptist Church over on 687 Gaskill Street, on the Southeast side of town."

Allen expressed his appreciation to Mr. Andrews, before adding, "Oh, I have one more thing I want you to take care of. At Mrs. McCray's job there's a funeral fund—a Mrs. Bernice Bonilla is in charge of it. When she brings those funds to you, I want you to see to it that Mrs. McCray's family is given all of that money."

"No problem, Mr. Williams. I'll make sure that Mrs. McCray gets every dime."

As Allen turned to leave, Mr. Andrews revealed that he had performed the funeral service for Carl Ray Sr. nine months prior. And that the death of Teresa's child, compounded with the death of her husband, had left her despondent. Allen sat back down in stunned silence for a long moment, contemplating what he'd just been told.

Finally, he parted his lips, whispering, "Poor Teresa. Poor Teresa. I had no idea her husband was dead, too."

Mr. Andrews, somewhat surprised by Allen's reaction, asked, "Sir, when was the last time you talked to Mrs. McCray?"

"Oh, it's been a while…do you know how Mr. McCray died?"

75

"Rumor has it that he was killed with a shank by a fellow inmate."

Allen, subdued, rose slowly. As he departed from the building, he thanked Mr. Andrews for everything.

Moments later, Mr. Andrews phoned Teresa's home and spoke with Ms. Hunter. Remembering the promise, he'd made to Allen, he told her that a friend of Carl Ray's had come in and paid for the funeral in full. Ms. Hunter was grateful that a stranger had come to the family's rescue, yet the kind gesture didn't ease the pain of losing her grandson. Two hours later, Teresa and her mother went to the mortuary to finalize the arrangements.

It was midnight, and Teresa was sitting on the side of her bed, holding a small picture of Carl Jr. Clutching the photo to her bosom, she began to cry uncontrollably. Although Teresa tried to muffle her crying, like most intuitive mothers, Ms. Hunter overheard her and knocked softly on the bedroom door. When Teresa didn't answer, she called out gently, "Honey?"

"Yes, Mama, what is it?"

"May I come in?"

"Yes, come in."

She entered the room, and when she saw Teresa's red, puffy eyes, she instinctively felt her daughter's heart breaking into pieces. Even though she also wanted to cry, for her daughter's sake she garnered enough strength to maintain her composure. Still clutching the picture, Teresa said to her mother, "Mama, why didn't God heal my baby? Why did he have to die?"

"Teresa, I can't answer that question. All I can say is that God's will be done. You remember last month when we prayed, fasted, and we asked God to heal him? When you think about it, God loved him more by taking him to heaven. Know that he's not suffering anymore...he's in a better place now."

Teresa screamed, "I don't want to hear that, Mama!

76

ONE MORE MIRACLE

What I want is him here in my arms, or sleeping in his little bed.
I don't want him in a better place. I want him here with me."
        She collapsed onto the floor, sobbing uncontrollably.
Ms. Hunter quickly sat down next to her, raised her head off the
floor, and placed it on her lap.
        She began to rub Teresa's neck and shoulders as she
said, "Child, please stop all this crying. You're going to make
yourself sick. I know how you must feel."
"No! No! Don't say that; say anything but that! How could you
possibly know how I feel? You've never lost a child before,
Mama. God has taken the sunshine from my life. My son is
gone. He was my pride and joy. I'll never be happy again. Why
has God taken that from me?"
"That's not true, baby. And even if it were, who else but God
could restore your happiness? Not me, not the twins, not even
Reverend Hayes. As much as I love you, Teresa, I don't have the
ability to mend your broken heart. Nobody but the Lord can do
that. You've got to keep trusting in Him and calling on Him.
Believe me, baby—this too will pass. God is going to see us
through this difficult time to happiness once again."
        The next day Teresa and her family assembled at
Friendship Baptist Church. Teresa's older brother, Tony, and his
family had driven down from South Carolina. Patrick, her
younger brother, a member of the US Air Force, had flown in
from Germany. The Hunters were seated on the front pew; a few
feet away was the small, steel, blue coffin that housed Little
Carl's body. Teresa sat next to her mother, followed by Mia and
Kendria. Patrick sat next to the girls, with his arms around them.
Tony; his wife, Yolanda; and their three children filled the rest of
the front pew. At Teresa's request, the coffin remained closed.
Teresa sat almost glued to her mother, holding her left hand
tightly, with a blank stare.
        The pastor, Reverend C. R. Hayes, was a few minutes
into the eulogy when Allen quietly made his entrance into the

church. He wore a dark European-cut suit and a London Fog raincoat that was slightly damp from the drizzle outside. He purposely sat on the back pew. From his vantage point, Allen could see Teresa and the family without being noticed. Allen assumed Patrick was her boyfriend, Rodney, because he was the closest male to Teresa. The small church was filled to capacity, but Allen felt isolated, surrounded by a sea of strangers. Allen had been christened Catholic and had never attended a Baptist church service before.

The service was nothing like he'd imagined. Reverend Hayes delivered a fervent and eloquent eulogy. Allen's compassion for people was often as deep as his pockets, and he truly shared Teresa's pain, so his eyes eventually became glossy with tears. He tried hard not to focus his attention on the tiny coffin, but his eyes kept gravitating toward it. The more he stared, the more anguish he felt.
Reverend Hayes paused during his eulogy and announced that Sister Tricy Dollard would sing a solo. She proceeded to sing "Precious Lord." A few notes into the first verse triggered an emotional outburst from a couple of members of the congregation.

Teresa suddenly cried out plaintively, "Ooh, my baby, I love you! I love you so much. Why did you have to go? Why? Why? Why?"

Her outcry was too much for Allen to endure. He quickly got up from his seat and walked out of the warm, dry confines of the church. As he left, Bernice waved to him, but her efforts went unnoticed. Outside there was a blustery downpour, but Allen took his time walking back to his car.

The soloist's beautiful soprano voice could be heard over the loudspeakers outside of the church. When Allen reached his car, he removed his rain-drenched trench coat and tossed it in the back seat. He turned on the engine and maneuvered the car out of the tight parking space. He drove slowly past the church, where he saw Mr. Andrews and his driver sitting in a black limousine. Mr. Andrews acknowledged him with a wave. Allen responded with a solemn nod.

The day after the burial, Tony and his family went back home to Columbia, South Carolina.

CHAPTER 11

A week later, Ms. Hunter and Patrick were sitting down eating breakfast. She had made pancakes for Patrick, his favorite breakfast since he was a child. She got up from the table to get some butter from the refrigerator.

"Ah, thanks, Mama." Patrick smiled.

Ms. Hunter remained quiet, reminiscing about past events. Life had become an aberration due to the untimely deaths of Carl Ray and Little Carl. Ms. Hunter, a strong, spiritual woman, took solace in knowing that her faith would sustain her throughout this ordeal. She was convinced that one day Teresa's life would once again have a sense of normalcy.

The telephone interrupted her thoughts. She instructed Patrick to tell whoever the caller was that she was unavailable. Within seconds, Patrick returned to the table, informing her that it was a wrong number. Ms. Hunter sighed in relief, returning to her original thoughts.

Several moments passed. Ms. Hunter revealed to Patrick that this morning she thought she heard Little Carl's voice when she woke up. Patrick respectfully assured her that she was probably dreaming.

Ms. Hunter concurred. Patrick went on to tell her that he believed when a person died, that person's spirit floated through the clouds, traveling toward eternal bliss, its final destination.

With a perplexed expression, Ms. Hunter stated firmly, "Well, son, as much as I love you, that sounds like nonsense. I strongly believe that Little Carl is in heaven with God. It is for that reason alone that I'm comforted."

Patrick reached across the table and lovingly gripped her hand as he said warmly, "Mom, you are such a strong woman. I know not to argue with you."

Smiling modestly, she thanked him and replied, "I'm not as strong as you think. As a matter of fact, the day that Little

ONE MORE MIRACLE

Carl died, I went to pieces, but nobody knew it because I locked myself in the bathroom and turned on the shower. I turned the hot water on full force, stood under the shower, and cried my heart out. I lost track of time and was startled by Mia pounding on the door, shouting, 'Granny, I got to use it!' Son, I grieved privately because I couldn't afford to break down in front of your sister and the girls."

Patrick said, "Mom, I'm so worried about Teresa. Not only has she lost a great deal of weight, but she seems spaced out. She's sinking even deeper into a state of depression."

Ms. Hunter confidently told her son, "Don't worry, baby. Teresa will be fine, despite the fact that she's been through a couple of terrible storms, and her life has been altered forever. After every storm there's a rainbow, and I believe that the Lord has a special rainbow in store for Teresa."

Patrick was both perplexed and inspired by what his mother had revealed to him.

The following day, Patrick prepared to return to Germany. As he sat in the living room, contemplating calling a former high-school classmate, he heard a car horn blaring directly outside the kitchen window. Ms. Hunter called out from her bedroom, "Son, the cab is outside."

He got up from his seat and headed down the hall toward the door, where he had placed his luggage. Teresa and the twins were standing at the door, waiting for him to gather his things.

Patrick picked up the two larger suitcases, leaving the smaller one for Teresa to carry to the cab. The driver continued to blow the horn impatiently. As Teresa and the twins followed Patrick to the cab, Ms. Hunter came out of the house, carrying a small bag of freshly baked oatmeal cookies. The driver got out of the car, opened the trunk, took the two large suitcases that Patrick gave him, strategically placed them in the trunk, and slammed it closed. Patrick placed the smaller case in the back seat. He walked over to his mother, who promptly handed him

81

the cookies. Patrick took a deep breath and smiled as his mother told him that she had baked the cookies especially for him. "Thanks, Mom. You are too good to me," he said with a bright smile.

He embraced her, placing an enormous kiss on her left cheek as he told her he loved her.

She gave him a tight squeeze. "I love you, too. I'll see you, baby. Good-bye."

Teresa was standing behind him. He turned around and embraced her. Momentarily looking at Teresa, he then turned back to his mother and said, "Mom, be sure to take good care of my big sister while I'm gone."
Ms. Hunter, teary-eyed, said, "Don't worry, son; I will."

Turning back, Patrick and Teresa stood staring into each other's eyes. Patrick felt as if his heart would burst wide open with sorrow. His sister's tears reminded him of how painful the ordeal still was. He stretched out his arms and hugged her tightly. He reminded her of the promise they had made the night before: not to cry when they said their good-byes.

Teresa spoke, her voice cracking. "Yes...I remember. I'm really sorry, Patrick, but my heart won't allow me to keep that promise. I'm really going to miss you, especially since it seems like the people I love the most are always leaving me."

"I'm so sorry to cause you pain by leaving, but we both know I have to go. Besides, I already told you and Mama that I'll be returning to the States next year," Patrick apologized.

At this point the cab driver began honking his horn again, reminding Patrick that the meter was ticking.

Patrick knelt down, faced the twins, and said, "Now, I want the two of you to give Uncle Pat a great big hug."

They honored his request with the biggest hug around his neck, a hug so tight he could hardly catch his breath. When they finally released him, he laughed and said, "Now, that's what I call a hug."

ONE MORE MIRACLE

He looked at Kendria and whispered, "Will you do your Uncle Pat a favor?"

She nodded.

"I want you to take good care of Mommy for me."

She replied, "Okay, Uncle Pat. I will."

He then looked at Mia and said, "I want you to take good care of Granny...would you be a big girl and do that for me?"

She giggled. "All right, Uncle Pat. I will."

He raced over to where his mother stood and hugged her a second time for an extended moment. This time, Teresa joined their embrace. They all knew his leaving was inevitable because of his military obligation. Nevertheless, it didn't lessen their pain. Patrick slowly pulled away from their loving embrace and turned to get inside the waiting cab. He waved good-bye as the driver pulled off. Ms. Hunter, Teresa, Kendria, and Mia looked sadly in the direction of the cab until it was no longer in sight. Then they went back into the house.

It was seven thirty, and Teresa had spent practically the entire evening addressing thank-you cards to friends and relatives who had supported her during her bereavement. Later, Bernice dropped by unexpectedly to see how she was doing. Once inside the house, Bernice waited patiently until Teresa completed her task. They sat and talked calmly for well over two hours.

Bernice's inquisitive nature wouldn't allow her to leave without asking Teresa, "Who was that white man who attended Little Carl's funeral?"

Teresa was surprised and asked, "What white man? There was no white man at Little Carl's funeral."

"Yes, there was. He was the same man who came to the job looking for you when you were out on funeral leave. He was tall, with long, dark hair, and blue eyes...very good-looking."

Bernice speculated, a whimsical smile on her face. "Girl, that man smelled so good, and was wearing a tailored suit that

83

had to have cost him a fortune. It fitted him perfectly."

She paused as she watched Teresa's expression change. It was as if she had just calculated a list of figures and somehow come up with the wrong total.

"Bernice...did the man say that his name was Allen?"

Bernice nodded with a smile.

Teresa sighed in frustration. "Why didn't you tell me this sooner?"

"Girl, I'm sorry...I guess I kind of forgot. I was in the midst of taking inventory when he stopped by. I was in so much grief with you and your family on my mind, so I forgot. He also told me to make sure to convey his condolences to you and your family. Oh, did I tell you that he left a donation for you?"

"I didn't see his name on the list of people who gave donations," Teresa said.

"Oh, that's because he never actually gave me the donation at the job. He didn't have any cash on him at the time. He gave his donation at the funeral home."

"How did he know where the funeral home was located?"

"I gave him the name and address."

Well, this is interesting, Teresa thought.

Bernice looked at her watch and said, "Teresa, it's almost ten. I didn't know I'd been here so long. Although I've enjoyed our visit, I've got to go. I'm going to go straight to the house, take a nice long, hot bath, and go to bed. I'm due in for work an hour earlier tomorrow morning, and I don't want to be late."

Teresa walked Bernice to the door and bid her good night. She closed the door. A thought came to her as clear and as bright as the morning sun. It couldn't have been one of Carl Ray's friends who paid for Little Carl's funeral. It had to be Allen.

Before daybreak, Teresa laid in her bed, pondering Bernice's visit. She experienced a blend of emotions. At one

84

point, she was comforted by the thought that Allen could be so generous as to remember her in her time of despair. But just as quickly, her pride attempted to resurface, because she was never one to easily accept handouts from anyone. As the thought circulated in her mind, she finally drifted off to sleep.

CHAPTER 12

The following morning, Teresa was awakened by the alarm clock. Staying faithful to her morning ritual, she got up and sat on the edge of her bed, her eyes automatically focusing on Little Carl's empty bed. She said, "Good morning. Mommy loves you, baby, and always will."

Her eyes filled with tears, but she managed to smile and cling to the thought that Little Carl's spirit would forever remain in the room. She reminisced for several additional moments. Then she focused on what she was going to wear. Afterward, she stood up, walked over to the dresser, picked up her hairbrush, and began to brush her hair. As she looked at her reflection in the mirror, her thoughts began to gravitate to Allen.

She contemplated what she would say to him, but most importantly how she would go about thanking him for all that he had done for her.

Teresa would be the first to admit that she knew very little about the male persona. The same question kept recurring in her mind. Why would Allen pay for Little Carl's arrangements, attend the funeral, but not once let me know that he was there? She kept reaching the same conclusion: Men can be so complicated.

Teresa's thoughts were suddenly interrupted by the sound of Mia's voice outside the door. "Mommy, are you ready to go? We don't want to be late for school."
She responded, "Just a minute, Mia…I'll be right out."

Ms. Hunter had prepared the girls' lunches and placed them in the refrigerator the night before. When Teresa made it to the front door, she found both Kendria and Mia waiting patiently. They then left for school.
A little while later, Teresa returned home from walking her daughters to school. When she reentered the apartment, Ms. Hunter was standing at the ironing board, holding up and

inspecting the dress she had just finished ironing.

After Teresa and her mom exchanged greetings, Teresa began to share the information Bernice had told her during their visit the night before. Teresa told her mom that Bernice talked to Allen, and he expressed his condolences to the family.

As she turned to put the ironing board in the closet, her mother glanced at her and asked, "Now, when do you plan to telephone Allen and tell him how much we appreciated what he did for us?"

Teresa responded, "I'm going to do one better, Mama. I am planning to go by his office this afternoon, before I pick the girls up from school."

Ms. Hunter smiled and said, "Then I'm going to bake a batch of tea cakes for you to take to him."

While Ms. Hunter baked the tea cakes, Teresa went to the post office to mail the thank-you cards.

Three hours later, Teresa entered Allen's law office. Martha, Allen's office manager, was watering a potted plant. She greeted Teresa cordially. "Good afternoon. May I help you?"

"I would like to speak to Allen Williams, please."

"Sorry, but he's in a meeting now, and he won't be able to see any clients today," Martha informed her. "Would you like to leave your name and phone number? I'll have Mr. Williams contact you once he's available."

Teresa's heart sank with disappointment. "Yes, I would like to leave a message."

Teresa suddenly had a bright idea. She decided to use a page out of Allen's playbook and handed Martha the batch of freshly baked tea cakes. She then said, "Please tell Mr. Williams that a very grateful friend left these for him."

Martha smiled and reassured her, "I'll make sure he gets the package."

Teresa turned, walked toward the glass doors, exited the office, and walked toward the elevators.

Roughly a second later, the conference room doors swung open. Allen walked out and asked Martha to make some additional copies for his meeting. Out of the corner of his eye, through the glass doors, he caught a glimpse of a woman walking to the elevators. At once, he recognized the woman as Teresa. He called out her name before realizing that she couldn't hear him. He sprinted to the door, opened it, and called out again. "Teresa...please, wait!"

Recognizing his voice, she stopped and turned to look in his direction. Immediately, their eyes locked.

Allen smiled widely, inwardly ecstatic to see her. He advanced toward her, uncharacteristically stuttering, "Ter-Ter-Ter-esa, w-w-w-what a pleasant surprise! What are you doing here?"

She replied softly, "I came by to say thanks to a wonderful man and to tell him how much I appreciated his generosity. Allen, I will never, ever be able to thank you enough for all that you've done for my family and me. Thank you for allowing my child to have a decent funeral and for allowing my family to maintain our dignity, so we wouldn't have to depend on the kindness of strangers."

Allen seemed almost embarrassed as he asked her, "How did you find out that it was me who paid for the funeral? Mr. Andrews didn't tell you, did he?"

Teresa answered tenderly, "No, Allen, he didn't. Some things are just meant for a person to know. I'll tell you what led me to believe that you were the person responsible for helping us. Do you remember the lady you spoke to when you came by my job?"

Allen nodded. "Yes. She seemed like a nice lady."

"Well, she's a really good friend of mine; her name is Bernice. She's the one who told you that my baby had died. When she asked you for a donation, you told her that you didn't have any cash with you, but you would leave a donation at the funeral home."

ONE MORE MIRACLE

Allen remarked, "Yes, I remember that day. When she told me the sad news, it seemed like suddenly everything went out of focus."

"Bernice told me that she tried to get your attention when she saw you at the church, but you did not see her. I thought it strange of you to attend the funeral and leave before the service was over. After all of the pieces of the puzzle were placed on the table, it didn't take me long to figure out the reason why you did not want to be seen. You wanted to remain anonymous. Oh, Allen, that was so gracious of you."

Allen gazed at her with fervent eyes as he smoothed the hair away from his face. His voice was almost at a whisper when he began to speak.

"Oh, Teresa, you've been through so much in your life, and it appears that life hasn't really been fair to you. When Mr. Andrews told me about your husband's death, I was numb. Even now, words fail me. All I can say is, you have my heartfelt sympathy."

Teresa's eyes soon became wet with tears. Allen reached into his pocket and handed her a white monogrammed handkerchief. Teresa's voice was barely audible, but she mustered up enough strength to thank him for his kind words. "It's still very hard to believe that both Carl Ray and Little Carl are gone. It's just like…a bad dream, a nightmare. I keep praying that I'll wake up and it will all be over, but I know that will never happen."

Allen looked at her and thought, I have never felt so helpless as I do at this moment.

He wanted to say something to her, but realized that words offered little or no comfort in the face of all the pain she'd had and was still experiencing. Allen then told her, "If there's anything else that I can do to ease your pain, don't hesitate to call me."

She embraced him tenderly. "Allen, you've already done

so much for me, and I am very appreciative. This type of heartache takes time, and I will have to deal with this misery one day at a time."

Allen and Teresa remained locked in each other's embrace for a long while. Allen didn't want the moment to end. He wished he could just hold her and protect her forever. His thoughts were interrupted by the sound of Martha clearing her throat.

"Uh, excuse me, Mr. Williams. I apologize for the interruption, but I have your copies ready. Was there anything else that you needed?"

Blushing at being caught in a tender moment, Allen thanked her and asked her to distribute the copies and tell everyone that he'd be returning to the meeting in a few minutes. Teresa said softly, "I didn't mean to keep you from your meeting. I just wanted to thank you for being so wonderful to my family."

"Please stay, Teresa; the meeting will be over shortly. I'd love to take you out for a bite to eat."

"Okay," she agreed. "I'll wait."

She followed him back into the office. She then called her mother and told her that Allen wanted to take her out to eat. She asked her mother if she could pick up the girls from school. Ms. Hunter readily agreed.

When the meeting was over, Allen took her to one of the city's top Caribbean restaurants on Roswell, Rob's Place (no relation to Allen's father). When the couple arrived at the eatery, it was only half full. They were greeted by a voluptuous young lady with braids and an infectious smile. She led them to their table, giving them a few minutes to study the menu. When she returned, Teresa ordered curried chicken with black beans. Allen ordered grilled red snapper, a baked potato, and green salad. To top it off, they shared a gigantic slice of rum cake. This was the first complete meal Teresa had eaten since Little Carl's death.

ONE MORE MIRACLE

Allen marveled at her ability to forge a smile. Behind the smile he could see the pain that she was trying to mask. He desperately wanted to tell her how much he loved her and wanted her in his life, but prudence wouldn't allow him to speak what was in his heart. He knew it was neither the time nor the place. Instead, he inquired about Rodney.

Teresa had once described Rodney as a "special friend," so Allen asked her if she was still seeing her "special friend."

Teresa shook her head. "No, I am not seeing Rodney anymore. My 'special friend' turned out to be a jackass."

"I don't mean to be presumptuous, but what happened? Why did you break up?"

"Oh, I really don't want to talk about it. I've had such a good day with you, and I don't want to ruin it by talking about him."

Allen respected her decision and simply nodded. "I understand. If you don't want to talk about it, please don't."

Inwardly, Allen was delighted. It provided him with a glimmer of hope. He believed he now had a legitimate chance to win Teresa's heart, but he was still compelled to ask Teresa if she was dating anyone else.

"Right now dating is just not a priority. My focus is on my family. The way I'm feeling right now, I may never date again."

Allen shook his head and responded quickly. "Oh, please don't say that. You're much too young to make that type of assertion. Besides, I'd like to take you out to dinner again sometime, whenever you feel up to it."

"I would definitely welcome the opportunity to go to dinner with you in the future. I consider you a close friend, who also happens to be one of the sweetest and kindest men I've ever met."

Allen replied, "It's gratifying to hear those words coming from your lips."

91

When Teresa glanced out of the window, she saw that it was dark outside. Her original intention had been to drop off the tea cakes at Allen's office, thank him, and then go directly back home, but she'd been away for more than four hours. Allen read her expression and motioned for the waitress. He paid the bill, and they walked outside to his car.

The drive to Teresa's apartment took less than thirty minutes. Once they arrived, Allen got out of the car and opened the passenger-side door for Teresa. He walked her to the door of the apartment.

They stood for a long moment, looking into the depths of each other's eyes.

Allen ended the silence when he said, "Seems like we've been here before."

"Yes, you're right. This is where we ended our first date."

He laughed. "Silly me, how could I have forgotten?"

Teresa laughed, too. "Yes, how could you have, but a lot has changed since the first time you were here. I was so happy then. My baby was still alive, although you never got a chance to meet him. Allen, I need to get away for a while; there are so many sad memories in Atlanta for me."

"You think a vacation is what you need?"

"Yeah. I think I'll take the girls up to South Carolina. My older brother, Tony, lives in Columbia."

"Maybe a vacation is just the remedy you need. Hey, I'm going on a business trip to New York City on Friday. Why don't you and the girls come with me?"

Surprised, Teresa pondered the idea.

"Am I hearing you correctly? You want the girls and me to go to New York City with you?"

Allen nodded. "Yes, you're hearing me correctly."

"Gee, I don't know. I'm sure you already have reservations for yourself. To make reservations for three additional people I'm sure would cost you an arm and a leg.

ONE MORE MIRACLE

Allen, you've done so much for me already; I'd feel guilty accepting your invitation."

"Teresa, I don't want to come across as being arrogant, but money has never been a problem for me. Let me worry about the cost. Just say you'll come."

"Okay, we will go with you. Man, the girls are really going to be excited. What time are we leaving on Friday?"

"Ah, to be honest, I don't know. Martha made the reservations. When I get to the office in the morning, I'll have her make the additional reservations. Once they are confirmed, I'll call you."

On that note they hugged and said good night.

Teresa stuck the key in the lock, turned it, and entered the apartment. She went straight to the living room, where she found her mother watching television. Teresa went and sat down beside her on the sofa.

"Hi, Mama; sorry I was gone so long. Allen and I went to get a bite to eat. Where are my little ones?"

"They're taking a bath. Did you thank Allen?"

Teresa smiled. "Yes, I sure did. Allen is incredible—one of a kind."

There was a brief moment of silence. Teresa continued to gaze at her mother. The silence was broken when Teresa said, "Mama, what do you think about me and the girls going to New York?"

"You and the girls going to New York? With whom?"

"Well, Allen asked me to go to New York, and he wants the girls to come with us. What do you think?"

"Teresa, you are a grown woman. I can't stop you from going."

Teresa looked at her and grinned. "Of course I'm a grown woman. I am not asking for your permission. I'm asking your opinion."

Ms. Hunter turned away from the television abruptly,

93

focusing her attention on Teresa.

"So you say Allen asked for the girls to come with the two of you?"

"Yes, Mama, he did."

"Teresa, I don't know about this. I just don't know if it's a good idea. Number one, they've never met Allen, and number two, he's white."

"Oh, Mama, what does him being white have to do with any of this?"

"C'mon, child. Be realistic. Allen being white has everything to do with this. These children haven't been exposed to that many white people. You know how mean-spirited people can be."

"What are you trying to say?"

"What I'm saying is white people seeing a black woman and two black children with a white man—they're going to look at you all funny, and they may even say or do some mean things. Heaven knows I don't want my grandbabies exposed to that kind of treatment."

Teresa snapped back. "Mama, it's not like he asked us to go to Mississippi with him. You're blowing this whole thing out of proportion. The girls are always exposed to white people. They go to school with white children. They had a white teacher last semester. New York City is a very diverse place, so I've been told."

"Okay, let me just shut up. Kendria and Mia are your children. You're a grown woman. I know I can't stop you, so I'll just shut my mouth."

"Thanks for your opinion. I'm going to take your advice and introduce the girls to Allen, and see how they respond to him. If they feel the least bit uncomfortable around him, then I won't take them. I may not even go either."

Ms. Hunter looked at her daughter and laughed. "I don't recall saying I wanted you to introduce the girls to Allen."

"Okay, Mama, maybe you didn't, but you did put the thought in

94

my head."

On the day before their departure, Teresa picked up the girls from school early. She and the twins met Allen at his office, and from there they went to Stone Mountain Park. The visit went extremely well. After the girls were introduced to Allen, it didn't take long for them to warm to him. The four of them rode the merry-go-round for what seemed like hours. The girls ate their share of hot dogs and ice cream. When the day ended, Allen took them home. The girls chatted happily in the back seat. Teresa was indeed satisfied and couldn't wait to tell her mother how much fun Mia and Kendria had had.

After hearing the details, Ms. Hunter changed her position and told Teresa the trip to New York was probably what she needed. Teresa then told her mother she was tired. She got up from the sofa and went to her room, leaving her mother to indulge in her private thoughts.

CHAPTER 13

On the day of the departure, Teresa and her girls were seated at the airport, waiting for Allen to return. He'd gone to check in their luggage. When Kendria saw him coming up the escalator, she nudged her mother. "Mommy, here comes Mr. Allen now."

Allen came and took a seat beside Teresa.

Teresa smiled. "You were gone so long that I thought you skipped out on us."

Allen returned the smile. "Oh, is that your way of telling me you missed me?"

She smiled again. "Um...maybe."

He looked at her lovingly. She looked back at him quizzically. "What?"

She knew what he wanted to hear, so she relented. "Allen, of course I missed you."

He took her hand, drew it to his mouth, and kissed it softly.

The girls suddenly jumped from their seats, both displaying restless energy, as they ran around in a circle, singing and dancing. Teresa silenced them with a stern stare and told them they were being too noisy. She ordered them back to their seats. Allen continued to look at Teresa. He could sense anxiety in her beautiful, brown eyes.

"What's the matter?" he asked.

"I'm just a little nervous. I have never flown before," she said.

"Don't worry. There's nothing to be nervous about. When the plane takes off, all you have to do is just hold my hand."

She nodded. "Thanks, I will."

A woman's voice came over the speaker. "Attention, please. Delta flight one twenty-eight to New York City, Boston, and Hartford is now boarding at Gate Seven."

Allen glanced at Teresa and said, "That's us."

Teresa turned to the girls. "Mia, Kendria, come on, let's go."

ONE MORE MIRACLE

The four of them headed for Gate Seven.

A few minutes later, they were in their seats on the plane. Teresa was about to complain about the heat, when the air conditioner suddenly came on. Soon they could hear the roaring sound of the engine, and the plane started to move slowly. Teresa glanced out of the window, watching an airline maintenance worker direct the pilot onto the runway. Once there, it stopped abruptly.

Mia called out to Teresa. "Mommy, why are we stopping?"

Before Teresa could utter a word, Allen answered. "Sweetheart, we're stopping because the pilot probably hasn't been given permission to take off."

"Who tells the pilot when to take off?" asked an inquisitive Mia.

"An air traffic controller in the tower behind us tells the pilot when to take off," Allen replied.

"What's a tower?" Kendria asked.

"It's like a tall, skinny building, or you could say it's a tall structure that overlooks the airport. It's a command center, where air traffic controllers communicate with incoming and outgoing airplanes. The air traffic controllers are the people who tell the pilots when it's safe to land and to take off."

Teresa was impressed with Allen's patience with the girls and how he explained to them what was going on.

The roar of the engines was more intense this time as the aircraft headed down the runway, picking up speed. Teresa's eyes stay fixed on the window as she looked out at the concrete pavement rapidly disappearing from view. The plane ascended quickly, soaring high in the Georgia sky.

Twenty minutes into the flight, Atlanta was all but a distant memory. Teresa continued to gaze out of the window with fascination, though the blue and white clouds shrouded her view. The girls sat rapt, taking turns looking out the window. Three hours later, Delta flight 128 was flying over the Hudson River. The pilot's voice came over the intercom, informing the passengers that the plane was now approaching JFK Airport. He also told the passengers seated on the right-hand side of the aircraft that they could see the state of New Jersey from their vantage point. As the plane began to descend in the night sky, the amber lights of the city below created the perfect canvas for a panoramic view of New York City. The Big Apple is considered one of the world's most electrifying cities. Allen, like most New Yorkers, found the city's energy and majesty unequaled.

Two hours later, Allen, Teresa, and the girls were settled in at the hotel in midtown Manhattan. Allen had reserved a two-bedroom suite at the Plaza, overlooking Central Park. After freshening up and changing clothes, the four went down to the main lobby, to the Platinum Room, one of the restaurants located inside the hotel.

Teresa sat awestruck by the decor: the purple velvet chairs, the luxurious royal-blue-and-gold carpeting, the finest crystal glasses, and exquisite china. The food was also superb. It was beautifully arranged on giant platters. Allen's smoked salmon, shrimp, crabmeat with wild rice, and steamed broccoli were whisked in by a flamboyant waiter.

The same dramatic flair was demonstrated when he delivered Teresa's prime rib, baked potato with all of the trimmings, and asparagus with hollandaise sauce. Mia and Kendria feasted on cheeseburgers, fries, and milkshakes. Allen and Teresa skipped dessert, but the girls thoroughly enjoyed their towering banana splits; Teresa and Allen laughed at them in their attempts to devour their desserts.

After dinner, the four of them returned to the suite, and to Teresa's surprise, Allen turned in early. He was looking forward to an early morning meeting with two potential business partners. Teresa and the girls, too wired to sleep, stayed up well into the night. Teresa watched a couple of movies, while the energetic girls played with their dolls. It was almost midnight when Teresa ordered them to bed. About forty-five minutes later, Mia and Kendria were sound asleep.

Teresa found herself staring out of the large showcase window, glancing down twenty-four stories at the wave of humanity, looking like a sea of marionettes. The multitude of lights from the vehicles cascading down both sides of the street caused Teresa to say to herself, It's well after midnight, and all these people are still on the street. Does this city ever sleep? Another thought occurred to her. If anyone would have told me I would be in a hotel in New York City with Allen, I would have called them crazy.

At two o'clock in the morning, the hotel suite was quiet. Teresa sat upright on the sofa. For some reason she couldn't sleep. Maybe it was the unfamiliar surroundings. She wondered, what does Allen really want from me? It can't be just sex. Allen is too rich and handsome to be hung up on someone like me.

Teresa knew she was pretty, but she was too modest to ever admit that to anyone else, only herself. Nevertheless, she found it quite intriguing not really knowing what Allen's intentions were—what type of relationship he wanted, or if he would be content just being friends.

Teresa's intuition was leading her to believe that by the time they returned to Atlanta, her questions would be answered. With those thoughts in mind, Teresa finally drifted off into a deep sleep.

At eight thirty that morning, Teresa dragged herself out of bed. Kendria and Mia were missing from the room, but they could clearly be heard in the suite's living room, laughing. It was obvious they were watching cartoons on television. Teresa was concerned that the noise would bother Allen, so she raced to the girls and told them to turn it down and not to wake Allen. Kendria then told her that Allen had already left. Mia informed her that Allen had left her a note. The girls were sitting on the couch, with two breakfast trays in front of them. Allen had phoned room service to bring breakfast for them, before leaving for his meeting.

Teresa was touched by this kind gesture. She could only shake her head in pleasant disbelief. What a sweet guy. He is amazing.

She strolled over to the coffee table, picked up the white sealed envelope, and opened it. To her astonishment, Allen had left five crisp one-hundred-dollar bills and a note that read:

My dearest Teresa,

I don't know how long I'll be gone. I anticipate that this meeting will last all day, so please take this money, and you and the girls go sight-seeing. You can catch a tour bus in front of the hotel every hour until 2:00 p.m. So go and have a good time. Have fun.

With deep affection,

Allen

Teresa took Allen's advice. She bought the tickets, and at ten o'clock she and her daughters boarded the tour bus in front of the hotel. The first stop was the Empire State Building. The tour of this famous landmark lasted two hours.

The second stop was Central Park. Then from there they went to Liberty Island to see the Statue of Liberty. It was four o'clock when the tour bus pulled back up in front of the hotel. When Teresa and the girls entered the lobby, they bumped into Allen, who was getting off the elevator. The girls ran to him with outstretched arms. Allen knelt down, gave them a hug, and said, "Well, I sure am glad to see you. Are you glad to see me?" Both girls replied, "Yes, we are glad to see you!" Allen stood up and smiled at Teresa. "Well, what did you guys do today?"

Teresa filled him in on how the day went. She started with the tour, telling him how excited she and the girls were, going to see the Empire State Building and Central Park. "What an awesome city New York is."

Teresa asked Allen how his meeting went. He was upbeat and optimistic about the two potential partners with whom he'd met. They wanted to start a construction business and have offices in New York and Atlanta. Allen would run the Atlanta office.

He didn't want to go into details, though, because he was superstitious and never liked discussing pending deals until they were finalized. Nevertheless, he appeared to be in a jovial mood and wanted to celebrate, so he whisked Teresa and the girls out of the hotel and took a taxi to Fifty-Seventh Street, to his favorite Chinese restaurant.

After a quick meal, Allen took them to Macy's on a shopping spree. Teresa pleaded with Allen not to be so lavish in his spending on them. However, trying to convince Allen to be thrifty was like trying to convince the French that wine was bad for them. Allen spent over $3000 on toys and clothes for Teresa and the girls. He was actually planning on spending more, but the store was closing and they had to leave.

Twenty-five minutes later, they were back at the hotel. It had been a long day, so Teresa ran a shower for the girls. After they took their showers, they waited on Teresa to come read them a bedtime story. It was Teresa's nightly routine which they eagerly awaited.

Teresa informed Allen she would be with him shortly; she was going to read a bedtime story to the girls. He asked Teresa if he could read to the girls. She agreed and invited him into the room. When she told the girls that Allen would read them a story, both girls shrilled enthusiastically, "Yes! Yes! We want Mr. Allen to read us a story!"

Mia handed him a book and he took a seat on the bed by both of them. Teresa sat at the foot of the bed, while the girls cuddled next to him. Allen read several stories out of the big white book that Mia handed to him. If the girls would have had their way, they would have had Allen read the whole book, but Teresa soon put the story-reading to a halt. She told the girls it was time to turn in.

He reluctantly said, "Sorry little ones. Mommy wants you to go to bed now, so I guess we will have to stop for tonight."

He bided them goodnight, gave them a hug and left the room.

Teresa told him, she would join him shortly. Kendria and Mia said their prayers. Once they were done, they gave Teresa a kiss on the cheek. Teresa turned off the lights and joined him on the sofa in the outer suite.

Allen had room service bring a bottle of Merlot for himself and a porcelain kettle of hot chocolate for Teresa. She sat down beside him. He poured the hot chocolate from the kettle into a cup for her. He then poured himself some wine in a crystal goblet.

Teresa held her cup up to him and proposed a toast. She looked at him and said softly, "Allen, let this night be the beginning of a special friendship, one that I hope will never end."
Looking at her with admiring eyes, he nodded his head, "I concur!"

He toasted her cup with his glass, and they both sipped their respective drinks. Allen appeared tired, so he leaned back on the sofa. Teresa loosened his neck tie, then bent down and removed his shoes.

Surprised, he remarked, "Oh, Teresa, you don't have to do that; I am not that tired!"

His heart seemed to melt at her thoughtfulness.
Teresa then looked into his eyes. Captivated by his gaze, she

whispered softly, "You have such beautiful eyes."
He smiled, "Only because I am looking at you."
"You always seem to say the right things at the right time."
"Well, it's true, Teresa."
Thinking that she was keeping him from resting, Teresa said,
"Allen, I should let you go to your room and get some sleep,
since you had such a long day."

"No, no, Teresa, I am fine. I would like to spend the rest
of the evening talking to you."
"Alright Allen, let's talk"

Without warning, she rested her head on his chest. That
was the second intimate close encounter they shared since being
on the trip. Teresa and Allen began to talk generally about life.

Teresa bewailed, "The past nine months of my life have
been hard to come to terms with."

He then comforted her with, "I know words offer very
little consolation to you, but for what it's worth, I will always be
there for you."

He told her the same thing at the sandwich shop in
Atlanta. He was just reiterating his feelings.

She grabbed his hand and responded, "Oh Allen, I could
never repay you for all the wonderful things you've done for me.
You have been such a God send!"

They continued to stare into each other's eyes. He pulled
her close to him and kissed her on the lips. She kissed him back,
running her fingers through his hair. Without hesitation, their
lips met. The series of kisses lasted for an extended moment,
before Teresa suddenly pulled away and said, "Oh, Allen, what
are we doing? We shouldn't be doing this. You're committed to
someone else; in fact, you are committed to two people!"

Peering into her eyes, he responded, "I'm not committed
to anyone, Teresa. I'm probably the most unconventional man
you'll ever meet. I've pretty much danced by the beat of my own
drum most of my life. I've traveled the world. I've made lots of

money. Teresa, I have to be honest, and I don't know how you're going to take this, but I've had my fair share of women. But you know what's amazing? I'm still not happy! There's still something missing in my life...and you know what? That something is you! Yeah, I am seeing two ladies, but I am not in love with either one of them and would gladly give both of them up for you. You may not believe in love at first sight, but I do. No, I've never made love to you, but the first time I laid eyes on you, I fell in love with your *Spirit*. What I feel for you, I can't explain. You consume most of my thoughts. You may not believe me but I have to say it. I'm in love with you. I'm truly in love with you and that's GOD's honest truth."

"Allen, I'm sort of concerned when you say that you've always *danced by the beat of your own drum*...does that mean that you're not capable to being committed to one person?"

"Teresa, I've never met anyone that I wanted to be committed to...until now. I know I love you with all of my heart."

Astonished, she energetically shook her head, "No Allen, you can't love me. We are from two different worlds. You're rich and I'm poor; you're white, I'm black. You're educated, I'm not. I know I've repeated this often, but I feel I have nothing to offer you."

He took a deep breath and responded sincerely, "In my world, color is not an issue and neither is money."
He posed a question." Teresa, how do you define love? Do you define love in dollars or how many degrees an individual has?"
"No, Allen, that's not how I define love."
"Well, Teresa, answer these questions for me. Could you love me if I weren't rich or if I weren't white?"

"Allen, how do you know I don't love you already?"
"Are you saying that you DO love me?"
His eyes suddenly dazzled.
She answered softly, "Yes, I think I love you, but I'm conflicted.

ONE MORE MIRACLE

I don't know how to describe my true feelings.
I know that I DO love you, but I'm not sure if I am IN love with you. Allen you have done so much for me and have been so generous; any decent person would have to love you."
Looking slightly crest-fallen, he responded, "Teresa, I appreciate your honesty. I realize that the flame of love doesn't burn in your heart with the same passion as mine. I strongly believe there is a spark in your heart for me and given the chance, I know I can turn that spark into a flame. I know one day you'll feel the same way, too. Please, just give me a chance! Teresa, your husband is gone now, so there is nothing standing in our way. I have to be candid. Teresa, I know that I love you. And I don't want a long courtship...I WANT TO BE YOUR HUSBAND NOW!"
Allen, I don't doubt your love for me, yet still find the idea of you wanting to get married is quite unsettling. There's no doubt you are a good and generous man," she continued, gesturing in deference, "but I have to ask you one question. *Can I completely trust you?* I know woman are attracted to you. If we were to get married, would I have any reason to be concerned about your faithfulness when you're out of town on business trips?"
With compelling eyes, he assured her, "Teresa, trust is important to me also. I was raised in a house with two parents who love and are committed to each other. They have been married for over thirty years and have a splendid marriage; that's the kind of marriage I want us to have. To answer your question, sure you can trust me! I promise I'll never betray your trust, Teresa. I love you so much, and I know we're meant to be together. I would say it's Fate. Knowing you, you probably would say it was a blessing from Heaven, but whatever the case, I'm in agreement with it. I hope you feel the same way."
"Yes Allen, I feel the same way. I hate to beat a dead horse, but let's be candid. You're going to be marrying a black

105

woman with two black children. I know it's not an issue with you, but other people may have a problem; the world still sees things in black and white."

"That's true Teresa, and it's sad. But truth be told, all of us are mixed; very few people are pure anything. In your bloodline, I know you have some white ancestry in your family. I have some black ancestry in my family, also."

"Allen, you're absolutely right, but I don't have *enough* white blood in me to be white, and you don't have *enough* black blood in you to be black. Therefore, you'll never see the world the way I see it. Society will always treat you better simply because of the color of your skin. So Allen, what about your family and friends? Will they accept me and my girls? I have to think about my children, and how they would be affected by us getting married."

With sincere eyes and an ardent voice, he said, "Teresa, this definitely applies to my family and small circle of friends. If by chance any one of them refuses to accept you and your children and not give you the respect that you deserve as my wife, then, as far as I am concerned, they're *'persona-non-grata'*. Teresa, if I have to, I will protect you and your children with my life. That's how much you mean to me. As nice as people say I am, I can be just as nasty with anyone who attempts to harm the people I love."

Reassured, she nodded, "I believe you, Allen. Honestly, I do."

Then with a look of mock vexation, she verbally scolded him.

"Mr. Attorney, let's get one thing straight. In the future, when we're having a conversation, let's stick to plain old English. By the way, what does *persona-non-grata* mean?"

"Forgive me for using a legal expression, honey. I was just caught up in the moment. *Persona-non-grata* is a term usually applied to diplomats. When a foreign government refuses to recognize an individual's status as a diplomat in a particular country, they're unacceptable or un-welcomed. The term is Latin in origin."

Teresa nodded, "Thank you very much, Sir!"

She then stared deeply into his eyes, trying to reconcile their interaction with the battle going on within herself. She mused about how this man had never been with her sexually, yet his feelings were so strong. *Wow, the way this whole scenario is playing out, I'm convinced we're meant to be together.*

She then expressed to Allen, "Everything that you've just said to me has convinced me that we are meant to be together."

"So will you marry me?" He asked tenderly.

Tears flowing down her cheeks, she finally accepted his proposal.

"Yes, Allen, I'll marry you."

With an exuberant smile, he responded, "Oh, Teresa, you've just made me the happiest man in the world!"
He drew her to him, holding her in a long embrace, his voice low and deep as he murmured, "I love you."
He continued to kiss her neck, then her lips. She felt his breath blowing gently in her ear. Her body began to moisten all over as her desire intensified.

It was his turn to be stunned when she said, "Allen, do you want to make love to me?"

His heart skipped a beat. He quickly grabbed the glass of wine, took a big gulp, placed the glass back on the small coffee table, and looked intensely at her.
"Teresa, of course I want to make love to you, but not for just one night! I want to make love to you every night, every night for the rest of our lives! Do you know what I want more than anything?"

"No, what's that?"

"I want the first time we ever make love to be on our wedding night."

Teresa certainly wasn't ready for *that* response. She slowly rested her head on the couch's armrest.

"Allen, I'm blown away. I just don't know what to say. All I can say is that's one of the sweetest, kindest things that any man has ever said to me. You've said many wonderful things to me tonight, but this tops them all!"

They stared at each other for a blissful moment before Teresa finally asked, "Allen, when you look at me, what do you see? Please don't describe me physically?"

"That's pretty easy to do," He smiled:

When I look at you, I see in you a woman who has been through an awful lot of emotional pain. I can still see the pain in your eyes and in your face. I see a woman who is resilient, ambitious and a wonderful mother.

I see a woman who hasn't enjoyed the finer things in life. I see a woman whose Spirit has been shattered, but somehow She's still whole. I see a woman surrounded by poverty, but rich in character. A woman who possesses a heart of gold. Most importantly, I see in you my future; my soul mate."

Like a good lawyer who'd just finished his final summation, he concluded by saying, "I rest my case."

Teresa's mouth began to twitch into a smile.

"Why are you smiling?"

"I'm curious, Allen. What if I would've pushed the issue? Would you have made love to me, then?"

He smiled and said, "Wow, that's a hard one."

"Oh, so you're saying you *wouldn't* have done it, under *any* circumstance?"

"Come on, Teresa, don't make me lie…let me be perfectly honest. I've charmed enough woman out of their panties in my lifetime. This time I want it to be different. By both of us agreeing to wait until we're married, we will only *strengthen* our bond. You won't have any doubts about my love for you this way.

108

ONE MORE MIRACLE

"Allen, that's so beautiful! We both know this isn't the perfect setting with my children in the next room, although you had me sizzling.

"I know what I'm going to do, Teresa. Go take a nice, cold shower."

But contrarily, he pulled her closer and they began to kiss again. The kissing was breached when Teresa said,

"Allen…Allen…remember what you said about the *cold* shower?

She then gave him a quick kiss in the lips and departed from the room. His eyes followed her as she entered the bedroom, closing the door behind her. He picked up the glass of wine and finished it. He then leaned backward on the sofa, resting his tired back and smiling. Inwardly, Allen was elated because he was about to embark on a new life with Teresa. He knew his feeling of euphoria would be in sharp contrast to the way Heather and Wendi would feel once he revealed to them his plan to marry Teresa. That dilemma weighed heavily on his heart.

CHAPTER 14

The next day, back in Atlanta at around 11:30 a.m., Allen dropped Teresa and the girls off at their apartment. Teresa explained to Allen that she wanted to break the news to her mother in private. Allen respected her decision. When they got out of the car, he assisted them with the luggage.

The girls got out of the car and raced to the door, shouting, "Granny! Granny! We're back!" loudly banging on the door.

Kendria said, "Mommy, Granny isn't answering the door."

Mia followed with, "Mommy, why isn't Granny opening the door for us?"

"Maybe she's taking a nap, Mia."

Teresa removed her key from her purse, stuck in the lock and opened the door. The girls ran into the house, while Allen helped Teresa bring the luggage inside the apartment. She thanked him, gave him a quick kiss, and he got back into the car and drove off.

The girls ran to their grandmother's room, as Teresa shouted, "Mama! Mama! We're home!"

The girls quickly returned to the front room, telling their mother that their grandmother wasn't in her room. Teresa immediately went to the kitchen, where she assumed her mother would've left a note on the refrigerator door, which was her custom when she left home.

She found a note, which read:

Dear Teresa,

I've gone to play Bingo at the Community Center. I'll be back around 3:00 p.m. I cooked a pot of chicken noodle soup, so you can feed the girls, if they're hungry.

Love, Teresa.

ONE MORE MIRACLE

It was a 2:45 p.m., when Ms. Hunter entered the apartment. When the girls saw their grandmother, they ran up to her, screaming, "Granny! We're back! We're back!"
Ms. Hunter smiled, "I can see," as she knelt down to hug them. Her cheeks were wet with kisses from both girls.

Teresa sat on the couch smiling. Ms. Hunter walked over to the couch, holding both girls' hands. Teresa rose to her feet, giving her mother a big hug. "We missed you so much, Mama!"
"I missed you too. The house has been so quiet, I couldn't sleep."
Ms. Hunter's eyes quickly focused on the couch, where she saw all the Macy's bags. "What in the world is all of this?"
"Mama, Allen took the girls shopping, while we were in New York. There's stuff in the bags for all of us."

The girls were excited, telling their grandmother about all the new toys they had. Teresa wanted to talk to her mother in private, so she asked the girls to go to their room for a while. The girls grabbed two of the bags and headed for their room.

Ms. Hunter looked at her daughter with curiosity. "Teresa Gail, what is it you want to tell me?"
Teresa hesitated. "Well, Mama, I don't know how you're going to take this, but Allen asked me to marry him, and I said yes."

Ms. Hunter looked at her with a probing stare. "What?! He asked you to marry him? Is that how he tricked you into sleeping with him?"
Teresa looked at her, "Mama, what are you talking about?"
"Did that man take you up to New York and voodoo you or something?"
"Mama, that sounds off the wall! Allen doesn't know anything about voodoo, and neither do I!"
"Teresa, have you lost your senses? You know darn well that white man is not going to marry you! Teresa, if you slept with the man, I don't have anything to do with that. That's your

111

business."

Teresa looked at her mother, stunned.

"Mama, I'm so surprised that this is what you think of me. Do you honestly think that I'm that loose? Mama, you don't know what you're saying, Allen loves me, and I love him!"

Ms. Hunter shouted, "Teresa, just because you sleep with a man one time doesn't mean that he loves you! He probably just loved you for that moment!"

Teresa looked at her mother angrily. "Mama, I didn't sleep with Allen! And he didn't pressure me to sleep with him, either. You know what? He said the first time we sleep together; he wants it to be on our wedding night. In spite of whatever you're thinking, Allen is a man with character! What kind of man would pay for your child's funeral, but never want you to find out about it? What kind of man would offer to take you on a trip and then ask you to bring your children? Mama, I know you have a hang-up about black and white, but I don't see Allen as a white or black man, I just see him as a special man. Whatever you think or however you feel, I'm going to marry him. I would love to have you at the wedding, but if you choose not to come, so be it!"

Teresa turned and walked to her room, slamming the door behind her in anger. Ms. Hunter sat mortified, feeling as if all the oxygen had been sucked out of the room.

Hours later, Ms. Hunter knocked on Teresa's bedroom door. "Teresa?" she called out softly.

Teresa answered dryly from behind the door, "Yes, Mama, what is it?"

"Can I please come in, so we can talk?"

"Mama, I don't want to argue about this anymore, okay? Too much has been said already. Let me sleep on it for now. I'll talk to you in the morning."

"Okay, baby, I understand. We'll talk in the morning."

The next morning, Teresa got up and went into the

112

kitchen. She found her mother sitting at the kitchen table drinking coffee. She had also fixed breakfast.

Ms. Hunter looked at Teresa and said, "Teresa, please let's talk before the girls get up. I'm sorry that I misjudged you. Like most mothers, I'm guilty of trying to run your life. I have to realize that you're a grown woman. I seem to forget that you're a mother also, but to me, you'll always be my little girl. I am so sorry for yesterday. I know you may not be able to do it today, but I hope one day you'll forgive me."

Teresa wanted to be firm, but when she looked at her mother and saw tears in her eyes, her demeanor instantly softened.

"Mama, of course I forgive you."
Ms. Hunter grabbed her around the neck and held her tightly.

"I'm so sorry, Baby, so sorry!" she murmured.

"Okay, okay, Mama, please stop! You're going to make me cry."

CHAPTER 15

Meanwhile, Allen sat in his office, busily reviewing work that had piled up while he was on vacation.   Upon his return, Martha, his office manager informed him that she had been inundated with messages. The primary caller was Heather, who had called numerous times. After reviewing his messages, he then told Martha to hold all of his calls except for Teresa's. From his desk, he tried to reach Heather at her office. Her secretary informed him she was in a meeting with the boss. Allen asked her to give Heather a message that he would be at her place around 6:00p.m. Allen then engrossed himself in his work. He lost track of time. When he finally looked at his watch, it was a quarter-to-six. He put a stop to his activities and gathered his belongings. The last thing he retrieved was a black leather briefcase. He then headed to Heather's place.

It was 6:15 p.m. when he let himself in with a spare key. Although he had visited her penthouse apartment many times, he'd always felt transient there. While making his way through the apartment, he heard the sound of running water coming from the bedroom shower. He didn't want to startle Heather, so he called out her name. He did this several times, but apparently she didn't hear him. The shower continued to run for about ten minutes. When the water suddenly stopped, he called out to her again. This time she answered, "Allen, is that you?"

"Yes, it's me," he replied in a loud and clear voice. When she stepped out of the shower into the bedroom, she was wearing nothing but a bath towel draped around her head. She found Allen standing, with his back against the wall. She ran and kissed him. He barely kissed her back. He stood silently for a brief moment.

"Heather, you're getting me wet!"

"Yes, I know. Sorry Allen, aren't you glad to see me?" she asked with a wary smile.

114

"Sure, of course I am!" he nodded.

"Well, how was your trip to New York?"

"Oh, it was fine."

"You know, Allen, since you left for New York, you've become quite the elusive bird. I called you several times while you were there, but you didn't return any of my calls."

"Sorry, Heather, but I was very busy up there. I do apologize."

"Really," said Heather, dryly.

"As a matter of fact, I did call your office today, and your secretary told me you were in a meeting with your boss. Didn't she give you my message?"

"Oh Allen, she did tell me you called. Now, it's I who should apologize. Well, why are you still standing? Make yourself comfortable; sit on the bed or better yet lie down!"

"I'd rather not," he said guardedly.

Heather sensed Allen was preoccupied and had something heavy on his mind.

"Allen, what's up? What's on your mind?"

"Heather, don't you think it's a little chilly in here? Aren't you cold? Why don't you put on some clothes?"

"What?! Allen, let's get one thing straight. I don't like being told what to do in my house! I'll wear clothes when and if I want to! You've never had a problem with me walking around naked before!"

"Okay, okay, Heather, I understand this is your house, but it is a little cold in here. That's why I suggested you put something on."

Allen was actually lying. He felt tempted, watching this nude woman with whom he'd spent the night less than a week ago.

"You know, Allen, there is a chill in here thanks to you! Since you got here, you've been cold and distant."

She then walked over to the closet, grabbed a purple silk bathrobe, and slipped it on. She took a seat on the edge of her

115

queen-size, Victorian-style bed, her arms folded tightly.

Allen remained standing, looking uneasy. The silence was finally broken when he said, "Believe me, this is one of the hardest things I've ever had to do…. I'm afraid I'm going to have to end our relationship."

Heather's mouth suddenly went slack and the muscles in her face started to quiver. She felt her heart falling to the pit of her stomach. She couldn't believe those words came from his lips.

"Allen, this is a joke, right? You can't be serious! Please tell me you're joking!" she said, her voice cracking, tears welling to her eyes.

"No, Heather, I'm not joking,"

"What did I do to deserve this, you heartless bastard?! Why did you come over here, to pour salt on the wound?! Why Allen? We get along, I don't crowd you. I give you your space. Why are you doing this to me?"

"Oh Heather, it's time! We've gone as far as we can go. It's just time!"

"Allen, that's a bunch of bullshit! When you left for New York last week, everything was fine between us. Now, here you come with this bullshit! If you want out be a fucking man and tell the fucking truth!"

"Okay, Heather, I will tell you the truth. I'm getting married," he replied calmly.

"You're getting married? *Married?!!* Don't tell me, I know who it is. It's that little wicked bitch Wendi, isn't it? So she won out after all."

"No, it's not Wendi…"

"Allen, if it's not Wendi, *then who is it?*"

"Heather, if you must know, her name is Teresa."

"Well, how long have you known her?"

"A little over two years."

"Allen, are you *really* in love with her?"

ONE MORE MIRACLE

With tears rushing down her cheeks, she said, "Allen, I just can't get over this. Last week you were in my bed making love to me. Now you're telling me you're going to marry some other woman! I was holding on to the hope that one day you and I would be married!"

"Heather, you were holding on to false hope and you know it. Remember last week when you brought up the subject of marriage? I told you then we weren't going to get married. I also suggested that you start seeing other people. So in my heart, I know that I didn't do anything to foster your hope."

"Allen, this woman must be one hell of a lay to get you to commit to marriage."

"Well actually Heather, I've never slept with Teresa."

Heather laughed sarcastically, "Oh, you've been screwing me for over three years, but you've only known this woman for two, and you say you have never had sex with her?! Allen what is she wearing, *a chastity belt*? On your wedding night will she surrender the key and then you'll get the prize? Allen, I know you. I know you too well! You love sex, and you're nothing but a skirt chaser and *that's all you'll ever be!*"

"Heather, you don't know me at all. You're wrong, dead wrong! For the sake of the truth and to use your metaphor, I've never been a *skirt chaser*. I'll admit with chagrin that I've had skirts chase me. But that part of my life is behind me now."

"Allen, what the hell do you mean, *that part of your life is behind you now*? Are you saying you no longer desire other women? What's so special about this *Teresa*? Has she put some sort hex on you?"

"Heather, the short time I've known her, my life has been transformed. Words are inadequate when it comes to describing her. Physically, she's beautiful and her Spirit's beautiful as well."

The egotistical Heather, with a protracted stare, wondered, *'Who in the hell is this woman? She couldn't be all*

117

that! She can't be as pretty as I am! I know she can't please him the way I can!'

"Allen, I can't believe those words came out of your mouth!! Where did you find this little pristine debutante? I hate to think you got her from one of the prep schools around town! I hate to think that you're robbing the cradle! You remember that *gun* you bought me? You better be glad I loaned it to my sister! If I had it here right now, you would be the recipient of nine bullets!! ALLEN, I HATE YOU!!"

"No, Heather. Teresa is a sophisticated woman with two children."

"Oh, really, two children! So, Allen, that means you'll be an instant dad! How terrific! I'm sure it's every man's dream to support some other man's brats!"

"Heather, why don't you knock off the sarcasm! Come to think of it, I am looking forward to becoming a father, even if it means being an *instant dad*. When you love the woman, you love the children. It's a package deal!"

"Allen, you can't possibly be in love with a woman you've never slept with. You're not that kind of man. I'm sure she's beautiful. More than likely you are just infatuated with her beauty. I can prove it to you."

"Heather, there's no need to prove that to me."

She suddenly opened her bathrobe, exposing her body.

"Allen, make love to me! I know I can make you forget all about her!"

"Heather, I don't think you understand, I'm serious! I'm getting married, so I can't do this anymore!"

"You bastard! You're refuse to make love to me after three years of being with me? Tell me again why you can't screw me now?! You owe me that much!"

"Look Heather, you're more than a cheap thrill. You shouldn't have to beg *any* man to make love to you. I have too much respect for you to just screw you and walk away, like you meant nothing to me. I think it's time for me to go, okay?"

He turned and headed for the door.

She followed behind him, screaming, "Go on and go, then! I don't need you! Give me back my fucking key."

He removed the spare key from his key-ring and placed it on the brass table in the foyer. He glanced back at her for the final time. Her emerald eyes were slightly red with tears. Even in her present state (no makeup; her hair wet and disheveled), she was still seductive with captivating eyes.

He took a deep breath, "Well Heather, I guess this is good-bye. Take care of yourself. I'm so sorry it had to end this way."

"Allen, *please make love to me* one last time. When we're done, you can go and never come back. I'll never bother you again. This woman Teresa will never have to know. *Please Allen*," Heather pleads, making one last desperate attempt to seduce him by completely disrobing and quickly walking towards him.

He shook his head, "No, Heather, I can't."

"Why not? My request isn't about her."

Allen stared at her for a long moment with remorseful eyes. "Heather, listen to me. I can't make love to you because everything I do now is about Teresa. I don't want to begin my life with her by cheating. I just can't do that; it wouldn't be right."

"You bastard! I hate you! I wish you were dead! Get the hell out of here! I never want to see you again!"

He quietly strolled out of the apartment and closed the door behind him, stifling the barrage of insults hurled at him by Heather.

He went directly to Wendi's place to end that relationship, too.

Unlike the break-up with Heather, this exchange went a lot smoother. Allen told Wendi all about Teresa. Wendi was deeply hurt. She tried hard to put on a happy face, but inside she was falling apart. She took solace in the fact that he didn't dump her for Heather. Wendi thought of an excuse to get him out of the house to avoid breaking down in front of Allen. She told him that she had to get up early the next morning to drive out of town on a business trip.

"I understand," he said sadly, as he turned to leave. She walked him to the door. As they hugged, she whispered, "I wish you and Teresa the best."
He kissed her softly on the cheek and said, "Take care, kid. I hope you find the right guy, someone who's worthy of you. You're a special lady."
She forced a smile and said, "Goodbye. I love you, Allen."

"I love you too, Wendi." He then walked out. She immediately closed the door.

With her face pressed against the door, she finally began to cry. She looked through the peep-hole and could barely see Allen waiting for the elevator. The elevator door opened, he stepped in and the door closed. That's when the finality of it all set in. She realized there wouldn't be any more "late night phone calls" or visits. No more love-making or breakfasts in bed. No more trips to Europe or new cars. Allen was always generous to the ladies he dated. Wendi's face turned red as she continued crying with her face pressed against the door.

Allen was a few minutes into his drive, avoiding the freeway and taking the long route home. He wanted to clear his head and unwind. It had been a long and emotional day, filled with highs and lows. The highlight of the week was knowing that now he has a future with Teresa.

The despairing part of the day was ending the relationships with Heather and Wendi. Allen's concern was mostly for Wendi because emotionally, she wasn't as tough as Heather. He knew that Heather had the mentality of an alley cat. It didn't matter how many times she was knocked down, ultimately, she always landed on her feet. It was almost midnight

when he made it home. Before going to
bed, he called Teresa. The conversation was short, since she
insisted that he go to bed and get some rest.

CHAPTER 16

The following day, Allen was lounging in his office chair talking to his mother on the phone. She had called to tell him that she and his father were back from New Orleans, where they had attended a medical conference. Martha suddenly buzzed the second line to notify him that the client he was waiting for had arrived. Allen ended the conversation with his mother, telling her he would see her and his dad for dinner. Allen surmised that after dinner would be the perfect opportunity to break the news to his parents about his decision to wed Teresa.

At 6:45 p.m., Allen drove to meet his parents for dinner. They usually ate at their favorite spot, **Aquiliana's**, on Thursday nights. It was an extravagant, Nouveau-Italian restaurant, known for serving authentic Italian cuisine. Because of traffic congestion, Allen was running a little late for their 7:00p.m. dinner date. He arrived at twenty minutes after seven.

He weaved his way through the crowded restaurant, making a beeline to his parents' table. He greeted his mother with a traditional smack on the lips, exchanging smiles and hellos. Allen's dad rose to his feet, shook his son's hand and asked him how his day had gone. He replies, "Oh Dad, the usual daily grind," as he took a seat. His father then summoned his favorite waiter, Frank. Deni ordered the chef's special, Eggplant Parmigianino; Rob ordered veal scaloppini, and Allen ordered Chicken Rollantina. They each also enjoyed a glass of rare pinot noir with their meals.

After dinner, he broke the news to his parents, telling them that he'd decided to get married.

Allen's mother asked, excitedly, "Who 's the lucky girl? Is it Wendi? She's such a sweet girl. Or is it Heather? She's not so bad, either."

For a moment, Allen remained silent with a whimsical expression on his face. Both parents stared at him in anticipation, waiting for an answer.

Allen's dad repeated the question, "Well Bug, who's the lucky girl, Heather or Wendi?"

"Neither of them. Teresa's the woman I am going to marry."

"Who is Teresa?"

"The woman I'm in love with, Dad. I've known her for a little over a year. We met in my office building."

"Bug, is she also an attorney," his mom asked.

Allen knew where this conversation was heading, so he muttered, "No."

"Well, what's her occupation, then?"

"Mother, she's a domestic worker and a student."

Allen's parents were speechless. His father looked dismayed.

Deni asked with a muddled stare, "Excuse me son, did you say *domestic worker*?!"

"Come on son, you can't be serious! We can understand you *mingling* with the help, but you certainly can't be serious about *marrying* one of them," Rob asserted.

"How dare you refer to Teresa as *'the help'*? She is a very intelligent woman. I won't allow you or anyone else to speak about her in such a derogatory fashion. In the future, I wish you'd keep your caustic opinions to yourself."

"Bug I'm sorry. I used a poor choice of words. Please accept my apology," Rob relented.

Allen replied sharply, "Yeah, sure!"

"My dear, your father and I only want the best for you, so even if this woman is a domestic worker, she must be pretty extraordinary to have captured your heart. Darling, when will we get to meet your lady?"

"Mom, you will soon. But I want you and Dad to listen to me. I love this woman. I love her like I've never loved any other woman before. And just so you know, she has two children...and she's also black."

"Honey, I don't care what color she is, as long as you love her," Deni utters.

"Bug, is this the woman you told me about a few months ago?"

"Yes dad she is," he confirmed.

"Bug, please tell me you weren't dating a married woman this whole time!"

Allen gave his dad a hollow stare.

"Dad, I'd never date another man's wife. That's not how mother and you raised me."

"But when we talked about her before, didn't you say the woman you loved was married?"

" Dad, Teresa's husband is dead now. He was killed—I am not going into any details. About a month ago, her three-year-old son also died. That poor child had a lot of medical issues since birth. This has been a tumultuous year for her."

"Oh my dear, my heart goes out to her," Deni exclaimed sympathetically. "Bug, are you sure it is love you feel for her and not pity?"

"Mother, I'm absolutely sure it is love. She's always in my head and heart. Even talking about her makes me feel good inside."

"Certainly sounds like love to me," she smiled.

"Son, I don't want to sound like a pessimist, but how can this relationship possibly last? You have nothing in common with this woman. You need to think this thing through. I can't tell you whom to marry, but don't you think Heather or Wendi would be more suitable choice."

"Dad, you are right. You can't tell me whom to marry. As far as Wendi and Heather are concerned, I'm not in love with either of them. Dad, nothing you can say will change the way I feel. I am going to marry Teresa and that's the bottom line. So, if you and mother will excuse me, I'm leaving. Obviously, I am not in a good mood."

He got up from the table and left the restaurant. Deni and

Rob sat giving each other an unsettling look.

"Rob, Bug is going to marry this girl, and if he's in love with her, she must be pretty amazing. He is far from naïve, especially when it comes to women."

"Deni, Bug is still a man. He is not immune to the power of a woman. A clever woman can break down the strongest of men."

"Yes, Rob, that's true. But that works both ways."

"I'm going to talk to Bug one more time. Hopefully, I can talk some sense into him."

"No, you are not," said Deni in a harsh tone. "Bug is an adult, and we're going to stay out of his personal affairs. His mind is already made up. He's going to marry her. Rob please, I want you to back off and make up with Bug."

"Okay," he conceded reluctantly. "If that's what you really want, then that's what I'll do."

The next morning at the breakfast table, Allen's father apologized for his behavior at the restaurant. Allen is a lot like his father. He inherited his stubborn demeanor, but he accepted his father's apology. Allen's mother was quite pleased that the tension between her husband and son was over.

Deni, a loving, doting mother, had a strong relationship with her children. Her husband, Rob believed she was always partial to Allen. Maybe it was because he looked a lot like her or it could have been because he was the firstborn. Rob once said when it came to Allen, Deni would support him in almost any endeavor, short of bombing a building. But she often accused Rob of being partial to their daughter Katie, whom Deni referred to as the "apple of his eye."

Once peace had been restored at the Williams' household, Deni focused her energy on preparing to meet Teresa. Allen phoned Teresa to tell her that his parents would host a dinner for her and her family on Wednesday night. He requested that they be ready around seven o'clock. This would be the first meeting between the two families. Teresa was truly looking forward to meeting Allen's parents, but she was also experiencing some anxiety. She wondered if Allen's parents would accept a woman with two children, not to mention a black woman with children. One fact was certain: after the dinner date, she would know one way or the other. When she ended her phone conversation with Allen, she went to her mother's bedroom to tell her about the dinner invitation.

She asked her mother to wear her best dress.   Ms. Hunter wasn't too thrilled about accompanying Teresa because she didn't want to be an intruder.

"Mom, the invitation is for the whole family; Allen will be disappointed if you don't attend."

Ms. Hunter acquiesced and finally said, "If it means that much to the both of you, I'll come."

When Allen arrived at Teresa's apartment, he was carrying a special surprise in his coat pocket. He stopped by one of Atlanta's most expensive jewelry stores and purchased an engagement ring. The eight-carat platinum ring was stunning. The center stone was a brilliant four-carat diamond, with two additional two-carat diamonds on each side. The ring set him back thousands of dollars. Before giving Teresa the ring, Allen got down on his knees, proposing for the second time, while Ms. Hunter and the twins looked on.

"Will you marry me?" he asked.

Not knowing he had the ring in his pocket, she said, "Would you let me think about it?"

She paused for a long moment and then replied, "Of course I'll marry you."

Smiling tenderly, he carefully removed the ring from his coat pocket, took it out of the case, and placed it on her left hand's ring finger.

"Oh Allen, it's beautiful! Thank you, thank you so much," she said, overcome with joy.

ONE MORE MIRACLE

"No, Teresa, thank you. I'm just happy you like it."

"I love it Allen; really, I do."

"Ooh, Teresa, that's one beautiful ring! I would be afraid to wear such an expensive ring," said Ms. Hunter.

Teresa lifted her hand, showing the ring to her daughters. "Do you all like Mommy's ring?"

Both of them nodded, "Yes!"

Allen looked at his watch and said, "Hey guys, we don't want to be late. Let's go!"

Shortly after seven, Allen and his passengers drove up to his family's estate. He pulled up at the gate and punched in the secret code on the key pad. The white, wrought-iron gate slowly rolled back on its tracks, allowing them access to the property. Allen then drove about seventy yards to at the main residence.

After the car came to a stop, Allen got out, followed by the twins; he then walked around to the passenger side of the car, and opened the door for Teresa and her mother.

The setting sun seemed to cast a golden shadow over the off white, stucco two-story, Mediterranean-style mansion. Teresa and her mother stood in awe as they viewed the 12,000 sq. feet home that sat on three acres of land.

To the far right, about two hundred yards behind the main residence stood a 2,000 sq. feet guesthouse with three bedrooms and three bathrooms, a mere fraction of the size of the five bedroom, six-bathroom mansion.

Allen and his guests ventured on into the house. They went directly to a formal den where his family often receives guests before serving dinner. Allen opened the walnut-colored French door to the room. Teresa and her family were awed by the antique crystal chandelier that hung high from the ceiling, illuminating the spacious room. Standing in front of the fireplace was a woman with dark, short hair. She was adjusting a photo frame on the mantle.

As she turned in their direction, Allen spoke out, "Mother, this is

Teresa, her mother, Ms. Hunter, and her daughters, Mia and Kendria."

The lady greeted her guests with a dazzling smile. She had striking, blue eyes. Her main focus was on Teresa. The two of them locked eyes, sizing each other up.

"Hello, Teresa. I'm Denique Williams. It's such a pleasure to finally meet you. My son has told me so much about you," she said gently in a French accent, as she hugged Teresa. Teresa smiled, "I'm glad to meet you, too."

Then she turned and hugged Ms. Hunter, "Ms. Hunter, it's a pleasure to meet you, also."

"Likewise, Mrs. Williams."

Kendria stood next to her mother, while Mia stood behind her grandmother, hiding her face. Deni decided to play peek-a-boo with Mia saying, "I can't see you."

Mia then stepped from behind her grandmother. Deni looked at her and quickly glanced at Kendria.

She was surprised. "Oh my God, they're twins! Identical at that. They are so beautiful!" she exclaimed gleefully.

Teresa looked at her girls. "What are you going to say to Mrs. Williams?"

They responded in what seemed like the same voice, "Thank you, Mrs. Williams."

"Teresa, I'm sure you have so much fun with them," Deni said. Teresa admitted," They can be a handful at times, but I wouldn't trade them for the world."

"Where's Dad?" Allen asked.

"Oh, my darling, he's upstairs in his office, taking an important business call. He'll be down shortly."

"I'm going upstairs to take a shower and change. I won't be long. I'll let Dad know we're here."

Deni entertained Teresa and her family during her husband and son's absences. Teresa couldn't help but notice the large diamond earrings Deni was wearing and how blue her eyes were.

ONE MORE MIRACLE

"Now I know where Allen gets his eyes."
"Yes, Bug gets his eyes and dark hair from me. My dark hair comes from my mother who was Greek; my dad was French. I was born in Athens and raised in Paris."
"Then it's safe to say you speak French?" Ms. Hunter asked. Deni nodded with a smile. "In fact, I also speak German and Spanish."
"What about Greek," Ms. Hunter continued.
"Well, my Greek isn't that great. I understand it but I sometimes have a hard time communicating it."
Deni then complimented Ms. Hunter, telling her that she looked young enough to be Teresa's sister.
"Thank you," Ms. Hunter said, "I only wish I felt as good, Mrs. Williams."
"Why don't we call each other by our first names. Mrs. Williams and Ms. Hunter are so formal." Deni suggested.
Although Ms. Hunter didn't feel comfortable with the idea, mainly because of Deni's social status, she reluctantly agreed.
Deni told Teresa that once she and Allen tied the knot, she'd liked to be called Deni or Mother.
Teresa's response was very clever, "I promise you this: I will call you one or the other."
They both smiled. Deni looked at the girls and told them she was going to be their new grandmother. She told them she had other grandchildren. Her son, Paul had a son and a daughter. Deni asked if she could give them pet names.
"We're not pets! We're little girls!" Kendria said.
"A pet name is a nickname," explained Teresa.
"Oh!"
"I never meant that you and your sister were pets. You are far too pretty to ever be pets," Deni expounds.
"Then what is my pet name?" asked Mia.
"Candy Apple. Because you're so sweet," said Deni.

129

Mia giggled.

Deni looked at Kendria and said, "And your pet name, Kendria, will be Sweet Peach, because you're pretty as a peach. Now, what do you think of your pet name?"

Kendria responded, "I think it's silly!"

Deni burst out into an exuberant laugh.

"Kendria! Now you apologize to Mrs. Williams." Teresa demanded.

"Oh, please don't scold her, she said nothing wrong. I had that coming. She never asked for a pet name. It goes to show that one should never underestimate the honesty of a child. It's too bad we adults can't be as honest as children," Deni expounds.

Kendria looked at her mother and saw the disconcerted expression on Teresa's face. Kendria concluded she must have said something terribly wrong. She turned to Deni with remorseful eyes and in a sweet innocent tone, she apologized, "I'm sorry, Mrs. Williams."

Deni kneeled down with extended arms and in a dulcet voice she told her, "You don't have to be, Little Angel. You said nothing wrong."

Kendria quickly hugged her back. Not to be slighted, Mia went and hugged her, also. Deni grabbed both their hands and led them into the dining room. Teresa and Ms. Hunter followed. Before they entered the dining room, the sounds of footsteps were heard coming down the hardwood staircase.

Walking down the steps was a man slightly taller than Allen, with brownish gray hair and deep dimples in both cheeks.

He wore dark blue pants, white Italian-style loafers and a starched white dress shirt. When he reached the bottom of the stairs, he immediately apologized to the guests. Deni beamed proudly as she introduced Teresa and her family to her "tardy" husband. Teresa stood waiting with nervous anticipation until Rob made eye contact with her.

ONE MORE MIRACLE

"You must be Teresa."

"Yes," she smiled timidly.

"Hi, I'm Rob Williams, Allen's father."

"Nice to meet you, Mr. Williams," Teresa said, as they shook hands.

"Oh, feel free to call me Rob."

Teresa then introduced her mother and her daughters.

"It's a joy to meet you, Ms. Hunter and these two lovely little girls," Rob said.

"The feeling is mutual," Ms. Hunter responded politely.

When he smiled, Teresa thought his teeth were extremely white, and if her eyes were closed, she would swear she was listening to Allen's voice. They sounded so much alike! Allen then made his way down the stairs, much to Teresa's pleasure, since she felt more comfortable with him by her side.

"Now you've met both of my parents," Allen said proudly.

"I don't know if that's good or bad," Rob joked.

"Oh, it's a great thing because meeting this wonderful son that the two of you produced is confirmation enough for me that you're great people also," Teresa declared.

Deni walked over to her and gave her an affectionate hug. Obviously, Teresa had captured her heart. "Oh, I love you already," she confessed.

"What a gracious thing to say," Rob smiled as Allen looked on approvingly.

Everyone went into the dining room except Deni, who went to the kitchen to consult with the caterer about the food.

Teresa was amiably surprised when Rob locked arms with her and pulled out her chair at the dinner table. Allen did the same for Ms. Hunter. Rob then seated Mia and Allen seated Kendria, just as Deni walked into the room. Allen did the honors for his mother. Thirty minutes into dinner, Deni couldn't help but notice how attentive Allen and Teresa were to each other.

131

When Teresa wanted more tea, Allen filled her glass. When Allen wanted an extra baked potato, Teresa was quick to share hers with him. When dessert was served, the two of them shared a slice of strawberry cheesecake from the same plate.

Deni was so amazed by her son's behavior. She'd never seen him act this way with any other woman. It was obvious he was smitten like a high school boy experiencing his first crush. However, Allen was far smarter than a school boy. There were two things that he excelled in: practicing law and courting women!

Deni possessed a keen sensibility. She was astute at analyzing situations as well as people. She knew it didn't matter how well a man thought he knew a woman, it took a woman to see through another woman's façade and not be blinded by her beauty, charm, sexual prowess, and physique. In spite of the unusual circumstances that brought Allen and Teresa together, Deni was convinced that Teresa loved her son and that's all that mattered to her! After dinner, Deni took Teresa and her family on a tour of the house.

The 12,000 square-foot structure had five bedrooms: one master suite and four sizable guestrooms. Each bedroom had its own fireplace and was layered with Brazilian Cherrywood floors highlighted with large Persian rugs. Crystal chandeliers hung from the ceilings in each bedroom. On top of all of that, the Williams' owned a vast collection of artwork, including early American, as well as Contemporary. The paintings were said to be worth millions. Teresa and her family were witnessing opulence at its finest!

The tour was cut short because the girls were getting sleepy and they had to go to school early the next morning. Deni and Rob escorted their guests out to Allen's car. Deni warmly hugged Teresa and her mother, while her husband looked on, waving goodbye with a smile. Allen buckled the girls in the back seat.

ONE MORE MIRACLE

Rob, being the ever concerned father, called out to Allen, "Drive carefully, son!"

Teresa and Ms. Hunter got into the car. Once they were settled in, Allen started the car, made a U-turn in the driveway and drove off.

An hour later, Deni was sitting in front of her vanity applying cleanser to her face. Rob was lying in their custom-made bed reading a medical journal. When she finished her facial, she got up and walked over to the foot of the bed stretching out and looking up at her husband.

"Well Rob, what do you think, now that you've met Teresa?"

"She's a very lovely young woman, but I still have misgivings about this wedding. Why are they in such a rush to get married? That's what I don't understand? Why don't they take a little time to get to know each other first?"

Deni suddenly removed herself from the bed, faced her husband and shook her finger at him.

"Rob, you keep saying you don't understand why Bug is proceeding with this marriage. Well, maybe some things aren't meant for you to understand. Our son is an adult, and what he does with his life is his own business. Rob, this is déjà vu, old news, and, frankly, I'm tired of talking about it."

"Deni it amazes me how cavalier you can be when it comes to such an important matter."

"Okay Rob, what's really eating at you? Is it because Teresa isn't white?"

"How could you say such a terrible thing? My biological mother was black! You know that!" Rob replied angrily.

"Yes, I do Rob! But, how many other people know that?"

"Deni, you know perfectly well that was mother's decision. She didn't want anyone to know. She believed that society would look at me differently, knowing that my mother was black. I was never ashamed of her. She was a beautiful

133

lady."

"Well Rob, is it Teresa's economic status that you can't come to grips with? Is it because she's from the projects in the inner city? Is that a problem?"

"Deni, perhaps that's what I'm grappling with. You and I both know Bug never dated anyone who didn't have a college education."

Deni shook her head in disappointment saying, "Shame on you, Rob! If the only reason you can come up with is she doesn't have a college education, then you are an elitist and that's petty. She's in school. She's trying to get a degree."

"Deni, you always seem to misconstrue what I say. Her not having a degree isn't the sole reason I don't think they shouldn't get married right now."

Deni suddenly threw her hands up in frustration. "Rob I don't want to hear any more of your other reasons why you think they shouldn't marry. You're giving me a headache. This wedding is inevitable. You're beginning to sound like a broken record rehashing this. I'm not going to have this argument with you anymore. Teresa and I will be planning this wedding next week."

Deni proceeded to get into the bed.

Rob conceded as he lowered his head, closing the medical journal he was reading.

"Okay Deni, you've made your point. As far as I'm concerned, this issue is put to rest. Our son has made his decision and I'll have to respect that."

"Thank you! Thank you!" Deni replied with pleasure.

They kissed goodnight before turning off the lights, honoring a commitment they made to each other when they first got married: vowing never to go to sleep angry with each other.

CHAPTER 17

A week later, Deni and Teresa were seated at the **Downtown Sheraton Hotel**, having lunch with one of Atlanta's top wedding planners and impresarios, Logan K. Smith. She was a young, aesthetically pleasing, bleached-blonde woman. She possessed a radiant smile and effervescent personality.

She welcomed Deni with a genuine hug. Deni then introduced her to Teresa, who also embraced her. During the conversation, Teresa learned that Deni was Logan's godmother. Logan's father, Dr. C.R. Smith, was a long-time friend of the Williams family.

Logan had an extensive resume orchestrating many special events, including cruise ship weddings, weddings on the French Riviera, the Caribbean, New York, and Hollywood just to name a few. She catered to the rich and famous. If you were on a tight budget, Logan wasn't the wedding planner for you. As far as money goes, most of her clients seemed to share the same belief that the sky's the limit! Logan usually shot for the stars. She believed as long as the client was happy, that's all that mattered. During the discussions, at Teresa's request, Deni did most of the talking. Logan listened intently, jotting down ideas and suggestions on a legal pad. When the luncheon ended, the three agreed to meet at Logan's place of business the following day.

After leaving the luncheon with Logan, Teresa and Deni paid a visit to the **Cathedral of Christ the King** on Peachtree Road Northeast. Deni had arranged a meeting with the Monsignor there. When they arrived, Teresa and Deni were received right away by a short, stocky, freckled-face man with an Irish brogue. "Monsignor Michael Matthews," he introduced himself.

The Monsignor was aware that Allen had been married before and the marriage had been annulled. When Allen was a student at USC, he befriended a young woman from Bolivia. She

135

was in the country on a student visa. When she took off a semester without notifying immigration officials, her visa was revoked and she was ordered to leave the country. Allen stepped in and married her to keep her from being deported. After meeting with INS, she was ordered to leave the country and go back to Bolivia and would have to reapply to come back to America. After two months had passed, she finally wrote Allen and told him she'd changed her mind about coming back to the States. Consequently, the marriage was annulled.

Monsignor Matthews told Teresa that he didn't anticipate any problems with her being married in the church, since her husband was deceased. He went on to explain to her the three most important steps of getting married in the Catholic Church. The first step was establishing freedom to marry by completing necessary paperwork. The second step was receiving counseling with a Priest or Deacon. Step three was to attend workshops approved by the Archdiocese. Deni assured him those obligations would be met. Before leaving the church, Teresa scheduled the six-week workshop for her and Allen to attend.

The following morning, Teresa and Deni arrived at the offices of **Logan K. Smith and Associates**. When they entered the ornate suite, they were greeted by Logan and the renowned fashion designer Ashley Elaine Hall. They didn't waste any time. Teresa was shown a multitude of pictures and sketches of bridal gowns that Ashley had designed. Teresa spent over an hour looking at pages of photos, trying to make up her mind. After looking at dozens of photographs of bridal gowns, one dress in particular caught her eye. It was a sophisticated open-back, mermaid-styled dress.

Deni also liked the dress, but then remembered that the church did not approve of brides wearing open back dresses during any wedding mass. Deni asked Ashley if she would make a shawl to cover Teresa's back. Before Ashley could answer, Teresa agreed to look at some of the other dresses. She continued

136

to look through the embroidered photo album. After about twenty minutes, she discovered a dress she liked even more than the first one.

The dress she decided on was a stunning bridal gown with a sweetheart neckline, made of pure **Dupioni** silk. Since she had been married before, she chose not to wear a traditional white wedding gown. Instead, she selected a pale blue color that appeared to be off white. For the bridesmaids' dresses, she chose Mediterranean-blue matted satin. Logan chose navy tuxedos for the groomsmen. (She thought Allen's tuxedo should also be pale blue in order to match Teresa's wedding dress.) After the wedding attire plans were finalized, it was time to begin the process of selecting wedding cakes. Logan excused herself for a moment and immediately went next door to tell the Executive Pastry Chef, Brenda Louise, that it was time for her meeting. Chef Louise had a distinct reputation for making any cake taste as if it were baked in one's mother's oven. The sweet scent of her cakes tempted many customers to reach out and taste the icing, even before the cake was cut. Several of her customers professed that the fresh symphony of ingredients imploded in their mouths each time they took a bite. Chef Louise's reputation extended from coast to coast.

As usual, Chef Louise was well prepared. She was professionally dressed in a crisp, white jacket and a tailored black skirt. Logan opened the door for her as she wheeled in a small cart, adorned with a crisp white table cloth, fresh flowers, water and various samples of her best tasting wedding cakes.

Her black and gold captivating photo album was neatly placed on the left hand corner of the table. Logan followed in after Chef Louise.

"Teresa and Deni, it is indeed my pleasure to introduce you to Chef Brenda Louise."

Chef Louise extended her hand, greeting both ladies. She then reached for the photo album, filled with the eloquence of

137

true epicurean delights, and handed it to Teresa. Teresa's childlike smile brightened the room as she took the album and placed it on her lap. The aroma within the room was wonderfully intoxicating. As Teresa and Deni viewed the items on the table, they simply did not know where to start. Each miniature cake looked more appetizing than the next.

The very first cake Teresa tasted was the charm. The vanilla cake with butter cream icing was more than just pleasing to her palate, it was breathtakingly delicious.

"Oh, yes! Yes! This is the one! This is my wedding cake!" Teresa exclaimed.

"Ma'am, you haven't even tasted the other four samples," said Chef Louise, apprehensively.
"Oh, no... I don't need to sample any of the other cakes. This is the one I want for my wedding," said Teresa, licking the icing from her fingers.

Not wanting to hurt the chef's feelings, Deni tasted the Italian cream cake, as well as the strawberry filling cake and the lemon chiffon cake and found that the taste of each superb. Chef Louise recommended that the Italian cream cake be selected for the groom.

Deni informed Teresa that Allen's favorite cake flavor was lemon chiffon.

"Lemon chiffon it is!" said Chef Louise, nodding in agreement. Chef Louise then asked Teresa if there were any special designs or particular theme she wanted the Groom's cake to reflect.

"Not really. I can't think of anything," she nodded with a smile.

"You are the expert. I have faith that you'll come up with something that everyone will be pleased with."

"Well, since Allen is an attorney, how about we do a model of the *Scale of Justice* on his cake?"

"That's perfect. Why don't you look through this photo

138

album and see if there's anything you like for the Bride's cake?"

Teresa took the photo album and began to look at some of the pictures. She scanned the pages until she got to page seven, where she saw a cake that impressed her. It was six tiers, and each octagonal tier was decorated with strawberry floral. The cake was topped with a golden bird's nest with two lovebirds cuddled together on a bed of fresh moss. This was the perfect cake for Teresa!

CHAPTER 18

Three months later, two days before the wedding, out of town guests began to arrive. Allen's brother Paul and his entire family of four, flew in from Boston. Paul looked like a perfect combination of his Mom and Dad. He had reddish-brown hair and blue-green eyes. Both brothers stood over six-feet tall.

Their sister Katie and her husband, Steve, flew in from San Diego. Katie stood about 5'8" with a slender frame and a well-developed derriere.

Teresa's elder brother, Tony and his family of five, drove down from Columbia, South Carolina. Teresa's maid of honor, her childhood best friend Jada Rachal, flew in from her hometown of Houston. The wedding party stayed at the downtown Hilton.

The day before the wedding, Logan had scheduled a dinner and rehearsal for the wedding party. In one of the hotel ballrooms, Logan and her staff assisted the bridesmaids with the fitting of their dresses. Once the fittings were completed, the staff focused their attention on the groomsmen's tuxedos. Everyone's attire appeared to fit perfectly. Teresa had tried on her dress earlier that day at Ashley's Boutique. She was very pleased with the elegant fit of her wedding gown.

Allen and Paul left before the dinner was over in order to attend Allen's bachelor's party, given by his colleague Jonathan on the south side of town. Steve planned on accompanying Allen and Paul to the bachelor party, but Katie was feeling under the weather, so, Steve elected to stay with his wife.

Before leaving the dinner, Allen and Teresa shared a tender moment in the hall-way outside of the ballroom. They couldn't wait to embrace each other. They immediately started to passionately kiss each other.

Both their bodies were hot with desire, as Teresa began

to moan, "We'd better stop this now!"

Allen replied, "Let's go up to your suite, right now!"

Teresa smiled, "Remember, you were the one who wanted to wait until our wedding night to make love, so, I'm going to hold you to it."

Allen grabbed her in his arms, started kissing her again and gently squeezed her breasts. Teresa responded, "You've got me sizzling. C'mon let's go to the suite right now!"

He pleaded, "Give me one more kiss."

As they kissed, Paul walked out of the ballroom, interrupting them with a devilish grin on his face, "Oh, did I come out at a bad time? Bug, it's time to go to the bachelor party! Teresa, he'll be all yours after the wedding ceremony!"

Teresa forced a smile, "Yes brother-in-law, you're absolutely right!"

Allen looked at Paul, thinking to himself, "Some things never change! This isn't the first time my little brother has spoiled my romantic plans!"

Allen and Teresa looked at each other and both snickered. She gave him a quick kiss and admonished, "I expect you to be on your best behavior."

"Darling, you don't have anything to worry about."

"Is that a promise?" Teresa joked as she pushed him away.

He smiled at her with blistering desire.

"This is going to be the longest twenty-four hours of my life!"

Teresa said to Paul, "Get him out of my sight!" She shook her finger at Paul and said, "Take care my man!"

As they left, Teresa thought to herself, "I could use a cold shower, right about now!"

It was well after 10:00 p.m., when Allen and Paul made their entrance into the exclusive **Gentlemen's Fantasy City Club**, located on the south side of town. When Jonathan spotted them, he immediately stood up on his chair and began to vigorously wave his hands. Paul and Allen looked in his direction at the same time and made their way over to the table where Jonathan and at least twenty other men were seated. It seemed that a section of the club was closed off for Allen's bachelor party. Just as soon as Allen and Paul were seated, four semi-nude dancers appeared and began to slowly twist and strut toward the table. Allen's smile grew wider and wider.

He asked, "Okay, who's responsible for this entertainment?"

Allen's law partner Jonathan Christopher laughed, threw up his hands and said, "Guilty as charged."

Two of the four exotic dancers danced their way towards the head table, where Allen was seated. The taller dancer with the blonde hair introduced herself first.

"Good evening, boys. My name is Lisa Love. Am I right to assume that this handsome man sitting at the head of the table is the bachelor?"

"Your assumption is absolutely correct," said Allen.

The slightly shorter dancer, with long black hair, chimed in, "Hello Honey! You can call me Chocolate Pudding."

As Lisa Love and Chocolate Pudding seductively swayed their hips right to left and front to back, Lisa slightly raising her voice over the music announced, "We are your private dancers for tonight!"

"Well ladies, it is an honor to meet you both," Allen quipped.

"At the end of tonight, Bachelor Boy, you're gonna change those words. Instead of saying it is an honor to meet Chocolate and me, you will say, it is an EXTREME PLEASURE to have met us."

As Lisa gently touched the top of Allen's thick dark hair, her hand slowly and gently outlined the left side of his face. By the time she allowed her hand to rest in the middle of his chest, she had his full attention. Lisa then effortlessly saddled him. She began to bump and grind as vigorously as she knew how. Her movements ignited the crowd to chant, "Go Lisa! Go Lisa! Go Lisa!"

As her routine became more and more provocative, Allen became more uncomfortable. Jonathan was oblivious to Allen's emotions. He summoned the waitress and ordered more drinks for the group.

Chuck Oliver, another one of Allen's Law colleagues, stopped at the table and said, "Atta boy, Allen! I'm sure glad that I didn't miss *this* party!"

By this time, Lisa had removed herself from Allen's crotch and begun to entertain the other guests.
Chuck asked, "What do you think of these two dancers?"

With a giddy expression plastered on his face, Allen replied, "Chuck, I think they both look like two sexy **Playboy Centerfolds** with very big butts!"

Chocolate soon made her way back to Allen, flexing her body skillfully like a belly dancer. She then ended up on Allen's lap. Chuck went over to the group where Lisa was performing, twerking with both of her palms placed squarely on the floor. He marveled as he observed one of the recently hired law partners spanking her backside.

Meanwhile, Chocolate seductively placed her arms around Allen's neck and whispered, "I didn't think your friend would mind if I spent a few moments with you, especially now that Lisa is busy with the other guests."

He leaned towards her right ear, and he told her that one of the things Chuck was known for was his ability to be long-winded. Chocolate gently pushed Allen's shoulders back. She changed positions, turning her back to him and opening her legs; sliding her buttocks backwards until she landed in the center of his tight slacks, creating a rise in him. She locked her thigh muscles around Allen's thighs, and squeezed them together. Then she began grinding methodically.

He quickly lifted her from his lap exhaling, "Whoa!

143

Whoa! Let me cool off for a moment, please!"

Chocolate, being the consummate professional, never missed a beat as she made her way over to Jonathan.

By this time, Paul, who had witnessed the whole encounter, was laughing uncontrollably, jokingly saying, "Oh, I see Teresa has sent you a subliminal message."

Allen looked perplexed at Paul, who was still laughing, "Little Brother, you certainly seem to be enjoying yourself. *Veronica* would be surprised that you're having so much fun here..."

Paul cleverly retorted, "Hey man, I may have a wandering eye, but I do have a faithful heart."

Chocolate left Jonathan momentarily, danced her way back to Allen and asked, "What's the matter, Pretty Boy? Don't you want me and Lisa to jump start your motor for your wedding night?"

"Well, I was sort of looking forward to my wife handling that responsibility."

"Pretty Boy, you and I both know the reason men attend bachelor parties is to enjoy one more night of pleasure as free men. Why are you resisting the inevitable?" Chocolate inquired licking her lips.

Allen pulled Chocolate close to him and whispered, "You're right, Chocolate! Go get Lisa, and both of you meet me in the **Champagne Room** in about five minutes."

Chocolate got up and motioned to Lisa, who recognized the signal right away. Lisa said in a loud voice, "It is intermission time, gentlemen. Chocolate and I will be back shortly. Sparkle and Ginger will pick up where we left off so don't even think about leaving! And fellas, come on now, let's make it rain in here...and I don't mean no **Washingtons**, either. Only **Grants** and **Benjamins**, now!"

Lisa noticed Chocolate heading to the Champagne Room out of the corner of her eye and followed quickly behind her. As the guests began to gear up for Sparkle and Ginger, Allen gave Paul a quick glance and said, "Little Brother, let's get out of here."

"What are you going to tell your buddies when they ask you why you are leaving so soon?"

"I am going to tell them the truth! I'm tired and sleepy, and I have to get ready for the biggest and most exciting day of my life!"

Paul, knowing his brother practically better than anyone, thought for a moment and said, "No Allen, that's not why we're leaving!"

"Well maybe it's not the entire truth, but that's what I'm going to tell them."

Allen then walked over to Jonathan and got his attention. He spoke in a loud voice so that everyone could hear.

"Thank you all so very much for coordinating and attending this exceedingly stimulating event. However, Paul and I must be leaving now, so that I won't fall asleep during the festivities tomorrow."

Chuck shouted, "Allen... you must be kidding! Are you seriously going to leave the *best party* I've attended in years?!"

Allen just waved in the most modest manner, patted Jonathan on the back, thanked him again, and headed towards the front door. Jonathan and the other guys were disappointed at Allen's departure, but the still enjoyed the rest of the night.

(Lisa and Chocolate were both upset and a little embarrassed after they realized that Allen had duped them into believing he would share some private time with them. However shortly afterwards, they both agreed that Allen would make some lucky girl a great husband).

Allen and Paul made it to the car and began the drive home. During the ride home, Paul told his big brother how proud he was of the man Allen had become. He also commended him on not going to the Champagne Room and "indulging" with the

145

dancers. Allen told him that the decision was a no brainer because he wanted to start his marriage with a clean slate.

Paul leaned over to him and shouted incredulously, "What has this woman done to you?"

The volume of Paul's voice shook Allen out of his trance. He couldn't help but reflect on how he and his bride-to-be almost went all the way.

Paul then laughed, "Bug, did you even hear a word I said?"

"I apologize for being preoccupied. You're definitely correct, Paul. Indeed, I'm a changed man and I owe it all to Teresa. She's such an awesome woman. In fact, I love her more than I ever imagined I'd ever love any human being."

Paul concurred. "I've seen a change in you. Not only are you in love, but your response just let me know that you are *crazy in love*. I never thought I'd see the day that a woman would capture your heart, but I'm glad it happened. It is time for you to settle down. You and I both know it. I used to be envious of all of the exotic, beautiful women I've seen you with over the years, but now it appears that you have something real and hopefully, lasting. Mom has shared some really wonderful things with me about Teresa and if mom gives her stamp of approval, then she has to be something special."

Allen smiled as his chest appeared to swell with pride.

He said, "Yes, I have finally found the perfect woman for me, and to have mom's blessing is icing on the cake!"

Paul reluctantly asked, "How does dad feel about Teresa?"

"Funny you should ask. Little Brother, you know dad as well as I do. You know he really believes that he knows what's best for everyone. To be painfully honest, dad told me that I was making the biggest mistake of my life by marrying Teresa."

Allen sighed, leaned back and said, "Contrary to what dad thinks, I happen to believe that *not* making Teresa my wife

146

would be the biggest mistake of my life. I also believe that dad will eventually change his mind about her."

Paul shook his head, "I hope so. Hey Bug, congratulations again! I love you, Big Brother!"

Allen returned the smile. "I love you too, Little Brother."

It was well after midnight when they arrived at their parents' estate. Allen decided to telephone Teresa's hotel room just to wish her good night. To Allen's surprise, when Teresa answered the phone, she sounded alert and energized.

"Hello sweetheart, I was just calling to say good night," he whispered.

"Allen, you will never believe what I am about to tell you! I'm so excited I can barely speak. My baby brother, Patrick, just flew in from Germany! I didn't think he'd be able to make it, but he's here!!"

"What a surprise," he exclaimed.

She continued, "Patrick called from the airport as soon as he landed. He had a week of R&R left over from last year and he decided to fly home for our wedding. He'll be in Atlanta for five whole days! Now both of my brothers will be with us on our special day! Everything is working out better than expected! Allen, words can't convey how happy I am!"

"I'm elated, Teresa. I can't wait to meet your brother. Well baby, I'm exhausted. I just wanted to hear your sweet voice before I see you tomorrow. Teresa, I love you and I can't wait until you become my wife!"

"Yes Darling, I'm so ready to be your wife. We'd better get some sleep because it will be daylight soon."

"I am going to make you the best husband in the world! I love you! Goodnight…well, I guess I should say good morning! Rest well."

Teresa slipped the receiver back into its place. She leaned back on the bed, stretched her legs out, and reminisced about the kiss she and Allen had shared before he departed for his bachelor party. Looking up at the high ceiling, smiling, she mumbled, "If he thinks that kiss was something, *just you wait until our wedding night!"*

Allen undressed and headed for the shower. He couldn't wait to wash the smoke from the party out of his hair along with the perfumes of the women he'd come in contact with. After showering, he found he couldn't sleep. Teresa also found herself experiencing anxiety, thinking about her big day. She only got a few hours of sleep before the morning light broke forth and filled the hotel suite.

At 9:00 a.m., Allen was awakened by his mother's voice and her light tapping on his bedroom door.

"Bug? Bug?" she called out. "Honey, are you decent?"

Allen's fatigued voice was barely audible, "No Mother, I'm in bed. Is there something you need?"

She partially opened the door and peeped in. "Bug, get up! Would you please come downstairs and have breakfast with us? We are all in the dining room. We would love for you to join us."

"Certainly, Mother. Give me a few moments to get dressed."

"No, no dear, just put on your robe and come down."

"Okay, Mother, I'll be down in a minute."

"Okay, my darling, don't tarry."

Allen was fully awake by this time. In a single motion, he rapidly turned over on the king-sized bed, rubbed his bloodshot eyes, and focused on the **Howard Miller grandfather clock** located next to the door.

He jumped to his feet and yelled, "Alright, Mother! Alright! I need to freshen up. I'll be right down in a minute."

Allen proceeded into the bathroom. After he washed his face and brushed his teeth, he put on his robe and headed downstairs to join his family. When he reached the dining room, he greeted his family saying, "Good morning all."

ONE MORE MIRACLE

He took a seat next to his sister, Katie, and her husband, Steve. He looked up and smiled at Paul and his wife, Veronica, who along with their son, Paul, Jr. and daughter, Mary-Christine, sat directly across from them.

Shortly afterwards, Mrs. Nancy, the housekeeper, entered the room. She poured freshly squeezed orange juice and coffee for the adults. After everyone glass was full, Katie lifted her glass to propose a toast:

"Hear ye, hear ye, everyone! To the man of the hour, my big brother, Bug, may this day bring you and your new bride all the happiness you deserve. May the two of you live happily ever after."

The rest of the family chimed in, "WE'LL DRINK TO THAT! SKOAL! SALUT!"

CHAPTER 19

Meanwhile, at the **Downtown Hilton**, Teresa was having breakfast with her family and Maid of Honor, Jada. Patrick tried coming on to Jada, who laughed at him saying, "No thank you. You just got out of pampers yesterday."

Ms. Hunter and Tony started laughing. Patrick gave Jada a smoldering look.

"I'm not a kid anymore. I'm twenty-one years old! I'm a grown man!!"

"*Whooptie-doo*! I'm twenty-five years old and you're still a kid to me. Besides, I'm an engaged woman now!"

"Where is your fiancé, then? Why didn't he come here with you?"

"If you must know, he's in Houston starting a new job and couldn't take off."

Tony interjected, "Just give it up, Little Brother. You don't have a chance with Jada!"

Patrick looked at Tony, "Hey man, I'm not a deadbeat! I'm serving my country! I'm in the Air Force!"

Jada saluted, mocking him. Patrick cut his eyes back at her, "Girl, you know that man of yours doesn't really have a job. He probably still lives at home with his Mama!"

Patrick burst into laughter. It was as if he couldn't help himself. He *actually enjoyed* the exchange between he and Jada. He could barely contain his wicked sense of humor and whatever he threw at Jada, she was always able to throw it right back at him. So he turned his attention to Teresa.

"Sis, you mean to tell me that out of all the black men we've got here in Atlanta, you had to turn to a white boy? Come on now, Sis, what's up with that? You know that your whole identity is going to change now. You are going to be talking proper, and my little brown-skin nieces are going to talk like little white girls. I don't know if I can handle that."

Patrick first snickered, then burst out in a loud, irritating laugh. Several seconds later, he noticed that he was laughing all by himself.

"What's the matter with you guys? Why are you looking at me like that?"

Patrick's behavior sent Ms. Hunter into an uncontrollable rage. "Patrick Robert Hunter! You need to shut your mouth! I mean shut it right now! Your sister and I are tired of your silly antics! Why do you always have to act a fool? Cut it out! I mean it! Right now!"

Teresa chimed in, visibly upset, "Patrick, for an intelligent man, you really can be silly. There you go stereotyping people again. Just as all black people don't speak the same way, neither do all whites. Please do me a favor— don't say anything else to me today, okay?"

She then abruptly got up from the table and went back to her hotel suite.

He sat like an embarrassed child, before deciding to go to Teresa's room to apologize. Tony dissuaded him, "Give her some time to calm down. Obviously Teresa appeared to be vexed before she came down from her room."

Patrick nodded his head in agreement and told Tony, "Man, I really need to grow up!"
Tony concurred with a smile, "Yes, you do!"

Two hours later, Patrick knocked on Teresa's hotel suite door. He heard voices inside of the room. It seemed everybody was talking at the same time. One of the wedding staffers answered the door. He told her that he needed to talk to his sister, but before the staffer could relay the message, Teresa saw Patrick's reflection in the mirror. She got up from the makeup table and met him at the door.
"Sis, I need to talk to you."
"Well, I don't want to talk to you!"

151

"Ahh, I'm sorry, Sis. I really didn't mean to upset you, really I didn't."

She glared at him hard for a short moment, then melted into a smile. "I know you didn't mean to upset me. Come here Baby Brother, give your big Sis a hug. I was already upset before you said anything."

"Yeah, I could tell. Why were you upset?"

"I thought Aunt Emma was coming to my wedding. Then she started mentioning the fact that Allen is white, and then she asked me how old he is. When I told her he was thirty, she said, *Girl, don't you know that the average serial killer is a white male aged 21-30? Girl, you must don't read newspapers.*"

"What about Uncle Joe? Why isn't he coming?"

"He called last night and said he couldn't make it, either. Oh, he started telling me about when he marched with Dr. King during the **Civil Rights Movement**. How white people beat him down and called him the N-word. He said he just developed a bad taste in his mouth for white people. He started ranting and raving about Allen saying, *'He may be good to you now, but white people can turn on you like a junk yard dog.'* Pat, I wonder why Uncle Joe can't let go of the past. What he's failing to realize is that all white people aren't bad, and all black people aren't good. Allen's family are wonderful people. They've accepted my girls and I. They've treated us just like family."

Patrick looked at her sincerely, "Sis, Uncle Joe has the right to feel the way he feels because of his experiences with white people. Sis, you can say white people have done some wonderful things for you, but on the other hand, he can say they've done some terrible things for him. Like our Father used to say, *'never judge a person until you have walked in their shoes.'*

"Yes, but he also said that *one shouldn't judge people as a group but as individuals.*"

"I'm in total agreement with that."

ONE MORE MIRACLE

"It still hurts to know that my Mother's only sister and my Father's only brother will not be at my wedding, but I'll get over it."

"Sis, what's Mama's take on all of this?"

"Well, Mama says I shouldn't be concerned about anybody who doesn't want to be here."

"I'm with Mama on that one!"

Teresa agreed, "You and Mama are right! I'm not going to let anyone spoil my special day!"

Patrick gave her a heartfelt hug. He changed the subject, revealing to her that Logan had supplied him with a tuxedo, which was delivered to his hotel room earlier.

He then remarked, "Sis, Allen's people must be loaded! I know this wedding must have cost a fortune!"

"Allen's parents are very wealthy people. I would've just settled for a small wedding, but Allen and his Mother insisted on an extravagant wedding. Pat, you know me; I'm not into all this fanfare."

"Sis, let me give you some advice. You're marrying into money, so, you may as well get used to an extravagant lifestyle."

"Pat, you know Allen told me the very same thing. Look, I have to get back to getting dressed. We're okay now. Go get ready and I'll see you at the church. Thanks for coming to apologize."

Teresa then went back inside her suite and closed the door.

CHAPTER 20

It was 4:10 pm when two white limousines pulled up to the **Downtown Hilton**. Teresa and the wedding party left the seventh floor hotel suite, went outside, and entered the waiting limousines. After a fifteen-minute drive, they arrived at **Christ the King Cathedral**. Allen and his family had already arrived. Their limousines lined the church's parking lot.

The limousine carrying Teresa and her group drove around to the back of the church to prevent the bride from being seen before the wedding. The other limousine stopped in front of the church. Ms. Hunter, her two sons, daughter-in-law, and four grandchildren got out of the car and entered the church.

Meanwhile, inside the church, Logan was giving last minute instructions to the participants. She told the bridesmaids once they marched in with their respective escorts, they should go to the left side of the altar and stand there. She then instructed the groomsmen to take their place at the right side of the altar.

She concluded, "Ladies and gentlemen, listen to me. When Teresa marches in with her brother down the aisle, Allen will receive her and they will lock arms. Ladies, I want you to go and take your seats in the front pews on the left side of the altar. Gentlemen, I want you to do the same thing on the right side. For those of you who are not Catholic, the bride, the groom, and the Priest are the only ones who stand at the altar during the Wedding Mass."

She rushed back into the room to be with Teresa and her wedding staff. Ms. Hunter and Deni were also in the room. Teresa stood in front of a large mirror while her mom helped her with her veil. Deni stood at Teresa's right.

Deni declared, "Teresa, why you're a beautiful bride!"

Teresa smiled, "Oh, Thank you, Mrs. Williams. Thank you for everything!"

Deni looked at her with soft eyes. "Oh my darling, is that wan to call me?"

Teresa remembered the promise she made to Deni: once she and Allen were married, she'd no longer call her Mrs. Williams. Teresa returned the look and smiled, "Oh, thank you, *Mother*. Thank you for being such a generous lady."

Deni smiled as she grabbed Teresa's hand, "That sounds better. I was hoping you'd choose Mother."

Ms. Hunter also expressed her deepest gratitude to Deni. She modestly replied, "Oh, Ethel, it's only money. When you die you can't take it with you."

Logan interrupted them, "Ladies, I don't mean to be rude, but I'm going to ask the two of you to take your places out there in the church. We need to finish with Teresa."

They apologized and immediately left the room.

Logan gave Teresa a final once over, bending down and straightening out her train. One of the staff handed Teresa the bouquet. The arrangement was called **Purple Haze** and it was made up of purple lilacs and hydrangeas.

Logan stood up and looked at Teresa. "You look flawless! You're so beautiful! You look just like doll!"

"How can I ever thank you?"

"When you're showing off all of your fancy wedding pictures to your friends and family and they ask who coordinated your wedding, just tell them Logan Smith did it."
Teresa nodded with a gracious smile, "Sure, I can do that." Logan smiled and glanced at her watch. "C'mon let's get this show on the road!"

The wedding started on time at 5:00 pm. The pews were decorated with purple and white ribbons. Katie and Steve were the first couple to march in. They were followed by Teresa's niece and nephew, Tara and Keith. Veronica was accompanied by Allen's cousin, Marion. Jada was escorted by Allen's law partner, Jonathan. Ms. Hunter was escorted down the aisle by

155

Patrick. Deni and Rob marched in together. Mia and Kendria served as flower girls. Allen and Paul, who was the best man, walked in from the back of the church and took their places at the right side of the altar. Monsignor Matthews stood in front of the altar, wearing a white robe trimmed in gold. Behind him was a life-sized statue of **JESUS on THE CROSS**. The array of lights surrounding the statue illuminated the altar.

The lights dimmed instantaneously as the ushers opened the church doors. Standing at the threshold was the   bride-to-be with her brother, Tony. The glow on her face matched the sunlight that poured into the church. The organist began to play "**The Wedding March**."

The congregation rose from the pews as Teresa and Tony ambled down the aisle. Tony appeared to be well composed, but Teresa, on the other hand, was a bit nervous.

She whispered to Tony, "Wow, so many people are in here! All eyes are on us."
Tony played the big brother role perfectly. "Just lean on me, Little Sister; I've got your back!"

The march to the altar seemed like a mile away, but the closer Teresa came to Allen, the calmer she became. When she and Tony reached the altar, the dimmed lights quickly brightened. Allen took his place beside Teresa, and they were absorbed in each other's gaze. Tony released her from his arm and found his way to his seat.

Monsignor Matthews welcomed the congregation. "On behalf of Mark and Teresa, I want to thank all of you for coming to share in this blessed event."

He began the Mass with a prayer from the **Missalette**, a Catholic prayer book. As the congregation stood, with heads bowed, Monsignor Matthews prayed:

"FATHER, YOU made the bond of marriage a HOLY MYSTERY, a symbol of CHRIST'S LOVE for HIS CHURCH.

ONE MORE MIRACLE

Hear our prayers for Mark and Teresa. With Faith in You and in each other, they pledge their lives today. May their lives always bear witness to the reality of that love. We ask YOU this, through our LORD, JESUS CHRIST, YOUR SON, WHO LIVES and REIGNS with YOU and THE HOLY SPIRIT, ONE GOD, FOREVER and EVER, AMEN."

Deni immediately left her seat, entering the pulpit. She walked over to the podium, adjusted the microphone, opened the **Missalette**, saying to the congregation,
"This is a reading from the **Song of Songs**":

"Hark, my lover! Here he comes, springing across the mountains, leaping across the hills like a gazelle or a young stag. Here he stands behind our wall, gazing through the windows, peering through the lattices. My lover speaks. He says to me, 'Arise my beloved, my dove, my beautiful one and come! Oh, my dove in the clefts of the rock, in the secret recesses of the cliff, let me see you; let me hear your voice; for your voice is sweet and you are lovely.' My lover belongs to me and I to him. Set me as a seal on your heart and as a seal on your arm; for stern as death is love relentless, as the nether world is devotion. Its flames are a blazing fire. Deep waters cannot quench love nor floods sweep it away.
THE WORD of THE LORD."

The congregation responded, "Thanks be to GOD."

After Deni returned to her seat, Rob got up and went to the podium to read the second reading. He opened the **Missalette** and read the second reading from the book of **Proverbs**:

"When one finds a worthy wife, her value is far beyond pearls. Her husband entrusting his heart to her, has an unfailing

prize. She brings him good and not evil, all the days of her life, she obtains wool and flax and makes cloth with skillful hands, she puts her hands to the distaff and her fingers ply the spindle. She reaches out her hands to the poor and extends her arms to the needy. Charm is deceptive and beauty fleeting, the woman who fears the LORD is to be praised. Give her a reward of her labors and her works praise her at the city gates. THE WORD of THE LORD.

The congregation responded, "Thanks be to GOD." Rob went back and took his seat besides his wife.

Monsignor Matthews continued with a prayer:

"Oh, GLORIOUS GOD our FATHER, THE MAKER of HEAVEN and earth, all that is seen and unseen. We ask that YOU bless this union between Mark and Teresa. We pray that YOU will bless them with good health and that YOU would increase them with more children. FATHER, JESUS said that marriage shall be between one man and one woman. FATHER, anyone who would willingly subvert YOUR WILL is not of YOU. Brother and sisters, we know that love is the fabric that unites us all. Love transcends color and race. This couple are living witnesses, for love is the glue that will bond any marriage. Love is patient, love is kind, love is forgiving and love should be stronger that lust. HEAVENLY FATHER, we pray that the commitment Mark and Teresa make here today, before YOU and the CHURCH, will never be reduced to broken promises and hollow words. FATHER, we pray that YOU will strengthen them with YOUR LOVE and MERCY. In THE NAME of THE FATHER and THE SON and THE HOLY SPIRIT, AMEN".

Monsignor Matthews focused on the pair with an

esteemed smile.

"Indeed, this is a beautiful couple. Both are unique in their own way. She's black, and he's white. They come from two different worlds. It's amazing how GOD can make the impossible possible. Love is the greatest experience one can feel. GOD THE FATHER'S LOVE is perpetual. After spending some time with Teresa and Mark during pre-marital counseling, I learned that Teresa is a young woman of deep faith. She strongly believes that GOD brought her and Mark together. Brothers and sisters when GOD gives you something, nobody can take it from you."

Monsignor Matthews continued looking at Allen and Teresa and smiled again.

"When I said this couple is unique, that's just what they are. After reading their wedding invitation, I was totally confused when I read the last paragraph. It stated: **'We are registered at the church. Please don't bring any monetary gifts.'** Brothers and sisters, I'm sure all of you were just as baffled as I was, upon reading the invitation. We all know that when couples get married, this is a great opportunity for them to receive some pretty good wedding gifts. Most couples are usually registered at big-named Department Stores. Mark and Teresa turned down the opportunity to get some nice gifts like fine china, kitchen appliances, comforters, maybe some nice drapes, things of that nature. This couple doesn't want any monetary gifts. The gift that they want most from you is the gift of prayer. Mark and Teresa want all of you to pray for their union together. I think that's beautiful and powerful. I've been a Priest for over twenty-five years. I've done my share of weddings, and believe me, this is the first time any couple has made such a benevolent request."

He paused for a short moment and then began again, saying, "JESUS said, in **Matthew 18:19-20**: *'Again I say unto you. That if two of you shall agree on earth,*

as touching anything that they shall ask, it shall be done for them of MY FATHER, WHO is in HEAVEN. For where two or three are gathered together in MY NAME, there I AM in the midst of them.'
In my estimation, just looking at the crowd we have here today, I'd say there are over one hundred guests. So right now I'm going to ask each one of you to grab the person's hand next to you. By so doing, we all are touching and agreeing. I have a strong feeling that JESUS is definitely in our midst."

Monsignor Matthews then faced the couple and said:
"Mark and Teresa, you have come together in this church so THE LORD may seal and strengthen your love in the presence of the church, ministers and this community. CHRIST abundantly blesses this love. HE has already consecrated you in baptism and now HE enriches and strengthens you by a special Sacrament, so that you may assume the duties of marriage in mutual and lasting fidelity. And so in the presence of the church I ask you to state your intentions."

The Monsignor then said to the congregation, "Mark and Teresa have composed some special vows they would like to say to each other."
Allen went first. He turned and faced Teresa, looking into her enchanting brown eyes and said,

"Teresa, you are the beacon that lights up my world. Your eyes are the morning sun.
Your lips are the fruit that feeds my heart.
Your love is the energy that completes me.
When I found you, I found my soul.
You are my North Star. Wherever you are, that's where I want to be.
Teresa, I know your father is no longer with us, but I've got a

feeling he's in Heaven watching all of this. So I want to say to
your mother, I am eternally grateful to you and your husband
for conceiving this beautiful woman and allowing our paths to
cross.
Mom, Dad, I also want to thank the two of you for conceiving
me, because without the two of you, I wouldn't be standing
here today.
Teresa, I will always put you first and I will love you
unconditionally.
I will honor and respect you. I will give you everything in life
that you deserve.
I want our love to serve as an inspiration to my   new-
found daughters.
It's my desire that they know how a woman should be treated
purely because of the way I'm going to treat you.
When they become women, they will surely know that a woman
should be respected.
So, when they enter relationships, if they are not treated in the
same manner as their mother, then they will unequivocally
know those men aren't worthy of them. Teresa, I pray that our
love will be impervious to gossip, rumors and lies.
I believe if we stand together, nothing can separate us.
You are my queen, my perfect angel.
I love you with all my heart."

With tearful eyes, she whispered, "I love you, too!"
She paused for a long moment before speaking. She then
nervously squeezed Allen's hand tightly, staring into his eyes.
She turned and faced the congregation.

"Oh…boy, I've forgotten most of what I wanted to say.
I'm so blown away by what my husband just said. Oh, well, he'll
be my husband in a few more minutes. What I want to say is,

161

*I believe in my heart without a doubt that GOD has ordained
this time, this place and this day.
You see, I prayed for this day. In my heart I knew this day
would eventually come.
I have some words of wisdom for all of you.
Before you make any major decision, in fact any decision,
consult with THE LORD.
Pray on it, and meditate; trust me, it works.
There are times when our Blessings are within our midst and
we don't always accept them.
We tend to embrace what's wrong for us and run from what's
right for us.
When you let GOD guide your footsteps, you'll never go wrong.
When you pray and if you're sincere,
THE LORD will grant you your heart's desire.
I'm a living witness.
When I prayed and asked GOD to send me a husband, I
wanted him to be special."*

She spoke with profound emotion as she turned back to
Allen and looked deeply into his eyes,
*"You are the essence of a man. You are strong, but also gentle.
You are firm, but also patient. You are all I ever wanted in a
man. You're:*
Altruistic
Loving
Loyal
Empathetic
Noble
*With all of these attributes, it's no surprise that I'm standing
next to the man of my dreams.
Allen, you've brought me solace at a time in my life when I
needed it most.*

162

ONE MORE MIRACLE

You've given me felicity when I didn't think I'd ever smile
again.
Allen, everyone who knows you would agree that you have a
way with words.
I could never be your equal when it comes to words.
But I promise I can match you with my fidelity and
commitment. I Love you so much."

Allen smiled, "I love you, too!"

Monsignor Matthews looked at Allen and Teresa and asked, **"Have you come here freely, without reservations, to give yourselves to each other in marriage? Will you love and honor each other as man and wife for the rest of your lives."**

He answered, *"I will."*
She repeated, *"I will."*

The Monsignor said,
"Since it is your intention to enter into marriage, join your right hands, and declare your consent before GOD and HIS CHURCH. Mark, do you take Teresa to be your wife? Do you promise to be true to her in good times and in bad times; in sickness and in health; to love and honor her all the days of your life?"

He said sincerely, *"I do!"*

"Teresa, do you take Mark to be your husband? Do you promise to be true to him in good times and in bad times; in sickness and in health; to love him and honor him all the days of your life?"

She answered softly, *"I do!"*

The Monsignor asked the couple for the rings. Paul and
Jada came forth and presented the rings. After receiving the rings
from Paul, his best man, Allen placed the ring on Teresa's ring
finger on her left hand. The ring that Teresa received from Jada,
she placed on Allen's ring finger on his left hand.

The Monsignor then blessed the rings,
"LORD, Bless and Consecrate Mark and Teresa in their love
for each other.
May these rings be a symbol of their true faith in each other
And always remind them of their love.
Through CHRIST our LORD, AMEN.
By the power entrusted in me by the Holy Catholic Church
and the State of Georgia, I now pronounce you man and
wife.
In the name of THE FATHER, the SON and the HOLY
SPIRIT.
What GOD has joined together, let no human being separate.

The happy couple fell into each other's arms with a long
and amorous kiss. The congregation applauded and cheered. The
bride and groom marched down the aisle, followed by the
wedding party. They immediately marched back into the church
to greet the guests and take pictures. After the photo session,
Allen and Teresa and the wedding party boarded the limousines
and headed back to the hotel for the reception.
When the bride and groom entered the Grand Ballroom,
they witnessed an exquisite layout. Each table was covered with
a red tablecloth and a three-foot tall plated vase, laden with fresh
flowers. A huge ice sculpture was next to a pink champagne
fountain. The menu consisted of: rack of lamb, prime rib, three

varieties of fresh-baked breads, baked potatoes and a host of fresh fruits and vegetables. The bride had her six tier vanilla cake, while the groom had his *Scale of Justice* lemon chiffon cake.

The first song the newlyweds danced to was an upbeat tune, *"Aint Gonna Hurt Nobody,"* by the group **Brick**. Allen displayed some pretty smooth moves on the dance floor, surprising his wife, whom was an excellent dancer herself. Four hours into the festivities, the celebration was drawing to a close. The bride and groom were handed a microphone.

Teresa did the honors, "Allen and I want to thank you all for coming to share our special celebration. It's been a long and exhausting day, but a beautiful one, none the less. We're both tired and we want to go up to our room and get some rest."

Allen's friend, Chuck, shouted out, "Yeah! You're going to get some rest, *alright!*"

Allen smiled coyly. "Thank you, Chuck! Good night!"

Teresa then continued, "Once again we'd like to thank all of you, from the bottom of our hearts. Drive safely. We love you, and may God Bless you all!"

After saying goodbye to all of the guests, Allen and Teresa went down to the table where Ms. Hunter, Mia, and Kendria were sitting. The girls hugged and kissed their new father.

Teresa looked on pleasantly as she waited for her turn. Her daughter stood at her waist and gave her a robust hug.

Teresa then kissed them, saying "I love you and I'll miss you. Mommy we'll be back in a week."

Both girls responded, "We love you Mommy, we'll see you soon!"

After a final group hug with Ms. Hunter and the girls, Ms. Hunter covertly pulls Teresa to the side and whispers in her ear, "I'm sure the devil is going to be ice skating tonight for sure!"

"Oh mama, you have a great memory."

"Yeah most mothers do, Honey."

Then Allen and Teresa left for the honeymoon suite. They stood impatiently, waiting on the elevator doors to open. Allen could hardly resist the temptation to undress his wife right there in the elevator. But before temptation could overtake him, the elevator stopped on the 16th floor, where their suite was located. They strolled to suite #116. Allen opened the door, picked up his bride and carried her over the threshold.

As they entered the suite, they were pleasantly surprised at how Logan's staff had romantically decorated the room. The floor leading to the bedroom was covered with rose petals. Scented candles lined the whole suite, including the spacious Jacuzzi bathroom. The Jacuzzi was filled with pink and blue bubbles. A bottle of **Cristal Champagne** was chilling in a stainless steel container of ice. *His* and *Hers* crystal wedding flutes were placed on a table fit for a King and Queen. Although the room was magnificently decorated, Allen and Teresa paid little, if any, attention to the décor. They were focused on consummating their marriage. Allen couldn't take his eyes off his bride, who was ravishing from head to toe.

Allen could be described as a *ladies' man*, a title that he reluctantly embraced because he didn't think of himself as a *womanizer*. This was debatable. It all depended on whom you asked. Because of Allen's countless sexual rendezvous with so many women, their wedding night would prove to be an epiphany for him. For the first time in his life, Allen would be physically, emotionally and spiritually connected to a woman.

They began to kiss passionately. The kisses were warm and fervent. Allen's temperature rose as he felt an erotic sensation travel through his entire body. Teresa suddenly broke away from his grip, turning her back towards him. She then demanded that he unzip her dress. Without delay, he accommodated her. Teresa stepped out of her dress, letting it fall to the floor, then stood still as Allen unbuttoned her bra and slowly removed her panties.

He leisurely turned her to face him, savoring her beauty. This was the first time Allen had seen his wife in her natural glow. She grabbed his hand, leading him to the bathroom. They entered the steamy water in the Jacuzzi and continued to kiss. The water was too hot for Allen. He wanted to make passionate love to his wife in the bed. They emerged from the Jacuzzi. He picked her up and carried her to the bed.

When they got to the bed, he laid her down gently. He instantly palpated her nipples with his lips. Her nipples hardened. She softly explored his phallus with her hand. His desire elevated; he couldn't wait any longer. She opened her legs and welcomed him in, so he connected inside of her. Her body went into a sexual frenzy, she grimaced with pleasure. To Allen's chagrin, he was finished before he started. He was embarrassed, to say the least!

Teresa didn't allow him to wallow in self-pity. She told him not to move, even though he was still inside of her, deflated. Teresa's constant kissing and sensuous voice proved to be the perfect aphrodisiac. In an instant he reenergized, and she felt his firmness again. Their bodies began to move in perfect rhythm. The hot, steamy, prolonged lovemaking lasted well into the morning hours. Teresa reached the *apex of stimulation* six times! If one were keeping score, he unloaded two and a half times. Allen satisfied her in a way she'd never had experienced before!

The next morning, the happy pair awakened enmeshed in each other's arms. When Allen opened his eyes, Teresa was looking at him smiling pleasantly.

"Are your eyes always this lambent early in the morning?"

"Baby, what does lambent mean?"

"Well, one definition is *softly radiant*. That definition fits you the most."

She playfully pinched his nose. "Baby, I'll be expecting you to tell me something romantic every morning!"

Gazing into her eyes, he replied, "I can do that and that's a promise!"

"Baby, what did you do to me last night…I've never had *that* done to me before…"

"Well, did you like it?"

"No…*I loved it*!"

She casually got up to go to the bathroom. Allen's eyes followed every move she made. Her stunning cinnamon brown skin, perfect ten body, and her beauty was so splendid that it was angelic. He believed he was a blessed man simply because Teresa was *his* angel. Minutes later, when she returned to bed, she gave him a big kiss.

He smiled, "That's not fair!"

"What's not fair?"

"You went and brushed your teeth."

"Yes, I did! My breath has to be fresh."

"I need to freshen my breath, too!"

He jumped out of bed and went to the bathroom. Moments later, he returned smiling, "Now we both have clean breath!"

"Sweetheart, what time does our flight leave for Paris?"

"It leaves at 3:45 this evening."

Teresa pulled him over to her giving him a tender kiss and whispered, "Come on and take a shower with me. Then let's go down to the restaurant and have breakfast. I'm hungry."

Allen responded, "Oh, Sweetheart, let's just order in. I don't feel like going down to the restaurant."

Teresa nodded her head, "Okay, that's fine. Honey, you call room service and I'll go and run the shower."

At 6:00 p.m., Allen and Teresa had been in flight for a little over two hours. The honeymooners were flying First Class. Teresa leaned back in her seat, her face gleaming, but she appeared to be in deep thought.

Allen observed her and asked, "What are you thinking about, Sweetheart?"

She smiled. "Oh, my mind is inundated with lots of thoughts. I'm thinking about us, I'm thinking about my babies and my mom."

Allen looked at her affectionately, "Your mind shouldn't be wandering. You should be focusing on our honeymoon and the great time we are going to have in Paris."

"Oh, Baby, I do apologize, but this is the first time I have ever been away from my babies for a long period of time."

"Sweetie, I do understand your feelings. Hey, the first thing we'll do when we get to Paris is call the girls."

She smiled, "Okay, Baby, then that's what we'll do."

When the plane landed, Allen and Teresa went through customs then on to the hotel. They checked in at one of Paris's posh hotels, **Hotel Deville Mairie de Paris**. The couple planned to spend five days in Paris. Since Allen had traveled to Paris on three previous occasions, he was somewhat familiar with the city. He gave his new bride a grand tour of Paris.

They visited **Notre Dame Cathedral**, the **Eiffel Tower**, the **Arc de Triumph** on the **Champs Elysees**; the **Plaza de la Concorde**; and they walked the left and right banks of the **Seine**, then booked a dinner cruise sailing down the river. Without a doubt, Paris, *The City of Lights*, was truly a place for lovers! Teresa couldn't help but be caught up in the pageantry and mystique of Paris. On the other hand, Allen was mainly caught up in his wife's majestic beauty, since in his eyes, Teresa purely added grandeur to the city.

After spending five days in Paris, they returned to Atlanta to embark on their new life together. Allen and his new family resided on his parent's estate and occupied the guest house for almost a year, while having a 11,500 sq-ft Spanish-styled mansion constructed. Once completed, the mansion had six bedrooms and seven bathrooms on two acres of land, near outside of Atlanta. The master suite was 300 sq-ft., with *His* and *Her* bathrooms, and *His* and *Her* walk-in closets. Leading out of the bedroom was a 150 sp-ft. balcony equipped with a dining set. The 500 sq-ft. kitchen had an island that seats seven, and a stainless steel, commercial style stove with six burners and a matching stainless steel refrigerator. The kitchen also had limestone floors that lead out into an enclosed, plexi-glass patio. Lastly, the mansion was equipped with an infinity pool and custom made lawn furniture that completed the back yard. A month after settling in, Allen and Teresa threw a lavish house-warming party.

The guest list was a collage of people from various backgrounds. Teresa invited some of her former neighbors from Grady Homes and some of her ex-coworkers. Allen's guest list included several law colleagues and their wives. His parents and some of their associates in the medical field were also in attendance. Ms. Hunter invited a few members from her church.

CHAPTER 21

A year and a half later, Teresa was a full-time student at Georgia State University. On the advice of her husband, she changed her major from Education to Business Administration. She was now ten semester hours away from obtaining a Bachelor's Degree in Business, while Mia and Kendria were excelling in an all-girls Catholic School.

Allen was truly the consummate father, helping the girls with their school work and most mornings dropping them off at school. The girls truly loved their new father and he genuinely loved them, too. To Allen's delight, the girls had elected to call him "Daddy."

Allen wanted to become the girls' legal father, so he suggested to Teresa that he legally adopt the girls. Obviously, their last name would be changed to Williams. He told Teresa that he wanted the girls to be entitled to all the privileges that came with the Williams name. Teresa was jubilant, thinking to herself, *'This man is just too good to be true!'*

She and Allen carefully explained to the girls about the decision to adopt them and their subsequent name change. The girls were thrilled. Allen, being a lawyer, judiciously did the legal work to get the name changes done. Within a few weeks, the twins became Kendria and Mia Williams.

On Wednesday around 2:30 p.m., Teresa suddenly became ill at school. Allen received a call from the University's Administrator, who happened to be a friend of the Williams family. Allen rushed over to the University to see about his wife. Teresa was running a low-grade fever and was thought to have a stomach virus. Allen took her to Grady Memorial, which was the closest hospital. It was Teresa's request to be taken there.

When they arrived at the hospital, Rob and Deni were already there (Allen had called them beforehand). The hospital staff wasted no time attending to Teresa. A distant cousin of

171

Rob's, Assistant Chief Resident Dr. Marvelyn Williams, was in charge.

The doctor ordered blood work and conducted a series of tests. Teresa had been hospitalized for about four hours. Dr. Williams came back to her room to deliver the results of one of the tests. At Teresa's bedside were Allen and his parents.

When the doctor entered the room, Rob greeted her with a smile. "Oh, hello, Marvelyn. Now I know my daughter-in-law is in capable hands."

"I saw Bug and his wife in **Admitting**, he told me his wife wasn't feeling well. I went and pulled her chart and I decided that she was going to be my patient."

"It's good to have family in high places!"

She smiled, "That would apply more to you than me. I have good news for the husband and wife here."

When she revealed the diagnosis, Deni burst into tears. Allen and Rob appeared to be pleasantly surprised, while Teresa began to cry. Allen asked the doctor in a cracking voice, "Are you absolutely sure Teresa is pregnant?"

Rob then asked Marvelyn, "Are you sure this diagnosis is accurate?"

She nodded with confidence, "I'm one-hundred percent sure."

Before leaving the room, the doctor congratulated the expectant parents. They thanked her for the wonderful news.

Allen's parents bent down and kissed Teresa, then exclaimed with joy, "This is one of the happiest days of our lives! We are so happy for the both of you!"

The diagnosis came as a complete but pleasant surprise. It had been medically documented that the chances of Allen fathering a child would be slim-to-none.

Teresa revealed to her in-laws that she had been praying to get pregnant ever since she and Allen were married. Now that her prayers had been answered, she was ecstatic!

Deni looked at her beaming and gushed, "Oh my Darling, you

have made this possible and we owe it all to you!"

Teresa shook her head, "No, I don't deserve any of the credit. All the credit goes to GOD. We should thank HIM."

Rob agreed. "You're right! When I go to Mass on Sunday, I'm going to say a special prayer."

Teresa said with sincere eyes, "Oh, we don't have to wait until Sunday; we can pray right now!"

Deni and Rob looked at each other, almost reading each other's minds. They both believed that prayer should be done in a private setting.

Allen agreed with his wife, "No, we don't have to wait until Sunday; we can pray right now!"

Teresa requested that they all join hands and pray together. Deni and Rob reluctantly joined hands with Allen and Teresa as she began to pray.

Eight months later, on Christmas Day, Teresa and Allen were doubly blessed. To the surprise of Teresa's doctor, Dr. Tracy Blanks, she had given birth to identical twin boys: Joshua Allen and David Anthony. Teresa honored her late father, Anthony Hunter, by using his first name for David's middle name. Joshua and his dad shared the same middle name. Teresa was now the mother of two sets of identical twins. The odds of this happening was 1 out of 70,000. This was one of the most exciting Christmases this family had ever celebrated. Teresa's hospital room was filled with family and friends.

The girls were ecstatic to know that they were going to be big sisters and were thrilled to bring some of their toys to the hospital. The family had Christmas dinner in Teresa's room. They had been there all day. It was well after 8 p.m. when Teresa stated that she was tired and wanted to get some rest. Before they left, she hugged the family and thanked them all. Once everyone was gone, Teresa was finally able to rest.

Four days later, Teresa was at home with her new babies in her bedroom sitting up in bed. The babies' cribs were on both sides of the bed. Ms. Hunter abruptly walked into the bedroom with a cup of cinnamon tea in her hand.

"I made you some tea," she said, gazing at Teresa. Teresa sat in silence as her face quivered in despair. Ms. Hunter sensed right away that something was wrong. "What's the matter, baby?"

She gently lamented, "Nothing mama, I'll be alright." Ms. Hunter said, "You should be happy you've got these two little bundles of joy next to your bed. That in itself should make you happy."

"I'm happy, mama."

Her mom looked closely at her. "If you're happy, then why do you look so sad?"

Teresa suddenly began to cry profusely. "Oh mama, I woke up this morning thinking about Little Carl and how much I miss him. When we moved away from Grady Homes, it felt like we left him there."

Ms. Hunter immediately placed the tea on a coaster on the white Victorian dresser and rushed to her daughter's aid. She put her arms around Teresa and encouraged her to vent, saying in a soothing voice, "It's okay, Teresa, let it out. It's okay, Baby." She continued to cry, saying, "Mama, I love my baby. I will *never* stop loving him."

Ms. Hunter looked attentively at her daughter. "Teresa, baby, I too think about Little Carl every day. He was just as much my baby as he was yours. I kept him when you worked nights and he slept in the same bed with me. Baby, Little Carl is in our hearts and that's where he will always be. Wherever we are, he will always be with us, Teresa. Little Carl is in Heaven now. He's playing with the other little angel children. Teresa, we will never forget him and we will never stop loving him. Look at how awesome GOD is! HE called Little Carl home. Plus, HE turned around and blessed you with two healthy baby boys. So let's be thankful for that reason alone."

She regained her composure. "Mama, I am thankful, believe me."

Teresa's mood mellowed as her eyes drifted towards Joshua's and David's cribs.

She sighed, "Mama, I am thankful. I thank GOD every day for the new lives HE has given me. 1 know I am Blessed. I have a great husband, beautiful children and a beautiful and great mother."

Ms. Hunter smiled, "Thank you, honey; now you're going to make me cry."

Teresa confessed, "Mama, I am so embarrassed."

"Why are you embarrassed?"

"Well, because I'm a 24-year-old woman crying like a baby."

Ms. Hunter looked at her maternally and said, "I'm going to let you in on a little secret. Yeah, you're 24 years old, but you'll always be *my* baby."

Teresa fondly rested her head on her mother's shoulder and whispered, "I can never tell you enough how much I love you."

Ms. Hunter replied, "Oh Teresa, if you never tell me again, that'll be just fine, because you show me everyday how much you love me."

CHAPTER 22

Five years later, David and Joshua were first graders. Mia and Kendria were freshmen at a Catholic high school. David and Joshua developed into two extremely handsome little boys. They inherited their physical features from their mother, such as their brown skin and captivating dark brown eyes. But both boys' hair was like their dad's: very dark and straight. These two pint-sized Romeos adored Teresa and they truly were the apples of her eyes. But she'd never admit such in front of Mia and Kendria.

Allen occasionally joked with Teresa saying having two other males in the house turned out to be a mixed blessing, since he never imagined he would have stiff competition for his wife's affection. Teresa always contended before David and Joshua were born, she used to compete with Mia and Kendria for his affection. Allen, the astute litigator, often won all arguments in court, but seldom won arguments at home.

After earning her MBA from Emory University, Teresa began working with her husband Allen as they had formed **Twin Enterprises**, a Real Estate and Development Company. Allen and Teresa were both real estate brokers. The company employed roughly twenty-five people, including two attorneys. The company was appropriately named **Twin Enterprises** because Teresa and Allen were proud parents of a set of identical twin daughters and a set of identical twin sons.

Twin Enterprises was housed in a four-story building in Downtown Atlanta on Forsyth Street. Allen and Teresa were the primary owners of the building. The fourth floor was exclusively occupied by **Twin Enterprises**.

The other three floors were leased out to other businesses. This provided a substantial income for the Williams family, along with Allen's other business interests. Teresa juggled being a wife, mother, and business executive quite adequately. One advantage she had over the other employees was being married to the boss. Her salary was guaranteed.

A year later, Allen and Teresa were blessed with another child. It was Teresa's third daughter. She named this child Mallory Jassiah, and this child was unique in many ways. At an early age, she displayed some remarkable physical and mental skills. She began to walk at 7 months old and by the age of two, she could speak clearly. When she was 4, she could read on a second grade level. At the age of 8, she was advanced to the fifth grade, where she was an A-student. Like all of Teresa's children, Mallory was blessed with great physical attributes. Her pecan color complexion and sparkling blue eyes caused her to stand out. Mallory definitely inherited her father's and grandmother's eyes. When she looked at you, her gaze was so intense it was like she could read your thoughts.

Mallory's fifth grade teacher, Sister Octavia   La Point, a nun from the Holy Family Order, was quite impressed with Mallory. Sister La Point often observed Mallory's willingness to help the other students with their work. On Friday mornings when the class would attend Mass, Mallory was eager to read the scriptures from the **Missalette**. For an eight-year old, she had a deep passion for the Bible.

Sister Octavia developed a special interest in young Mallory. Teresa trusted Sister Octavia enough to share her delivery room experience with her. It had been eight years since she had last spoken about the ordeal with Mallory's delivery with anyone except her mother.

Sister Octavia believed that Mallory had a special destiny because of what Teresa experienced in the delivery room. Sister Octavia really wasn't a stranger to Teresa. They'd forged a friendship a few years ago when she was Mia and Kendria's fifth grade teacher. Sister Octavia had been reassigned to a school in New York City, where she worked for three years before returning to **St. Mary's Academy**. Teresa was delighted to be reacquainted with her.

The following day, Teresa had lunch with Allen. They discussed the conversation she'd had with Sister Octavia the previous day. Teresa revealed to him that Sister Octavia believed Mallory had a *Spiritual Destiny*. He found what she revealed to him somewhat amusing. He discounted the comment on the Spiritual aspect of what Teresa told him. Allen knew that academically his daughter was gifted, and that's all he wanted to believe. However, he had to admit, at various times in her young life, she'd exhibited some clairvoyant skills.

One example was when her grandfather Rob couldn't find an 18 ct. gold pocket watch, a family heirloom. Given to him by his late father-in-law, it had more of a sentimental value than a monetary value to Rob. It had been missing for well over a month when Mallory happened to be visiting her grandparents. It was a bright, sunny day. The three of them were relaxing on the patio, across from Deni's rose garden, at a white wrought-iron table with a large bright red umbrella shielding them from the bright sun. The sweet fragrance from the roses filled the air. Rob and Deni were enjoying frozen strawberry margaritas, while Mallory indulged herself with a chocolate milk shake. Rob suddenly glanced at Deni's almost empty glass and asked, "Dear, can I get you another drink?"
She nodded, "Sure."
He grabbed the pitcher from table and filled her glass almost to the brim. He then placed the Crystal pitcher back on the table. Deni looked at him and said, "Thank you, my Darling."
He smiled, "Oh, you're quite welcome, Dear.
Mallory looked at Rob and said, "Grampee, do you mind going inside the house and getting me some cold water?"
He smiled, "Why Angel, it will be my pleasure."
He went back inside of the house, returning shortly with a glass of ice water. He then handed the glass to Mallory.
She responded, "Thank you, Grampee. Thank you very much. You are the best!"

178

"You're very welcome," he said with a smile.

Deni made eye contact with Rob as she asked, "Oh my Darling, did you ever find that missing gold watch that my father gave you?"

He shook his head with regret, "No, Dear, I didn't. But I'm hoping it will turn up soon. I'm sure I've overlooked it, somehow. It has to be around here somewhere."

She sighed, "Well, I certainly hope you're right."

Out of the blue, Mallory said to Rob, "Grampee, are you sure you've looked everywhere for this watch?"   He paused briefly, in deep thought as he muttered, "Um, I believe I did."

He then added, "Angel, I'm certain I looked everywhere I could possibly think of."

She looked at him as she tightened her lips, "Grampee, did you look over in the guest house?"

He nodded, "Yes, I think I already looked there."

Rob suddenly began to concentrate as he thought to himself, '*Wait a minute, the last place I remember having the watch was in the guest residence. I took a shower there after jogging. On that particular day, we were replacing the two water heaters in the main house. What I need to do is go back and look again.*'

Rob's thoughts were interrupted when Mallory said to him, "Grampee, I have a good feeling you are going to find your watch in the guest house."

With a smile, Deni said to Mallory, "My dear sweet Angel, what makes you think he will find his watch in the guest house?"

Mallory replied, "I really don't know. I just have a positive feeling."

Deni said to her, "Well my Darling, I certainly hope that your inclination is right."

The very next day, Rob walked out of the main residence and took the short walk through the rose garden, which led to the guest house. Once inside, he went straight to the master bathroom. He found a dark-brown velour monogrammed bath robe hanging on a hook outside of the closet. Rob searched the inside pocket of the bathrobe and literally struck gold. There it was—the solid gold pocket-watch!

Thrilled, he broke into an enormous smile. Rob felt like a kid in a candy store. The watch meant so much to him not just because it was a gift from Deni's father, but it was also a family heirloom. It had been in Deni's family for well over a century. The watch was first given to Deni's father by his father. Deni didn't have any brothers to carry on the tradition, so her father gave the watch to Rob as a sign of admiration for being a great son-in-law. Rob felt very fortunate to have found it. Just as Rob was about to leave, a thought occurred to him, *'If it weren't for Angel, I may have never found the watch.'*

Rob continued to search his mind, trying to figure out how Mallory instinctively knew he would eventually find the watch in the guest house. He knew that he had not mentioned to her that he was ever in the guest house. *That was simply amazing*, he surmised. In the end, Rob shrugged it off as just a coincidence.

Four months later, Mallory's clairvoyant abilities came into play once more, when twelve-year-old Melissa Payne went missing. She was last seen walking home, alone, from school. The girl's parents described her as being very happy and outgoing, with no disciplinary problems. Melissa was also a student at the same school Mallory attended. It had been over 24-hours and there was still no trace of the missing girl. A picture of Melissa Payne had been shown on all the television stations in Atlanta and nationwide.

It had been established that the child was not a runaway; therefore, the police were profiling all known child molesters in the area. The FBI had been called in to help with the investigation. The child's parents, Alex and Joy Payne, had been interviewed twice. The police were convinced they were not suspects in the girl's disappearance.

Thirty-six hours later, there was still no sign of the missing child. Friday morning, Mallory and her sixth grade classmates were leaving the classroom to attend 9 a.m. Mass at the school. Sister Octavia led her class in a special prayer for Melissa's safe return. When school ended, Teresa picked up Mallory. When her daughter got in the car, Teresa instantly knew something was wrong.

Teresa gave Mallory a serious stare and asked, "What's on your mind? What's bothering you, Angel?"

She sighed, "Mom, you seldom call me Angel. Daddy usually calls me that."

Teresa looked at her and said in a dramatic fashion, "Oh, well, I'm *awfully sorry* I called you Angel. I suppose your daddy is the only one who has that privilege."

Mallory giggled, "Mom, don't be so sensitive. I never said you couldn't call me Angel."

Teresa smiled, "Why, thank you, Ms. Mallory Jassiah Williams, for allowing me the *privilege* to call you Angel."

"Mom what's for dinner tonight?"

"I don't know. What do you want?"

Mallory replied, "I don't know, Mom; maybe a hamburger."

Teresa gave her a long look and said, "Stop trying to be like your father."

"Mom, how am I trying to be like Daddy?"

"By camouflaging what's really bothering you. You never answered my question."

She looked at her with a sad expression, as she readjusted the seatbelt and leaned against the passenger door.

"Well mom, I guess I'm sad because one of my school mates is missing. I was thinking about how her parents must be feeling."

Teresa shook her head and said with compassion, "I can't

181

even imagine how I'd feel if you or one of your sisters or brothers went missing. Your dad and I would be devastated."

"Mom, when my classmates and I went to 9 a.m. Mass, we said a special prayer for Melissa. I hope GOD will let her be found safe."

"Yes Mallory, so do I."

"Mom, do you think GOD takes children prayers seriously?"

Teresa answered earnestly, "Oh, sure, HE does, Angel; without a doubt! I can assure you that children's prayers resonate the loudest. Their prayers are more sincere and innocent. And I also believe children have favor with GOD. I don't think children bother GOD as much as we adults do."

"Mom, I hope GOD will allow Melissa to return to her mom and dad."

"Yes, Angel, so do I."

"Mom, before we say grace at dinner tonight, can we say a special prayer for Melissa?"

"Most definitely, Angel."

The following morning, Mallory came down from her bedroom to have breakfast with the family. She was disappointed to find that her mother and grandmother were absent. Teresa had gone to drive her mother to the airport. Mallory wasn't aware that her grandmother would be going out of town. Ms. Hunter was on her way to Colorado Springs to visit her younger son, Patrick.

Teresa's brother Patrick had been married four years now. He and his wife were expecting their second child. Ms. Hunter's plans were to spend some time with them and to help Patrick's wife, Carmen, with the new baby due in a few days.

Mallory was somewhat disappointed after learning her mother wouldn't be there for breakfast because she was anxious to share her dream with her. Mallory was frustrated to the point of not wanting to eat breakfast. Her father insisted that she eat something, so she had a bagel and a cup of hot chocolate.

ONE MORE MIRACLE

At 7:30 a.m. Allen glanced at his Rolex. He then said to all five of his children, "C'mon gang, let's get a move on. You guys don't want to be late for school."

Of course, he was referring to Mallory, Joshua and David, since Mia and Kendria were seniors at **Georgia Tech University**. Both had developed into two gorgeous young women. The older they became, the more they looked like their mother. Mia was a pre-law student. Allen was inordinately pleased with her decision to become a lawyer. Kendria was a pre-med student. Her decision was pleasing to Deni and Rob because, as far as *they* were concerned, the family couldn't have enough doctors.

Both young ladies drove late model sport cars. Buying cars for their older daughters paid dividends for Allen and Teresa, since Mia and Kendria were often asked to drive their siblings to school.

On that particular morning, Mia drove Joshua and David to school. Kendria drove Mallory to school.

During the ride to school, Mallory tried to tell Kendria about the dream she had. Apparently, Kendria wasn't too interested because, she turned the volume up on the radio. The music was so loud, it prevented Kendria from hearing what Mallory had to say.

Each time Mallory tried to speak to Kendria, Kendria would to say, "Mallory, wait a minute. I can't hear you."

Mallory became so annoyed, she stopped talking. A few minutes later, when they pulled up to the school, Kendria noticed that Mallory was upset.

She asked her, "What's the matter, Angel baby?"

Mallory replied in frustration, "I was trying to tell you something, but you weren't paying me any attention. You were playing radio so loud I couldn't hear myself speak. That's so rude, Kendria!"

Kendria's spirit suddenly sank as she whispered, "So

183

sorry baby, forgive me? You're absolutely right. That was rude, Mallory...can 1 make it up to you?"

"How are you going to make it up to me, Kendria?"
"I'm getting out of school early today. I'll call Mom and tell her that I'll pick you up from school. We can go to the library to check out some books. Then we'll go over to **Fà Reals Pizza**, over on Auburn Avenue. You'll be hanging out with your big sister. Would you like that?"

Mallory said with a big smile, "Sure, Kendria!"

"Hey, can we solidify this deal with a hug?"

Mallory nodded, "Yes!"
She then wrapped her arms around Kendria and gave her a tight squeeze. Before getting out of the car, Mallory said, "Kendria, Mia says she is my big sister."

Kendria shook her head, "No, she's not your big sister. I'm your big sister and I'm also her big sister."
An inquisitive Mallory inquired, "Kendria, how can that be so when the two of you have the same birthday and you are the exact same age?"
Kendria smiled, "I was born three minutes before Mia, so *technically*, that makes me older."

"Oh, Kendria, that's just like you to focus on technicalities and find a loophole!"

"Little girl, you're too smart for your own good. Now go on, get out of my car. Get out now! I love you, little woman."

Mallory smiled, "Yeah, I love you too" as she got out of the car.

She walked down the dark-green carpeted concrete sidewalk, then through the gilded glass doors, finally entering the red brick building. Once inside, Mallory made her way down the hall, (on what appeared to be) freshly waxed terrazzo floors. When she arrived at her classroom, Sister Octavia was standing in front of the door. The nun was greeting her students, which was her daily ritual.

ONE MORE MIRACLE

Once all of the students were inside, the students would stand at their desk. They would automatically lift their head's to the sky and would say collectively, "Good morning, **HEAVENLY FATHER.**"
Then they would turn their focus to Sister Octavia and say, "Good morning, Sister."
She would respond, "Good morning future saints." The students would then bow their heads and recite the LORD'S PRAYER.

Next, they would say the pledge of allegiance to the United States flag. After completing the daily routine, Sister Octavia would select one of the students to call the roll. Then the school day would begin.

It was 11:30 a.m., lunch time when Sister Octavia began escorting the class to the cafeteria. When they arrived there, Sister Octavia stood outside the door while Mallory and her classmates went inside. Sister Octavia didn't want the students to know that she was fasting and the smell of food would make her nauseated. After leaving the students in the cafeteria, she walked across the courtyard, past the statue of Mother Mary, and entered the church. Once inside, she made her way to the altar, lit a candle and made the sign of a cross.

Sister Octavia had an unorthodox style of praying. There were times when she'd chant the name of JESUS for long periods of time, before actually praying. Sometimes, she would appear to be in a trance while praying. Sister Octavia would often ask GOD to let her experience some of the agony of the people for whom she was praying.

She fervently believed that she had a special connection with GOD. She wouldn't ever share her belief with anyone because she didn't want to be seen as arrogant or sanctimonious. Sister Octavia used the entire thirty-minute lunch break praying for the missing child. She then went back, collected her students from the cafeteria and escorted them back to the classroom.

At 2:15p.m., the children were being dismissed from

185

school an hour early. Mallory was still in the classroom, waiting for her big sister Kendria to pick her up. In the meantime, she was engaged in a conversation with Sister Octavia. Mallory told Sister Octavia about her dream. Sister Octavia was overwhelmed with joy. She believed Mallory's dream could possibly be the answer to her prayers. She was now confident that Melissa would be found safe.

Mallory revealed to her that in the dream, she saw Melissa talking to a man in a white pick-up with some lawn equipment on the bed of his truck. Melissa appeared to be talking and smiling with the man, as if she knew him. Sister Octavia asked Mallory to describe the man in her dream. Mallory told her she didn't have a clear picture of the man because Melissa was the primary focus of the dream. Sister Octavia, sounding like a seasoned detective, then asked her, "Was the man black or white?" Mallory told her the man appeared to be white and he was wearing a dark colored baseball cap. Sister Octavia sat in deep thought, trying to mentally digest what Mallory had revealed to her. Her concentration was interrupted when Kendria opened the door to the classroom and walked in.

Sister Octavia greeted her with a sincere smile, and said, "Hello, my child, how is my former student?"

Kendria returned the smile saying, "I'm blessed, Sister. And you?"

"I'm extremely blessed! I'm doing fine for an old lady."

Kendria shook her head with a wide grin and acknowledged, "Sister, you haven't changed one bit! You don't look any different now than you did ten years ago, when Mia and I first started school here."

"Thank you, Kendria. You're so kind! When you and Mia were in my class, the two of you were the cutest, most disciplined students I'd ever taught."

She smiled softly, "Oh, thank you, Sister. I appreciate the compliment."

186

Mallory impatiently looked at her sister. "Kendria, are you ready to go?"

"Give me a minute and then we can go."

Kendria walked over and gave her a hug. Sister Octavia walked them to the door. Her parting words were, "GOD BLESS THE BOTH OF YOU."

They responded, "And you also, Sister."

CHAPTER 23

After Mallory and Kendria left, Sister Octavia
immediately phoned the Fulton County Sheriff's Department and
asked to speak to Lieutenant Drew Hamilton, a detective and
Sister Octavia's former student. He was more like family because
Sister Octavia grew up with his mother on the island of
Martinique. They were still close friends. Sister Octavia revealed
very little information over the phone. She only told him she had
a possible lead in the Melissa Payne case. She made it absolutely
clear that she needed to speak with him in person. The lieutenant
left immediately.

It was 4:45pm when he arrived at the school. He wasn't
alone. With him was an extremely attractive female officer
whom he introduced as Sgt. Jasmine Everette. She stood about
5'8" tall, with hazel-brown eyes, chestnut-brown hair and a super
figure. She could certainly be described as eye candy. But then
again, so could Drew, standing at 6'4", with movie star good
looks and smooth dark-brown skin. He, being slightly over 200
pounds, had the body of an athlete and a warm, trusting smile.

After exchanging greetings, Sister Octavia said, "I'm
sorry I can't offer you a seat. I know these desks are too small for
you, but we can go into the teacher's lounge if you'd like."

He responded, "We're okay, we've been sitting all day."

She looked at him and said, "Well, Drew, what I'm about
to tell you is sort of complicated."

She then focused on Sgt. Everette, saying to her, "My
child, would it offend you if I spoke French to Drew?"

Sgt. Everette shook her head with a disconcerted
expression, "No Ma'am, it wouldn't."

(Sister Octavia was fluent in French, understandably so,
because French was her native language. The island of
Martinique was a French-colonized country. Drew's mom, also
being from Martinique, taught him and his sister French.)

ONE MORE MIRACLE

Sister Octavia said in French, **"Eh bien Drew, ce que je vais vous dire est assez mystique, pour dire le moins. Cette information m'a ete donnee comme un rêve. Un de mes ètudiants a vu en rêve Melissa Payne monter dans un pick-up blanc avec un homme, Melissa semble l'avoir connu."**
("Well Drew, what I'm about to tell you is quite mystical, to say the least. This information was given to me in the form of a dream. One of my students dreamt she saw Melissa Payne getting into a white pickup truck with a man that Melissa appeared to have known.")

He looked at her as his eyes narrowed.

"Ma Tante," il murmura un mot doux, qu'il utilise chaque fois qu'il s'adresse à elle. Après une longue silence, il finit par dire, **"Ah! tu penses vraiment que je vais poursuivre la piste d'un rêve? Honnêtement, Je ne sais comment! Je ne suis pas un faiseur de miracle ou un génie, je suis un officier de police répond-t-il la regardant droit dans les yeux."**

("My Aunt," he murmured a term of endearment he always used when addressing her. With a long pause he eventually said, looking her straight in the eye, "Aww, do you expect me to follow up on a dream? To be really honest, I don't know how. I'm not a miracle worker or a genius. I'm a police officer.)

She said sardonically, **"Drew, tu sais que je suis dingue ou cinglée, mais je sais que c'est vraiment difficile pour toi de comprendre. Parfois Dieu révèle des choses aux gens de façon compliquée. Drew, le plus souvent, si on prie et demande la sagesse, nos prières sont exaucées en général."**

("Drew, you know I'm not nut or a crackpot, but I also know this is very difficult for you to comprehend. Sometimes the way GOD reveals things to people is complicated. Drew, more often than not, if we pray and ask for wisdom, our prayers are usually answered.")

"Ma tante, je suis un fervent croyant de cela."

189

("My Aunt, I am a firm believer of that.")

Sgt. Everette felt like the proverbial third wheel, being left out of the conversation.

She suddenly cleared her throat, interrupting them, saying to the lieutenant,

"Excuse me, Drew. I'm going to wait for you in the car. I need to phone someone."

He nodded, "Okay, Jazz, I won't be long."

Sister Octavia said to her, as she departed,

"It was so nice meeting you. I hope I didn't make you feel uncomfortable by speaking French to Drew."

Sgt. Everette replied with a smile,

"No, Ma'am, you didn't at all," but as she closed the door she thought to herself, *'I'm such a liar!'*

He then said to Sister Octavia in French,

"On peut parler Anglais maintenant?"

("Can we speak in English now?")

She responded in French,

"Bien sûr."

("Sure we can.")

"Now I know why you wanted to speak French in front of Jasmine. You're such a wise lady. Jasmine wouldn't have believed any of this. She is one of the biggest skeptics I've ever met."

"Well, my nephew, I can't say you were over-zealous either, even when I told you about the dream."

He nodded, "You're absolutely right, and that's putting it mildly. I'm not into the supernatural."

"Neither am I, Drew, but I'm certainly into the HOLY SPIRIT, and the HOLY SPIRIT reveals himself in many ways. This particular little girl told me the dream. I believe, without a doubt, that she's been touched by the HOLY SPIRIT. Look Drew, you don't have to share this conversation with your fellow police officers, if you don't feel comfortable."

190

"Trust me, I have no intentions of doing that!

"Drew, don't the Police Force keep a list of pedophiles in this area?"

"Yes, we do."

"Well, when you get back to the station, I'm not trying to tell you how to do your job, but maybe you can look at that list and see if any pedophiles or child molesters live in or were in this area when the child came up missing."

"Yes, Ma'am, that's what I intend to do. I almost feel silly asking this question, but did she describe what the man looked like in the dream?"

"Well, she gave a vague description of the man, but she didn't get a clear image of the man in the dream. She believes he's white and the key-factor is that he was wearing a dark baseball cap."

"Dark baseball cap? That's it, Sister?"

She continued, "Not really. She said that in the dream, he was driving a white pick-up truck and the truck appeared to have lawn equipment on the back of it."

With a smirk on his face, he asked, "Well, in the dream, did she get the truck's license plate number?"

Sister Octavia responded with a half-smile, "No, she didn't."

He had been in the Law Enforcement for almost ten years. This was the first time that he had ever received information concerning a case by way of a dream. He reconciled in his mind that this was, by no means, an ordinary tip.

Lieutenant Hamilton stood for an extended moment, reflecting. Sister Octavia inquired with a serious look in her eyes, "What are you thinking about, my nephew?"

He explained, "I was just thinking about this make-believe information I just received from you and I was wondering what I was going to tell my colleagues."

She said, with a soft smile, "Well, you can always tell them the truth."

He shook his head, "Oh no, I can't do that! My fellow officers couldn't handle the truth, in this situation. Well, My Aunt, I must be going now. My partner's outside waiting for me. I promise I'll follow up on this information."

"Drew, I pray this information doesn't turn out to be make-believe, as you call it. I pray that it will lead to something positive."

Before leaving, he gave Sister Octavia an affectionate hug.

She bid him good-bye and said in French, **"Que DIEU vous benisse, mon neveu."**
("GOD bless you, my nephew.")

He smiled and responded, **"Que DIEU vous benisse aussi, ma tante."**
("GOD bless you, my aunt.")

Before meeting with Sister Octavia, Lieutenant Hamilton was hoping to get a concrete lead. Now he was leaving her with only a dream (and no ordinary dream at that). Heading out the door, Lieutenant Hamilton reflected on the past.

When he was twelve years old, Drew was diagnosed with leukemia and given only months to live. His mother solicited Sister Octavia's help in praying for his recovery. Sister Octavia went on a thirty day fast and prayed to GOD, asking HIM to heal Drew. After her fast was complete, when Drew went to his follow-up visit, the doctors found no trace of leukemia in his blood. He was miraculously healed!

Twenty years later, he's still cancer-free. Reminiscing, he remembered that Sister Octavia is no ordinary woman!

The following day, Lieutenant Hamilton headed a team of officers who rounded-up over sixty convicted child predators, in the Atlanta Metropolitan Area. Within a
72-hour period, all were questioned. Fourteen of the   ex-felons were held for parole violations. The remaining forty-six had solid alibis and were released.

192

ONE MORE MIRACLE

This had been another grueling 12-hour day and Melissa
was still missing. Lieutenant Hamilton didn't have a good
feeling about this case. He had begun believing that the outcome
of this child's disappearance wouldn't be good because
statistically the longer someone remained missing, the less the
chance of their being found alive.

Monday morning, Lieutenant Hamilton left Douglasville,
Georgia, his home, heading to work. He had driven for ten
minutes before turning on the police radio. Within seconds, a
patrol officer checked in with dispatcher, saying,

*"This is unit 1274. Please be advised, I just pulled
over a white pick-up truck. My location is the 285 North Loop,
near Mangum Manor. The license plate number is Jack
Timothy Robert 222. Routine stop. It seems brake lights are
not working on the pick-up."*

Suddenly, a light came on in the Lieutenant's head.
Thoughts of the conversation with Sister Octavia, crossed his
mind. Lieutenant Hamilton's thoughts began to run rampant,
saying to himself, "I'm not even going to think that this could be
the suspect, but, I'm going to hope like crazy, that it is."

His palms began to sweat as he gripped the steering wheel
with anticipation. He quickly switched to one of the back
channels and communicated with the officer in unit 1274.

"This is Lieutenant Hamilton; do you copy?"

The deputy responded, *"I copy lieutenant, go ahead."*

Lieutenant Hamilton said, *"Give me a run down on the
occupants of the vehicle."*

"What do you want to know?"

"Are you confirming it's a white pick-up?"

193

"Affirmative!"

He paused and took a deep breath, *"Is your microphone secure?"*

"I'm still in my patrol car, Sir."

"I'm curious, what's on the back of the pick-up truck?"

"Sir, it looks like lawn equipment."

Lieutenant Hamilton said to himself, *'In my gut, I believe this is our guy.'*
He then asked a follow-up question: *"How many occupants are in the truck?"*

"The driver is a white male and the female passenger is also white; she looks like a child, no more than eight or nine years old."

"By chance, Is the driver wearing a dark baseball cap?"

The deputy responded, *"Yes Sir, he is wearing a dark baseball cap."*
Lieutenant Hamilton struck the steering wheel with his fist and shouted with excitement, *"Yes! Yes! I think this is our guy!"*

Lieutenant Hamilton instructed the deputy to stall for a few minutes, get the suspect out of the truck, take him into custody. Back-up would soon be there. Lieutenant Hamilton got back on the radio and said,
"All units, please be advised, code 1 at 285 and Mangum

ONE MORE MIRACLE

Manor! Repeat, code 1 at 285 and Mangum Manor."
He then told the deputy in unit 1274, *"I'm on I-75, on the way to the scene."*
Within minutes screeching sounds of sirens echoed in the wind, as caravans of patrol cars converged on the scene. Moments later Lieutenant Hamilton arrived at the location. Nine patrol cars were already there. Lieutenant Hamilton exited his unmarked vehicle. He observed the suspect in the back of unit 1274's patrol car. What captured his attention was that the suspect was wearing a blue **Atlanta Braves** baseball cap. He thought about what Sister Octavia had revealed to him, about the suspect in Mallory's dream. *"Mallory DID say the suspect in her dream was wearing a dark baseball cap!"* He shook his head, *"This is more than remarkable!"*
Melissa was five cars away from the suspect. She was sitting on the front seat, with a female patrol officer.
Lieutenant Hamilton made his way over to her saying, "Are you okay, honey?"
Without making eye contact, she said, with teary eyes, "Yes sir, I'm alright. I just want to see my mom and dad."
"You will see them shortly. We need to take you to the hospital. Your parents will join you there."
The female officer gently caressed Melissa's hand and reassured her she was safe.
Melissa's parents were notified by the police department and were brought to the hospital, where they reunited with their daughter. In the meantime, the suspect was identified as a twenty-seven-year-old Walker Gillette, a yard man. He was charged with kidnapping of a minor. The strange thing about this suspect was he had no prior criminal history, which made Mallory's dream more significant.
At 12:10 p.m. Atlanta's Police Chief L.M. Harvey, surrounded by members of the various Law Enforcement Agencies, held a live news conference. He spoke for more than

fifteen minutes, paying tribute to the FBI, the Georgia State
Police Department, the Atlanta Police Department, and the
Fulton County Sheriff's Department. Chief L.M. Harvey also
gave considerable praise to Lieutenant Hamilton. He told the
Media that if it weren't for Lieutenant Hamilton, Melissa would,
possibly, still be missing.

He was about to leave the stage, when a news reporter
from CNN, inquired of the Chief, "Is it true that you received an
anonymous tip about the suspect caught today?"
Chief L.M. Harvey explained, "I think so, but I'm going to
introduce to you the man who may have the best answer to your
question. At this time, I would like to ask Lieutenant Michael
Drew Hamilton, of the Fulton County Sheriff Department, to
step to the microphone."

When Lieutenant Hamilton stepped up to the podium, he
adjusted the microphone because of his height, Chief Harvey
stood at about 5'8" and the Lieutenant was over six feet tall. He
began by saying, "I'm pleased to report that Melissa Payne was
found safe today. Yes, we DID receive an anonymous tip that led
to the suspect's capture."

One reporter shouted from the back of the room, "Was the
child sexually assaulted?"

Lieutenant paused for a moment and replied, "I don't
know. We do know she was taken to the hospital to be examined
by the doctor. As far as I know, I don't think she has been
released yet." Lieutenant Hamilton continued, "Before we go
any further, I'd like to acknowledge one of the officers, from my
department, unit 1274 Deputy Willie Jones, who stopped the
suspect on 285 this morning. Deputy Jones was traveling behind
the suspect, when he noticed that the suspect's brake lights
weren't working properly, so he pulled him over. He thought it
was a routine stop, but this routine stop turned out to be the catch
of the day."

Reporter Helen Ross of the **Atlanta Journal**

ONE MORE MIRACLE

Constitution raised her hand. Lieutenant Hamilton acknowledged her with a nod of his head. She asked, "Lieutenant, my sources tell me the suspect you arrested today, one Walker Gillette, had no prior criminal history. Can you tell us about the person who gave you the tip? Was it a friend or a relative of the suspect?"

With a serious stare, he said, "I'm not at liberty to say who gave us the information. Let's just say, *we had some help from above.*"

"Are you saying, you received this tip from a Higher Power, maybe an angel?" she asked with a smirk.

He paused, "That's a good analogy, Ms. Ross."
She smiled again, "I didn't think my question was rhetorical. If you want to frame it in that context to protect the source of your information, then I guess you have the right to do so."
"Thanks for your understanding," he nods sarcastically.
On that note, the news conference ended.

An hour later, the Lieutenant went to his office to call Sister Octavia. It appeared she had already heard that Melissa had been found safe. She revealed to the Lieutenant that when she first heard the news, she fell on her knees and thanked GOD. She told him she also thanked GOD for him.
Drew modestly said, "Without Mallory's dream, none of this would have been possible."
Sister Octavia quickly corrected him, "Without GOD, none of this would have been possible."

He concurred, offering no argument. Before ending the phone conversation, he asked Sister Octavia to extend his gratitude to Mallory, adding, "I wish we could thank her publicly. Maybe one day she can be acknowledged, but that's not for me to say."
"Take care, Drew. GOD bless you."
"Thank you, my Aunt. May GOD bless you, too."
They ended the conversation.

At 7:40 the next morning, Teresa was driving into the parking lot at **Pine Crest Catholic School** in her BMW sedan. Teresa and Mallory exited the car and headed down the walkway into the building. Sister Octavia phoned Teresa the previous day, asking her to drop by the school. When they entered the hallway, Sister Octavia was standing in her usual place outside the classroom. She looked at Teresa and Mallory with a bright smile and said, "You are two minutes late, but since you're with your mother, you won't be marked tardy."

Mallory smiled, "Thanks, Sister Octavia."

"Mallory, go on inside the classroom. I need to talk to your mother privately."

Mallory entered the classroom and closed the door behind her. Sister Octavia and Teresa looked at each other with anticipation.

Sister Octavia clasped her hands and spoke first, "Well, it's obvious Mallory told you about the dream."

"Yes, she told me last week."

Teresa took a deep breath and continued, "Deep inside, I don't think it was a fluke that the police found this man. My child played a significant role in this matter, yet it's hard for me to come to grips with this whole ordeal."

"Your daughter told you about the dream she had, and it played out just like a script."

" I'm glad things turned out positive, but the whole situation is still unsettling. Sister Octavia, what is your take on all of this?"

She responded, "Teresa, more often than not our untrained imagination can't always comprehend the HOLY SPIRIT. I know that GOD has blessed some of us with special gifts, and Mallory's dream wasn't a coincidence or happenstance. Teresa, you're a Spiritual woman. If anyone knows about miracles, it's certainly you. Teresa, remember what you told me about your delivery room experience?"

She nodded, "Yes, Sister."

"What happened to you that day when you gave birth to Mallory

198

was indeed a miracle."

"Oh Sister, I know it was a miracle."

"Teresa, sometimes GOD gives some of us special gifts. I believe Mallory has been blessed with a particular gift. Teresa, that's what my heart tells me, but only time will tell."

Teresa stared at her, slowly shaking her head. "Sister, at this point my prayer for her would be that she will have a normal childhood."

Sister Octavia gestured with her hands and said, "Teresa, it's obvious I don't have any children, so I'm going to resist the temptation of telling you what's best for your child. I'll say this: any person who dedicates his or her life to GOD doesn't always have an easy life. Sometimes people will say your way of thinking is not with the mainstream and they will even call you crazy. Teresa, I've lived long enough to know that people, places, and events change, but THE WORD of GOD NEVER CHANGES."

"Amen, Sister."

"At the end of the day, I have no regrets about dedicating my life to THE LORD. Whatever GOD'S plan is for Mallory; I pray that she will embrace it to the fullest."

Teresa locked into her gaze and said with equanimity, "Sister, that's a prayer that I'll pray for all my children."

Sister Octavia responded, "Teresa, I'll make it my lifelong mission to pray for you and your family."

Teresa smiled, thanking her. They ended the conversation with a warm embrace.

Friday night, Allen and Teresa were in downtown Atlanta at **Kris's Oyster Bar**, having dinner with an old friend of Allen's. Tom Sanders and Allen were former Marine buddies. Tom was joined by his wife of ten years, Janet. Allen and Tom had lost contact with each other due to the fact that Tom had spent the last seven years working in Canada as Vice President of a major Canadian oil company.

Last Summer, Tom had been re-assigned back to the United States. During dinner, Tom expressed to Allen his love of Canada, especially its massive wild life and abundance of freshwater lakes. Tom knew that Allen was quite the outdoors man. Back in the day, Allen and Tom had taken several hunting trips together. In fact, Tom and two of his business associates were planning a hunting and fishing excursion to Canada. Tom invited Allen to join them. Allen graciously accepted the invitation. It had been well over three years since Allen, his Dad and brother had gone hunting. Before leaving the restaurant, Allen assured Tom that he would clear his schedule for the last week of September.

CHAPTER 24

Two nights later, without any knowledge of her dad's pending hunting trip, Mallory dreamt that five people were killed in an airplane crash. A few nights later, Mallory had the recurring dream. This time it was most disturbing to Mallory because she'd learn her dad was going on a hunting trip with three other men. In the dream all four of the people were killed, including the pilot. She woke up sweating; she was so upset, she couldn't go back to sleep, so she got up from bed and went to her grandmother's room. Mallory didn't even knock on the door. She just opened it and went in. Ms. Hunter, being a light sleeper, woke up immediately.

The room was dark and Ms. Hunter's eyes were not focused clearly. All she saw was a diminutive shadow. Instinctively she knew it was Mallory.

"Angel, is that you?" She asked softly.

Mallory replied, "Yes, Granny, it's me. I had a nightmare and couldn't go back to sleep. Can I sleep in here with you?"

"Sure you can, baby. Come and get in bed with Granny." She hopped into bed with her grandmother, cuddling with her, then drifted off to sleep.

The next morning Teresa was taking Mallory to her pediatrician for her yearly checkup. Before leaving for the doctor's visit, Teresa made Mallory breakfast. That's when she told her mother she didn't want her daddy to go on the hunting trip. Teresa was unresponsive, as she went to get some cheese from the refrigerator. She placed two slices of cheese on two pieces of bread, then placed them in the toaster oven on the counter top and set the timer. In less than three minutes, the bell sounded.

Teresa removed the grilled cheese sandwich from the oven, placing it on the plate. She gave it to Mallory, then poured a glass of fresh-squeezed orange juice for her.

201

Mallory flashed a bright smile, thanking her mother, "Oh, Mom, thank you so much. You're so good to me. You're the best mommy in the world."

Teresa smiled, "Oh, Angel, you're such a charmer, just like your daddy." Teresa then sat down and watched her daughter eat breakfast.

Shortly after Mallory finished with her breakfast, she told Teresa about her dream. When Mallory disclosed details of the dream, Teresa sat silently for a long moment, before saying, "Angel, are you sure about this dream?"

"Mom, of course I'm sure about what I dreamt."

Teresa then asked, with a concerned look, "Angel, do you feel that daddy would be in some kind of danger if he went on the trip?"

She paused for a brief second, before saying, "I don't know, Mom, but I don't want him to go."

"Angel, in your dream, how many people were on board the airplane?"

Mallory replied, "Four people, Mom."

Chills ran down Teresa's spine, simply because Mallory had no way of knowing how many people were going on that trip. Teresa was now emotionally tormented, thinking about what she and Sister Octavia had discussed about Mallory, the possibility that Mallory may possess a spiritual gift. Teresa was faced with the fact that she'd have to tell Allen about the Melissa Payne incident. She had her own reasons for not wanting to tell Allen that their daughter played a major role in finding Melissa Payne.

Teresa knew that he was the ultimate skeptic. Allen was the kind of man who believed, if he couldn't touch it, see it or feel it, more than likely, he wasn't buying it. However, she knew that telling Allen about the Melissa Payne story would add significance to Mallory's dream.

That's what she was hoping, because two nights later,

202

ONE MORE MIRACLE

Allen and Teresa were lying in bed. Allen was almost asleep, when Teresa nudged him in the back with her elbow, then said to him, "Baby, baby, wake up!"

With a long yawn, Allen whispered, "Yeah, sweetheart, what's up?"

"We need to talk."

"Ok, what about?"

Teresa looked into his eyes. "What if I asked you not to go on this hunting trip?"

Allen took a deep breath. "Sweetheart, why don't you want me to go?"

"Well, I just don't want you to go."

He laughed, "Sweetie, I've already paid for the trip."

Teresa responded, "Well, I'll give you your money back."

He suddenly raised his head and said in a serious tone, "Ok, Teresa, what's the real reason you don't want me to go on this trip?"

Teresa stared into his eyes. "Angel doesn't want you to go on this trip." Teresa paused, then said, "I really don't know how to tell you this but Angel had this recurring dream about a plane crash."

"What does this have to do with me and my trip?"

"Well Allen, you're going on a trip and you're going with three other men."

"And…?"

"You don't get it? Four of y'all are going on a trip!"

"Teresa, we're flying on a commercial plane to Canada; there'll be more than four people on the plane!"

"Yes, but when you get to Canada, you're going to charter a flight!"

He shook his head. "Teresa, I think you're making too much out of this dream! Ok, did Angel actually tell you she dreamed I was in a plane crash?"

203

"No, she didn't."

"Well, sweetheart, what is your concern? Why are you putting so much stock in this dream?"

Teresa sighed, "Well, it's more to this dream than meets the eye." Teresa then told him how Mallory dreamed about Melissa Payne's disappearance.

"Who's Melissa Payne?"

"She is Mallory's school mate who was abducted but was found safe."

"Teresa, what are you saying? What does all this mean?"

"It was Mallory's dream that facilitated the safe return of the child. She gave the description of the suspect as he appeared in her dream."

"Sweetheart, do you really expect me to believe this?"

"Yes, Allen, it's true!"

Allen shook his head in disbelief, as Teresa finished telling him the whole story.

"Teresa, all of this is so hard to believe. As a matter of fact, it's impossible to believe."

Teresa adamantly said, "Allen, whether you believe it or not, Angel's dream played an instrumental role in finding that child."

All of a sudden, Allen got out of bed, went over to a small, room-sized refrigerator next to the closet. He got a can of soda, peeled off the aluminum lid and took a few swallows. He then sat the can on top of the refrigerator, looked at Teresa and said, "Sweetie, don't you think this situation with Angel and this Payne kid is just a coincidence?"

Allen then took his right hand and rubbed the back of his neck. He then paced back and forth for a short minute, mumbling to himself, "No! No! No! This isn't possible!" When he stopped pacing the floor, he suddenly looked at Teresa and asked, "How were the police made aware of Angel's dream? Teresa, please tell me you didn't let the police interview our daughter?"

ONE MORE MIRACLE

With soft eyes, Teresa murmured, "No, baby, I'd never do anything like that without consulting you. Allen let me say this to you. Obviously it was GOD'S will that Melissa Payne be found, and I'm alright with it. Maybe, unlike you, I happen to believe all things are possible with GOD."

With a disappointed look, Allen responded, "Teresa, that's a cheap shot. You act as if you have a monopoly on GOD."

Teresa replied remorsefully, "You're right, baby. That was a cheap shot. I'm sorry. I had no right to question your faith. Baby, please forgive me!"

Allen whispered, "Sweetheart, I forgive you."

He then went and sat on her side of the bed and held her in his arms saying, "Teresa, let's not argue about this."

"Allen, I don't want to argue with you either, but I want you to consider not going on this trip."

"Teresa, that's a promise I'm not going to make! Just because Angel had this dream doesn't mean anything is going to happen."

"Allen, Angel is really tormented because of this dream and she doesn't want you to go on this trip."

"Teresa, I'll talk to Angel and put her mind at ease."

"Thank you, baby, because if there's anybody who can put her mind to rest, it's you."

The next day, Mallory finished doing her homework at the kitchen table and was about to get up when her parents entered the kitchen.

"Are you finished with your homework, already?" Allen asked.

"Yes Sir, I'm finished."

"Can we talk for a few minutes?"

"Yes, daddy."

He sat beside her at the table and Teresa sat across from them. He began by saying, "Your mom told me about your

205

dream. Angel, do you remember when you had that dream?"

"What dream, daddy?"

"When you told me you were falling off a building? You woke up crying, and I came to your room and sat with you until you went back to sleep?"

She nodded her head, "Yes daddy, I remember."

"Well, have you fallen off a building, lately?"

"No daddy, of course not!"

"Do you remember the dream you had where a werewolf was chasing you?"

"Yes daddy."

"You woke up crying again and your mom had to come comfort you. Well, has a werewolf ever chased you?"

She poked out her lips. "Daddy, I was only six years old when I had that dream!"

"Angel, that was only two years ago! Did that dream come true?"

"No Sir, it didn't!"

"Baby, the point I'm trying to make is that nightmares and bad dreams seldom come true. Angel, we can't let dreams and nightmares control our lives. Ninety-nine percent of the time these nightmares are just a figment of our imagination. One thing we can't do is live in fear of the unknown. Angel, what does daddy do for a living?"

"You are a lawyer."

"What did daddy tell you about the law?"

"Daddy, you said that the law isn't based on conjecture or hyperbole, but the facts!"

Allen then gave her a warm hug and said, "Angel, you're smart. You remember everything I told you about the law. Angel, life and law are similar. In life, we have to deal with facts. Something we can touch, something we can see. We don't base our lives on make-believe and dreams, do we?"

Mallory contemplated for a short moment, then replied,

ONE MORE MIRACLE

"No daddy."

Teresa looked on with a superficial grin. She thought to herself, "Angel's father can get her to believe almost anything! The two of them are so much alike. I know if she had to choose between me and her dad, she'd drop me in the grease in a New York minute! When it comes to Mia and Kendria, the jury's still out on them; they love Allen dearly, but my beloved sons, David and Joshua— I know they love me more."

Mallory suddenly looked at him and said, "Daddy, I know we're not supposed to put much stock in bad dreams and nightmares, but how do you explain a positive dream?
Sister Octavia says sometimes dreams are similar to reality. She told me how GOD would speak to prophets in dreams."

Allen looked at her for a long moment, thinking to himself, "This little girl is just like Teresa! Just when you think you've convinced them of something, they'll throw a curve ball at you."

Allen shifted his eyes to Teresa. She was smiling, saying to herself, "That's my baby. You just can't convince her that easily! Now, she's playing his game, cross-examining him."

He answered, "Angel, Sister Octavia is exactly right! Yes, GOD would speak to prophets through dreams. But Angel, do you consider yourself a prophet?"

She responded, "Of course not, daddy! Sister Octavia also said that GOD can use whomever HE chooses to convey HIS message."

Allen looked at her in amazement and said to her, "Angel, to put your fears to rest, what I want you to do is pray to GOD and ask HIM to protect your dad and his friends on this hunting and fishing trip. Will you do that for me?"
"Yes daddy. I have a better idea. What about you, Mommy, and me say that prayer together right now?"
"Angel, I have no objection at all."

Mallory led the prayer. She asked GOD to watch over

her dad and the other men while they were in Canada and to bring them all safely back home. After praying, Mallory's concerns were put to rest.

Sunday morning, Allen was preparing to leave for his trip later on that day. It was 6:43a.m. when Teresa awakened to find her husband missing from the bedroom. She kicked away the comforter that covered the bed and flinched as her feet felt the cold hardwood floor. She then reached for a pair of furry white slippers at the foot of the bed. Slipping the slippers on, she walked over to her closet, and grabbed a matching robe from the rack. She then went downstairs in search of her missing husband.

When she reached the kitchen, she heard the sound of a whistling tea kettle. She walked over to the six-burner, restaurant-style stainless steel stove. She turned off the front burner and suddenly a buzzing sound of the alarm was heard, indicating that someone was coming into the house. It was Allen, walking from the garage. When he saw Teresa, he asked, "Why are you up so early? I'm the one who wakes you and the children up, every morning, remember?"

"I'm going to help you finish packing."

"Oh sweetheart, I'm done already, but that was certainly sweet of you, wanting to help me."

He strolled over to her and held her in a big embrace. Feeling the lingering heat from the extinguished stove, he quickly moved her away, pinning her against the counter top, kissing her softly, while staring at her beautiful face.

She then whispered, "Oh, Allen, I love you so much!"

"Sweetheart, I can never tell you enough times how much I love you. Teresa, you were really passionate last night, I mean extra passionate! What was that all about?"

With a sensuous smile, she said, "What's wrong with a wife being aggressive in bed with her husband?"

He kissed her again, returning her smile. "You have no complaints from me!"

ONE MORE MIRACLE

"The real reason I was extra passionate last night is I know my husband is going to be gone for five days. I wanted to do something so he would think about me."

With a sincere expression, he said tenderly, "Oh, baby, everything you do makes me think about you. The way you roll your hair. The way you drink your coffee. Even the way you eat your eggs. Teresa, the day you were born is the day my destiny began."

"Oh baby, after all these years, you still know how to push my buttons," said Teresa.

Allen whispered in her ear, "Sweetie, do you think we have time for a quick encore of last night?"
With seductive eyes, she replied, "Of course, we do!"

Allen suddenly lifted her off her feet, carrying her back upstairs to their bedroom. When they got to the top of the stairs, they encountered two stumbling blocks, in the form of David and his brother, Joshua. The boys were surprised to see their dad carrying their mom. With a concerned face, Joshua said, "Mom, are you okay?"
She replied, "Yes darling, I'm fine!"
David followed with, "Dad, why are you carrying Mom like that?"

Allen responded in frustration, "What do you mean, why am I carrying my wife like this? I didn't know I needed anyone's permission to pick up my wife! Besides, why are you guys up so early?"

David answered, "We're hungry. We wanted Mom to make us pancakes for breakfast."
Allen's chance for a little romance with his wife was now nullified. He gently lowered Teresa to the floor. She kissed him with a coy smile, saying, "I'm sorry, honey, but I've got to feed my babies."
With a half-smile, Allen said, "Go on and feed your babies!"
Teresa said, "Well, they're your babies too!"

It was now 10:30 a.m. The family was gathered in the family room; however, David and Joshua were not present. Teresa looked at Mia and Kendria and asked, "Where are your brothers?"

Both of them shrugged their shoulders at the same time. Then Mia said, "Mom, I think they're still in their room."

Teresa responded, "They should be down here saying goodbye to their father."

Ms. Hunter exclaimed, "I'll go up and get them!"

Within minutes, Joshua and David came marching down the stairs, like little soldiers, with Ms. Hunter as their drill Sergeant. She admonished them, "Get your lazy behinds down here!"

When they stepped into the room, Teresa looked at them, "Why didn't you come down here to say goodbye to your father?"

David whined, "I was asleep and Josh didn't wake me up. He was watching cartoons."

Teresa, still being perturbed at the boys for being "spoilers," said to David, "That's no excuse! You got up this morning before seven and you didn't need anyone to wake you up then!"

Both boys apologized, "We're sorry, Mom."

Allen glanced at them, agreeing with his wife, "Yeah! You got up early this morning!" He turned to Teresa. "Give them fifty lashes, after I'm gone."

David responded, "Dad, don't you think the punishment is a bit severe?"

Allen nodded, "Yeah, I guess you're right! Just give them twenty lashes."

He soon turned his attention to Ms. Hunter, lounging in a Lazy Boy chair, catching the morning sun. "Come on Mama, where's my hug?" he said, smiling.

She slowly got up and ambled over to Allen. Looking up at him, with her head tilted to the side, she countered, "Well, I

210

was just waiting my turn." They engaged in a warm embrace.

After the hug, Ms. Hunter then said, "You're such a popular man in here!"

Allen smiled, "Well, Mama, that may be true with the ladies in here."

He promptly made eye contact with Joshua and David. Joshua smiled, "Come on Dad, you know you're the man!"

Allen seriously looked at his sons and said, "Okay, guys, I'm going to be gone for five days. I expect you to be on your best behavior. Remember, Mom's in charge." Laughing, he said, "Wait a minute, what am I saying? Mom is in charge even when I'm here!"
Teresa looked on, nodding her head. Allen grabbed Teresa's hand and the two of them proceeded to walk out of the door.

All five children chanted, "Bye-bye, Dad!"

Allen waved good-bye; then he and Teresa closed the door behind them. Mallory quickly ran behind them, opening the door, going outside to get a final hug from her father. Allen gave her a kiss on her forehead.

Mallory stood at the door, watching her parents proceed to the car. When they reached the car, Teresa and Allen gave each other a final embrace. Allen got into his white Mercedes Sedan and backed out of the driveway, heading to the airport to meet with his friends. Teresa walked back into the house and grabbed Mallory's hand; they entered the house together.

The next morning, Allen called Teresa from the hunting site in Canada. He told her they had a smooth flight and we're looking forward to some good hunting and fishing. He assured her that he would call her every morning to see how she and the children were doing.

CHAPTER 25

It was day three since Allen had been gone from home. Teresa was just returning home from taking Mallory to school and dropping her mother at the Grady Homes' Day Care Center, where she volunteered as a foster grandmother three days a week. Teresa had a slight headache, so she headed upstairs to the medicine cabinet in the bathroom.

Excedrin was the medicine that worked best whenever Teresa had a headache. She shook two pills out of the bottle into her hand. She then opened the cupboard door, pulled out a paper cup, turned on the faucet and filled the cup with water. After swallowing both pills, she went back into the bedroom, decided to inform her secretary, JoAnne, that she would be running late. After the phone call, she took off her clothes and got back into bed.

Teresa closed her eyes and waited for the medication to take effect. She had been sleeping for at least forty minutes when the ringing telephone prompted her to wake up. The telephone was lying on the bed within arm's reach. When she answered, it was her mother on the line, stating that she had left her purse in her car. Teresa promised her that she would take her purse out of the car and bring it into the house.

Immediately after hanging up, Teresa got out of bed. She noticed that the pain from the headache had subsided. Teresa was about to open the door to her walk-in closet when, without any warning, a loud clap of thunder rang out. She rushed to her bedroom window and opened the closed blinds. The sky was dark as the night. The gusting winds began to rattle the window pane. Sheets of rain started to fall; she quickly closed the blinds.

All of a sudden the mansion took on an eerie atmosphere. This was the first time Teresa had ever been alone in the house. Usually the house was filled with sounds of laughter, and at other times, the sound of children arguing.

ONE MORE MIRACLE

Teresa began to be somewhat concerned about Allen. "I am really surprised that Allen has not tried to get in contact with me, today." The sound of her voice startled her, for she was not aware that she was speaking out loud. She quickly dismisses her mounting concerns that something could possibly be wrong with Allen.

She slowly lay back on the bed, crossed her legs, grabbed the remote control, turned the television on and began to channel surf, stopping on the Weather Channel. The weather lady reported that the Atlanta metropolitan area was experiencing a severe thunderstorm. After hearing the report, Teresa made the decision not to report to work after all.

She picked up the telephone, dialed the phone again, and waited for the secretary to answer. When JoAnne answered, Teresa informed her of her plans not to report to work due to the storm. Before Teresa concluded the call, she paused for a moment before asking if Allen had called. JoAnne told her that she had not heard from him. Teresa thanked her, said good-bye, and hung up the telephone.

The sound of rain drops tapping against the window relaxed her. She felt herself drifting back to sleep, when out of the corner of her eye she noticed the *"News Bulletin"* sign flash across the screen and the newscaster's voice announced, *"This just in! There has been a plane crash in Northern Canada."*

Teresa immediately sat up as her eyes focused directly on the television screen. The newscaster continued,

"This just in: a private plane crashed around 6:30 a.m.! Onboard the plane were four businessmen from Georgia and a pilot. Canadian authorities have reported that there were no known survivors. The plane was chartered through Blue Bird Aircraft. We'll have updates when more information is available.

Again, we repeat for those of you who are just joining us, there's been a deadly plane crash in Northern Canada. Flight

213

*2465 crashed this morning. Four businessmen from Georgia,
and the pilot were killed.*"

Teresa's thoughts were frozen and unable to connect
clearly with her brain. She knew that Allen and his friends had
chartered a **Blue Bird Aircraft** because she had read Allen's
itinerary. She recognized the flight number, but hearing that
there were no known survivors of the plane crash caused her
heart to sink.

Teresa literally could not move her legs, paralyzed with
grief. She lay there attempting to scream, but she could only
murmur, "Oh, my GOD…Oh, my GOD…please help me," she
continued to murmur, "I need to get up. I need to get out of this
house!"

Time seemed to have stood still. After a few minutes,
Teresa managed to move her body to the edge of the bed. She
fell and laid on the cold hardwood floor in the fetal position for
what seemed to be an eternity. Her thoughts began to weigh
heavily on her heart. She ultimately mustered enough strength to
stand.

Teresa finally began to scream hysterically, "Oh my
goodness! I need to have my babies here with me! Mia! Mia!
Oh, Kendria! Kendria!"

The grief was compounded by the fact that her children
were now fatherless as she cried, "My babies have no father!
He's gone!"

She managed to maneuver over to the dresser, holding
on to it trying to collect her faculties, but her mind began to run
rampant. She thought, '*Why has this happened to me? Why did
GOD take Allen?*'

Her thoughts were also on her first husband, Carl Ray.
She said, "What have I done to deserve this?"
She aimlessly wandered out of the bedroom, and down the stairs.

When she finally reached the bottom of the stairs, the
lights flickered on and off. It was obvious that Teresa was

214

mentally discombobulated, because she suddenly made a right turn into the kitchen. She stumbled to the back door, opened it, and walked outside. It was as if she were in a trance. Teresa never stopped to close the door. She proceeded past the covered patio into the backyard. The force from the driving rain hit her squarely in the face. She trudged on about twenty yards passed the pool, where she sat down on the wet ground, resting her back up against the cedar fence.

Soaked all over, she began to rock back and forth, thinking to herself, *'Why has this happened to me?! This is the second husband I've lost. I'm not going to make it. I want to die! I really want to die!'*

Then the voice of reason chimed in, 'You *can't die. You have five reasons to live.'*

"Yes I have to go on. What would my children do without me? Oh GOD, I need you!"

The house was completely without power she realized as she continued to rock back and forth, but in her present state of mind that was the least of her concerns.

Half an hour later, Mia arrived home from the University. She turned into the driveway and carefully parked her car on the side of Teresa's car.

'Mom must have stayed home from work,' her inner voice said. Mia sat in the car for a few moments, then opened the car door and made a mad dash toward the house to avoid the heavy rain.

Once inside the house, Mia attempted to turn on the light in the foyer. To her surprise it didn't come on. She assumed that the light bulb had blown out. She then went to the bathroom next to the kitchen and attempted to turn the lights on there, but encountered the same results. That's when she figured out that the power had been knocked out because of the storm. She walked on into the living room, calling out to Teresa, "Mom, mom, I'm home!"

215

She continued to call out, "Mom, I'm home!"
She then thought, *'Mom must be asleep.'*
She walked on into the kitchen. When she saw the door open and the floor wet from the rain coming in, she ran to close the door. That's when she saw Teresa sitting against the fence in the rain. Mia sensed something was dreadfully wrong.

She screamed, "Mom, what are you doing?! Why are you sitting out there in the rain?!"

Mia quickly ran to Teresa, panting, "Mom, why are you out here on the ground? Please get up!"
Teresa looked up at Mia, murmuring, "Mia, daddy was killed in a plane crash this morning."

Mia stood for a moment, trying to grasp what her mother had just told her before repeating, "Daddy was killed?"

She then screamed, "NO, MOM! IT'S NOT TRUE! IT CAN'T BE TRUE!"

Teresa looked up at her and nodded, "Yes it's true, Mia! It's true!"

Mia suddenly collapsed onto the ground next to her mother, sobbing uncontrollably. Teresa slowly moved towards her, trying to comfort her. Mia and Teresa continued to sit on the wet ground in a tight embrace, consoling each other.

A few minutes later, Kendria arrived home. It was obvious to her that Mia and Teresa were home because both of their cars were parked in the driveway. The electricity had finally come back on. Kendria sat in the car for a few minutes. She suddenly began rummaging through the back seat in search of an umbrella that she didn't find. She decided to brave the rain. She opened the car door and ran into the house.

Once inside the house, she observed that all the lights were on. She went straight to the kitchen (the family's favorite hangout in the house), expecting to find her mother and sister. She didn't see them, so she began to call out, "Mom! Mia! Where are you guys?"

ONE MORE MIRACLE

Thinking that her mother and sister were probably upstairs, Kendria advanced further into the kitchen. That's when she suddenly observed the door open and the water-soaked floor. Water was pouring into the house like someone had opened up the flood gates. Kendria ran towards the door to close it. There, she witnessed her mother and her sister sitting on the ground in the blistering rain. Her instincts told her something was definitely wrong. She rushed out of the house, screaming, "MOM, MIA, WHAT'S WRONG? WHAT ARE YOU DOING OUT HERE? MOM, WHAT'S THE MATTER? WHY ARE YOU AND MIA OUT HERE IN THE RAIN?"

Mia cried out, "KENDRIA, DADDY IS DEAD! DADDY'S DEAD!"

Kendria shouted, "WHAT ARE YOU TALKING ABOUT? DADDY IS NOT DEAD!"

Mia screamed, "YES, KENDRIA, IT'S TRUE. DADDY IS DEAD! HE WAS KILLED IN A PLANE CRASH!"

With a grim expression, Kendria looked at Teresa and said, "MOM, WHAT IS SHE TALKING ABOUT?"

Teresa could hardly talk. She was taking shallow breaths as she finally muttered, "Yes Kendria, its true! Your dad is dead. He was killed in a plane crash this morning."

Kendria began to back away screaming, "No! No! I don't believe it! It's not true!"

She walked over to the cedar fence and began to pound it with her fists screaming and hollering, "No it's not true! It can't be true! Oh GOD! Why did this have to happen?"

Suddenly, she realized that her dad would never walk her down the aisle and give her away to be married. Allen wasn't her biological father, but he was the only father she and Mia had ever known. Without a doubt, Kendria believed this was the worst day of her life. She suddenly fell to her knees and started to sob. The sobbing became so intense that her body began to

217

convulse.

Teresa immediately snapped out of her haze of despair when she saw what was happening with Kendria. She literally crawled to her daughter, lifting Kendria's head off the wet grass and placed her head on her lap, trying to console her.

Teresa whispered, "It's going to be okay. It's alright, baby; it's going to be okay. We will get through this together."

Kendria looked at her mother with sad eyes. Without mouthing a word, just shaking her head, she uttered, "No....no it's not...it'll never be alright again."

Mia soon joined her mother and sister, saying to Teresa, "Come on Mom, let's go in the house. We can't stay out here any longer."

Kendria lifted herself from the ground first. She and Mia reached down and grabbed Teresa, who held onto both daughters' hands and rose to her feet. The three of them locked arms with Teresa in the middle. They sorrowfully walked back into the house as the rain continued to pound them in the face.

Later on that evening, the house was filled with family and friends. Allen's father, Rob, had arrived and was pretty much in control of everything. While displaying a calm demeanor, internally his heart was shattered like broken glass. Losing his son made him feel as if a part of him had died.

Allen's mother, Deni, was attending a medical conference in Switzerland. There was no way Rob was going to call her and convey such catastrophic news over the phone. She would be returning home on Saturday morning, and Rob felt it was best for him to tell her then.

In the meantime, Rob had been on the phone practically all evening with the Canadian authorities. He was trying to find out if any parts of the wreckage had been recovered yet. He was told by Canadian officials that the area was very remote and mountainous. The plane had hit a mountain and upon impact, had burst into flames. He was also informed that the wrecked plane was spotted earlier by a search helicopter, but due to inclement weather, the search had to be called off. The man assured Rob that the search would resume in the morning, weather-permitting. Further search was made difficult because of the heavy snowfall. Before hanging up the phone, Rob informed the gentleman he was trying to get a flight to Canada as soon as possible.

CHAPTER 26

Teresa's three youngest children were upstairs in her bedroom with their grandmother. Kendria and Mia were gathered in the large family room with their mother and a host of friends and employees of **Twin Enterprises**, the family company. Ms. Hunter was quite concerned about Mallory. Since being brought home by Teresa's close friend, Bernice, Mallory hadn't uttered a word to anybody. She seemed to be in shock. Ms. Hunter sent David downstairs to get his mother. Teresa rushed upstairs to her bedroom, where she found Mallory staring out of her bedroom window. When Teresa approached Mallory, she had a blank stare on her face. Teresa gently pulled her away from the window.

"Mallory, you have to talk to mommy because if you don't, I'll have to take you to the hospital. It's okay to cry. I've been crying; so have your sisters and brothers. Even Granny has been crying, Angel. Things are going to get better. As a family, we're going to get through this, trust me. We'll never forget daddy. When I look into your eyes, I see daddy. When Joshua eats his cereal, he chews his food slowly just like daddy. When David walks, he walks just like daddy. So we'll always have all these great memories of daddy. Your grandfather and your daddy sound just alike. It's almost like the same person talking. Your daddy has left me three wonderful gifts, you and your two brothers. So I'll always have a part of him because of the three of you. One day, when we get to heaven we'll see daddy again."

Mallory suddenly burst into tears, and she said, "I don't want to see my daddy in heaven. I want to see my daddy here! Right now!"

Teresa embraced her, holding her close to her chest, saying softly as tears ran down her eyes, "Angel, it's okay to cry. Your daddy was worth crying for. It's okay Angel."

She continued to cry, as her body began to tremble forcefully.

ONE MORE MIRACLE

Teresa continued to hold Mallory tightly, softly stroking her long curly locks.

Rob suddenly entered the room. He took a deep breath, informing Teresa that he had just notified Paul and Katie of their brother's death. Naturally, both were devastated and were making plans to fly into Atlanta first thing in the morning. Rob then told Teresa of his impending plans to fly to Canada. He was waiting on more information from Canadian authorities concerning retrieving the bodies from the wreckage.

Two hours later, it was almost dark when Allen's law partner and good friend Jonathan Christopher and his girlfriend, Zena Gordon, arrived at the house. Jonathan and Zena had been on vacation in the Bahamas when they learned of Allen's death. He immediately returned to Atlanta. Once inside the house, Teresa greeted Jonathan with a warm hug. Jonathan then introduced his girlfriend, Zena Gordon, to her. Teresa gave her a tender hug and said, "Nice to meet you, Zena."

"Nice to meet you, too, but sorry for meeting under these circumstances. You have my deepest sympathy."

Clutching Teresa's hand, Jonathan interjected, "Teresa, no words can express how I'm feeling right now. Allen was more than my boss and my friend; he was like a brother to me. He loved you and these children more than life itself."

Teresa smiled softly, "If there's anything in life that I'm sure of, it's Allen's love for me and the children. I know that for sure!"

Jonathan said to Teresa, "I'm a nervous wreck! I really need a drink!"

Teresa said, "Well, Jonathan, you know where the bar is in the den."

Jonathan excused himself. He went to fix himself a drink. When Jonathan left the room, the conversation took on a different twist. Zena suddenly put on her reporter's hat, acting like she was sitting at her anchor's chair with an earpiece on, waiting on the nearest director to cue her on when to start.

Zena inched closer to Teresa asking, "How long were you and Allen married?"

"We were married twelve years."

"Was there any added pressure on you being an interracial couple?"

"We really didn't see ourselves as an interracial couple, just two people in love."

"That's a good answer."

Teresa then added, "Well, it's the truth!"

Zena inquired, "What kind of a husband was Allen?"

"He was the best! He was my best friend, a great father and an all-around great guy."

Jonathan reemerged with a glass of **Chivas Regal** on the rocks. Zena didn't even acknowledge his presence as she continued to bombard Teresa with a plethora of questions. Jonathan became annoyed by Zena's behavior. He thought to himself, *'This heartless bitch must be out of her mind!'*

She went on to ask Teresa, "Now that your husband is gone, will you serve as the new CEO?"

Teresa blinked and said, "Zena, I'm definitely not in the mood for an interview right now. Maybe in a few weeks you can contact my secretary and I'll sit down with you and we can have a talk."

She laughed nervously with an embarrassed expression on her face.

"I sincerely hope you don't think our conversation was an interview because it wasn't my intention to interview you. If I came across that way, I am truly sorry."

Before Teresa could respond, Mia called out to her from the top of stairway, informing her that her brother Patrick was on the line. Teresa then excused herself and went up the stairs to her bedroom to answer the call.

Jonathan suddenly grabbed Zena by the hand and whisked

her into the foyer.

With a contentious stare, he blurted out, "What's your problem? That poor woman has just lost her husband and you're trying to get an exclusive for your TV station!"

"No I'm not, Jonathan. Maybe I did come on a bit too strong, but I guess that's just the journalist in me."

"Well, where is the compassion in you? Or do you have any?"

They stared at each other for a short second. She appeared to be contrite as her voice dropped, "I am so sorry. Maybe I did come across as being insensitive. Maybe I need to go and apologize again to Teresa."

Jonathan shook his head, "No, just leave well enough alone for now. I'm going upstairs to say goodbye to Teresa. Wait down here for me."

It was now 1:15 a.m., and all of the guests were finally gone and house was relatively quiet. Teresa, Kendria, and Mia were in the family room. Sitting on the couch, Mia was drifting in and out of sleep. For the fourth time, Teresa suggested that Mia go on upstairs to her room and go to bed. With sleepy eyes, Mia shook her head, saying, "No, Mom, I'm not sleepy."

Kendria glanced at Teresa and said, "Mom, I'm sleepy. Come on, Mom, let's go upstairs and go to bed. Mia and I are sleeping in your room."

The three of them slowly walked up the stairs. When they reached the top floor, Mia and Kendria went into their mother's room, while Teresa went to David and Joshua's room and opened the door. She looked in on them for a brief moment. They appeared to be in a deep sleep. Teresa quietly closed the door. Teresa then went to her mother's room and carefully cracked the door open. Mallory was nestled in her grandmother's arms, sleeping soundly. Ms. Hunter was wide awake.

She looked in Teresa's direction and then whispered, "Angel has been asleep for a while now."

Teresa responded softly, "Okay, that's good Mama. Hopefully

223

she can rest all night. I'm going to bed now."

"Teresa, why don't you just lie in here with us?"

"No Mama, I'm going to my room. Mia and Kendria are already there. They're going to sleep with me tonight."

Ms. Hunter nodded, "Alright."

"I love you, Mama."

"I love you too, Baby."

Teresa carefully closed the door.

It was 2:30 a.m. and Teresa was lying in bed, sandwiched between her two daughters. Her mental state is precarious at best. Her heart was definitely broken. Her eyelids were heavy, but her subconscious wouldn't allow her to fall asleep. A sudden thought occurred: *'Did I activate the downstairs burglar alarm?'*

Thirty minutes later, Teresa was still restless. *'I need something to help me sleep,'* Teresa thought out loud, *'Oh yeah, I have some Benadryl in the medicine cabinet.'*

She slowly uncovered herself and carefully crawled over Mia, so as not to disturb her. When her feet hit the floor, Kendria's eyes suddenly popped open.

"Mom where are you going?" she whispered.

"I'm going to the medicine cabinet, Pumpkin Pie. I need some **Benadryl** to help me sleep."

Kendria laid her head back down on the pillow as she smiled and thought to herself, *'Mom hasn't called me Pumpkin Pie since I was a little girl.'*

After taking two Benadryl capsules, Teresa walked back into her bedroom. It was obvious that she had activated the upstairs burglar alarm, but she wasn't quite certain about the downstairs one. So she walked over to the key pad and deactivated the upstairs burglar alarm, so she could go downstairs to check.

When Teresa got halfway down the stairs, she clearly heard a noise coming from outside the front door. It was like someone was trying to pick the lock. Teresa stopped dead in her tracks. The noise became louder, so she called out, "Kendria, please come quick," as she hastily backpedaled up the stairs.

Both Mia and Kendria raced out of the bedroom and met their mother at the top of the staircase. As the noise got louder, all three of them retreated back into the bedroom. Teresa then said, "Kendria, dial 911."

Kendria followed her mother's instruction.
Mia attempted to follow her mother out of the bedroom.
"Mia, stay in the bedroom with your sister!"
"No, no Mommy. I'm going with you."
Teresa screamed in a panic, "MIA, DO AS I SAY, NOW!"

Mia reluctantly stayed in the bedroom. Teresa's inner voice said, *'What else could go wrong? My husband was killed today and now someone is trying to break into my house!'*

Teresa then remembered that Allen had a nine-millimeter handgun in his closet. She quickly ran back to the bedroom, opened the closet and retrieved the gun from the top shelf while Kendria pleaded with the 911 operator to send help immediately. Mia's eyes widened in shock as she saw the gun in her mother's hand. Teresa raced back to the top of the staircase, with Mia following her this time. Kendria soon joined them.

Ms. Hunter suddenly opened her bedroom door, shouting, "TERESA, WHAT'S GOING ON OUT THERE?!"

"Somebody's trying to get into the house! The police are on the way! Go back in your room and lock the door!"

When Ms. Hunter saw the gun in Teresa's hand, she asked nervously, "Where did you get that gun?"

"Mama, please go back in your room and close the door! Please! LOCK IT!!"

Ms. Hunter stood there frozen in shock; then she quickly closed the door to the bedroom and locked it.   Teresa then said, "Kendria, go to David and Joshua's room and stay in there with them! Lock the door! Mia, what did I tell you to do?! Go back to my bedroom NOW!"

Mia cleverly disobeyed her mother by stepping behind a wall, out of view. The jimmying sound at the door suddenly stopped but Teresa stood vigilant at the top of the staircase aiming at the front door with her hands squarely on the trigger. All of a sudden the lock turned and the door slowly swung open. A figure stepped inside of the house.

Teresa shouted, "STOP! I SWEAR I'LL SHOOT! I HAVE A GUN!"

When the light in the foyer suddenly popped on, Teresa relaxed. The gun slowly slipped out of her hand, falling onto the thick carpet, her legs wobbling like jelly. She could barely move them.

She stood holding onto the railing of the staircase, murmuring, "JESUS! JESUS! JESUS!"

Mia quickly stepped from behind the wall. She looked down into the foyer and screamed at the top of her lungs, "DADDY! DADDY! DADDY! DADDY! OH MY GOD! OH MY GOD!"

It was indeed Allen who had stepped into the house. Teresa, still gripping the rail, collected herself. She promptly ran down the stairs, running and stumbling to Allen's outstretched arms.

Mia continued to scream, "DADDY! DADDY! DADDY! YOU'RE NOT DEAD!"

Teresa looked into Allen's eyes and said, "Please tell me this is not a dream! Please tell me that you're here?"
He smiled, "I'm here baby. It's really me. What's going on?"

Mia responded with excitement, "MOMMY, IT'S DADDY! IT'S REALLY DADDY! IT'S NOT A DREAM, BECAUSE WE CAN'T ALL BE HAVING THE SAME DREAM!"

When Kendria heard all the commotion, she rushed out of David and Joshua's room. When she arrived at the top of the stairs, and she glanced down at the foyer. She couldn't believe

226

her eyes.

She began to yell, "OH MY GOD! OH MY GOD! THANK YOU! THANK YOU!"

A stream of tears rolled down her face. She immediately headed down the stairs to join her mother and sister in the celebration.

Ms. Hunter swiftly opened her door after hearing Kendria's piercing scream in the foyer. She was screaming so loud Ms. Hunter thought she was outside her door. When she opened the door, Kendria was nowhere in sight. Joshua and David, awakened by all the noise, soon streaked past her.

When they reached the ground floor and saw their daddy, both boys burst into laughter, saying excitedly, "DADDY! DADDY! WE'RE SO GLAD YOU'RE ALIVE! WHERE WERE YOU? PLEASE TELL US WHAT HAPPENED!"

Ms. Hunter quickly walked back to her room and awakened Mallory, shaking her vigorously, "Angel! Angel! Get up now!"

"Why Granny? Is it morning yet?"

"Just get up, Angel! Get up right now and go downstairs! Please hurry up!"

Mallory jumped out of bed and flew downstairs. When she saw her dad spread out on the floor with all her siblings and her mother surrounding him, tears flowed from her eyes as she joined the pile. Allen suddenly sat up saying, "Let me hug my baby!"

Mallory was squeezing his neck for dear life! She wasn't going to let go!

"Daddy, I'm so glad that you came back home! We thought you were dead! Somebody told a lie! We thought you were dead!"

"Angel, let his neck go! You're going to choke the man to death!" Joshua yelled.

"Shut up, Joshua!"

227

Teresa looked on smiling. She thought to herself,
*'Normalcy has now been restored in my family! Oh, JESUS, I
will never ever doubt you again!'*
Teresa glanced up at her mother, sitting on the top of the
staircase. "Mama, come on down here!"
"In a minute. Just let me sit here for a while. I need a
minute so I can exhale."\

Ms. Hunter continued to sit at the top of the stairway,
ruminating:

> ***"FATHER, I prayed for strength. I prayed that you would
> restore happiness to this house of grief, but I had no idea you'd
> do it today! All I can say is THANK YOU.
> I GIVE YOU ALL THE PRAISE!"***

Ms. Hunter sat shaking her head, glancing down at her
family sitting on the floor hugging Allen.

She thought, *'If there ever was a Kodak moment, this is
truly it! When this bedlam is over, I'm going to make these
people a huge breakfast.'*

The celebration was soon interrupted by flashing lights
from three police cruisers arriving at 1928 Sarah Lou Lane.
When the police rang the doorbell, Teresa told the children to
help Allen to his feet and let him answer the door. One of the
officers informed Allen that they had received a call about a
possible break-in at that address.

Allen explained the reason for the misunderstanding,
saying to the officer, "I just returned from a hunting trip and
wasn't expected home tonight. When I arrived home, the porch
light was out, and I was having trouble locating the right key in
the dark. I have six keys on my key ring, so I had to try every
key until I found the right one."

He went on to tell the police officers, "Evidently, my
wife heard me at the door and thought I was an intruder. To
complicate matters, because of misinformation reported on the
news that my hunting party and I had been killed in a plane

crash, my family wasn't expecting me to come back home *ever*!"

One of the officers said, "I can only imagine the hell that your family went through."

Allen sighed, "It certainly wasn't a good time for them."

"Okay Sir, just to confirm your story, would it be okay for us to come in and talk to the other family members," the taller of the two officers asked.

"Sure, come in!" Allen assented, nodding his head.

"By the way, I think it prudent for you to know that I am an attorney."

When the police officers entered the house, they talked with the three youngest children first. They were satisfied with their answers. They then asked Mia and Kendria a couple of questions. Everybody seemed to corroborate Allen's story, so the police officers quickly left.

A few minutes later, the entire family was seated at the kitchen table. Allen explained to his family why he and his group weren't on the plane.

He took a deep and said, "On the night before the flight, I came down with a stomach virus. A health care worker at the lodge provided me with medication. Basically, I didn't know one of the side effects of the medication was drowsiness and dizziness. I ended up oversleeping the next morning. We were supposed to leave at 8 a.m., but I didn't wake up until 8:45. It was my job to notify the guys that morning, so I phoned their rooms. I still felt a little lightheaded and barely managed to get dressed. It took about fifteen minutes for us to get to the landing strip. There were four other men there from Augusta."

"Wow, the news media could have saved me a lot of heartache if they only would've reported the four people onboard were from Augusta!" Teresa interrupted with her hand over her heart.

"Like I was saying, because our group was thirty minutes late, the pilot decided to take the Augusta group to the

229

hunting site first. Evidently, the paperwork wasn't updated, because when the plane crashed, Canadian officials assumed we were on board that ill-fated flight," Allen lamented, shaking his head sadly, "minutes after the plane took off, the weather bureau issued a weather alert. A massive snowstorm was heading toward the camp site. Everybody at the camp was evacuated to Quebec. From there, we caught a flight heading home."

Teresa looked at Allen and said gently "Baby, you need to call your father, your brother, and your sister right away! I know they're going through such agony thinking about you."

David walked over to the kitchen countertop, removed the receiver from the cordless phone, and handed it to his father. He dialed his parents' phone number; his dad picked up on the fourth ring. Rob knew the call came from his son's home because of caller ID.

He answered by saying, "Teresa, is that you?"

Allen replied "It's me, dad!"

Rob was stunned in disbelief as he choked up. After a long pause, he spoke in a trembling voice, "Bug? Son, is that really you?!"

"Yes dad, it's me!"

"Son, what happened?"

"Dad, I overslept. But that's why I'm alive."

"Good grief, son! *What are you talking about*?"

"Dad, it's a long story, but I'll explain the whole thing tomorrow. How's mom holding up?"

"Son, your mom is fine…because we didn't call her. We thought it would be best to tell her the news when she got home. But there's no need to; now that you're home safe!"

"Thank God you didn't tell her, dad. It was bad enough you guys had to go through this."

"Well, I'm glad that you overslept, son. I'm ecstatic! I'm overjoyed! It's so good to hear your voice. I've got to call Paul and Katie and tell them the good news! Bug, why don't you call them?"

"I will dad, as soon as I get off the phone with you, I'll call."

"Okay son, enjoy the time with your family. I love you…I'm so glad we still have you, Bug!"

"I love you too, dad! Talk to you later."

"Okay son, bye."

After hanging up with his father, he called his brother, Paul, first.

When Paul answered the phone, Allen said, "Paul, it's me!"

He replied, "Dad, is that you?"

Apparently, Paul was half asleep, thinking it was his father on the line.

So Allen said, "Paul, it's me, Bug!"

Paul couldn't believe his ears. He held the phone for a long moment, laughing nervously, "Bug, is that *really* you?"

"Yes! Yes, little brother, it's me!"

Paul held the phone to his ear, his voice cracking as he said, "Bug, you're not dead!"

"No, little brother, I'm not. I'm alive!"

"What in the hell happened, man?"

"Like I told dad, it's a long story, but I'll definitely fill you in on it later on today. All I can say is this: there was a lot of misinformation floating around."

"I couldn't care less what happened! I'm just happy to be talking to my big brother. That's all that matters to me."

"Hey Paul, later on today I'm going to do a conference call to all the family members and friends explaining to everybody what really happened. Stay on the line, I'm dialing Katie's number now."

When the phone rang, Katie's husband, Steve, picked up the receiver.

When he heard Allen's voice, he yelled in disbelief,

231

"Bug! Bug! Is it really you," startling Katie out of her restless sleep, "how did that rumor get out that you were dead?"

"Everybody will be filled in on all the details later on, Steve. Right now, I'm mentally exhausted. Please let me talk to my little sister."

Steve handed the phone to his ecstatic wife.

"Bug, I'm so grateful God spared your life!"

"So am I, little sister. I'm so sorry you had to go through this temporary grief."

After hearing his voice, Katie broke into tears. It was hard for her to contain her emotions.

Paul chimed in, "Hey after all this excitement, I need some sleep. I'll talk to you both later on today. I Love you." They echoed, "We love you too!"

After Paul hung up, Katie talked briefly to Allen, tears flowing once more. When she finally composed herself, she said to Allen, "Bug, this whole day has been disconcerting. My head is still spinning, but my Soul is at peace. My heart has been healed now that I have my big brother back!"

Allen hesitated with emotion, "Thanks little sister, that is so touching to say. It warms my heart."

"Bug, I'm going to hang up now. I know that if I keep talking, I'm going to start bawling all over again. Give my love to Teresa and the kids."

"Hey, I'm going to switch you on speaker and you can do it yourself."

"Okay."

Allen switched the phone to speaker. Katie then said, "Teresa, kids, and Granny Hunter, I love all of you!" They all replied, "We love you too Katie!" Katie ended the conversation saying that she loved Allen. He repeated the same words to her.

An hour later, daylight slowly replaced the darkness. Ms. Hunter made breakfast for the family. The smell of ham, hash browns, scrambled eggs, and homemade biscuits permeated the spacious kitchen. When breakfast was ready, Ms. Hunter summoned everyone to the large table in the dining room.

She said *Grace* over the food. She then thanked GOD for Allen's safe return, and said a special prayer for the families of the men lost in the plane crash. When breakfast was over, Teresa announced to the three youngest children they didn't have to go to school this morning. Joshua and David cheered with joy at her announcement, but Mallory had mixed feelings. She didn't like missing school for any reason. Obviously, she was mentally and physically tired. Teresa insisted that she stay home.

Mia and Kendria had afternoon classes, so they had the luxury of sleeping in.
Mallory suggested to her mother and father that she and her siblings go up to their parent's room, and all get in the bed together like the good old days. Ms. Hunter advised against that idea. She told Mallory that her parents needed some privacy. Allen gave his approval with a wink and a smile. Allen and Teresa left the table first.

The children proceeded to leave the dining room, when their grandmother suddenly said, "Hey nobody's going to their room until the kitchen is clean and the dishes are washed and dried."

An hour later, Allen and Teresa were lying in bed, relishing the afterglow of lovemaking. As they snuggled in each other's arms, Teresa gazed at him with tired eyes and whispered, "Allen, just hold me. Please hold me and never let me go."

He said softly, "Baby, I'll never let you go as long as we both live."

He was gearing up for a long conversation with his wife, but Teresa wasn't having any of it. She looked at him and said, "I'm going to sleep now; when I wake up, we can talk about whatever you want to talk about."

A month later, Mallory was still having problems

sleeping. She was afraid that if she dreamt something tragic, then it would come to pass. Mallory had begun sleeping in her grandmother's room. Allen and Teresa were very concerned about her behavior. Allen was pushing for professional counseling. Teresa was conflicted by the idea. The thought kept popping in her head what Sister Octavia had told her about the possibility of Mallory's special gifts from GOD.

Allen, who was not on the same level Spiritually as his wife, wasn't buying that theory. He demanded that Teresa seek professional help for Mallory. She relented. With the help of Deni, Teresa and Allen were introduced to one of Atlanta's leading child psychiatrists, Dr. Julia Shekita Jackson.

Upon meeting Mallory, Dr. Jackson found her to be very precocious and quite pragmatic for an eight-year-old. After three therapy sessions, Dr. Jackson decided to place Mallory on medication to help her sleep. The medication seemed to work well, but Teresa wasn't pleased with the side effects. Some mornings, Mallory would move around like a zombie.

After talking to Dr. Jackson about Mallory's reaction to the medication, Dr. Jackson told Teresa that it was necessary for Mallory to continue taking medication and that in time, Mallory's body would adjust to it. Teresa didn't agree with Dr. Jackson's assessment. She decided to take Mallory off the medication. However, she allowed the therapy sessions to continue. After four months of therapy, the old Mallory seemed to come back.

CHAPTER 27

Eleven years later, Kendria was married and was the mother of two sons. She was an Assistant District Attorney in Washington, D.C. Her husband was a junior partner in a local law firm. Mia was living in Baltimore, fulfilling her dream of becoming a Pediatrician. She worked at Johns-Hopkins Hospital and was married to a Pharmacist. David and Joshua had also finished college. Joshua was in Los Angeles, pursuing a Master's degree in Mechanical Engineering. David was a Captain in the Marine Corp, stationed in South Carolina.

It was Friday morning, the beginning of a picturesque day in Atlanta. The leaves on the ground were turning yellowish-brown, a true indicator that winter was right around the corner. Mallory, who was now a Junior at Georgia Tech, had just arrived at the University. She was thirty minutes early for her calculus class. This was normal for Mallory. She usually arrived at her classes early, so she could spend more time with the professors. Being an "A" student, Mallory's desire was to maintain a 4.0 GPA. Mallory's calculus professor was the renowned Dr. Ron January, one of Georgia's top mathematicians.

When Mallory entered the classroom, Dr. January was preoccupied with a student. Not wanting to interrupt them, she started to back pedal quietly out of the door. Just then, Dr. January looked up and stopped her, saying, "It's okay, Ms. Williams. You can come in. We were just finishing up now."

She advanced forward, smiling as she apologized. "Oh, I didn't want to disturb you."

The young man that Dr. January was tutor was trying to be inconspicuous, but couldn't control the urge to cut his eyes back and forth on Mallory with interest. Dr. January introduced the young man as his nephew, Tyson January.

Tyson was the star basketball player on Georgia Tech's team. He was intrigued by Mallory's beauty and sex appeal. He was captivated by her angelic blue eyes. He then thought to himself, *'They're probably, contact lenses'* because he had never seen anyone with blue eyes and brown skin. He then wondered if she was African-American or some other race.

Apparently, there was some chemistry between them because she found him to be a very attractive man. He had a nice smile. He stood well over six feet tall and the tight muscle shirt he wore accentuated his chiseled chest and well-developed biceps. This dark skin young man was quite pleasing to Mallory's eye! Before leaving the classroom, he asked Mallory, "Are you a basketball fan?"

She instantly responded, "Yes!"

In reality she wasn't much of a basketball fan but when he invited her to the next home game she readily agreed to take him up on his offer. While Dr. January looked on, they exchanged phone numbers.

Two weeks later, Mallory and her classmate Vanessa, a petite blonde with a giddy smile, attended the game between Georgia Tech and Maryland. The home game was a nail-biter. At half-time, Tech led Maryland by twelve points. In the second half, Maryland fought back. The lead changed hands nine times. The game came down to the wire. Maryland took the lead by one, with seven seconds left on the game clock. After Maryland scored, Georgia Tech's coach used his final time-out to design a play. Georgia Tech had one last chance to win the game. When the time-out was over, Georgia Tech's point guard, Cameron Carey, inbounded the ball. He was immediately double teamed, yet he skillfully dribbled his way out. With only two seconds left on the game clock, he spotted Tyson out of the corner of his eye, slashing toward the goal. He lobbed an *Alley-Oop* pass. Tyson caught the ball in flight and slammed it just as time expired, giving Georgia Tech a one-point victory. Chaos erupted in the arena as Tyson was mobbed and knocked to the floor by his teammates' exuberant celebration.

ONE MORE MIRACLE

After the game, Tyson texted a message to Mallory, asking her to meet him and some friends at a pizza place. She obliged him, showing up with her best friend Vanessa. When Vanessa and Mallory arrived there, the place was packed. It was standing room only. Tyson and his teammates had not arrived yet. Within minutes, he walked in with several members of the Georgia Tech's basketball team. When he entered the restaurant, everybody started chanting, "TY-SON! TY-SON! TY-SON!"

It was like radar! Tyson spotted Mallory and her friend right away. When he approached them, Mallory gave him a hug first, follow by Vanessa. They congratulated him on the game-winning shot.

They could barely hear themselves talk over the noise. Mallory then complained about not having anywhere to sit. Tyson looked at her and told her, "It's no problem! The owner of the place has reserved a section for members of the basketball team." Tyson and his friends escorted Mallory and Vanessa to that section.

After partying with Tyson and his friends for a couple of hours, Mallory was approaching her curfew; she had to be home before two a.m. She whispered to Vanessa, "It's time for us to leave."

Vanessa wasn't all that thrilled about leaving, but she didn't have a choice. She was spending the night with Mallory. She looked at Mallory and asked, "Why do we have to be in the house by two?"

Mallory replied, "That's the house rules, plus, my mom has a saying that after 2 a.m., the only thing open is legs and Denny's restaurants. She wanted to make sure that my sisters and I were always in the house before 2 a.m."

Vanessa burst out into a laugh saying, "That doesn't sound anything like what Mrs. Teresa would say."

Mallory responded, "Oh trust me, she says it."

Mallory then told Tyson she had to leave. It was getting late. He escorted her to her car. His teammate Cameron came along to talk to Vanessa. After engaging in small talk for a few minutes, Vanessa gave Cameron her phone number. They headed to Mallory's home.

The next day, Tyson called Mallory and asked if she was still on campus. She told him, "Yes."
"I need help with some math problems; can you meet me at the student library?"
"Sure."

Fifteen minutes later, they met at the library. Tyson brought a total of ten math problems for Mallory to help him solve. Mallory found the math problems simple. However, what was usually complicated for most people, came easily to her. She worked out a formula for Tyson to do the math. She patiently showed him how to solve each problem, step by step. She then wrote an extra problem and gave it to him to solve.

When Mallory saw he was having trouble with the problem, she showed him an easier way to do them. She looked at him and thought quietly chuckling, "This boy is dumber than I thought."

He appeared to struggle, but that was just his game.

After the math session, Tyson continued to stare at Mallory, making her feel slightly uneasy. She then asked, "Why are you looking at me like that? Please don't tell me it's because you think I'm so beautiful, that's sickening. I hear that all the time."

Tyson responded, "Well, that's part of the reason I'm looking at you."
"What is the other reason?
"Oh, I was just wondering what ethnicity you are?"
"Does it matter?"

He shook his head, "Oh no, no, it doesn't matter. I know you're probably sick and tired of hearing this, but you are a beautiful woman, whatever ethnicity you are. Why don't you like compliments?"

"Well, I know physical beauty isn't as important as inner beauty because physical beauty fades. What's inside you stays. I think I look okay, but I've seen girls on campus that look much better than me."

"No, I don't think so. If there were, believe me, I would have seen them by now."

"Getting back to my race, I'm biracial. My mother is African-American and my dad is Caucasian. Because of my brown skin, society dictates who I am so I don't have a problem being a black woman."

"Mallory, I see you are a very secure woman."

"Mmhhm, thank you!" She says dryly.

"But, I'm sure that you have to admit there are very few black women with blue eyes. I'm assuming that you get your eyes from your dad."

"Yes that's true, but there's more to my dad than his blue eyes. My dad is such a sweet and wonderful man. I would love him even if he were a Martian."

"Mallory, I know some people of mixed race who look more white than black. They don't want to associate with the dark side of their family."

"Tyson, those people are really silly. I don't have time for those kind of people."

"Who would you say you look more like? Your mom or your dad?"

"Well, it all depends on whom I'm with at the time. When I'm with my mom, some people say I look just like her. When I'm with my dad, people say I look just like him. Obviously, his skin color is different from mine, but if you saw us together, you would say, *That's paradoxical. Here's a white man with his black biological child*...hey, hey, hey what's up with all this *black and white* stuff?"

"Sorry, sorry, geez! I was just telling you about some of

my pet peeves, that's all. Mallory, I'm going to tell you what
really gets under my skin."

"What's that, Tyson?"

"With some of these brothers and sisters who are mixed,
when people ask them what race they are, they start rambling,
'I'm Indian, I'm Irish, I'm Italian' or whatever.' And I sincerely
doubt they're mixed all that. Most of them are as black as I am!

She looked at him and sighed, "Geez Tyson, you're
really persistent, aren't you? Well, life is too short for you to
worry about other people's idiosyncrasies and silly hang-ups."

"I have a question for you?"

"What's that, Tyson?"

Tyson's naïve mentality started to inwardly irritate
Mallory, as he continued to ask.

"You've seen some of those legal forms at the DMV?
The ones where some boxes state African-American, Asian,
Native-American, Caucasian, Hispanic or Other. They ask you to
check the box for your race. What do you check?"

She repeated, "Like I told you Tyson, *I don't have a
problem being black.* Of course I check the box that says
African-American. Checking a box that says *'Other'* reduces you
to an anomaly, and that's not what I am. Can we now put this
race issue to rest, *please?*"

"Oh yeah, sure!"

He pleasantly looked at her for a long moment, smiling.
His inner voice said, *'So, her daddy's a cracker. Shit, I ain't mad
at him! he certainly helped produced a pretty little cinnamon
Graham cracker. I can't wait to get a little bite of that
sweetness.'*

A week later, Tyson was in the apartment he shared
with his teammate, Cameron. He was excited about receiving an
"A" in English. It was hard for Cameron to believe that Tyson
had earned an "A." Tyson was very gifted athletically, but what
he had in athleticism, he lacked in scholastic ability.

Cameron looked at him suspiciously. "So, you got an "A" in English?"

Tyson nodded, "Sure did! And between me and you, I think Professor Boxdell really likes me!"

Cameron inquired, "She likes you, huh? What do you mean by that?"

"I mean, she likes me. I mean, like in really *likes* me. I've been over to her crib before."

Cameron laughed, "Man, get out of here!"

"Naw dude, it's true!"

"You mean to tell me proper, conservative Dr. Boxdell? Whatever man, that's hard for me to believe!"

"Hey, believe it! She's like Dr. Jekyll and Mr. Hyde! Yes, in the classroom, she's very proper; very conservative, like you say. Once you get her in the bedroom, she has no inhibitions! *That chick is a freak!* And You know I'm a freak, too; when two freaks get together, it's a sexual explosion! Guess what, Cameron? She has a Capricorn sign tattooed on her ass. It's really cool!"

"Tyson, isn't that chick *married*?"

"Yeah, she has a husband. He's an officer in the Navy. He goes out on his ship once a month," Tyson grinned, "when he's out to sea, I'm at his crib."

Cameron began to smile, rubbing his chin.

With a baffled expression, Tyson asked, "Hey dude, why are you smiling like that?"

"Now I know how you got the "A" you didn't deserve."

"Hey dude, I earned that! Believe it or not, I had to work *hard* for that **A**!" Tyson laughed.

"How are things going with you and Mallory?"

"They are going according to plan. Everything is on schedule."

"So you saying you haven't hit that yet?"

"Not yet, but it's coming. When I see her tomorrow, I'm going to ask her to be my girl. I know she likes me, so I *know* she's

241

going to say yes."

Tyson was a very deceptive young man. Everything about him was a façade. He was the father of two young children back in his hometown of Houston. He had been charged with failure to pay child support for one of the children, but because he was a star athlete on a major college team, the coaches funded the money to the young lady to keep her from pursuing a court settlement.

The following day, Tyson met with Mallory and asked her to be his girlfriend. She accepted. This much was true: Tyson liked Mallory. But it was probably more of an infatuation, since being the type of person that he was, he was incapable of ever really loving anybody. It was all about the chase. Innately, Tyson didn't have much respect for women because of how women treated him at an early age. His drug addict mother gave him away to some friends to raise when he was a child. His foster mother never showed him much love either, since she was an alcoholic. Tyson learned to guard his heart and treat women as means to an end. Tyson's true intentions was only revealed to his roommate, Cameron.

Mallory and Tyson had been dating for a month when one Sunday afternoon, Mallory invited him over for dinner to meet her family. Tyson arrived at the Williams residence and rang the doorbell; Mallory answered it. She greeted him with a quick kiss before leading him by the hand into the dining room. Waiting for him were Mallory's mother, father and grandmother. Mallory introduced Tyson to the family. He was given a warm reception, but Tyson could barely keep his eyes off of Teresa, saying to himself, *'Damn! This girl's mama is finer than she is!'*

Allen, being a sports fan, was pleased to have the star basketball player on Georgia Tech's team in his home! He considered Tyson a celebrity. During dinner, Tyson was the consummate conversationalist, comfortably dividing his time with each family member. Teresa found him to be quite engaging, with a beautiful smile.

'Angel has pretty good taste,' she thought to herself.

Ms. Hunter, on the other hand, had a different opinion of him. She observed how Tyson commented on everything that was discussed.

'If anybody talks that much, they've got to be lying,' she thought suspiciously.

Ms. Hunter, being old school, knew from experience when person talked too much and knew something about anything and everything, they were most likely a big, fat liar.

Ms. Hunter was also perturbed that Tyson's eyes seemed to follow Teresa's every move, his eyes always focusing on her, whether it be either her breast or her butt. Even though Teresa was in her mid-forties, she still had a youthful look. All those hours spent at the gym paid dividends. Her body was tight! She was often mistaken for Mia and Kendria's big sister. But that was no excuse for his lascivious behavior. Ms. Hunter formed a negative opinion of Tyson, thinking, *'Angel deserves better than this boy!'*

The next day at school, Mallory and Vanessa sat at a table in the student center discussing Tyson's premiere dinner date with the family. She became giddy with every mention of Tyson's name. She told Vanessa how impressed her family was with him. Vanessa could sense by the gleam in her eyes that she was falling for him. With a girly smile, Vanessa asked her, "Have you and him done it yet?"

Mallory forced a smile, shaking her head, "Oh girl, no! That's light years away!"

"What do you mean, *that's light years away*," inquired Vanessa, frowning, "you like Tyson and he likes you. Not to mention he's the star basketball player. Girl, he's quite a catch! If you're not willing, there're plenty of girls on campus who are."

"I'm not worried about that; besides, Tyson's not pressuring me."

"But Mallory, aren't you concerned that some of the girls on campus might be getting your man's goodies?"

"Well, his goodies are his goodies, and my goodies are mine. I was raised to believe that a man is not yours until you marry him."

"Mallory, can I ask you a question?"

"Sure!"

"Have you ever had sex with anybody?"

Indignant, Mallory answered, "No, of course not!"

Vanessa laughed. "Girl, this is 2010! What are you waiting for?"

"I'm waiting for my husband and my wedding night."

"Mallory, don't tell me you're one of *those girls* who believe in *Prince Charming* are you?"

"No, I'm not. I just believe that the most precious gift a woman can give a man is her body. That comes with your heart and soul. Then the two of you belong to each other. Vanessa, married people *make love*; unmarried people *have sex*."

"That's purely semantics, dear Mallory! Making love and having sex are one and the same. For your information, *sex* is good for you."

"Vanessa, a woman can always find a man to have sex with. That's not hard. But finding the right man to love you is. Of course I'm not speaking from experience. But I only can imagine that would be the best orgasm in the world!"

"*Oh, you church-goers think you know everything!*" Vanessa said, a hint of sarcasm in her voice.

"No, I don't. I don't think I know *everything*! I hope I haven't offended you by saying these things…I don't want to come across as being *holier-than-thou*. I just *choose* not to have sex."

Vanessa looked at her and said, "Okay, let's change the subject."

On Sunday morning, Tyson met Mallory at church for

the 11:00 o'clock Mass. Although he was an atheist, Tyson made an all-out effort to win Mallory's heart by coming to church. He never told Mallory that he didn't believe in the existence of GOD.

Tyson's efforts seemed to be working. He had a three-month plan to break Mallory down. Obviously Tyson wasn't starved for sex. Being a star basketball player, he had access to his share of female groupies. He just liked the challenge of seducing such a sweet, innocent woman.

CHAPTER 28

On July 14th, Mallory and her family planned to fly down to Jamaica to visit her grandparents at their Summer home. Before leaving, she had an extensive phone conversation with Tyson. Mallory wanted him to come on vacation with them, but he had other commitments. He was assisting one of the Atlanta Hawks' star players with a basketball camp for inner city children. They ended their conversation with Mallory telling Tyson that she loved him.

After hanging up with Mallory, Tyson sat with his feet propped up on the cocktail table. *'It won't be long now,'* he thought smugly, a smile plastered on his face, *'soon, she's going to be naked in my bed.'*

At 7:30 p.m. that evening, Tyson pulled in the parking lot of **Fa Reals' Pizza Place**. When he entered the popular spot, naturally all eyes turned to him. Before making his way to a table, he exchanged greetings with several other athletes. He finally made his way to a booth.

One of the staff soon arrived to take his order.

"What's up, Big Dog?"

Tyson responded, "What's up, Mackey?"

"It's all good in the hood! I can't believe my eyes!"

"What you talking about, dog?"

"You're in here by yourself. No honey?! What's up with that?"

"Well, these days I'm keeping a low-profile. I still have a couple of freaks on the side. But I got to make my girl think that she's the only one, so I don't want to be seen with anyone else in here."

Mackey nodded and said, "I feel you," as they bumped fists. "Hey man, what can I get you tonight?"

"I'll take a medium pizza with Italian sausage, ham, ground beef, olives, extra mushrooms and a pitcher of Bud

ONE MORE MIRACLE

Light."

Mackey nodded his head, "Alright, gotcha! Coming right up!"

A short time later Vanessa entered the restaurant. She didn't see Tyson, but he saw her and called out to her. When they made eye contact, he waved for her to come over. They hugged each other.

"What's up Vanessa?"

"Nothing much, just chilling. What's up with you?"

"Doing the same. Chilling."

"What's that cologne you're wearing? It smells good!"

"It's called **Guilty, by Gucci**. As you know my girl's gone to Jamaica with her parents. If you're not meeting anybody, why don't you join me and share some pizza."

"Well, I'm not meeting anybody…yeah, I'll share a slice with you."

"Haven't seen you at the apartment lately. You and my boy Cameron not kicking it anymore?"

"Man, you know we both see other people; we're not anything serious. He's out of town for the Summer; won't be back until school starts."

"Yeah, he's a country boy, I don't think Atlanta's his cup of tea."

"Hey Tyson, there is some talk around campus you may be drafted in the NBA next year."

With an arrogant smile he replied, "No, it's not true. I toyed with the idea but I waited too late. The NBA draft was held last month…but I definitely won't be coming back to school my senior year, that's for sure."

"Tyson, do you think you and Mallory will get married after you go pro?"

He chuckled, "Damn, who said anything about *marriage*? I haven't even got to first base yet! I guess I should really say I haven't *been on the field* with her."

Vanessa smiled, "Yeah, Mallory is going to be a tough nut to crack."

With a sly grin Tyson replied, "Any nut can be cracked. All you need is the right tools."

Looking at him pointedly she asked, "So you think you have the right tools?"

Through veiled eyes, he responded, "Yes, of course I do!"

"That remains to be seen." She said with a smirk.

Two hours later, Tyson was walking Vanessa to her car. He thanked her for sharing a pizza with him. She, in turn, thanked him for extending the invitation. Vanessa suddenly glanced at her watch, remarking, "It's only 9:00 p.m. I thought it was much later!"

"Well since it's so early, come to my apartment and watch a movie with me then."

Vanessa had mixed feelings.

Tyson sensed this and said, "We could call Mallory from my apartment to see how she is doing in Jamaica."

"Oh okay, sounds like a plan!"

Vanessa followed Tyson in her car to his apartment. When they entered, the thermostat read 65 degrees; that was too cold for Vanessa.

"Hey, Tyson, can you turn up the thermostat?"

He smiled, "No problem," and turned it up to 78 degrees, which suited Vanessa just fine. Tyson then popped a movie in the DVD player. Vanessa made herself comfortable on the couch, slipping off her red flip flops. Tyson sat on the floor, in a traditional Bean bag chair.

A few minutes into the movie, Tyson asked Vanessa if she'd like a glass of Sangria.

"Sure."

He went to the kitchen, poured her a glass of wine and got himself a beer.

ONE MORE MIRACLE

Coming back into the living room, he asked, "Vanessa, you smoke weed?"

She replied with an impetuous smile, "Sure! Do you have some?"

"Yeah, I've got a couple of joints."

He left the room, went to his bedroom and stayed there for a moment. When he returned, he had two joints in his hand. "I'll smoke just one with you. I have to drive home."

Tyson suddenly grabbed her half-empty glass of wine and went back into the kitchen to refill it. What Vanessa didn't know was that he also had taken an **rohypnol** pill from his bedroom desk. He crushed the pill, covertly slipped it into her glass of wine, and stirred the wine to dissolve it thoroughly. He then added some crushed ice to the glass to keep her from detecting any remnants of the drug.

When he returned to the living room, he lit one of the joints. He took the first hit, held the smoke in for a few seconds, then exhaled. He passed the joint to Vanessa. He purposefully let her smoke most of it. As part of his devious plan, he wanted her to get high quickly.

He continued to watch her, like a hyena watches its prey. Soon, Vanessa's speech became slurred.
She looked up and told him, "I'm feeling a little light-headed. This weed has quite a kick!"

"Lie down for a few minutes, I'll wake you up." He suggested.

"Don't let me sleep too long. Promise me you'll only let me sleep for a couple of hours." She stretched out on the couch and immediately fell to sleep.

Tyson observed her for a few minutes. When she began to snore, he knew the roofie had taken effect. Tyson slipped off his pants, then his underwear. He went over to the couch and removed Vanessa's blue jeans and underwear. He went back into the bedroom and got a condom out of a top drawer. He came

249

back into the room, saying out loud, "Can't have any DNA evidence, Baby."

After slipping on the condom, he went back over to the couch, spread Vanessa's legs wide, and penetrated her. He had his way with her for a while. When he finished, he removed the condom and walked back into the kitchen to discard it in the trash bin.

While in the kitchen, he poured himself a glass of wine. He went back into the living room, sat on the floor next to the couch and stared at Vanessa, naked as she slept.

Turned on, Tyson went back into the bedroom, got another condom, slipped it on, then came back and raped her again. When he finished the second time, he repeated his activities, going back into the kitchen, taking off the condom, and discarding it in the trash bin. After that, he went to the restroom, got a towel, wiped Vanessa off, and put her clothes back on.

Concluding his plan, he went to the bathroom, showered, and put on the same clothes. He went back into the living room, sat down on the Bean bag chair, and fell asleep. Vanessa lay sleeping all night, oblivious to what had happen to her. Tyson was indeed the epitome of a low-life bastard!

Around 9:00 a.m. the next morning, Vanessa's eyes slowly opened; she was almost unaware of her surroundings. Her body felt somewhat sore. As her eyes scanned the room, her mental faculties slowly came into focus. Her eyes landed on Tyson, sleeping on the floor in the Bean bag chair.

She realized that she had overslept and spent the night at Tyson's apartment. She finally sat up, calling Tyson's name. He was unresponsive. She got up from the couch, went over to the Bean bag chair and shook him, "Tyson, wake up!"

When his eyes opened, he pretended to be surprised that she was still there. "What happened?"

"What happened? I should be asking you, what

happened! What was in that damn joint?"

He shook his head, "Nothing, just some damn, good weed! It knocked me the hell out! I guess it was the combination of the weed and wine."

"Look, I've got to get out of here! I need to go home. I still feel like I'm out of it. I feel so tired and drained."

"Come on, I'll walk you to your car." Tyson walked her outside to her car. She got in and drove off, as he waved goodbye. She ignored his wave.

When she got home, she still didn't feel right. When she went to urinate, she felt a burning sensation. Vanessa began to take her clothes off. She removed her jeans and then her underwear. For some reason she felt dirty. As she ran her bath water, she stared at her reflection in the mirror.

She pulled the polo-style shirt over her head. While removing the shirt, she caught whiffs of Tyson's cologne on her clothing. She brought the shirt to her nose to smell it closely. The shirt smelled like Tyson's cologne. Everything was clear now. She didn't remember being in close enough contract with Tyson for his cologne to be on her shirt!

Vanessa became furious inside, as she thought to herself, *'THAT BASTARD RAPED ME! That weed must have been laced with something!'*
Vanessa examined herself for semen but, didn't detect any.

Vanessa was almost right, it wasn't the marijuana, but it was what was in the wine! Vanessa's eyes began to tear up, as she thought, *'How am I going to tell Mallory what happened? She will never understand! This whole damn thing is my fault! I shouldn't have taken my ass over there.'*

She stepped into the bathtub. The warm water and the bubbles were very relaxing and melted away some of her soreness. She closed her eyes, laid back, and extended her legs the length of the tub. *'I can't tell Mallory what happened! I don't want to ruin our friendship!'*

251

Then her thoughts shifted to Tyson. *'He is a dangerous guy! Mallory doesn't need to be with him!'*

Eight days later, Mallory and her parents came back from their vacation in Jamaica. Since returning home, Mallory hadn't heard from Vanessa, so she decided to call her. When Vanessa's cell phone rang, she was driving on I-85, heading into Downtown. She gazed at the phone's caller ID and saw that it was Mallory calling her. She didn't answer the call and let it go to voicemail.

Ten minutes later, Vanessa pulled into the parking lot at the bank. She turned off the car's motor, picked up the phone, and listened to the voicemail message.

"Hey, girl! What's up? I called you a few times from Jamaica, but you never returned my calls. And I haven't heard a word from you since I've been home. I've texted you twice and still no response. What's up with that? Call me! Love you."

After listening to the message, Vanessa took a deep breath and whispered, "I need to call her. I can't let what Tyson did to me ruin our friendship. I can't tell her…I'm going to forget about it…. Completely forget about it!" She then dialed Mallory's number.

The phone rang a few times. Mallory looked at the caller ID and knew it was Vanessa.

With an ebullient shrill, she answered, "Hey! Hey, Vanessa! What's up? How have you been?"

"I'm okay!"

"Girl, I've been home two days. I called you. Why haven't you returned my calls? I called you more than once! I even texted you!"

"Oh, Mallory, I apologize. Please forgive me. I've been going through something."

"What is it? Is it something you care to talk about?"

Vanessa paused for a long moment, then replied, "No, not really. It's a family matter."

"I understand. Well, if you change your mind, I'm here for you."

"Thanks, Mallory. I appreciate that."

"Sure, anytime. Hey Vanessa, let's go and hang out!"

"Okay, where do you want to go?"

"Let's meet at Fa Real's around 4-ish."

"Okay Mallory, I'll be there."

Three hours later, Mallory and Vanessa met at the restaurant. They were there less than an hour when Tyson walked in. They were sitting at the front counter on bar stools, the kind that swivel. When Tyson and Vanessa made eye contact, she shamefully looked away. He walked over to Mallory, put his hands on her shoulder and spun her around. When the stool came full-circle and stopped, Tyson kissed her on the lips.

Mallory stood up and embraced him. Tyson suddenly turned to Vanessa with out-stretched arms. "White Chocolate, where is my hug?"

Mallory looked on, smiling. Vanessa stood up, turned her body sideways and gave him a half-hearted hug. She immediately sat down, then flew right back up.

Looking directly at Mallory, she said hastily, "Oh, ah, I forgot to go to the dry cleaners and pick up my clothes. They're going to close in half an hour. I'll call you later."

"Okay, talk to you later," Mallory responded as Vanessa rushed out of the restaurant.

Tyson looked at Mallory, "What's up with her? She seems jumpy!"

"Oh, she's having family issues, that's all. She'll be all right."

"I certainly hope so, because she's really a nice girl," he said, caressing Mallory's hand.

253

CHAPTER 29

For Tyson's birthday, Cameron reserved a hotel suite, which he offered to Tyson as a birthday gift. Tyson met with Mallory on campus. He told her of Cameron's gift and presented the idea of spending the night at the hotel with him.

"Tyson, you know I can't do that. Come on. Let's go to a nice restaurant for dinner. My treat, for your birthday."

Tyson responded, "No, I don't want to go to a restaurant. Let me cook dinner for us, at my apartment."

"Tyson, it's your birthday. I should be cooking for you... but I can't cook," she said bashfully.

"Don't worry about it, Baby. Let me cook for you. Do you think you can come over to the apartment tonight? We'll just chill on the couch and watch movies all night."

"Well, I'm going to have to come up with something to tell my parents. What time do you want me to be there?"
"Around eight."
"Okay," she said. "I'll see you then."

Mallory left to go home. During the drive, Mallory thought about what she would say to her parents. She came up with a plan. *'I'll ask mom if I could spend the night with Vanessa. Oh, I just hate lying to my parents but it's Tyson's birthday and I have to be there for him."*

When she arrived at home, her father wasn't there. She went to her mother's room and asked, "Mom, is it okay if I spend the night at Vanessa's? We want to go to a late-night movie."

Since Mallory and Vanessa were best friends, Teresa had no problem consenting. Mallory went back to her room and packed an overnight bag and left the house.

When she arrived at Tyson's place, she rang the doorbell. After a few rings he answered the door, welcoming her with a smile. When she entered the apartment, the savory smell of food delighted her nose.

ONE MORE MIRACLE

"Did you cook?"

Smiling, he said, "Yes, I guess you can say I made a little *something something*."

Mallory sighed, "I feel bad."

"Why do you feel bad?"

"Because it's your birthday! I should be cooking for you."

He then hugged her, "Oh Baby, it's okay. I don't mind cooking for my lady even though it's my birthday."

She kissed him. "You're too sweet."

He kissed her back. "Ready to eat?"

She nodded her head. "Yes, I'm famished."

"Well, let's go eat, Baby."

They entered the small dining area, where the table was already set with a splendid array of food: baked salmon, collard greens, sweet potatoes, and cornbread muffins. Mallory looked at the table with a girlish grin.

"Did you really cook this?"

With a straight face he answered, "Yes, I sure did."

"I'm impressed. How did you know I liked baked salmon?"

"Your mother told me. When I was at your house for dinner, you went to your bedroom to get something, and I asked your mom what was your favorite food.

She told me everything you like. I also have some **Pralines and Cream Blue Bell Ice Cream** in the freezer."

Mallory clapped her hands like an excited child and exclaimed, "*Pralines and Cream*—my favorite ice cream in the whole world!"

He slipped his hand in hers. "Let's eat."

Tyson pulled out the chair for her. A bottle of **White Zinfandel** sat chilling in a bucket of ice on the table. Tyson opened the bottle and poured himself a glass. When he attempted to pour her a glass, Mallory stopped him. "Tyson, I don't drink!"

With a surprised look, he remarked, "You don't drink?"

"No, I don't drink."

"Come on, you have to have one drink with me. White wine goes well with salmon."

"No, Tyson, I don't drink. I never developed a taste for alcohol."

He looked at her for a quick moment then shrugged, "Okay, more for me. What would you like to drink?"

"Do you have tea or a diet soda?"

"Yes, I have both."

"I'll take a diet soda."

He went to the fridge and got her a diet soda. Tyson was vexed because his plan was to get Mallory tipsy and then make his move, and she was throwing him a curve.

After dinner was over, Mallory continued to praise Tyson for the wonderful meal. He reveled in her approbation, detailing how he made the salmon, how he marinated it overnight, and how long it had taken him to cook the entire meal. In reality, he had purchased the food at one of Atlanta's most popular soul food restaurants, Busy **Bee's**.

He tried to create a romantic mood by popping in a **Maxwell** CD. Enjoying the music, they began to kiss, but when he tried to touch her breasts, she grabbed his hand.

Irritated, he said, "Mallory, what's the deal here? We've been seeing each other for over three months now. You *say* you love me."

"Tyson, I do love you."

"Well, if you love me, prove it. Let me make love to you."

She took a deep breath, "I'm sorry, Tyson. I just can't."

"No, don't say you just can't. Be honest and say you *just won't*."

"Tyson, it's not that I don't want to. I just can't!"

"Come on Mallory, tell me the truth."

With sincere eyes she responded, "Tyson, when I was fifteen I made a vow to GOD that I wouldn't have sex until I was married."

ONE MORE MIRACLE

He looked at her and laughed. "You made a vow to
GOD? That's crazy, and besides, that was before you met me.
Now I know GOD is not going to hold you to that. Mallory, you
were only fifteen when you made that vow; now you are almost
twenty! You're a woman now. There's nothing wrong with
making love. That's what people in love do."

Mallory looked at Tyson and said, "Yes, Tyson, you're
right. I was only fifteen years old when I made that vow, but I
was old enough to understand what I was saying. Now that I am
almost twenty, I can't go back on my vow."

Tyson stared at her and said, "Mallory, you should've
told me about this. You should have been up front with me and
told me about this vow that you made to GOD."

Mallory nodded her head, "Tyson, maybe it was naïve of
me to take for granted that sex wouldn't be an issue in our
relationship. I just thought I would finish my education, you'd go
to the NBA, and afterwards we would get married, settle down,
and have kids."

"Mallory, that could still happen, but it's up to you. It's
your call, Baby."

Mallory gazed into his eyes, saying tenderly, "If you
want me to go home, I can. If you start seeing somebody else
Tyson, I would understand. But I do love you, and I want you to
know that. There's always another option," she quietly said, "we
can get married."

Tyson sat subdued for a long moment thinking to
himself, *'This chick is really stupid! She has a lot of book sense,
but that's all she has—but no street smarts!'*
A devious thought occurred to him. "I have one more **rohypnol**
pill (roofie) left. I'll still be able to get what I want."

The silence was broken when Tyson said, "Well, let me
think about what you just said. Marriage is such a serious
commitment. I'm not sure if I'm ready to take the plunge. I think
this something we should discuss later…Would you like a cup of

257

tea?"

"Sure," she enthusiastically agreed, glad the tension between them had dissipated.

"Hold on tight while I'll go and make us some."

Tyson stepped into the bedroom first and went to the top dresser drawer to retrieve the roofie. He then came out, went into the kitchen and turned on the burner under the tea kettle. Once the kettle started boiling, Tyson retrieved two cups from the kitchen cabinet. One blue, the other, white. He made sure he could tell the difference between the cups. He poured some hot water in the cups, put a tea bag in each cup, then took the roofie out of his shirt pocket and dropped it into the blue cup. He let the pill dissolve thoroughly, then added lemon to the blue cup to camouflage the pill's taste. He called out to her from the kitchen, "Baby, would you like some honey in your tea?"
"Yeah sure, I like honey."

When he reentered the room with the two cups of tea in his hands, he suddenly tripped over a barbell that was on the side of the sofa, spilling both cups of tea onto the carpet. Mallory jumped up and raced over to him to help. She said with concern, "Are you hurt, Baby?"

He rose to his feet. "I'm okay, but I made a terrible mess here."

"Please, Tyson, let me help you. You've been waiting on me all night. Please just let me help you clean the carpet."

Tyson was visibly upset. His plan had gone awry and that was the last **rohypnol** pill he had. He looked at her in frustration, "No! Mallory, you don't have to help me. *I got this!* Just have a seat; I'll clean the carpet."

Mallory said softly, "Okay, if that's the way you want it. I only wanted to help, but if you don't want me to, that's fine." She took her seat back on the couch.

After Tyson finished cleaning the spilled tea on the carpet, he returned to the couch. Mallory had become distant.

ONE MORE MIRACLE

Her feelings were hurt because he wouldn't allow her to help him
clean the carpet and because he had snapped at her. He knew that
he had upset her, so he sat beside her, held her hand, and
apologized for hurting her feelings. He reiterated that she was
the guest and since it was he who had made the mess, it was no
more than right that he cleans it up. He then gave her a quick
kiss on the lips. Mallory gave in, smiling, telling him that he was
forgiven. They resumed watching the movie, cuddling and
kissing.

Mallory began to get sleepy, so she told Tyson, "I'm
ready to turn in; if you don't mind, I'll just sleep on the couch."

"There's no way you're sleeping out here, Mallory. You
can take the bedroom; I'll sleep on the couch."
She looked up at him, "Are you sure?"

He smiled, "Yes, I'm positive. Now go on into the
bedroom and get ready for bed. I'll get you a pillow and a
blanket. Don't worry about me; go on and go to sleep."
She gave him a long passionate kiss; then she got up off the
couch and went into the bedroom. Although Tyson was sexually
frustrated, he continued to watch the movie.

Mallory had been in the bed for a while when Tyson's
cell phone rang. It was his standby, Professor Boxdell. She told
Tyson, "I need to see you. Can you come over?"

"Sure. No problem. I'll be there in a few minutes."
Tyson pondered whether he should leave Mallory sleeping or
wake her up and tell her that something important came up and
he had to leave. He felt it best that he'd wake her up.
He entered the bedroom and shook her softly. When she
awakened he told her, "I just got a call from one of my
teammates. He's been arrested and needs someone to come and
bail him out of jail."

Mallory jumped up out of bed, already dressed, and said,
"Well, I'll go with you." Tyson told her, "No, that won't be
necessary. I want you to stay here and just rest. I'll be back as

fast as I can, after I bail him out. Now please come and lock the door, and put on the deadbolt."

Mallory did as he instructed. Meanwhile, Tyson covertly headed over to Dr. Boxdell's place.

Within twenty minutes, Tyson pulled up in her driveway. He got out of the car, walked up to the front door, and rang the door bell. She looked through the peep hole and then opened the door. When the door swung open, she was completely nude! Tyson displayed a wide grin and walked inside, closing the door behind him.

At 1:45 a.m., Mallory awakened from a restless sleep. She looked at the time on her cell phone and decided to call Tyson to see how things were going with his friend in jail. When she punched in his number, his cell phone rang, but he did not answer. A few minutes later, she dialed his number again. This time, he answered. Mallory was impatient.

"What's took you so long to answer your phone?"

"Baby, it takes a while to bail someone out of jail. When I got here, I discovered he hadn't been processed yet," he answered, whispering,

"Why are you whispering?"

"Baby, I'm talking low like this because, obviously I don't want anybody to hear me."

"How much longer is it going to take?"

"Baby, I don't have any idea!"

"You mean you have no idea when you'll be home?"

"Baby listen, I'll be there when I get there. Okay?"

Mallory snapped, "What do you mean 'you'll get here when you get here'?!"

Tyson's voice softened, "Okay, Baby, I'm sorry. I'll be there, soon as I can. Mallory, I love you."

"I love you too, Tyson." She then hung up.

He rolled over and started kissing Dr. Boxdell.

"You're such a good liar."

ONE MORE MIRACLE

With a wicked grin, he said, "I only lie when it's necessary."

The following morning, Mallory awakened almost late for class. Obviously, Tyson did not come home. She checked her phone for messages. Tyson had texted her at 5:00 a.m., apologizing, telling her that it would be another hour or so, before his 'friend' would be released from jail. He ended the message with, "I'm sorry Baby, I'll make it up to you tonight."

As promised, Tyson took Mallory on a make-up date for leaving her alone all night in his apartment. They arrived at the **Cheesecake Factory** in the Buck Head, one of Atlanta's most exclusive areas. Mallory and Tyson were in the restaurant for almost an hour, when two unexpected visitors approached their table.

Obviously Tyson knew one of the young ladies because his mood quickly changed from calm to angst. One of the women looked directly at him, before cutting her eyes sharply at Mallory, saying, "Who is she? The new flavor of the month?"

Tyson responded, "No, she's *the flavor* I hope to spend the rest of my life with. Dede, let me introduce you to my *fiancée*, Mallory."

Mallory was delighted by being referred to as his fiancée. "Pleased to meet you, Dede."

"Yeah, pleased to meet you, too. This is my friend, Raquel.

"It's a *pleasure* to meet you, Mallory."

"Same here," Mallory said politely.

Dede turned to Tyson saying, "I need to talk to you. You need to step outside, now."

"No I don't, Dede. Anything you have to say to me, you can say it here in front of my future *wife*."

"Tyson, don't make me cause a scene in here."

"Look Dede, I have nothing to say to you. Will you please get away from our table? If you don't, then I'll have Security get you away from here."

"You know what, Tyson? You're one evil bastard! You romanced me for two months, but after I gave in to you, you dropped me. All you wanted was sex. You don't give a damn about me or any other woman!"

"Dede, you and I both knew what the deal was. We went out, we had a good time and that's all it is to it. I never told you I loved you."

"You're a damn lie! Every time we had sex, you told me how much you loved me," Dede shouted.

Tyson calmly said, "Dede, come on, you and I know that's not true. You're just trying to cast me in a bad light in front of my fiancé."

Mallory looked on with mixed feelings. In her heart, she felt empathy for Dede, but she was impressed with Tyson for referring to her as his future wife. That proved to her that Tyson had nothing to hide.

Dede's voice grew louder as she became more emotional, prompting one of the restaurant's employees to come over and ask her to leave.

Before leaving, she shouted, "Tyson, you may be on top now, the big man on campus, the superstar basketball player, the superstar player of women, but your day is coming! You can't keep treating women like this and lying. Your day will come, you phony bastard! Something or someone is going to hurt you really badly. Tyson, you're the scum of the earth! *You're no-good*!"

Raquel suddenly grabbed her by the hand, forcing her to leave.

He looked at Mallory with sincere eyes, saying, "Baby, I'm so sorry that you were subjected to that clown show."

She responded, "Tyson, she obviously cares a lot about you. When people are hurting, they don't always choose the proper time nor place to express their feelings. Tyson, I'm not naïve. I realize that girls are attracted to you. Number one, you're the star basketball player on the team. Number two, you have a great body, and number three, you're a devastatingly handsome guy. I know you've probably slept with a lot of girls. I don't care about that. The only thing I care about is that we're together now. I just want to know, can you be faithful to me? I need to know that."

Tyson caressed her hand and looked into her eyes. "Baby, I'm going to *try* very hard to be faithful to you. I've never dated just one girl. I've also never been in love with anybody, but I can truly say I'm in love with you and I'm going to do my best. Girls seem to throw themselves at me all the time. I know I can be faithful to you, because I love you. I don't want to lose you."

"Oh, Tyson, I love you too. I want you to promise me this though. If it's too big of a challenge for you to be faithful to me, please be honest with me. Come to me and tell me that you want to start seeing other people. I know it will hurt and it'll be hard for me to accept, but I will always have respect for you knowing that you came to me as a man and told me the truth."

"Mallory, I'm going to be faithful to you. You'll see; just trust me."

He reached down and grasped her hand. He landed a light kiss on the back of her hand. They ended the conversation there, with him kissing her hands softly and murmuring reassurances to her.

A month later, Mallory and Tyson attended a farewell party at the **Downtown Ritz-Carlton Hotel** for Tyson's uncle. Professor Ron January was leaving Georgia Tech for **Yale University**, where he had accepted a position as Head of the Math Department. Dr. January was being honored for bringing noteworthy repute to Georgia Tech's Math Department.

Dr. January received a much deserved send off. The black tie affair was attended by some of Atlanta's most prominent educators. When the dinner was over, Tyson asked Mallory to accompany him to his apartment. She agreed.

Shortly after arriving at the apartment, the pair ended up on the sofa, kissing. Tyson soon rolled on top of Mallory. As the cuddling and kissing became more intense, Tyson began to gently squeeze her breasts. When he attempted to unbutton her shirt, she grabbed his hands, holding them tightly. They continued to kiss. Tyson was fully aroused as he attempted to center himself between her legs. Mallory's body was moist with desire.

Suddenly a red flag went off in her head, *'What are you doing? You have to stop this now!'*
She abruptly stood up, pushing him away.

He started to plead with her, saying, "Please, Mallory, Baby. I know you want this as much as I do. Come on Baby, don't turn me off like this. Please, Baby, please!"

"I'm sorry, Tyson. I want to, but I can't. I just can't!"

Tyson suddenly glared at her with a look of disdain. He didn't take his eyes off her. When Mallory looked into his eyes, she was actually frightened. She had never seen that look in his eyes before. Mallory refused to show any fear as they continued to stare each other down.

Tyson blurted out, "You know what Mallory? You ain't all that! It's lots of girls who are throwing themselves at me! I don't have to put up with this shit!" Come on, let me take your crazy, baby-ass home!

Mallory quipped, "Wow, what a difference a few minutes make. At first I was your sweet baby, now I've been reduced to a crazy baby-ass! You can take me home now! Nobody talks to me like this!"

He snapped, "Yeah, I'll take you home."

They drove to her home in complete silence. Mallory felt bad because she let things escalate. In her heart, she knew that going to Tyson's place was a mistake. Then she thought, *'How is going to your fiancé's apartment a mistake? I'm so confused! Why did I make such a vow to GOD not to have sex until I was*

264

*married? That is so unfair to Tyson! I am going to have to let
him go so he can be with someone else—Someone who's
normal.'*
    When they arrived at Mallory's house, Tyson pulled into
the spacious driveway. The motion lights instantly came on.
Tyson kept the engine running. He looked at Mallory and said
dryly, "Well, goodnight and goodbye!"
    "Can you please turn off the engine," Mallory asked.
He honored her request but he didn't make any eye contact with
her. When she began to caress his hand, he finally looked at her.
    "Tyson, I truly love you, but I'm not going to be able to
sleep with you. Neither of us are ready for marriage, so the right
thing for me to do, and it pains me to do this, is to let you go. I
want you to break up with me, then you'll be free to be with
whomever you please. I know there are lots of women who
would relish the opportunity to sleep with you. I'll be jealous, I'll
be hurt, but I'll get over it. I want to sleep with you. I love you,
but the time is not right. And I don't expect you to wait until the
time is right."
    "Mallory, are you finished?"
    "Yes, I'm finished."
    "Well, I think you're right. I'm going to have to find someone
else. I guess this relationship wasn't meant to be. Nothing more
needs to be said."
    She looked at him with tears in her eyes, responding,
"Ok, Tyson, I understand your position. I guess this is goodbye."
    She ambled into the house. Once inside, Mallory went
up to her room. She sat on the bench in front of her vanity, stared
into the mirror and began to cry.
    Tyson wasted little time driving off. He felt cheated.
All of the time and effort he spent with Mallory had been
wasted. He began to think, *'She never wanted me. She only
wanted to be seen with me. She just wanted to be with me
because I'm the hottest guy on campus. If given the chance, I*

would have given her the best sex of her life. She played me, but that's alright. I'm going to find a way to get even with her, and nobody can get even like I can.'

In Tyson's profane way of thinking, he actually thought he was entitled to every woman he wanted.

CHAPTER 30

For a few days, Mallory was in a deep state of depression since breaking up with Tyson. She made several attempts to call him, but he never returned any of her calls.

Two weeks after their breakup, training camp for the Georgia Tech basketball team began. Tyson was excited going into his senior year. NBA scouts had him rated as one of the top five college basketball players in the country. If Tyson could match the kind of season he'd had last year, he was guaranteed to become an instant millionaire and perhaps be drafted number-one.

The first day of training camp turned out to be catastrophic for Tyson. Less than an hour into the practice session, while trying to make a cut to the basket, he elevated. He landed awkwardly on a wet spot on the floor and felt his knee pop.

Trainers and coaches immediately rushed to his side. Oblivious of those hovering around him, Tyson, in a state of torment, held his knee tightly with both hands. He was rushed to **Emory Medical Center** by ambulance. When he arrived at the hospital, emergency room doctors took X-rays of his damaged knee. They revealed that he had torn his ACL. At that precise moment, he realized that his Senior year was over and possibly his career in the NBA was in jeopardy.

Later that evening, Tyson underwent surgery to repair his knee. The Head Surgeon came out and spoke to the media. He told reporters that the surgery had been successful. Tyson was now faced with at least a year of intense rehabilitation. The word quickly spread throughout the city about Tyson's injury.

When Mallory heard what had happened to Tyson, she said a prayer for him. She agonized within herself about going to see him, but the battle was short-lived. Mallory called the hospital trying to get information about him, but because Tyson was a basketball star, the hospital wasn't able to release any information to the public about him. All questions were directed to the Georgia Tech Athletic Department. Mallory phoned Cameron. He gave her Tyson's room number but warned her, "I know you and Tyson broke up, so please don't let him know I gave you his room number."

"I won't," Mallory promised Cameron.

Later that day, Mallory went to the hospital. It was late in the afternoon when she arrived at Emory Medical Center. She parked her car, got out and entered the building. She caught the elevator to the fifth floor, where the Orthopedic unit was located, and went straight to Tyson's room. When she walked in, Tyson was watching television. He appeared to be in some pain. They stared at each other for a brief moment.

Mallory asked softly, "How are you feeling?"

Tyson remarked sarcastically, " I'm in a lot of pain; my knee is busted up. Things couldn't be any better. What are you doing here?"

"Tyson, I came because I was concerned about you, but if you don't want me here, just say the word and I'll leave."

"Yeah? Okay, why don't you leave?"

Mallory blinked. "Alright, I'll leave."

She turned and headed for the door, then instantly did an about face.

"Before I go, let me say this. Tyson, you've certainly fooled me. I thought you were this kind, sensitive guy with a beautiful smile. You are nothing like I thought you were. You seem to be very angry inside. I've done nothing but try to be a friend to you. I love you very much! But in time I know I'll get over you. I'm going to make you a solemn promise, after today I'll never bother you again."

Tyson stared at her as tears streamed down her face. She could never touch a soft spot in his heart, because he had no heart! Tyson was, indeed, a charlatan. Maintaining a facade was very important to him; therefore, exposing him would render him

268

ineffective in maintaining that façade. So he was forced to show
some compassion. Mallory didn't realize that she had touched a
nerve with Tyson. He begged her to stay. Mallory was pleased
that he asked her not to leave. She quickly went to his bedside
and carefully draped her body over him.

Feeling vulnerable because of his injury, Tyson said to
himself, '*I don't know how this knee is going to heal. Damn! I
hope everything will work out fine, but in case it doesn't, I need
to stick with Mallory because her people have lots of money. I
might need to get my hands on some of that wealth in the future.*'

As Tyson held her in his arms, he began to smell her hair,
thinking to himself, '*Her hair really smells good! She is so
different from these other airheads that I mess with. I may have
to just marry her. That seems to be the only way I'm going to get
her in bed.*'

A week later, Tyson sat at home recovering. Mallory had
been there waiting on him hand and foot. She would go to class
and afterwards, come over and bring him food. She also helped
him with his class assignments. Mallory felt herself falling
deeper and deeper in love with Tyson.

Tuesday night after his arrival home from the hospital,
Mallory had just finished having dinner with her family when
her cell phone rang. It was Tyson. Mallory told him she'd call
him back later after doing the dishes. A few minutes later,
Mallory called him back. Tyson asked her if she could come
over and spend the night. Mallory told him she would have to
discuss that with her mother. Tyson snickered, causing Mallory
to ask, "What's so funny?"

Tyson hurriedly responded," Oh nothing Baby, nothing at
all."

In Tyson's world, whenever he summoned a woman, she
came running, but Mallory was a horse of a different color. She
had to consult with her parents on every move!

Mallory then said, "I can't promise you anything, but I'll

269

see."

"Ok Baby, get back with me as soon as you know something."

When Teresa got out of the shower, she came down to the kitchen to make a cup of coffee. To her surprise, her daughter was still sitting at the kitchen table. "What are you doing still sitting down here?"

Mallory ignored the question. Instead, she looked at Teresa, a serious look on her face.

"Mom, may I ask you something?"

"Sure, go ahead."

"Mom, you know since Tyson had his surgery, I've been going over there helping him out with his school work and running errands for him?"

"Yeah baby, I know and I think that's good."

"Would you have a problem with my going over to his house to spend the night?"

Teresa paused and then said slowly, "Yeah, I think I would…and I do. "

"Why, Mom?"

"First of all, you're just twenty years old. You're not legally grown yet."

Laughing, Mallory said, "Mom, I can certainly tell you're married to a lawyer; that sounds like something daddy would say."

"Well, it doesn't matter who says it; it's still the plain truth. It just doesn't look good! Your two older sisters never spent the night at guys' houses, so we're not going to let you begin that tradition. Angel, *respectable girls just don't do things like that.*"

"Mom, I wouldn't sleep in the same room with Tyson. Don't you trust me?"

"Angel, yes I trust you. It's not a matter of me trusting you. I don't know if I can trust Tyson that's all."

ONE MORE MIRACLE

"Mom, Tyson can't go any farther than I'll let him go. What if I weren't living here? What if I were living on campus? You wouldn't know when I left out and came back in."

"Angel, what you're saying is irrelevant. You're not living on campus. You're living here and you have to go by the rules of the house."

"Mom, that is so unfair," Mallory pouted. "You sound like a dictator."

"Angel, you young people kill me with that term, '*unfair*'. Tell me what's so unfair about your life? You have a brand new car, a Visa, Macy's, and a gas card at your disposal. You have a checking account in which we deposit money for you. So, what's unfair about your life? Little girl, just stop and think about it. You're blessed beyond measure. You have way more than I had when I was your age."

Mallory sat quietly for a moment and then said to her mother, "Mom, I don't want you to ever think that I'm not grateful for what you and Dad do for me. I don't ever want to come across as a spoiled brat. I have the best parents in the world." Tears suddenly rolled down Mallory's cheeks, as she said, "Mom, you know I like helping people. Tyson doesn't have any family. I just want to help him, that's all."

Teresa extended her arms out to her tearful-eyed daughter and said, softly, "Come here."

Mallory stood up, walked over to her mother and received a comforting hug and a kiss on the forehead. Mother and daughter stood there for a long moment. After the embrace, Teresa finished pouring herself a cup of coffee. Before leaving the kitchen, Mallory asked, "Mom, would it be alright if I leave early in the morning and go to Tyson's apartment and make him breakfast?"

Teresa smiled, "I don't have a problem with that."

Teresa then went back into her bedroom. Allen was sitting at the computer. "Are you still drafting that bid for the job

271

in Seattle?" she asked.

He nodded his head, "Yes, I'm almost finished. What took you so long making your coffee?"

"Oh, I had a conversation with your daughter. As you know, she's been going over to Tyson's apartment since he's had the surgery."

"Yes, I know," Allen replied.

"Well, she asked if she could spend the night at his apartment." Allen quickly cuts his eyes away the computer, "Well how did you handle that?"

"I just told her, NO!"

"Sweetheart, she's twenty years old! In a few months, she'll be twenty-one. We to start loosening the leash."

"Allen, she's a twenty-year-old who pays *no* bills. I couldn't agree with you more. Yes, we do have to start letting her go, but only after she finishes college, moves out, and starts paying her own bills at her own place. Then, we will be able to let her go completely!"

"You're the boss." Allen replied.

Mallory patiently waited until her family went to bed; then she quietly left the house.

CHAPTER 31

When she got in her car, she called Tyson and told him she was on her way. What Mallory didn't know was that Tyson had made other plans. He had already invited some other female friend over to spend the night.

As Mallory talked to him, she detected a reluctance in his voice about her coming over. Tyson attempted to dissuade her from coming, saying, "Baby, it's so late. Why don't you just stay home and I'll see you tomorrow."

"No way I'm staying home. I've already left the house and I'm on my way. I'll be there, shortly."

After hanging up with Mallory, Tyson turned to the young lady who was naked in bed with him, fast asleep. He began frantically shaking her, telling her she had to go because his girlfriend was on her way over. Naturally, the young lady was quite upset. She started shouting obscenities at him. She looked at him and continued to shout, "Now that you've screwed me, you want me to leave? Well, I'm not going anywhere!"

He suddenly grabbed her by the throat and responded in a hostile voice, "LOOK BITCH, IF YOU KNOW WHAT'S GOOD FOR YOU, PUT YOUR CLOTHES ON AND GET OUT OF HERE, NOW!"

She became frightened by his sudden change of mood. She quickly got out of bed and started putting ON her clothes. When she finished dressing, she looked at Tyson, saying, "I'll never come back here again! How could you treat me this way? How could you treat me like trash?!"

He stared at her and said, "BECAUSE YOU ARE TRASH. NOW SHUT THE DOOR ON YOUR WAY OUT!" When the young lady left the apartment, she left the door wide open, on purpose.

Tyson could feel the draft blowing in, so he mumbled, "She didn't even close the damn door!"

273

He retrieved his walker, went to the door and closed it. He slowly walked back into the bedroom. It was difficult for him to maneuver because of the cast on his leg.

Suddenly, there was a knock at the door. The knocking became quite intense, prompting him to yell, "Okay, I'm coming! I'm coming!"

When he got to the door and opened it, it was Mallory. He locked the door behind her and gave her a hug and a kiss.

She then mentioned that on her way into the apartment complex, she was almost hit by a driver who was speeding recklessly.

Out of curiosity, he asked, "What kind of car was it?"

"A blue **Ford Focus**. You know the driver?"

Tyson knew that it was the young lady who had just left his apartment. Her name was Christy Wesley, a senior at Spellman College.

Mallory wasn't good at being deceptive. On this particular night, Allen had inadvertently left his computer in his car. It was about 1:00 a.m. when he went to get it. Allen and Mallory hardly ever park their cars in the garage. So when he to the driveway, to his dismay, Mallory's car was missing. His first thought was that perhaps the car was stolen.

He got his computer and went back into the house, straight to Mallory's room. He knocked softly on the door. When she failed to answer, Allen carefully pushed the door open. That's when he discovered that Mallory was not in her room. He went to their bedroom, awakened his wife and informed her that their daughter was gone.

Teresa was furious after learning that Mallory left the house. She immediately called Mallory's cell phone. The call went directly to voicemail. Teresa called her phone two more times, getting the same result.

She then texted Mallory: Where are you, young lady!

ONE MORE MIRACLE

Moments later, Mallory texted her back: <u>Mom, Im fine. Im @</u> <u>Tyson's place. I noe Im n hot water. Sry I betryd ur trust. C u aftr</u> <u>skool tmrw</u>.

Teresa let Allen read the message. When he finished, he remarked, "Teresa, I'm a little disappointed in Angel, but by and large, she is a good child."

"Yeah, she's a good child alright; a good child who betrayed our trust."

"Teresa, let's not be too hard on her; she's only human. We all make mistakes. Things could've been worse. At least she is not pregnant."

With a concerned gaze, Teresa gasped, "Oh Allen, please don't put that thought in my head."

At two o'clock the next day, Mallory pulled into her parent's driveway. Her grandmother was in the dining room, polishing the China cabinet when she saw Mallory enter. She cut her eyes sharply to her and asked, "Little girl, where have you been?"

Mallory walked over to her grandmother, giving her a warm, gentle hug. The gesture seemed to diffuse her anger. She asked her grandmother, "Why are you cleaning the furniture?"

"The cleaning lady didn't come today. She doesn't feel well. Now, answer my question, where were you last night?

"I was at Tyson's apartment. I know I was wrong. I'm sure everybody is angry with me."

With a reassuring smile, Ms. Hunter said, "Your granny isn't mad with you. We all make mistakes; no one is perfect."

"Granny, what I did I don't consider a mistake."

"Oh, you don't?"

"No, I don't!"

"Well, what would you consider it?"

"Granny, leaving the house without telling anyone, I must admit, was wrong. But mom and dad are still treating me as

275

though I were still a child. I'm a senior in college, for goodness sakes! I'm a 20-year- old woman!"

"Angel, why don't you get your own place?"

"I'm seriously thinking about that."

"Angel, let me give you some advice. If you move out it's okay, but don't move out just so you can be with that *boy* Tyson. Once you start sleeping with a man, there's less of a chance you will get him to marry you."

"Granny, please believe me, if I were to move out, I wouldn't move in with Tyson. I'd get my own apartment. Granny, I have values. I have respect for myself. *I'm not a loose woman.*"

"I know you're not a baby. You're a good girl."

"Thanks, granny. I love you."

"I love you too, little girl."

Forty-five minutes later, Teresa walked into the house and into the dining room, where Mallory and her mother were.

Teresa's posture was subdued, as she placed her purse and her monogrammed briefcase on the table near the door. Teresa greeted Ms. Hunter, "Hi, mama. How was your day?"

"It was fine. I slept most of the day."

Teresa and Mallory made eye contact. Mallory spoke first, "Hello, Mom. Did you have a good day?"

"I had a great day at work. How was school? Did you have a good day?"

"Yes Mom, I did."

Teresa gave her mother a quick glance, before saying, "Mama, would you excuse us, please? Angel and I need to talk."

"Sure, Teresa, no problem."

Ms. Hunter abruptly left the room. Teresa and Mallory eyed each other briefly. Mallory looked away but became anxious, as her eyes shifted back to her mother. Teresa finally said, "Angel, you really let dad and I down, sneaking out of the house like you did. I never could've imagined that you would betray our trust. Sleeping at Tyson's apartment is so disrespectful. Angel, never let a man lower your standards!"

Mallory displayed an uncharacteristic hostility when she spoke, "Mom, I haven't lowered my standards. That's unfair of you to imply that I have!"

"Oh, you think sneaking out of the house is right?"

"Mom, you keep saying I snuck out of the house. That's something a disobedient child would do. I'm not a child! I'm a woman! I just left because I wanted to leave. I wish you'd start treating me like the woman I am!"

"Angel, no one here treats you like a child. You're allowed to come and go as you please. Since your involvement with Tyson, you've certainly changed."

She responded angrily, "Mom, I haven't changed! I wish you would stop saying that! I'm still the same."

Teresa shook her head emphatically, "Mallory, I'm your mother. I know you better than anyone else. Mallory, are you sexually active?"

"Mom, that's none of your business! *That's personal!* You have no right to ask me that!"

Teresa moved closer, as she shrilled, "I'm your mother and I'll ask you whatever I want! Are you having sex with Tyson?!"

She stood up facing Teresa, forcefully saying again, "Mom, you have *no right* to ask me that!"
Teresa gave her an icy stare and ordered her to sit down. She took a seat, staring back at her mother, then asked, "Are you going to hit me because I won't answer your question?"

Teresa responded with her finger in Mallory's face, "Let me remind you of something. Don't be disillusioned by this Armani suit and these Prada stilettos. Underneath this veneer is still the same black mother who loves you enough to take five bullets for you if she had to. But one thing I'm not going to take is shit from you! And the next time you get in my face like you just did, I'll do more than hit you. *I'll beat your ass!*"

Mallory's face softened as she whispered, "Yes, Ma'am."

Teresa turned and stormed out of the room. She went into the kitchen and got a bottle of spring water from the refrigerator. Ms. Hunter was sitting at the kitchen's island sipping a warm cup of coffee. Noticing the angry expression on Teresa's face, she inquired, "Teresa, are you okay?"
"Yeah mama, I'm fine."

"I baked some chicken, made a potato salad and steamed some broccoli. May I fix you a plate?"

Teresa went over to her mother, squeezed her hand softly and said, "I'm not really hungry. I'm going upstairs to take a shower. I'll eat when Allen comes home."

"Alright, baby, that's fine."

When Teresa left the kitchen, Ms. Hunter went back to the dining room where Mallory was still sitting on the sofa with a melancholy look on her face. Ms. Hunter came and sat beside her. She placed her arms around Mallory.

"Okay, tell your granny what's bothering you."

Although Mallory wanted to be treated as a woman, whenever she was upset she'd revert back to being a little girl so she could be comforted by her grandmother. She rested her head on Ms. Hunter's shoulder and explained, "Granny, mom's attitude was terrible. She talked to me in such an acrimonious manner."

"Angel, what do you mean, she talked to you in an acrimonious way?"

"You know granny; her tone was strident."

Ms. Hunter looked at her, "Angel, you're sounding like your daddy and your big sisters using words that I'm not familiar with."

"Oh granny, I'm so sorry. Please forgive me. What I meant to say was, mom talked to me really badly. And she threatened to beat my butt."

ONE MORE MIRACLE

Ms. Hunter blinked, "What? She threatened to whip you? What caused her to say she will beat your butt?"

With an averted glance, Mallory sighed, "Well, I did raise my voice a couple of decibels."

"Angel, you know you were wrong. You had no right raising your voice at your mother."

"But granny, mom talked to me like I'm a child."

"Angel, you're acting like a child. Let me give you some advice. When you're wrong, the best thing to do is to humble yourself then accept responsibility. That's what adults do."

Mallory sat silent for a lengthy moment. With a serious look, she said, "Granny, I think I should move out and get an apartment near the campus."

"Angel, why don't you discuss this with your daddy?"

"Yes, you're right! I'm going to talk to dad."

Later that evening, Mallory and her dad were sitting on the deck in the backyard. She had just finished apologizing to him for leaving home abruptly. He graciously accepted her apology after telling Mallory that he didn't think her leaving the house the previous night was a really big deal. He was a bit surprised when she told him she was contemplating moving out. Mallory told her dad that she felt as if her mother was out of control because of the way she spoke to her.

He took issue with her statements. With a stern look, he responded, "Wait a minute, Angel. You're the one who acted irresponsible last night. You left the house without letting us know you were gone and when your mom reprimanded you, you have the audacity to say *she's out of control*? Angel, you broke the rules. You don't get to choose how you're going to be scolded."

"Oh, Dad, I knew you would take mom's side. You always do!"

He paused. "Angel, think about what you just said. Honestly, do you think that I never take your side? Is that what you're saying?"

She sighed, "No dad, that's not what I'm *really* saying. For the most part, you're always objective."

"Angel, if you feel the need to move out, I don't have a problem with it. But don't leave out of anger and rebellion. It's always best to leave under the spirit of harmony because that way you can always come back home without any provisions."

"Oh dad, I suppose I'm not your sweet little Angel anymore. I've become the black sheep of the family."

"Sweetheart, don't say that. You're not the black sheep of the family. I don't want you to flounder in self-deprecation, either. You're a good, young lady and I'm proud of you."

"Thanks, dad. That means the world to me, coming from you."

He smiled softly, "Angel, you remember when you were a little girl and you were upset about not being a twin?"

She chuckled, "Yeah dad, I remember. Dad, you always knew how to make me feel special. I'll never forget what you told me. You said Kendria was your right arm, Mia was your left arm, Josh was your right leg, David was your left leg. You told me I was your heart. You said you could live without your arms and legs, but you couldn't live without your heart. Daddy, am I still your heart?"

"Yes, Angel, you're still my heart."

"Daddy, may I ask you a question? If Mia and Kendria are your arms, Josh and David are your legs, and I'm your heart, then what is Mom?"

"Oh, Angel, mom is my *oxygen*. I can't breathe without her."

"Daddy, you and mom seem to have a perfect marriage."

"No sweetheart, our marriage is far from perfect. We have our moments, but the love we share covers all faults. Angel, I want you to make up with mom, okay?"

She nodded, "Yes, Sir!"

ONE MORE MIRACLE

The next morning, Teresa was getting ready for work. Her bedroom door was cracked open. Mallory suddenly walked in, "Mom, do you have a minute?"
Teresa tensely answered, "Yes, ma'am."
"Mom, I just want to tell you that I'm sorry I got all up in your face yesterday. I absolutely had no right to scream at you. It truly upsets me when you are angry with me. Mom, I hope you'll forgive me. I'm truly sorry about yesterday," She responded with tears in her eyes.
Teresa turned to face Mallory as her face softened, "Yes, Angel, I forgive you."
"Thanks mom, I hope you have a good day at work today."
Mallory then turned to walk out of the room, when Teresa said, "Young lady, aren't you forgetting something?"
She turned, went over, embraced her mother with a warm hug and said, "I forgot mom that's how we do it."
Teresa playfully pushed her away, "Go on, get out of here. I wanted to stay mad at you, but I just can't."
Mallory smiled, "I can't stay mad at you and you can't stay mad at me because we love each other so much."

CHAPTER 32

Four months later, while Tyson was getting out of the shower, he slipped and reinjured his knee, causing his rehab to take a serious setback. The knee had swollen severely. This time, the doctors only had to do **Arthroscopic surgery**.

Tyson saw his chances of going to the NBA slipping away. He decided to implement Plan B: he asked Mallory to marry him. She happily accepted. Mallory wanted a large wedding, but Tyson talked her out of it. He told her that once he made it big in the Pros, he would give her the type of wedding she deserved.

He convinced her that, getting her parents to pay for the wedding would be like charity and that's something he didn't want to accept. Mallory was disappointed but, with reservations, she went along with his idea of getting married in the office of the Justice of the Peace.

Friday morning at 10:45 a.m., Mallory and Tyson went to the **Fulton County Courthouse** and obtained a marriage license. Two hours later, they were married. Mallory was now Mrs. Tyson January. She was happy to be Tyson's wife, but was ambivalent about telling her parents what she had done, so she called her best friend Vanessa first and told her the news.

Vanessa was surprised, to say the least. For obvious reasons, Vanessa wasn't happy that Mallory and Tyson were married; nevertheless, she pretended to be happy. Since Mallory was married, she knew that Tyson would be taking up most of Mallory's time. She was certainly going to miss Mallory, because she truly loved her like a sister. Before hanging up, Vanessa couldn't resist asking Mallory if she was pregnant.

Mallory laughed, "How can I be pregnant, when I've never had sex before?"
They ended the conversation with Vanessa saying, "I guess that answers my question."

ONE MORE MIRACLE

It was 6:00 p.m., when Mallory and Tyson pulled up in her parents' driveway. Mallory was experiencing some anxiety, but Tyson was quite relaxed. They got out of the car and entered the house. Hearing the sound of voices coming from the living room, they proceeded on in there. Mallory's parents and her grandmother were watching a movie. Mallory went over and kissed her grandmother and then her parents, while Tyson stood in the doorway, watching Mallory.

Allen looked up at him and said, "Tyson, please come on in! Have a seat."

He walked toward the sofa, but before he could sit down, Mallory grabbed his hand. Looking at her parents, she said, "Mom, dad, we have something important we need to tell you."

Allen quickly grabbed the remote and muted the sound of the movie. Mallory stood, holding Tyson's hand as she spoke. "Mom, dad, and granny, Tyson and I are in love, you know that."

Both parents sat silently and waited.

"Well, today we went and got married."

Allen blurted out, shocked, "You got married?"

The whole time Teresa sat restrained, reflecting on when she first got married at eighteen, because she was pregnant. Teresa's inner voice said, *'I'm not going to judge her, I'm going to be supportive. That's how my mother was with me.'*

Teresa looked Mallory in the eyes and said, "Angel, I'm a little disappointed, because I would have loved to have given you the type of wedding that I gave your two sisters. But I guess you didn't want that. This was your decision, and I'll have to accept it. Congratulations!"

Allen rose to his feet, looking directly at Tyson, saying to him, "Did the two of you have to get married? Was there some compelling reason why you had to do this, now?"

Tyson said, "Well, Sir, if you are wondering if Mallory is pregnant, then no, that's not the reason. The reason is, we love

283

each other. That's what we wanted to do. I hope that I'm not being disrespectful by saying this. I don't want to embarrass Mallory, but this is something that we need to get out right now. Mallory is still a virgin."

Allen felt like a ton of bricks had been removed from his chest. He was quite relieved. He even echoed his wife's sentiments, "Well yes, a congratulation is in order, then! Welcome to the family."
He went over to Tyson and gave him a firm handshake and then hugged his daughter tightly and told her how much he loved her.

Ms. Hunter sat bewildered, not saying a thing but thinking to herself, *'There is just something shady about this boy! I don't know what it is, but, it's just something about this boy I don't like. And, who in hell is this boy? We don't know nothing about him or his people!'*

After spending an hour at her parents' house, Mallory and Tyson decided to leave. Teresa extended an offer for them to spend the night at the house, since they were married. Mallory said they were going to go some place and eat dinner and then go to Tyson's apartment. Allen also offered them a townhouse as a wedding present.

Twin Enterprises owned numerous properties in the city of Atlanta and surrounding counties. Allen also made the offer to let them stay in one of his Downtown high-rises, free of charge, as a wedding gift.

Tyson told Allen that they appreciated the offer, but that they would think about it and get back with him. Tyson and Mallory left her parents' house to go to dinner. After dinner, they returned to Tyson's apartment.

When they entered the apartment, they kissed at the door for a long time. Mallory went to the bathroom and showered. After taking a shower, she came out of the bathroom wearing her robe. Tyson went in and showered after her. A few minutes later, he came out of the bathroom with nothing on. Mallory still had her robe on. As she lay in bed, Tyson went over to her and removed her robe. This was the first time any man had seen her unclad.

Tyson looked at her body with delight, thinking to himself, *'This was really worth the wait; she has a gorgeous body.'*

They began to kiss and make love. Undoubtedly, the lovemaking was nothing like she imagined. It was very painful, and Tyson wasn't as tender and gentle as he could have been.

When it was over, Mallory lay next to Tyson; her body trembling, obviously in pain. He held on to her, explaining to her that it always hurt the first time. He assured her it would be better the next time. In his mind, he was thinking that the only thing he didn't like about deflowering a virgin was that it was never pleasant for her, and he would always have to end up teaching her how to make love.

A short time later, Tyson wanted to make love again, but Mallory told him she was too sore. She wanted to wait a while. He agreed as he hugged and kissed her.

Tyson was a very good actor. He knew how to say the right things to women. He told her that they would try again in the morning. She felt relieved. He held on to her the whole night. The next morning when they woke up, Tyson told her that he would just wait until that night, because he knew she had to go to school. Mallory got up, got dressed and went off to class.

Tyson and Mallory now had been married four months. Tyson's rehab was back on schedule. He had been working extremely hard, trying to rehabilitate his knee so he could have a shot at playing in the NBA. Tyson's agent called with some good news. He had set up a workout with a scout from the Sacramento Kings. They met at a local gym so he could evaluate Tyson's progress. Tyson worked out for a whole hour for the Scout, but he couldn't elevate like he normally did before. The knee just wasn't healing the way he thought it should. So, the scout told him he needed more time to rehabilitate his knee. Tyson felt very depressed.

Two weeks later, Tyson tried out for another scout, this time from the Portland Trailblazers. That scout didn't like the way he moved and told him maybe he would be better off thinking about pursuing another career, because the knee was just not healing to their satisfaction. Tyson was devastated. He became totally depressed. He wanted a life with fame and money. It looked like it would never happen. While Mallory slept one night, Tyson settled on the couch contemplating on how he would make some money. He came up with a very diabolical way of getting it.

The following day, Tyson talked Mallory into buying a two-million-dollar life insurance policy. He had money stored away that he had received from some of the Georgia Tech Boosters. Mallory was quite concerned about why they needed to get such a large life insurance policy.

Tyson told her that he wanted to go sky-diving, something that he always wanted to do. He felt that if something were to happen to him, he wanted to make sure that she was well taken care of and did not have to depend on her parents. Mallory was usually a firm person and stern in her beliefs, but Tyson had a way of manipulating her and pushing her buttons, so she relented. Little did she know he was planning on using that two-million-dollar policy to his advantage.

CHAPTER 33

Tyson decided to call on an old friend in Houston with whom he'd previously had some shady business dealings. Tyson dialed the number and someone answered saying, "Speak your piece?"

Tyson responded, "What's up, fool?"

"Who da hell is this?"

Tyson laughed, "Oh, you trying to make believe you don't know who this is?"

The person on the other end of the line paused briefly, "Oh, is this T.J.?"

"Yeah, it's your boy T.J. What's up? Hey, I got a job for you. I need you to make somebody go away. Do you remember how we helped that white chick, Ms. Wingate?

There was a pause; then the person on the other end said, "I don't know what the hell you're talking about."

The phone suddenly went dead. Tyson called back repeatedly, but he was unsuccessful in reaching his party. Tyson thought to himself, *'What's the matter with this fool?'*

A few hours later, someone called Tyson from a phone number he did not recognize. He let the phone ring for an extended period of time before finally picking up.

The caller said, "It's me, Sonny."

Tyson said angrily, "Dude, I called you about a job and you hung up in my face. You pretended not to know what I'm talking about, but now you're calling me back five hours later. What's your problem? Have you started smoking that shit you're selling?"

Sonny responded, "First of all, I haven't heard from you in over three years and you call me to discuss some crooked shit that we did back in the day. I didn't know if you were trying to set me up or what."

Tyson laughed, "Sonny, come on dude, get real!"

"I am real! I'm as real as a heart attack."

Tyson took in a deep breath, "Dude, you are serious aren't you?"

Sonny replied, "Yeah, all day long!"

"Sonny, what do I need to do to convince you that I'm not trying to set you up?"

Sonny paused and said, "Well, just say what we did."

"Okay, I will. You, me and Rafael helped that white chick, Ms. Wingate, whack her old man."

"Who was the master mind behind this?"

Tyson responded, "It was me, I was the brains."

"Okay TJ, now what's up?"

"I need you and Rafael to help me make my wife go away."

"Your wife? I didn't know you were married."

"Yes, I got married almost a year ago. I know you heard about me blowing out my knee, right?"

"Yeah, I saw something about it on ESPN one night, but that was way last year."

"Sonny, I'm rehabbing now, but I feel like in a year or so I should be ready. Spoke to my agent the other day and he said he had at least two teams that are interested."

"Ok T.J. getting back to this job, what are you paying?"

"A hundred thousand."

"You got that kind of money laying around?"

"Well, I don't have the whole thing. When I first got here at Tech I met a whole lot of those wealthy boosters. I'm sure I got over a hundred and twenty-five thousand out of those people, but I spent most of the money. I'll front you fifty thousand right now; after the job is done, I'll give you the rest."

"So, how long do I have to wait for the other fifty thousand?"

"Well, I don't know but you'll have to wait until the two-million-dollar life insurance policy kicks in."

Sonny took a breath and said, "Whoa! Two million

288

dollars! T.J., that's a lot of money, man! That's going to send red flags up!"

"Sonny, it may send red flags up and it may not. I thought this thing out carefully, I'm the one who made her go and get the life insurance policy. I told her that I wanted to go sky-diving and mountain-climbing and I told her that she needed to get some life insurance because if anything happened to me she would be well taken care of. She tried to talk me out of going sky-diving, but I told her it was something I always wanted to do. *She bought the policy*, so I think that's a pretty good cover for me."

"I didn't know you were playing with that kind of money; you know? Two million and all I'm getting is a hundred thousand? Do you think that's fair?"

Tyson paused, "Ok, Sonny, I'll give you two hundred thousand and that's it. That's all I'm going to give you. If you don't want to do it for that, I'll have to find somebody else."

"You don't have to get anybody else. I'm down. Two-hundred grand is fair. Yeah, I see you really have thought this thing out, because you know any time there's a murder involved between married people, the spouse is always the primary suspect. Cops aren't dumb. Remember that."

"Sonny, I have a perfect alibi. When the job goes down, I'm going to be on a fishing trip with her father. Sounds like a plan to me."

"T.J., I see you have an air tight alibi."

"Hey, Sonny, I'm assuming that you are going to get Rafael involved in this, right?"

"No, he's back in Colombia, but I got another guy; he's in Mexico right now. He comes and goes back and forth into the country."

"Is he legal?"

"Yeah, T.J., he's legal."

"Good. He's going to need the proper ID because he's

289

going to have to board a plane."

"If he doesn't have the proper ID, T.J., he can always drive here."

"Oh no, Sonny, he's going to have to fly, 'cause I don't want to run the risk of anybody driving to Atlanta. He could get stopped by the police or something. I mean coming here, he'll have to travel through three states, that's Louisiana, Mississippi, and Alabama. No, I don't want to run the risk. He's going to have to fly."

"Ok, T.J., that's fine."

"I'm going to let you handle all the details from your end."

"I can assure you, he'll have the proper ID to fly to Atlanta."

"When are you and her old man going on that fishing trip?"

"In about three weeks."

"Ok, that should give us enough time. T.J., tell you what I want you to do. Get yourself a *throw down phone*."

"What's a throw down phone?"

"It's a pre-paid phone. I suggest that you go to a flea market where you don't have to provide any ID. Just buy a phone with some minutes on it. And make sure that after you do that, you call me from that cell phone. Because any time it's a murder investigation, the first thing police start doing is a checking phone records. They check the phone records of the living spouse and the victim."

"Dude, you're pretty clever!" Tyson replied, "How did you learn all of this stuff?"

"I watch a lot of those cop shows like *Unsolved Murders*."

"I think I may start watching them too, Sonny."

"T.J., when you get the throw down phone, text me the number, so when you call, I'll know it's you."

"Ok, dude, later." They ended the conversation.

The following day, Tyson did just as Sonny suggested and purchased a pre-paid phone. Five days into the murder plot,

ONE MORE MIRACLE

Tyson sent Sonny pictures of the inside and outside layout of his apartment. He sent those pictures via email. He wanted Sonny to be somewhat familiar with his surroundings. He also took pictures of the street leading into the complex, so the hit man wouldn't have any problems getting back to the Interstate and to the airport when he made his getaway.

At 7:30 that evening, Tyson and Mallory were in the living room sitting on the couch. Tyson pretended to be a loving and affectionate husband. Mallory was laying with her head on his lap, watching TV. He leaned down and kissed her passionately. "I'll be glad when these two years are over and you'll have graduated with your degree and we can start our family."

She looked up and said, "Oh Baby, we're on the same page! I want to be a mommy so badly!"
"And I want you to be a mommy, too."

A week later, Sonny called Tyson and told him to wire him a thousand dollars for a plane ticket for the hit man, Marco. Tyson honored the request. He wired the money to a local **Kroger Store** in Houston. However, three days before the hit, there was a snag in the plan. Mallory had accepted a speaking engagement at a Parochial School in, of all places, Houston! When Tyson came home from school, Mallory broke the news to him. Obviously he was livid, because in his mind, he and Sonny had worked out the perfect plan. Now it seemed like a potential monkey wrench had been thrown in the plan. This was quite disconcerting to him.

Mallory and Tyson had a heated discussion over her surprise trip to Houston. Tyson repeatedly asked Mallory why she didn't consult him before accepting her Godmother's invitation to speak at the school. Mallory had a legitimate reason, saying to him she didn't think it was a big deal. He and her dad were going on a fishing trip out of town Friday, anyway. He was so angry with her that he stormed out of the house. He drove a few blocks down to a convenience store, parked there, and

291

phoned Sonny.

When Sonny answered, Tyson said dejectedly, "Hey man, I don't think this thing is going to happen."

Sonny responded in an angry voice, "What the hell you mean it's not going to happen?"

"She's not going to be home Friday morning. She's going to be in Houston."

"She's coming to Houston? What for?"

"Her Godmother is the principal of a school down there. She asked her to come and give a speech at some awards dinner. I think she's also going to be doing some recruiting for Tech."

Sonny was quiet for a few minutes, then said with excitement, "T.J., this may be the best thing in the world!"

"Why you say that?"

"Look at it this way. She can be whacked here and it may be easier. Think about it—all the focus will be off you. You're going to be on a fishing trip with her old man. Look at it this way: this trip to Houston is a gift! Nobody can tie you to anything! This is going to be a good day after all! I'll get back with you in about an hour. I'm going to have to tweak this plan. Talk to you later."

Tyson responded, "Okay, later."

An hour later, Sonny called Tyson back with a new plan.

"Hey, man, this is the new plan. I'll pretend to be a cab driver. I got a cousin who has cab, I'll borrow his and pick her up at Bush Airport here in Houston. By the way, what time does her flight get here?"

"She'll be landing in Houston at 9:00 a.m."

"Once she's inside the cab, I'll pick up Marco. We'll take her to a remote location, kill her and then text you a photo of her body. Man, make sure to tell her I'm your cousin, Sonny and I have some important papers to send you concerning some family property."

ONE MORE MIRACLE

Tyson was elated. He thought it was a fantastic plan
and couldn't wait for Sonny and Marco to carry it out.
Sonny continued saying to Tyson, "Once the job is done, I want
you to wire my money to a P.O. Box in the Dominican Republic.
I'll give you the address later. I have a girlfriend down there
who'll pick it up and wire it back to me in Houston."

Before hanging up, Sonny also told Tyson to make
sure the morning that Mallory was leaving to take some photos
of what she is wearing and text them to him, so he'll know
exactly what she looks like. They ended the conversation with
Tyson thanking Sonny for everything.

After driving around for an hour, Tyson returned home.
Mallory was already in bed. He went to the bedroom, but didn't
go in. He framed himself in the doorway, speaking softly, calling
her name, "Mallory, are you asleep? Mallory Baby, I'm sorry I
blew up at you."

She suddenly sat up and turned on a small lamp that sat
on the night stand. She turned and faced him, still angry and
said, "Tyson, I'm sick and tired of you storming out of the house
like a three-year-old every time we get into an argument or when
you don't get your way! Why can't we sit down and discuss
things! I'm an adult woman and you are an adult man! We're
husband and wife. We're two people in love. When a husband
and wife have disagreements, they should always find common
ground to resolve whatever they're going through. That's not
what we've been doing lately."

Tyson said softly, "You're right, Mallory. You're
absolutely right. I'm going to have to do better."

She was surprised by his candor and the fact that he was
willing to admit that he was at fault. He then told her he would
try to become a better husband. She quickly reached for him. He
maneuvered his way over to her.

She then said, "I'm going to try and become a better, more
understanding wife."

The next morning before going to school, Tyson revealed to Mallory that he had a cousin, Sonny, who drove a cab in Houston and he would arrange for him to pick her up at the airport. Mallory told him that wouldn't be necessary because her Godmother would be happy to get her. That's when Tyson told her the story that Sonny made up about some special papers his cousin had for him. She agreed to let the cousin pick her up from the airport.

On the morning of the trip, Tyson and Mallory got out of bed early. It was 5:00 a.m., when the alarm clock went off. Tyson got out of bed first, and Mallory soon followed. She proceeded on into the bathroom while Tyson used the guest bathroom to shower. Naturally like most men, within a few minutes he was finished. However, Mallory chose to soak in the bathtub for awhile.

It was 5:30 a.m. when Tyson opened the door to the bathroom saying to her,

"Baby, you need to get a move on! It's 5:30!"
She smiled, "Okay Baby, I'm coming out."

He then closed the door. He went to the kitchen and put on a pot of coffee. Mallory came from a family that thoroughly enjoyed an early morning cup of coffee. Tyson then reached into the refrigerator and got himself a beer. He demolished it in about three gulps, then put the empty bottle in the trash to hide the evidence. Mallory didn't approve of his drinking early in the morning. She soon appeared in the kitchen wearing her bathrobe. She poured herself a cup of coffee, then poured one for him. They sat for a few minutes and drank their coffee together.

It was 6:15 a.m. when Tyson helped Mallory put her luggage into the trunk of her car. She was dressed comfortably for her flight, wearing a pair of red, loose-fitting Capri pants, red Nike tennis shoes, and a white button-down blouse.

Tyson marveled at how beautiful his wife looked, saying to her, "Oh Baby, you look so sexy. You look like a Dreamsicle to me."

She smiled, "Thank you, honey."

He then embraced her, pulling her close to him, kissing her passionately for a long moment. When he released her, he suddenly removed the pre-paid phone from his top shirt pocket saying, "Wait a minute Baby, let me take your picture."

She accommodated him, smiling, displaying her best supermodel expression: throwing her head back, and leaning her body back with her hands on her hips. She went through a collection a poses, her final one being serious. The rising sun seemed to create the perfect backdrop, as the fragmented sunlight peaked through the clouds, creating an imaginary halo over her. Her blue eyes had never looked more brilliant. These photos were truly synonymous with the nickname she had been given as a child. Mallory indeed looked like an Angel.

When Tyson finished taking the last shot, Mallory noticed his pre-paid phone.

She asked, "Where did you get that little rinky-dink phone?"

He quickly explained, "Oh Baby, I dropped my phone in some water. When I took it to the phone store, they said they couldn't repair it. So, they gave me this phone. My **I-Phone** didn't have insurance, so I took the free phone."

"Tyson, you could have easily written a check or used one of our credit cards. You could have gotten you another **I-Phone**, if that's what you wanted."

"Mallory, we agreed to stay on a budget."

"Yes we did, but in this case you could have gone ahead and gotten another **I-Phone!**"

"No, I'm not! I'm going to stick to our budget."

She smiled, "You are really becoming the perfect husband."

He shook his head, "No, not yet. I'm trying to get there, trust me!"

"Come on Baby, give me a kiss. I've got to go. I hope

295

you and Dad catch the biggest fish out of everyone on the boat."
They kissed for the last time. Mallory got in her car and headed
for the airport. As Mallory drove off, Tyson texted the pictures
to Sonny.

Forty-five minutes later, she arrived at **Hartsville
Airport**. The flight left Atlanta on time, at 8:15 a.m., Eastern
Standard Time. The plane touched down at **Bush
Intercontinental Airport** at 8:45 a.m., Central Standard Time.
The two-hour flight was a smooth ride. Because of the time
difference, the passengers gained an extra hour when landing at
Bush.

It was 9:07 a.m. when Mallory retrieved her luggage
from the basement floor of the airport. She caught the escalator
to the main floor. Waiting for her was a tall, burly, brown-skin
man, carrying a sign: <u>Mallory January</u>.
"Hello, are you Mallory?"
"Yes, I am."
"I'm Tyson cousin, Sonny. Please to meet you."
"The pleasure's all mine."
After exchanging pleasantries, he helped her with her luggage
and they walked out of the airport's revolving doors. Waiting
outside was a cab driver, a Hispanic male with a heavy accent. It
was 9:20 a.m., when they left Bush Airport.

Meanwhile, back in Atlanta, Allen and Tyson were
relaxing on a fishing boat. Allen appeared to be undisturbed,
having a good time, but Tyson was on edge. He kept looking at
his watch in anticipation. It was 1:15 p.m. He thought to himself,
*'Mallory has been in Houston for almost five hours and nothing
from Sonny. I hope everything went off without a glitch.'*

One thing that made Tyson feel optimistic was that he
had dialed Mallory's cell phone three times and she had not
answered. He had left her three voice messages and he knew it
was not like her to not call him back.

At 3:05 p.m., Tyson received a text. He and Allen

were at their fishing stations next to each other. He turned to
Allen and told him he'd be right back; he had to use the restroom.
He went down to the cabin of the boat, took out his phone and
opened up the text.

Sonny sent him a photo of a woman lying face-down
in a field, with a gunshot wound to the back of the head. She had
on red Capri pants, red Nike tennis shoes, and a white blouse.
Standing over her body was a Latino man with a forty-five,
semi-automatic handgun in his hand. He had on a red bandana,
and he was giving the thumbs up sign over the body, a devious
smile on his face.

Tyson smiled, knowing that the devilish deed had
been carried out. In a few weeks, he'd be a very wealthy man! He
displayed tendencies of a true sociopath. He had no remorse for
what he had done. He had no feelings for anybody. In his own
conniving, befuddled mind, he felt entitled to the two million
dollars. He went back to the top of the boat and resumed his
position at his fishing station.

It was 7:00 p.m., when Tyson returned home from the
fishing trip. At 7:30 p.m., he received a call from Sonny, giving
him final instructions on how to send him the money to the
Dominican Republic.

After hanging up with Sonny, Tyson went into the
garage and removed a shoebox from a top shelf, where he had a
plastic bag of marijuana. He came back into the house, sat down
at the kitchen table, and rolled several joints.

He went to the pantry and took out a fifth of **Jack
Daniels** and poured himself a big glass. He drank half of it
straight, before sitting the glass down on the cocktail table. He
then lit one of the joints and began to smoke it. Talking loudly to
himself, he began, "Well, I don't have to hide anymore. I can
smoke all the weed I want, anytime I want! I don't have to worry
about her saying anything to me anymore."

It was 8:00 p.m. when the house phone rang. The phone

297

sat next to him. He looked at the caller ID and knew it was from the Williams' residence. When he picked up the phone Teresa was on the other end.

"Hi, Mom."

"Hello!"

Tyson could hear the desperation in her voice when she said, "Tyson, have you heard anything from Mallory?"

"No mom, I haven't. I've called her six or seven times and left messages, but she hasn't returned my calls. Have you talked to her?"

"No, I haven't. Her Godmother called a few minutes ago and said that she hadn't heard a word from her, either. I called the airlines and I know she got off the plane in Houston and apparently took a cab. That's all we know."

"Mom, this is so out of character for Mallory, because she always calls. I am really worried."

"Yes, so am I, son."

"Mom, if you hear anything, please call me. Please let me know immediately and I'll do the same."

"I certainly will, Tyson; I certainly will."

"Mom, does she know anyone else in Houston besides her Godmother."

"No, Tyson…no one else."

"I tell you what, Mom, if I don't hear anything from her tonight, first thing in the morning I'm going to Houston."

"Well, if that's the case, her dad and I will be going to Houston, also."

Before hanging up, Tyson said, "Mom, I love you."

Teresa paused for a long moment and then said, "Yes, Tyson, me too."

She then hung up.

Tyson then poured himself another glass of Jack Daniels and fired up another joint. Thirty minutes had gone by before Tyson called Mallory's cell phone again, knowing very well that she wasn't going to answer. When the voicemail came on, he left her a message, "Mallory, this is your husband. We haven't heard anything from you. Your parents are worried and so am I. Where in the hell are you? Please call me." He then hung up.

A few minutes later, he called her cell phone number again. It was almost like he had lost touch with reality or, perhaps it was the effects of the alcohol and marijuana. Tyson drifted off to sleep with his head on the kitchen table.

It was 10:42 p.m. when the house phone rang again. Tyson reached for the receiver picking it up, fumbling with it, then eventually dropping it to the floor. Still highly inebriated, he leaned forward, almost falling out of the chair. Finally, he picked up the receiver. It was Allen on the other end. Allen told him that Teresa had just gotten off the phone with Mallory's Godmother for the fourth time, and they still hadn't heard one word from Mallory. Mallory's Godmother informed the police of her disappearance.

Allen revealed to Tyson that he was leaving for Houston first thing in the morning. One of Allen's business partners had made his private liner jet available to him.

Tyson inquired, "I thought Mom was coming too?"

Allen explained that Teresa didn't want to leave her mom home alone. Ms. Hunter was also not feeling well. Tyson told Allen that he would be packing a bag tonight and would be prepared to accompany him to Houston in the morning. Allen agreed.

CHAPTER 34

At 8:22 a.m. the next morning, Allen and Tyson boarded the Liner jet, and left Atlanta heading for Houston. An hour and thirty minutes later, the jet landed at **Hobby Airport**. Allen and Tyson took a cab and went directly to Police Headquarters in Downtown Houston. Allen had talked to someone in the department prior to leaving Atlanta and was expected. When Tyson and Allen got out of the cab and entered the building, they emptied their valuables into two small containers, went straight through the metal detectors, and received them on the other end

They caught the elevator and went to the fourth floor where a female uniformed officer sat at a round desk.

Allen walked up to the desk and informed her that he was there to file a **Missing Person's Report** on his daughter. The officer buzzed her supervisor's phone. Within seconds, an office door opened, about fifteen feet to the right of them. A medium height, silver-gray haired man with penetrating eyes and a stoic face stepped out of the office. They exchanged greetings in the hallway. The man introduced himself as Senior Captain William Sampson of the Homicide Division. Allen introduced himself and then Tyson. Captain Sampson invited them inside his office.

Once inside, Tyson and Allen took a seat facing the Captain's desk. The Captain sat in a swivel chair and looked directly at them. Allen then said, "I'm here to file a Missing Person's Report on my daughter, Mallory Williams-January. I called and spoke with a night supervisor and made him aware of the situation. He told me that once I landed here in Houston, I could come straight here to the Police Department and file a report, so that's why I'm here."

With a trenchant gaze and a sympathetic tone, Captain Sampson said, "Gentleman, it grieves me to tell you this. Last night, a body was found by a night highway crew, about four miles East of Bush Airport. The body matched the description given to us by your daughter's Godmother, a Mrs. Jada Rachal. Identification found on the body pretty much confirmed, Sir, that the body is your daughter, Mrs. Mallory Williams-January. We found a Georgia drivers' license with her name and address on it. She had four hundred dollars in cash and two major credit cards, so that pretty much rules out robbery as a motive for this murder. Sir, we have your daughter's belongings in the property room. Once this interview is over, you can claim her belongings. We also found her cell phone. She had a series of missed calls, so obviously someone had been trying to call her. An autopsy will be preformed sometime today and then we'll release the body to you. Mr. January, Mr. Williams, I'm certainly sorry for your loss."

Tyson abruptly cried out hysterically, "No, this can't be true! No, I don't believe it! This can't be true!"
He buried his head into his hands, remembering what Sonny told him. He had traces of black pepper on his hands to make it easier for him to shed tears. Allen sat speechless, in a state of shock. No, he couldn't believe the news he had just heard. Allen appeared to have some difficulty breathing. Captain Sampson noticed it right away.
He shouted, "Mr. Williams, are you okay?"
He was unresponsive.
Captain Sampson shouted again, "Mr. Williams, are you okay?"
Still, no answer.

Tyson turned around and grabbed his hand, "Dad, dad, are you okay?"
Allen whispered, "I'm having some trouble breathing."

Captain Sampson ran to the door and alerted the female officer to call for help now!
Within minutes, the paramedics arrived, placed Allen on a stretcher and connected him to a heart monitor. The monitor

301

indicated that he had an irregular heartbeat. He was quickly whisked off to **St. Joseph Hospital** in Downtown Houston.

Tyson wanted to go with him in the ambulance, but was asked by Captain Sampson to stay and answer a few questions. He was told that when he finished with the interview, an officer would drive him over to the hospital to be with his father-in-law. Shortly after Allen was taken to the hospital, Captain Sampson and Tyson went back into his office. Captain Sampson closed the door, sat back down at his desk and faced Tyson.

"Mr. January, I'm not going to keep you long. I'd like to reiterate that I am really sorry for your loss. You have my deepest sympathy."

Tyson looked up at him and said passionately, "Thank you, Sir. Captain, I want you to promise me one thing."

He replied, "Well if I can, but normally I don't make promises. Let's hear what's on your mind."

"Will you please promise me that you'll catch the bastard who did this to my wife? Will you please promise me that you'll catch him?"

Captain Sampson stared at him for a long moment and said, emphatically, "SON, THAT'S A PROMISE I CAN MAKE AND KEEP! Mr. January, what's so mind-boggling about your wife's murder is that robbery wasn't the motive, she wasn't sexually assaulted and she was a stranger to this city. I find it so hard to connect the dots to this murder."

Tyson paused, "Oh, I guess it's crazy people everywhere."

Captain Sampson nodded, "I guess you're right. Mr. January, an autopsy is going to be done today on your wife. When it's finished, the Medical Examiner's Office will release the body to you."

Before Tyson could respond, there was an unexpected tap on the door. Captain Sampson shouted, "Come in!"

Two men entered the office. One was black, about 6'4", weighing around three hundred pounds. He looked as if he could have been an NFL defensive end. The other officer was a short Latino male with a bushy mustache and a receding hair line. Captain Sampson introduced the men as Sergeants D.J. Patterson and W.L. Cantu. He explained to Tyson that the two were detectives investigating his wife's murder.

Sergeant Patterson temporarily left the room and went across the hall to retrieve a chair from another office. He then came back to the office and joined the interrogation. Sampson looked at Tyson and said, "Mr. January, I'm not going to keep you long. I just want to ask you a few questions. I know you want to get to the hospital where your father-in-law is. Mr. January, what was your wife wearing when she left home yesterday morning?"

"She was wearing a pair of red Capri pants, a white blouse, some red tennis shoes."

"Mr. January, do you owe anybody any money?"

"No sir, I don't."

"Mr. January, who do you think did this? Have you made any enemies lately?"

"No Sir, I haven't. I don't have any idea who could have done a terrible thing like this."

"Sir, did you love your wife?"

"Yes Sir, with all of my heart!"

"Did you and your wife argue excessively?"

"No Sir, we never argued at all!"

"How long were you married?"

"We've been...er...we were married for ten months."

"Oh, no wonder you didn't argue much. You probably spent all your time trying to get to know each other."

"Yes Sir, that's about the size of it."

Tyson's eyes began to water again from the burning of the black pepper. He broke down again and started to cry, mumbling, "I don't know what I'm going to do without my wife! She was my world; she meant everything to me. I'm going to be

lost without her."
His body began to shake as he attempted to cry.

Captain Sampson continued to stare at him. He finally said,
"Mr. January, please try to calm down. Can we get you
anything? Water? A soda?"

Tyson looked up at him and said, "Yes Sir, I'll take a can of
soda."
Captain Sampson went in his wallet, brought out a dollar bill,
and tossed it to Sergeant Patterson, "Hey, go out to the coke
machine and bring him a soda."

Within minutes, Sergeant Patterson came back with a Coke
and handed it to Tyson. Captain Sampson's cell phone rang
suddenly. He reached into his coat pocket, pulled it out and
answered it. He whispered inaudibly to the party on the other
line. He then turned to the two detectives and said, "Hey, excuse
me. This is the wife and I'm going to have to take this call
outside. I'll be back in a few."
He stepped out of the office.

Detective Patterson resumed the interrogation, saying to
Tyson, "Mr. January, what time did your wife leave Atlanta?"

"I think her plane left a little after eight."

"When she arrived here in Houston, did she call you?
Did you call her?"

"Well, no Sir. Not as soon as she landed. I did try to
contact her several times during the day, because I was
concerned why I hadn't heard anything from her."

"Mr. January, did your wife know anyone else in
Houston besides her Godmother?"

"No Sir. As far as I know, she didn't."

"Was this her first trip to Houston?"
"Yes Sir."

Sergeant Cantu followed with, "Mr. January, how many
times did you try to call your wife yesterday?"

"I really don't know. I called her several times. Well I'll

say, at least five or six times."

"When you didn't hear from her, were you overly concerned?"

"Well, I don't know about overly concerned, but I was concerned."

"Oh, so you're saying that your wife was in a city that she'd never been to, you hadn't heard from her all day, and you were just *'concerned, but not overly concerned'*?"

"Maybe I said the wrong thing. I was deeply concerned; as a matter of fact, I was worried out of my mind."

"Mr. January, why was your wife here in Houston?"

"She was here on a speaking engagement. Captain Sampson asked me that same question. I'll tell you the same thing I told him. She was here to speak at this Parochial Girls' School. Her Godmother is the principal there."

"Oh, I'm sorry. I didn't know the Captain had already posed that question to you."

Captain Sampson then reentered the room. He apologized for his absence saying, "Gentlemen, I'm sorry I had to leave. That was my wife and you know how demanding wives can be."

He sat back down.

Sergeant Cantu began to stare at Tyson. He became extremely irritated. Sergeant Cantu finally said, "I know you from somewhere. I'm almost one hundred percent sure I know you."

Tyson shook his head, "Well, I don't know you."

Sergeant Patterson then said, "I think I know you, too."

Tyson shrugged his shoulders, "Well, maybe you do."

Sergeant Patterson stared at him, smiled and then said, "I know where I know you from."

Tyson asked, "Where do you know me from?"

"You played ball for Georgia Tech, didn't you?"

Tyson nodded, "Yes, I did."

Tyson thought to himself, *'That seems like so long ago.'*
Sergeant Patterson then turned to Cantu and said, "See, he
played ball for Georgia Tech. Is that where you know him
from?"

Sergeant Cantu shook his head, "No, I don't really keep up
with college basketball. I'm almost one hundred percent sure that
I know Mr. January from somewhere else."

Tyson then spoke with contempt in his voice, "Sir, I'm
absolutely sure I've never seen you before in my life!"

Captain Sampson then glared at Sergeant Cantu,
"Like Sergeant Patterson said, this guy was a star basketball
player. Maybe you've seen him on television. But if he says he
doesn't know you, I'm inclined to believe him."

Captain Sampson focused his attention back on Tyson
and said, "You see these two guys here? They're two of the best
homicide detectives in this department. They are also members
of our **Cold Case Unit**. Since they joined the CCU, in the past
three years they have gone back and solved four previously
unsolved murders! Four murders that no one thought would ever
be solved! So, you need to take this into consideration. These
guys will definitely solve your wife's murder case. But getting
back to Willie, sometimes he can be overzealous when
interrogating a suspect."

Tyson cut his eyes sharply at Captain Sampson, "Oh, you
consider me a suspect?"

With a serious expression, Captain Sampson responded,
"No, not at all."

Tyson's body relaxed as he sat back in the chair. Captain
Sampson said to him, "Mr. January, I hope you will indulge me
for a minute. I'd like to prove something to Willie here. When we
finish, I'll have them to take you over to the hospital so you can
see about your father-in-law. Mr. January, have you ever met a
famous athlete? I know that you are a celebrity in your own
right, but when you were a kid, did you ever meet one of your

sports idols?"

"Yes, I met Magic Johnson once."

"Were you excited?"

"Oh yes Sir, I was. He was my favorite basketball player."

"Mr. January, when I was a kid I tried my hand at boxing. My idol was Muhammad Ali. At the boxing camp that I attended as a kid, the boxing instructor was a friend of Muhammad Ali's. He arranged for Muhammad Ali to come and visit us at the Center. When I got my chance to meet him, it was like a dream come true! I got him to autograph one of my boxing gloves. That was icing on the cake! That was the best feeling in the world! I had finally met my idol! Like most people, when you meet celebrities, especially the ones that you idolize, man, you get so excited! You start experiencing endorphins in your brain. The excitement can be overwhelming. On the other hand, when I first met Sergeant Cantu here, about seven years ago, I didn't feel anything."

Sergeant Cantu looked at him and smiled.

"The point I'm trying to make is, when you meet a celebrity, somebody that you really admire, just their presence consumes you!"

Tyson flashed a deceitful smile as he thought to himself, *'What in the hell is this screwball, red neck talking about?'*

"Yep Mr. January, for a whole week the only thing I thought about was how my idol, Muhammad Ali, had shaken my hand. I showed his autograph off to everybody. Man, I was really, really, happy, because he was somebody important. You get my drift? You can also experience endorphins, when you're feeling pain or if you have been traumatized. In some cases, you might experience the feeling if you come across someone who happens to remind you of something bad that happened in your past. You experience those same endorphins, but in a negative way."

Tyson inquired, "Sir, is any of what you're saying, based

on scientific facts? And what about my wife? Aren't we supposed to be here to find out what happened to her?"
Captain Sampson continued to ramble, "Mr. January, I guess you could say some of it may be based on Science. Most of it is just based on my silly opinion, that's all. Mr. January, do you have a dollar?"

Tyson look surprised, "Yes Sir. Do you want your dollar back for the soda you bought me?"

Captain Sampson laughed, "Oh no, Sir, I'm going to play a little game with you."

He responded with anger, "Sir, I came here in search of my missing wife. When my father-in-law and I got here, we were faced with the grim reality that she was killed. Please don't trivialize her death by asking me to play a game with you."

"Mr. January, I'm not trivializing your wife's death by any means; we take murder seriously! Maybe I used the wrong terminology. This is not about a game. I'm trying to prove a point, that's all."

Captain Sampson then went in his wallet, took out a one-hundred-dollar bill and placed it on the table.
He gazed into Tyson's eyes, "Where is your dollar?"

Tyson reached into his pocket, unfolded some ones, and put it next to Captain Sampson's hundred-dollar bill. Captain Sampson then said to him, "I'll wager you a hundred dollars to one that I can get you to admit to something that you're not aware of."

Tyson showed his frustration, saying, "Look Captain, I don't want your hundred dollars and here's your dollar back. Let's get this over with, this contest, game or whatever it is, so I can get over to the hospital, and see about my father-in-law."

"Like I said, the first time I saw Muhammad Ali, I was gleeful and I was starry-eyed. The first time you saw Sergeant Willie Cantu, you were excited, and very happy, too. I guarantee you, you experienced the same endorphins I felt when I met

ONE MORE MIRACLE

Muhammad Ali."

Tyson went into a rage, "Sir, I don't know what you're talking about. I've never ever met this man. I've never seen Sergeant Cantu, nor Sergeant Patterson. You people are f-ing wack! Are you guys real police officers? Or are you a bunch of clowns? Captain, this line of questioning is stupid! What does any of this have to do with the price of tea in China?"

Captain Sampson laughed. "Mr. January it doesn't have anything to do with the price of tea in China or the price of coffee in Houston. Perhaps all the while, I was phrasing the question incorrectly. Maybe you haven't met Willie Cantu in person, but I guarantee you've seen him. I'm going to repeat, Mr. January, you are right, this doesn't have anything to do with the price of tea in China or the price of coffee in Houston, but it has everything to do with SOLICITATION OF CAPITAL MURDER!"

Tyson sat in his chair, stunned. Captain Sampson then said to Sergeant Cantu, "Willie, do you have that red bandana?"
He smiled, "Sure!"
"Put it on."

He went into his pocket, removed the bandana and tied it on his head. Captain Sampson informed Tyson, "It was Willie who texted you that picture, standing over your wife's body with a gun in his hand. Mr. January, I guess the main reason you didn't recognize Sergeant Cantu is that we doctored up his picture. With the help of photo shop, we removed his mustache. His bushy mustache is sort of a trademark around here. When he walked into the room, you would have recognized him right away, so we doctored up the photo. See, on the altered picture he texted you, he doesn't have a mustache."

Sergeant Cantu took out his cell phone, opened up the text and attempted to show the picture to Tyson. He refused to look at the picture.

Captain Sampson continued, "When he texted you that

picture, you saw him but he didn't see you, so I just had it mixed up. And another thing— your wife is not dead. She is downstairs in an office, along with her father. Your father-in-law didn't have a heart attack, Mr. January; he's fine. All of this was a plan, just like you planned to kill your wife. WE SET YOU UP! WE PLANNED TO CATCH YOU, AND WE GOT YOU!

Some information was brought to our attention that you were the mastermind in the *Wingate Murder* four years ago. We just couldn't figure out how we were going to get you to admit your role in that murder."

Tyson responded firmly, "Man, I don't know what you're talking about! I may be guilty of trying to have my wife murdered, but this other murder? Y'all ain't pinning this on me!"

Captain Sampson smiled, "Well, that's not the story your boy, Elroy 'Sonny' Brown, is telling. Sonny told us you were the mastermind in the Wingate Murder, and that Rafael Lopez was the trigger man. Mr. January, we have you on tape admitting that you were the mastermind behind the Wingate murder. Don't you remember when you called Sonny and he hung up on you, only to call you back a few hours later. We got you then. Sonny said all he did was help bury Mr. Wingate's body."

"That's entrapment!"

"No Mr. January, that's a confession."

With a clever grin, he continued, "I know you're probably wondering why Sonny would drop you in the grease now, after all this time. It's been almost five years since the murder was committed. Well, Sonny got himself in a little jam. Let me correct what I've just said— Sonny got himself in a *big jam*. When Narcotics Officers busted Sonny, they found ten kilos of cocaine in his SUV. Sonny, being a two-time offender, was looking at life in prison. That's when Sonny approached the D.A.

The D.A. then put a deal on the table for Sonny. If we could get you to confess that you were the mastermind behind

310

the Wingate murder, the cocaine charges could possibly go
away. Sonny would be looking at, hmmmm, let's say maybe five
to ten years in prison or perhaps probation, for his part of the
murder.

We tried to get Sonny to call you to try and set you up over
the phone. Sonny told us you were far too smart for that, and you
would never admit anything over the phone. Lo and behold, *you*
called Sonny with a proposition for him. You wanted him to help
'make your wife go away'. No one could have written a better
script, Mr. January. Everything you and Sonny talked about we
have on tape. Everything worked out in our favor!

The morning that your wife landed here in Houston, she
was met at the airport by Sergeant Patterson and Sergeant Cantu.
She was unaware that they were police officers. She thought that
Willie was the cab driver and she assumed that Darrell was the
cousin that you had lied to her about. She left in the cab with
them. When they were about, oh, I guess half a mile from Bush
Airport, we had a marked unit pull them over. That's when I got
out of the car with a uniformed officer and introduced myself.

I told her that I knew her dad's cousin, Captain Bill
Williams, with the **Atlanta PD**. We told your wife that you
plotted to have her killed for insurance money. Of course, she
didn't believe it. She cried uncontrollably. We had to have
Captain Williams to talk to her by phone to calm her down. Then
we played a tape with you and Sonny for her to hear.

After hearing the tape, your wife was forced to believe
the truth. When she called her mother, we briefed Mrs. Williams
right away. We did a three-way call with Captain Williams and
he filled your mother-in-law in on all the details. Your mother-
in-law convinced Mrs. January to cooperate with our plan. We
took her over to the field and had her lay down. We had some
help from a makeup artist to make it appeared as if she had a
gun-shot wound in the back of her head. It was Willie who text
you the picture. When your father-in-law got back home from

the fishing trip, Mrs. Williams filled him in. We wanted your father-in-law to bring you here to us. You were hand delivered here to HPD and that's exactly what we wanted.

As for the Wingate case, Ms. Wingate is now living in the Hamptons. We've contacted police there. She was arrested and is fighting extradition. In a week or so, she'll be back here in Houston to face charges. And as far as the trigger man, Rafael Lopez, is concerned, we learned that he was killed in Colombia by federal police. He was running drugs down there when fate caught up with him.   Mr. January, I think you're facing a long time behind bars."

With a deep sigh, Tyson asked, "Captain, do you think the D.A. has a deal for me?"

Sampson shook his head, "No, there was only one deal and Sonny got it. Mr. January, your wife really loved you. It took a lot to convince her to believe that you wanted to have her killed."

Tyson sat in the chair stone-faced. He looked up and said to Captain Sampson, "I need to see my wife! Please, just let me tell her how sorry I am. Please, that is so important to me; that's all I ask. I just need to see Mallory and tell her that *I'm really sorry*. I love her and I hope that she'll forgive me!"

"Mr. January, I'm going to go downstairs. I will deliver the message, and if she wants to see you, I'll bring her up here. Hold on for a minute."

He left the room and went downstairs, where Mallory and her father were. A few minutes later, he returned with both of them. If Mallory's scornful look could kill, Tyson would be dead in his tracks. Allen looked on with venom in his eyes.

Mallory finally cried out, "Tyson…how could you do this to me? *I loved you so much!!* All I wanted to do is be a good wife to you."

Tyson broke down sobbing, "I'm so sorry, Baby," digesting Mallory's disdain, as he reached out to her.

ONE MORE MIRACLE

"Tyson, you're not sorry!" Mallory's voice cracked as she jerked back from his touch. "You're not capable of being sorry because *you have no heart*! The only thing that you're sorry for is that your plan was foiled!"

"No Baby, no! I'm sorry, honest! You've got to forgive me. I must have been out of my mind...."

Mallory didn't allow him to utter another word as she charged over to him in blinding rage and struck him with a closed fist, drawing blood from his lip.

Stunned, Tyson replied, "I deserved that..."

Mallory turned and ambled out of the room in grave silence. Before he left, Allen said with deep disgust, "You're the worst piece of shit I've ever seen in my life. You have no idea how much I want to kill you right now."

Tyson lowered his head in shame as Allen walked out of the office.

After Mallory and her father leave, Sergeant Patterson reads Tyson his Miranda rights.

Captain Sampson looks at him, shaking his head, "Mr. January, all I can say is I really pity you. You had a beautiful wife and you both are so young! You had so much promise...to just throw it all away; it's really silly, really sad."

Tyson responded sadly, "I just wish I could change things. I just wish I could go back and change things..."

Sampson looked at him with no sympathy and replied, "Well, that's what all criminals say when they're caught!"

CHAPTER 35

A short time later, Mallory and her dad left police headquarters and headed to Hobby Airport. When they arrived there, the police officer took them to a private landing strip adjacent to the main airport. He parked the car, got out, and helped Mallory with her luggage. The pilot stood outside of the plane and greeted his two passengers. His co-pilot was still in the plane, checking the controls and the flight data. Allen turned to the police officer, gave him a firm handshake, and thanked him for the ride. The officer gave Mallory a sincere nod and a smile, which she returned.

Within minutes, Mallory and her dad were secure in their seats. One of the luxuries of flying in a private jet was one could escape the scrutiny of metal detectors and body scans. Soon, the plane was airborne.

Mallory sat quietly across from her dad who appeared to be taking a cat nap. She was in a sedate state of mind but, her body was still alert. Ingrained in her head were memories of Tyson. Her inner voice said, *'I can't think of him because, if I do, I'll only hate him. But I can't hate him because I'm not made that way. When you hate someone whose wronged you, then you're no better than they are. When I think about him, I only have pity for him in my heart.'*

Her father suddenly opened his eyes and looked over at her. "What's on your mind, Angel?"

"Oh daddy, *everything.*"

"Angel, don't think about everything, just focus on the good things, okay?"

She smiled, "I'll try. Daddy, how were you able to maintain your composure flying to Houston with Tyson?"

"Angel, it was one of the hardest things I ever had to do. I wanted to snap his neck! Angel, I hope Tyson hasn't destroyed your Faith in men."

314

"No, daddy. He could never do that. I'm blessed to have
four wonderful men in my life. Obviously, starting with you,
then Grappe, and my two knuckle-head brothers."
Allen smiled and said, "We are certainly blessed to have you
too!"
    Mallory said softly, "I am a Blessed child in more ways
than one."
    "Jada told me that you delivered a moving speech at the
awards dinner last night."
"Yeah, I think it was okay."
"Do you have a copy of it?"
"Yes Sir."
"Why don't you read it to me?"
"Daddy, I don't feel like reading the whole speech, but I'll read
you the last few paragraphs, okay."
    Mallory pulled out a folder from a large purse that sat on
the side of her. She opened the folder and began to read the last
part of the speech to her dad:

**"Young ladies, you should always strive to be the best; to be
resilient. Always know that there's a solution for every
problem. As students of a parochial school, you should
always be aware of the fact that GOD is as important as
Math and Science. A relationship with GOD can propel you
to heights unlimited. Forging a relationship with GOD when
you're young is essential. We live in a dangerous world!
Danger is all around us, seen and unseen. More often than
not, prayer will insulate you from danger. The HOLY
SPIRIT is a buffer that helps protect you. Young ladies,
there will be times in life that you are going to feel lost and
alone. Some of your friends are going to turn against you.
People are going to be '*hating*' you on Facebook; but pray
and ask GOD for strength. GOD will help you overcome any
issue that you are going through. Trust me, HE will.**

315

JOHN FENLEY

There's an old cliché that says, '*When you are at the end of your rope, tie a knot and hold on*', but I say when you're at the end of your rope, stretch out your hands to JESUS. HE is your only hope. JESUS will always catch you when you fall. It doesn't matter how bleak things are, or if you feel no one can save you. When you feel that there's nowhere else to turn, keep this in mind: THE CREATOR, THE GREAT COMFORTER, THE OMNIPOTENT ONE, YOUR FATHER IN HEAVEN IS ALWAYS CAPABLE OF PROVIDING...ONE MORE MIRACLE!

A week later, Mallory and Vanessa met for lunch. That's when Mallory told Vanessa about Tyson's plot to have her killed. Vanessa finally revealed to Mallory that Tyson had raped her. She lamented that the rape was her fault because she had no business going to Tyson's apartment. Mallory reassured her it wasn't her fault, and that she was at the wrong place at the wrong time with an evil man! Both women hugged and cried together.

ONE MORE MIRACLE

Epilogue

A year later, Tyson was tried and convicted. He received sixty years for his part in the Wingate murder. He received ten years for *Solicitation of Capital Murder* in Mallory's case. Both sentences would be served concurrently. That meant, under Texas law, Tyson would have to serve half of his sentence before he would be eligible for parole.

As for Sonny Brown, he received three years in the State Penitentiary for his part in the Wingate murder. Because of the illegal search and seizure of his property, his drug charges were subsequently dropped. Ms. Wingate is still awaiting trial.

Five years later, Mallory earned two degrees: an MBA from **Georgia Tech**, and a law degree from **Harvard University** (Allen's *Alma Mater*)
After having her marriage annulled, Mallory met Ira Hendrix, the true love of her life. He is a professor at **Morehouse College**. They met while attending **Christ the King Catholic Church** and have been married for two years. They are the proud parents of a one-year old son named Jayden. Mallory works at **Twin Enterprises**, the family business. She is the Vice President of the Construction Division.

Kendria has one son and two daughters.
Mia has two sons and a daughter.

David is married and the father of two sons. He and his family live in Los Angeles.

Joshua is also married. He is the father of four: two

daughters and two sons. He is a Major in the United States Marine Corp. He has done two tours of duty in Iraq. Presently, he is stationed in Florida. At the end of the year, his plan is to retire from the military (to the delight of his wife and mother). Joshua has pleased his parents by accepting a position at **Twin Enterprises**, when his discharge is final.

Teresa and Allen are proud grandparents of thirteen.

Granny Hunter is still cooking meals for Allen and Teresa, at least four-times-a-week, and is still a foster grandmother at Grady Homes Daycare.

Rob and Deni retired to their Summer home in Jamaica. They visit their Atlanta home, several times a year.

THE END.